*Daisy!
thank yo
so much
Love [signature]*

Dhariya
Prelude To A Dark Legacy

~ Reader's Comments ~

Your words have given me much inspiration in my search for honesty and pureness of heart as you gracefully lay your pen to paper leaving my soul in awe of a truly talented lady'

———

I find it is driven by its own power, the power of truth in your writing shines thru and that is the light.

———

Fascinating… good read!! More, more!! You have written such vivid images and emotions … Yes. Yes. This MUST be published!!

———

I didn't want it to end.

———

You are a very skilled and intense writer!!

———

Wow. Very profound and very well written. Your writing seems to flow lyrically through the castle as I followed the character's first visit. It left me very anxious to read more. Without becoming morbidly- descriptive and over- using clichéd phrases, your understated descriptions of places and events gave me, the reader a full visual picture of the textures and the smells that the character(s) were seeing. I will look forward to reading more.

———

Ok so I want more...get busy. :) This is wonderful.

You are a great writer!! I can't wait to hear the rest. very intense... very awesome!!

You sure have a way with words!! and things are heating up, with anticipation!! "And still he claimed her body with his gaze as his image claimed her mind;"......."he determinedly banked his need until the time was right, "More More!!

LOVED, LOVED, LOVED IT!! YOU ARE VERY TALENTED!!

Love your new excerpts and chambers!!
What is around the dark corners!!!
Wonderful writing.

I love your site and your writing. I am already drawn into Llyr's story and want more. Thank you for sharing the excerpts.

I HAVE JUST READ ALL OF YOUR WRITINGS AND YOU HAVE LEFT ME WANTING MORE!! YOU ARE AMAZING!!

As my eyes look upon your writings I feel your emotions run through me like a sudden breeze that's found its way to my soul. I stand in awe.

Copyright © 2008 Karel Wade
All rights reserved.

ISBN: 1-4392-1149-3
ISBN-13: 9781439211496

Visit www.booksurge.com to order additional copies.

~ This novel is dedicated to my Nana ~
She who taught me, through example, what it truly means to love and to give

Dhariya
Prelude To A Dark Legacy

Based on the personal journals and writings
of
Lady Dhariya • 1692–1722

by Karelleyn Brae Wade

> "So often I have wondered throughout the years;
> 'had I known the ending would
> I thus have chosen differently in the beginning?'
> But alas the answer to that question
> yet remains a mystery."
>
> ~ D ~

Table of Contents ~ Verse

~And the night comes
~And the shadows fall
~And o' how I seek the sweetness
  only dreamt of but never felt

~And I shall fear not the darkness~
~And thus, I wait upon the edge
  of twilight's beckoning call
~And the flames of desire arise
  to meet the coming of the midnight hour
~And the dark velvet passions pulse to life

~And what be this place where darkness touches light,
  where neither is yet each exits one within the other?
~And what doth one truly seek within the other?
  Could it be fulfillment of one's own self promise?
  Yet, perhaps it is more an opposite reflection,
  a hope of balancing some perceived weakness with
  naught but an overpowering extreme
~And the brighter the light, the darker the shadow

~And o' the night where be thy mercy?
~And o' the darkness where be thy solace?
~And o' the dream why doth thy vision lie?
~And still I am drawn by faith,
  that which sees promise of light,
  even within the depths of darkness

Elegy

I
~ And the night comes ~

*… It was but a singular night in a lifetime of many.
Who could have known it would prove to alter forever
all that was and all that ever would be—Evermore…*

Scotland ~ 20 November ~ 1709

~ I rode alone through somber blackness. Endless forest pressed in close against the way. The night storm had come, like some great dark winged thing spanning the sky, consuming the moon and stars.

There was no turning back now and nothing to turn back for. The darkness lay ahead as unrelenting as the darkness I sought to leave behind. So I followed by instinct a path I'd traveled hundreds of times. Sounds of hoof-beats against the sod and the panting breath of horse and rider filled the air—in the distance, thunder.

Pressing my booted heels to Andromeda's flanks, I urged the mare onward. We had to reach Skara Brae Castle before the storm broke full upon us and the ground became treacherous mire.

I could feel my composure beginning to shatter, like glass shards tearing me apart inside. Suddenly I was no longer a woman grown to seventeen years but a child abandoned in the night. Vulnerable, afraid, longing to cry out for the mother I'd lost only hours ago. Needing the comfort that only a maternal embrace could give and knowing those loving arms would never hold me again…

O' how stark and unyielding—is this lament of sorrow's song.

Rain was falling steady now, a parody of my own flowing tears. Drawing a deep ragged breath I brushed my cheeks with a fisted hand. Then turning inward, I prayed to God for strength to carry on while the storm crept ever closer—a beast taunting its prey.

~ D ~

~ Leaves rustled in the surrounding darkness. Lady Dhariya trembled with cold and fatigue as bitter winds blew in from the North Sea. The icy breath of winter's promise offered no mercy to the grieving young woman lashing thick wet tendrils of her hair against her, stealing-away her cloak's protective warmth and trailing its fluttering length in her wake, yet the heavy scent of brine it carried was indeed welcome for it bespoke the nearness of her destination.

The first glimmer of torch lamps soon pierced the foliage.

Moments later the gates of Skara Brae came into view. The sight was very nearly Dhariya's undoing, but she held fast and leaned down to murmur soft words of praise for Andromeda's steadfast efforts while her gaze reached beyond the lacy pattern of wrought iron where the black shadow of the fortress loomed large and imposing.

Wrapping the frozen fingers of both hands around the bell pull, Dhariya half stood in the stirrups and wrenched the rusted metal links downward, a feat that demanded the full weight of her slight body. A rewarding clang sounded in the tower above the gatekeeper, Crowley's, quarters and brought him scurrying out into the night. A glowing lantern held high in his gnarled claw.

Dhariya watched Crowley's hunched figure draw near, leaning into the wind as he fought his way toward the gates.

He had been gatekeeper here at this castle since before she was born. Although she knew him well, Dhariya did not speak. Feeling deadened by cold and grief, she sat motionless waiting for him to reach her.

Old Crowley's weathered face expressed grave concern as he squinted into rain soaked shadows. Once he realized the black-cloaked figure on horseback was not some dark specter come to claim his soul, but his lordship's niece the young Lady Dhariya herself, Crowley did not know whether to feel relief or more afraid, *aye with the pretty young miss out alone on such a night, 'aught surely must'v 'appened*, he thought. Yet he held his tongue and quickly bent to her bidding.

Skeletal trees lined the carriage path that snaked its way through the sprawling grounds toward Dhariya's place of refuge. The squeal of metal gates closing behind her was soon lost to the keening howl of the tempest and ceaseless clatter of barren limbs. Each angry gust tossed hard rain, like handfuls of tiny pebbles, bruising her tender flesh.

Despite feeling physically battered and spiritually wounded Dhariya's fierce determination never wavered, for there ahead Skara Brae stood tall, craggy points of spires and crenellated walls rising up out of the ever present mist in proud defiance against the ravages of time.

Most would look upon the ancient citadel with foreboding, to Dhariya however, it was her Uncle Tamas' home and always a welcome sight, more so this night than ever and she prayed that on this night *here* is where she would find him.

Soft golden light flickered behind the webbing of leaded panes as if offering greeting and warm relief from its brooding countenance. At her approach a young stable lad rushed forth to help her dismount and see to Andromeda's care. Though clearly surprised by the lateness of the hour and Lady Dhariya's wildly disheveled appearance, he dare not venture comment, just silently led the exhausted animal away.

Watching them depart, Dhariya leaned heavily against the Castle's outer wall. While trying to re-gather her resolve and force her legs to stop quavering, she noted how the mare's silver coat gleamed in the lamplight, knowing it was more from exertion than the pelting rain. Andromeda wearily followed behind the lad's small dark outline, being well acquainted with these surroundings she was instinctively assured that a dry comfortable resting place and nourishment awaited.

Dhariya hated that she had ridden the animal so hard. There had been no choice however, and she had no doubt that her beloved horse would soon receive more than adequate attention to make up for it. Her Uncle Tamas spared no expense when it came to the care of his own highly bred horses. The Lord of Skara Brae employed only the best equerry and grooms, ensuring his stables were always exceptionally run. Therefore it was unnecessary to give any verbal instructions and she turned her thoughts to the difficult task that still lay ahead of her.

As was her habit Dhariya made her way behind the castle and entered via the servant's small doorway—immediate warmth and the wafting scents of drying herbs engulfed her—all so familiar—so comforting—so very needed.

Sudden tears stung her eyes. She frantically blinked them away as the rawness of her grief threatened to come spilling forth in a drowning flood. Grasping hold of the iron will that had so often been her nemesis during her girlhood, Dhariya steadied herself, *not yet*, she inwardly commanded, *I will not give in yet! Dear God help me do what I must!*

When she felt some measure of her control restored, Dhariya followed along the narrow hallway where shelves climbed from floor to ceiling on either side, housing countless jars of costly spices and various cooking ingredients.

An archway at the end opened into the large kitchen where she found the houseman Urien and his wife Ffyonna sitting hearthside quietly sipping hot tea. Having known this kindly couple—now into their late-middle years—her entire life, they seemed more family than staff.

Both graying heads lifted at the sound of her entry. At once they were on their feet and coming toward her, Ffyonna's words accompanying their hasty steps. "Lord bless us all Lady Dhariya! Whatever has happened child?" Upon hearing the question Dhariya faltered, nearly collapsing into the four loving arms that enfolded her.

After aiding the weather-beaten young woman to a chair by the fire, Ffyonna removed her own woolen shawl and draped it around the lass's damp shoulders. While Dhariya, taking a few fortifying sips from the brimming sherry glass pressed into her hand finally managed to ask, "Is Uncle Tamas here at the castle?"

At the affirmative nods Dhariya felt a dizzying rush of relief. She closed her eyes on the swirling room about her and sent a profound thank you heavenward. She opened them a moment later and forced herself to speak.

Her voice shook with emotion and weariness as she began relaying the few known details of the carriage accident that had claimed her mother's life earlier that very day. Urien had drawn a third chair into the warm circle of firelight and he and Ffyonna now sat in shocked disbelief at the news. They both recalled all too clearly a tragic night years ago when there had been another accident, one that had claimed the lives of both Dhariya's father and brother and had nearly killed her as well.

"M-mother had gone yesterday…t-to the Chattan Estate out of town," Dhariya was saying, "s-she and Lady Catherine, t-they were to co-host a charity ball next month and needed to review their plans together."

Pausing for another sip, she placed the glass on the hearth and continued. "M-Mother was to stay the night and return t-today since the drive is s-so lengthy… it seems she'd not long left the Chattan's gated grounds this morning when her c-carriage went off the road and p-plunged over a steep e-embankment. N-no one yet k-knows w-why." Dhariya pressed her palms to her face.

Watching the courageous young woman struggle with her words Ffyonna marveled at the way she had ridden through a storm in the dark of night to get here, aggrieved and all. *Aye but our Dhariya's a strong one,* Ffyonna thought, remembering how her own hands had pulled the squalling infant from her mother's exhausted body, bathing and swaddling the precious new life, hushing her cries as she placed the babe in her mother's arms to nurse at her breast. It had been a long difficult labor. Both mother and child fought valiantly for their lives and succeeded.

There seemed a special bond forged between the three of them during the birthing that night. Now the lovely Lady Suriya was gone leaving her daughter alone, with no blood family, but for her uncle. Being the only remaining offspring, she was sole heir to all the wealth and estates of each parent. A heavy burden for the young shoulders of Lady Dhariya who sat there now looking for-all-the-world the image of the beautiful woman that she mourned, that they all mourned. *Dear Lord how were they ever to get through this?*

Urien puffed from his pipe and just listened, as was his way, cupping the small bowl in his palm in a comforting familiarity that Dhariya recognized and savored. Her gaze followed the lazy wisps of smoke he sent spiraling into the air above his head. Thus she did not notice the deep frown knitting his brow or that his eyes had misted.

There's been too much death in this family, Urien was thinking with grave sadness, *too many shadows, too much darkness and now this. Will it ever end?* He wondered, feeling each loss anew, as his memories of all those now departed floated to the surface.

"I had to come here myself tonight" Dhariya—feeling a little more composed—was saying, "I-I need to be the one to tell uncle. I know how hard he'll take it. Mother and he...

t-they were always so c-close." Dhariya looked away and stared with unseeing eyes into the fire, "She's to be laid out in the drawing room of our Edinburgh residence. I must return there tomorrow. Two of our loyal servants Josey and Maybel are sitting vigil while I'm gone. They've been with us a long time and are grieving also."

Dhariya turned back to them, her gaze sought the older woman's and as always she gained strength from what she found there. Ffyonna was like the grandmother Dhariya and her late brother DJ—Darrien Jr. had never had, since none of their own grandparents had lived long enough to see their children's children.

Urien in his own quiet way suited the role of grandfather well enough. Though his brand of care was a more distant one as bespoke his position, it was there nonetheless. By contrast, Ffyonna's love and devotion were infused in everything she did. In many ways she was a cornerstone for Dhariya's entire family as well as Skara Brae's household staff. She didn't coddle or patronize. Yet one could feel the love she gave, it was truer and far more real than any spoken words. She was strong and practical. She also had a tender heart, however, and she more than shared in the pain of this loss.

"Ffyonna…will you come and help me prepare her body for…b-burial?" Dhariya finally managed to ask.

"Of course child," the older woman replied as she reached over, her warm consoling hand enclosing Dhariya's icy fingers.

Dhariya's other hand immediately came overtop and she held Ffyonna's tightly between her two. "Thank you." She softly said. "I would only have those who are dearest bathe her body. Afterward M-mother shall be anointed with your special blend of herbal oils, of course. Then she's to be dressed in her bridal gown, 'Thusly garbed to reunite with her beloved husband for all eternity.' As was her expressed wish since his passing…The last touch upon h-her shall be of those who love her…A final tribute to the wonderful woman s-she w-was."

Dhariya sighed with a shuttering breath. "I'm sure Uncle Tamas will loan his carriage for our comfort. I must speak with him tonight so we can leave early in the morning."

Ffyonna's heart constricted in her chest as her eyes met Urien's and they shared a worried look; an unspoken communication also took place, one which silently conveyed a great deal and was clearly understood between a couple married many long years. The two servants then took things swiftly in hand, overlooking their own grief; concern for Dhariya's well being the utmost priority.

Urien, who had been all but silent up till now, finally spoke. "His Lordship dines in the formal chamber." He told her in his customary, dignified, man of few words demeanor. "I shall notify him at once." He rose to his feet, bowed his head respectfully to Dhariya, then turned—his reed thin form moving with efficient ease—as he went to inform Lord Tamas of his niece's arrival and of her need to speak with him once she had bathed and donned dry garments.

While his wife, always ample and sturdy, bustled in the opposite direction to see to her ladyship's rooms and summon servants needed to heat and pour the heavy cauldrons of bathwater, murmuring a prayer to the heavens as she did so.

The young woman left alone by the fire stared into the flames and sipped her sherry. After a few moments she set the empty glass aside, stood and straightened her shoulders purposefully—the woolen shawl falling away unnoticed to drape itself across the arms of the chair behind her—Having come to a sudden decision Lady Dhariya then walked out of the kitchen.

She did not go directly to her chambers.

II
~ And the shadows fall ~

...A single fragment of time, thus cast into dye upon my memory, like a given promise to fill the empty space with what might yet be...

*~ **The** graceful curve of rough gray stone arched high above my head, as I stood peering into depths of the cavernous, sparsely furnished dining chamber—with its silk tapestries, plush carpets and extraordinary outer wall of leaded glass. Yet the luxuriant hall stretching out before me was vacant, offering only evidence of a meal recently taken.*

A linger of pungent spicing mingled in the air with traces of sandalwood, white linen still draped the long table, upon it lay discarded serviettes and bits of cutlery. The multi-branched candelabrum suspended from the vaulted ceiling burned with fresh candles, as did the four matching ones standing tall in every corner. While fires blazed with new life in the granite hearths spanning the room's breadth at either end.

The two massive mahogany sideboards that completed the heavy, ornately carved dinning-suite loomed large on each side of the entryway; both laden with stacks of dirty dishes and sterling servers awaiting removal. How strange. Everything appeared deserted as if abruptly abandoned...but not so came the next thought accompanied by a rippling of sudden awareness.

More moments passed before I saw the lone figure seated in a high backed chair before the fire, at the far end of the linen draped centerpiece. A black silhouette haloed in flames and red glowing embers. I stepped forth to speak. He turned toward me and candlelight touched gently over his face. I halted. It was not my uncle. Only then did I recall seeing a 'pair' of silver wine goblets atop the table. A smooth eloquent motion brought him to his feet and the stranger's dark gaze locked in full upon me.

~ D ~

~ **D**hariya was held there spellbound and breathless in the moment, unable to tear her eyes from his intensely, intimate stare. Her pulse beat quickened. Her body stirred. A myriad of sensation erupted within her, penetrating the hazy shroud of bereavement, which had veiled over her senses.

Yet he made no other moves and neither spoke. Time stilled. The world fell away, leaving them alone together, suspended in a strange realm—face to face—across the shadowy expanse of the room. And somewhere in a world far away a storm raged, beating rain down hard upon the hundreds of mullioned panes, as the heavens cried out in thunderous roars, flashing its pure white light in against the darkness.

And still he claimed her body with his gaze as his image claimed her mind—tall, strongly built, darkly clad. His well-defined, hard-edged features chiseled into a rugged handsome-ness that far surpassed classic good looks. These lucid thoughts she stored safely away.

While the harnessed power of his countenance bespoke a silent warning *'Dangerous'* the word became flesh in every fiber of his being. Suddenly, Dhariya felt frightened of him and her body's unfamiliar response to his presence.

Just then—as if sensing her discomfort—he made to step toward her but the side panel door opened carrying the sound of Lord Tamas' voice echoing into the chamber… "I believe a night cap by the drawing room fire would be just the thing. Will you join me Llyr?"

…And the spell was broken. Thus, with a swirling whisper of cloak and skirts Dhariya fled down the long torch lit passageway without a backward glance.

Llyr was still reeling from recent events that had led him here to this castle not long ago. His mind had not yet fully comprehended the multitude of changes that were so quickly brought upon him—without warning—without choice.

Since his arrival at Skara Brae he had been treated like royalty and his every whim catered to. He had been given a magnificently furnished suite of rooms in the east wing. The lavish accommodation so far above his usual high standard he could scarcely believe his eyes. This world that he was thrust into certainly had its privilege, yet what it demanded in return, was far beyond any price.

Earlier he had joined Lord Tamas' for a late supper in the formal salon. They had feasted on an array of Indian curries, spiced vegetables, rice and flat breads still warm from the pan. All of which had been laid out in a colorful display for their dinning pleasure.

Llyr had found this unique blending of flavors was indeed a pleasure for his jaded pallet. Despite his years of world travel he had never tasted anything like it, all the while the finest imported wines had flowed freely, further complimenting the dining experience.

At the completion of the meal a footman approached and bowed before Tamas, a silver message salver in hand. The white sheet of parchment atop it, bearing His Lordship's name, luminous in the candlelight.

Tamas unfolded the missive his expression betraying nothing as he read in silence. Refolding and pocketing the note, the older man excused himself momentarily and followed the waiting servant out through a side door hidden amid the wainscoting. While Llyr—lulled by wine and the glowing ambiance of the room about him—sank back in his chair savoring the quietude.

That was when '*she*' appeared in the entryway. Swathed in candlelight and flickering shadow the face of one so unearthly fair, framed by long dark tresses that fell past her waist in a tumble of waves, windblown and glistening with raindrops. Her huge eyes had held to his in a haunting gaze of wonder that seemed to reach beyond all bounds, into eternity.

He had sensed her sudden fear. It had filled her eyes like those of a trapped animal in the woods. He knew she had been about to flee and he had been about to stop her from doing so. Now as he stood watching the stunning dark haired beauty vanish into the shadowy depths of the corridor Llyr knew it was too late. He also knew he had just experienced a moment of utter-perfection and that for the second time in as many days his world had—once again—been altered forevermore.

She was absolutely exquisite. There was something wild and untamed that flared in the depths her eyes—the glimmer of a passionate soul. Yet everything else about her bearing bespoke a woman of refinement and high birth, such an intriguing blending. He had to find out who she was. His immediate reaction was to follow after her and demand to know everything about her. Well that was out of the question with Tamas now striding toward him. How could he possibly explain such peculiar actions?

Moreover there were things that needed tending to before he could allow himself the indulgence of life's pleasantries however lovely they might be and this man before him topped that list. Llyr had a vast amount to learn before Tamas disappeared and he must remain focused upon his main reason for being here. So he forced himself to turn toward his generous host and courteously accepted his offer.

    Entering the main foyer Dhariya's mind was whirring in a state of bewilderment. Halfway across the massive expanse she encountered Lord Tamas' two beloved deerhounds, Lyos and Ellyon, sprawled languidly by the fire awaiting their master.
    Instantly recognizing her they arose and came forth in a sudden burst of speed to offer their own special welcome. Tails widely sweeping the air, the dark blue-gray of their wiry coats appeared almost black in the dimness as they writhed in happiness and vied for her attentions.
    Pausing to pet them Dhariya was grateful for this moment of normalcy amid so much else. Such an open natural response the animals gave, so innocent and unknowing of her immense life-shattering loss. She felt suddenly overwhelmed by it all. The next thing Dhariya knew she was kneeling on the cold flag stones encircling a dog in each arm as she fought the tidal flow of tears anew. Burying her face in the abundance of warm fur where the scent of the peat-fire lingered. She was so close to breaking. She sought comfort in this unconditional love and strength within her own soul.
    "Alright, away with you now," Dhariya told them a few moments later. Releasing them from her embrace, she drew her damp handkerchief from her cloak pocket and sniffled into it. The well-trained hounds obeyed without hesitation, taking themselves back to their previous fireside post, where they curled up on the carpet once again. Their large dark eyes watching her as she struggled to her feet before they closed and the dogs sank blissfully into sleep.
    Dhariya had felt her limbs tremble violently in her efforts to rise and steady herself. Yet she knew she was not only faltering beneath the burden of sorrow, but also from her unexpected encounter with the man in the dining salon, which had left her feeling unsettled on some deep level that she was far too distraught to deal with.

Thankfully her uncle had not seen her standing there gaping at his guest. Lord above! She had never before done such a thing, nor had she even considered the fact Lord Tamas might be entertaining. He always lived such a solitary life that finding someone else here with him had been a startling surprise to say the least.

Dhariya's acute sensing abilities should have forewarned of a stranger's presence. Yet tonight grief had numbed her to everything but the all-consuming pain of her loss, until it was too late. Now with exhaustion rapidly claiming what little strength remained she left the hounds slumbering peacefully and ascended the grand staircase to the second floor, her hand tightly gripping the balustrade with every step.

Then onward through the labyrinth of richly appointed passageways where arras and thick eastern carpets gave a sense of warmth to the otherwise barren stones. While exotic scents of foreign lands wafted from countless wall sconces as the fragrant flames of Ffyonna's specially blended candles lit Dhariya's way to her rooms.

Lord Tamas, having lost his wife and twin sons years ago, had always avidly welcomed his extended family into his home, keeping private quarters for each of them ever at the ready. It was here in the farthest reaches of the east wing Dhariya's own chambers lay ensconced within the rounded stonewalls of the tower.

This tower—her tower sat perched atop the jutting protrusion of the precipice. Overlooking the rocky shoreline where the North Sea came crashing-in wave after wave upon it. And *this* was Dhariya's most favorite place in the whole world.

With a click of the latch and a creak of aged hinges the heavy timbered door opened wide. Inside the familiar façade of her sitting room greeted her warmly with lamps lit and a crackling fire already ablaze in the oversized hearth.

Drawing her sodden cloak from her weary form Dhariya then dragged herself up the narrow curving stairwell. Her booted feet scuffing the stones, attesting to the effort needed to lift them.

Finally reaching her bedchamber on the next level, here too a hearth fire burned heartily, driving out the damp chill and reflecting its golden hues upon the pale tones of the exquisitely furnished room. Despite the warmth Dhariya's flesh prickled beneath her damp woolen gown, the black folds hanging limp around her as she hugged herself and rubbed her hands briskly up and down her arms. Yet nothing could dispel the icy coldness from within her.

Just then Ffyonna emerged from the adjacent bathing room where the fragrant aroma of her bathwater beckoned. No doubt some soothing herbal tincture as Ffyonna was wise in the ways of healing.

Bathing though not overly popular in this part of the world had always been a regular practice with Dhariya's family. A tradition that went back countless generations as the bloodlines of Dhariya's mother and uncle descended from India, where the daily ritual of bathing in the Ganges River began. For her family here in Scotland however, the ritual had evolved into bathing in a tub of fresh water that had been warmed over a fire. Thus, her uncle had installed specially designed bathing rooms beside the privy closet within in each suite.

These rooms though small, were spacious. The only furnishings being a marble bench and a large claw-footed brass tub placed on a rug before the fire—its one end curving up high to allow the bather to lean back and relax. The walls were surfaced completely in Spanish tile and Italian marble that varied in color to compliment the tones in each of Skara Brae's exclusively designed suites.

Tile shelving built out from one wall housed an array of herbal oils used to scent the water and clean toweling for drying. The marble hearth spanning the opposite wall warmed the air as it heated the cauldrons of rainwater that funneled down from the battlements and collected in numerous locations on the castle's upper floors. Since it rained so often the servants were usually spared the arduous task of hauling barrels of water up from the well near the gardens.

"Wherever did you get to child?" Ffyonna asked gently. Her pale blue eyes filled with concern. "Your bathwater's been drawn and growin' cold in the waitin'."

"I…I'm afraid I became a little distracted. Forgive me Ffyonna I didn't mean to keep you."

"Auccc well, never mind luv' 'tis all right now, I've just poured an extra bucket of hot water and some bergamont oil into the tub. 'Twill help ease your nerves and all that pent up emotion." The older woman came forth and began helping Dhariya disrobe.

Dhariya willing gave herself over to the beloved servant's capable hands, for Ffyonna had special gifts that led her way in caring for others. She had the uncanny ability of seeing past the surface of a person into the deeper depths, uncovering wounds and secrets that were hidden from most others. Although Scotland was Ffyonna's homeland and that of her predecessors for numerous generations, rumors ever whispered that her bloodlines actually descended from a long line of Welsh witches, stretching even further back to the women of the Mystical Isle of Avalon.

Whether this was true or not, no one knew and Ffyonna herself never spoke of such things. Yet her natural gift as a healer was remarkable, using insight and intuition, she responded to the greater unspoken need within the heart of each individual.

Peeling away the cold wet layers from the shivering girl Ffyonna's shrewd, assessing gaze missed nothing. *The child's far too thin* she was thinking, and knowing this death would only strip the flesh further from the fine delicate bones, Ffyonna's quick mind was already busy at work, mentally blending various herbal concoctions to fortify the willowy body against the ravages of grief.

Moments later Dhariya lowered her aching limbs into the steaming tub and closed heavy lids over tear tender eyes. Sinking back to rest her head against the wide brass rim, she released the heavy fall of hair she had been holding up—the silken spill of sable trailing down onto the rug like a dark waterfall.

While Ffyonna, aware that Dhariya was one who needed to face her pain alone before she could share it with anyone else, slipped quietly away closing the door after her. Leaving just the faint light from red smoldering cinders in the darkness where the smoky scent of peat melded into the soothing scent of bergamont.

And in the blanketing silence that followed the dark stranger's image was swept into deeper recesses. For reality would no longer hover at the edges of Dhariya's consciousness but came in like a rushing tide, full force upon her.

...How shall my life be now? Naught but lonely and empty without the one who'd always been there, she who, through her own body had thus given life unto me, was now gone. It's too much...mama–oh–mama I cannot bear it. I cannot bear that I shall never see you again... Lady Dhariya then bowed forth her head. Her slender body shaking as she sobbed her sorrow into the curve of her own cupped hands.

———

In the deep darkness of predawn Llyr was alone in the main drawing room, sitting back within the shadowy depths of the oversized chair. His right ankle—booted in expensive black-leather and polished to a mirrored finish—was propped upon his left knee, which was clad in the equal richness of ebony-damask. The chair's massive wings of burgundy velvet curled around each side of him giving the illusion of a comforting embrace.

Lord Tamas had long since sipped the last of his dram and the tall white haired man had taken his leave, the two deerhounds following at his heels. While Llyr's goblet was now filled for the third time, he turned the crystal stem between his thumb and forefinger watching the intricately cut edges glisten in the glow of dying embers.

Despite his relaxed appearance he was far from being at his ease and far too restless to seek sleep. All during these subsequent hours of solitude his thoughts kept returning the mysterious woman he had seen earlier.

Bloody hell, he hated complications. Yet he could not stop his mind from wondering about her, who she was—what had brought her here so late on such a stormy night—where he would find her again?

He knew she was only a visitor, Tamas had told him that he lived here at Skara Brae alone. The questions came once more, *who was she—why was she here—how long would she be staying?*

Though he had seen her only a scant few moments he knew he would never forget her. That she was extremely beautiful could not be denied. But then how many beautiful women had he already known in his past? How many sat even now awaiting his bidding? He could not possibly count their number with any degree of accuracy.

No. There was something else about this woman, something that would not let him be. It subtly worked its way through his mind. He could feel it burrowing deeper and deeper into the core of him. He could not stop it any more than he could define what it was. Though he knew it was something much more powerful, much more evident even than mere beauty alone, yet remained hidden and unseen as if her very spirit were shinning through.

Yes, that's it, he thought with a surging rush of realization. It was the essence of her being that drew him so, an untouched purity he wanted, perhaps even needed to claim for himself. Never before had he experienced such a thing as what had transpired between the two of them. The connection was truly startling.

His black midnight eyes narrowed in on the last spark slowly dying out in the hearth and she came again, flooding into his mind, filling him with longing. He sensed she was near and he wanted her liked he had never wanted any other before.

Hunger, raw and unbridled burned though his veins and ached in his loins. It was far too soon however. Llyr's mind knew it even if his body did not. He could not afford any outside interference at this crucial juncture.

But he *would* have her he consoled himself with this promise, just not quite yet.

Thus resolved, he determinedly banked his need until the time was right, a time when the old man was no more, only then would he be free to claim her.

III
~ And o' how I seek the sweetness, only dreamt of, but never felt ~

…Thus, I come to answer the call of the silent yet ever beckoning, only to find deeper mystery and the seductive lure of veiled secrets…

Skara Brae Castle, Scotland ~ *January* ~ *1711*

~ *I*'d seen him but once and fleeting. Back on that fateful night of my mother's passing, now more than a year ago. O' but I'd not forgotten him, how could I. When all through my mourning period—spent abroad with close family friends—his image had remained ever with me as if imprinted upon my innermost being.

How often I'd revisited those scant few moments shared with a man I did not know. Recalling too—the gamut of my emotions; how I'd cried like a babe while held and rocked in my uncle's arms. Yet earlier that same night when held by the gaze of a stranger, my passions had suddenly awoken and I'd never felt more like a woman.

And tonight I shall see him again…

The mere thought sent my senses reeling, and this very thought had been my constant companion earlier as I again rode the familiar path *to the gates of Skara Brae. This time had been different however, not only because the day was crisp and clear, but also because my uncle was off traveling in some unknown place.*

Thus in his absence I sought another within the castle walls.

The very one who'd been entrusted with the entire estate and given unlimited access to the vast wealth in Tamas' accounts, none other than that same mysterious stranger—Lord Llyr I'd since learned he was called.

~ D ~

~ **U**pon Dhariya's arrival old Crowley was the first familiar face she saw, murmuring his respectful acknowledgement in his usual manner. After passing through the front gates she was exuberantly met by—Lyos and Ellyon—the castle's two resident deerhounds and beloved pets of her uncle. They were both in fine form, barking their greeting, their large-lanky bodies running in gray furry circles around Andromeda's hoofs all the way to the stables.

An equally warm welcome awaited inside the kitchen, where the scarred wooden table was soon overflowing with scones, oatcakes and homemade preserves, all in honor of Dhariya's return after being so long away.

Urien and Ffyonna's twenty-year-old son Bryden had taken the place opposite hers. He was their only child born long after they had given up hope of having a family. He was a very good-looking young man. Tall with light brown hair and pale blue eyes. Being nearly two years older than Dhariya, Bryden was an integral part of all that was Skara Brae and they had so often played together as children.

Now he trained beneath his father to one day succeed his position as houseman, a family tradition that went back countless generations. Dhariya had always known by how Bryden gazed at her that she held his fancy. The way he was smiling today merely served as reconfirmation. And even though her own interests lay elsewhere she found this to be sweetly flattering.

Sitting with a steaming cup of mulled wine, Dhariya listened as the servants chatted on excitedly, talking endlessly of their enigmatic new overseer. Thus it was she came to learn the habits of the 'Dark Lord of Skara Brae'—a name by which they all covertly referred to him.

Annie, a pretty under maid in her mid twenties—of medium stature with a full figure and a mass of fiery red hair framing her round earnest face—pulled a stool up beside Dhariya. Having been on staff at the castle for number of years she had a much more familiar way than the others

Annie's large brown eyes were wide with awe as she began whispering to Dhariya about 'is 'andsome Lordship, 'ow 'e rides 'is great black 'orse across the misty moors like a wild man in the dead o' night and not returnin' till dawn. Sometimes 'e disappears for days on end, tellin' no one where 'e's gone or when to expect 'im." Dhariya made no comment to any of this. She knew she really should be discouraging such gossip, yet instead she found herself being most attentive, wishing to learn everything she could about this mysterious man who now ruled over her uncle's castle.

While Ffyonna sat back watching the young woman so newly returned to them, feeling a measure of pride and inner satisfaction. It was obvious to the older woman's discerning eye that her stringent instructions for daily herbal tonics had been adhered to. For Dhariya, despite the long months of mourning, was the absolute epitome of glowing health and fully ripened womanhood.

As different staff members offered forth their own bits of information on 'the Dark Lord', Dhariya silently noted how closely parts of Lord Llyr's routine mirrored that of her uncle's, for he too would remain ensconced within his chambers—under strict order to be left undisturbed—until he appeared in the main drawing room at precisely six o'clock each evening. *Men and their peculiar rituals*, she thought to herself with an internal shake of her head.

Then Ffyonna put a stop to the 'tale-telling' as she called it and the servants all scurried away to their various tasks like mischievous children who had been scolded by a stern parent, while Dhariya, feeling every bit as guilty as the others also hurried away, escaping to her own suite of rooms.

Later having rested, bathed and donned fresh garments, Dhariya stood before the looking glass finishing the last touches to gown and hair. She had chosen an off the shoulder design in the deepest shade of scarlet silk velvet—which complemented her dark features and naturally golden skin tone. Never being one for fancy adornments she fastened a single ornately crafted chain of silver around her throat from which hung a tiny garnet teardrop.

With no ladies maid at hand Dhariya decided to wear her hair loose in a style she much preferred. Drawing a few wavy tendrils from each side, she secured them in back with a silver garnet incrusted barrette, allowing the remainder of its heavy length to flow in glorious freedom to her knees. And as Dhariya gazed at the woman before her she found herself somewhat unsure, wondering if *'he'* would find her attractive.

She had never had such thoughts before this—before *him*.

A strange thing happened just then, all at once for the first time, she saw her mother's face reflected in her own features. Leaning in Dhariya studied each one closely. Recognizing the same heart shaped face, high cheekbones and strong jaw line, the same finely arched brows, straight nose and full lips the color of roses.

The large eyes of course, she thought, *but where mother's had been brown, my own are hazel, like father's. Why had I never seen this before? Though I'd known I resembled her and people had always remarked on the likeness, only now did I find her there, within myself.*

This both comforted and grieved Dhariya, for never did she feel her mother's loss more than this moment. *So many questions I wish to ask her,* she was thinking. Feeling the need to speak from her place as the woman newly emerging from the chrysalis, to the woman of worldly poise and experience that her mother had been, *if only she were here to help me understand my strong feelings for this man and all these changes taking place within me.*

Like a visitor to a foreign land Dhariya felt lost within the unknown wonder of awakening passions and womanly desires. Nor was there anyone else with whom she was comfortable enough to discuss such intimacies. She could only hope to somehow find her own way through. Dhariya did gain reassurance however, for her mother's beauty was legendary and wherever Lady Suriya had gone the eyes of men had ever followed. Thus, with renewed resolve Dhariya whispered '*thank you mother*' and blew her a kiss.

Then adding pinch of color to her cheeks and a drop of scented oil behind each ear, Dhariya drew on her long white gloves. Now she was ready—or so she hoped as she left her chambers in search of him.

And as Dhariya walked these passageways she had come to know so well, she recalled precious memories of a lifetime spent within them. Ghostly echoes of her brother's teasing, their innocent laughter as he and Bryden chased her into the shadowy depths of Skara Brae—where the intricately woven world of catacomb-ed tunnels twist in endless tangles. *How often I'd become lost in them as a child* she thought wistfully *and always, it was uncle Tamas who finally found me. Lifting me into his strong arms he'd kiss my tear stained cheeks assuring me I was all right now.*

Then as I clung to him, he'd carry me back to safety, scolding all the while for going where I'd been told not to. Yet his voice would be gentle and tender even as he tried to sound stern.

Why had her uncle refused to give any explanations for this trip? Dhariya wondered yet again. She had only been home a day when he had come to see her with the news of his going—no matter how she had pressed him for details—he would disclose nothing more and had left quickly.

So now Dhariya had come to Skara Brae looking for answers, something that might serve as an explanation. She hoped that by coming here and speaking with the man who had assumed Tamas' place she might gain some understanding of what was happening. For she had a strong suspicion that all was not as it seemed.

She truly worried so for her uncle. His behavior, though never what one would call normal, had changed radically after her mother's death. *Perhaps it was the result of losing his sister and only sibling,* Dhariya told herself. Heaven knows she could understand that having now lost all of her family but for him. Yet she felt she had lost him too and she was hurt by his up and leaving so suddenly offering no details of his travel plans or even when he might return. It felt as if he had purposely abandoned her.

…O' uncle where have you gone? … Her thoughts called out to him…*I feel your loss every bit as much as mother's… and I feel so alone…*

Her mind conjured the image of his thin kind face, the ever-present twinkle glinting in his pale eyes, his long white hair always worn straight and unbound to his shoulders. She smiled at that. Again remembering Dhariya the little girl, who, having never before seen anyone else with hair the color of snow, had been fascinated. She could still recall how her small hands ever sought to touch the soft silky strands.

Dhariya turned the next corner and the memories vanished as an icy coldness came sudden upon her, sweeping away the warm, the familiar. And she thought how very different Skara Brae seemed to become in that instant—the sadness—the emptiness—the pain. Such overwhelming feelings had never been there before.

Darkness in these corridors seemed to have now deepened, as if fewer sconces had been lit. Yet this was not so—for the shadows still danced in their flickering flames. While a strange sort of hushed stillness hovered in the air, without a single servant evident anywhere. Her flesh prickled at the abrupt change. However there was another feeling overshadowing all others.

It was a strong sense of this new lord she realized. It seemed to permeate the entire surroundings, absolute and everywhere present, as if something of him emanated from each and every gray stone. It sent a new kind of chill along her spinal column. And it was this very thing that drew her onward in spite of herself.

Llyr sat amid the shadows of the drawing room. No light burned but for the fire in the hearth, a tenebrous ambience to comply with his own brooding countenance, after all darkness was his home now and he was indeed finding a morbid kinship to this blackness.

He could never have imagined his life would change so quickly and so dramatically. He had once, not too long ago been the man about town, namely London as it offered such a variety of pleasures for a young titled male with means, one who was game for any amusement along with his circle of high-ranking cohorts—well those days were gone for good—never to return.

Yet neither was he the same person as before. He no longer even belonged to himself but was as a slave to other forces that now ruled his existence, offering him few choices of his own making. Though he admitted that road which brought him here was indeed one he himself had forged step by step. It was also one with no turning back.

He had often been impulsive and made unplanned decisions. Coming back home to Scotland had been one of these unexpected ventures and all that had transpired in this land of his birth even more so. Now that he had cut off all ties to that previous life, his world had narrowed to within these stonewalls that surrounded him, venturing out only for his nightly rides upon his destrier; his magnificent warhorse stallion—Taranis, to free the wildness in his soul for a time or to sate the needs of his body when the urges became beyond control.

The one person he had had any real contact with since was now gone…Tamas. Llyr was surprised to discover just how he much missed the older man's companionship. Right from the moment he had taken Tamas' place and assumed the role of Lord of Skara Brae, Llyr had never felt more alone. This feeling had not lessened with time.

When the final moment came it had been extremely difficult to bid Tamas farewell knowing he would never be returning.

And as surely as the turning of a key, Llyr had felt the full magnitude of his own fate lock firmly into place. How long he had stood staring up drive that night he did not know. Then with the new burden so heavily weighted upon him, he had turned and slowly made his way back toward the castle.

Strange were the things that stayed so clearly etched in his memory. The sound of his booted heels clicking against the stone steps and those that took him across the threshold. The groaning of aged hinges and muted thud that brought the heavy oaken door to a close behind him, sealing him off from the rest of the world. He relived those moments again now…

Releasing the cold metal latch from his grasp he strode forward into the foyer and as he stood there amid the gaping vastness of what was once the great hall, all the former splendor of Skara Brae's beauty suddenly faded away before his very eyes, leaving naught but vacuous tomb—a cold gray pall where only echoing stillness abounded—and so it had remained from that night forth.

He sought his refuge within the more sheltered confines of the darkened drawing room where he came to rest between the massive velvet wings of the oversized chair. Sinking back into the shadows of its embrace, a dram of whiskey cradled in his palm, just as he had done each evening since and just as he was doing now, always acutely aware of the heaviness upon the forefinger his left hand—Tamas' ring…

Llyr gazed intently at the large oval onyx set within four silver claws. It was an extremely well crafted piece incorporating the intricate weave of the Celtic symbol of eternity. It looked ancient enough to date back to the time of those historical people from which Llyr's own bloodlines had first sprung.

How often he had admired it upon Tamas' hand yet the strangeness now looking down and seeing it upon his own finger. It seemed more distant and surreal to him than ever. He did not think he would ever get used to it nor the immensity of all that it represented. Sipping from the crystal goblet he turned his eyes to the fire and tried not to think any more about it.

The peat glowed crimson. The whiskey burned. And he ached with a lonely pain. It seemed to claw at the very essence of his being with sharp talons that offered no mercy, a constant reminder of this solitary existence that was now his to bear.

Yet had he not always felt alone? Regardless of the fact that he once played a starring role in high society, being the most sought after guest at every function. Despite the fact that he openly defied the rules of the upper class and never hid his air of indifference, still, his attendance at any fete or gala ensured its success—which only served to prove what a foolish superficial world was-that of the high and mighty, the wealthy and powerful.

Though, in truth, he had never felt he belonged there or anywhere else for that matter. These feelings had only magnified since the change had come and he was no longer able to deny this to himself.

Even the hounds that had slumbered at Tamas' feet here before the fire each evening were conspicuously absent of late, he noted with cynicism. *Yes well, why not?* He thought wryly, *they owed him nothing after all, least of all their loyalty.*

His goblet nearly drained of its contents Llyr tipped his head back. Closing his eyes against the world as a numbing haze of unreality finally began to enfold him. And he was grateful its meager respite.

Finally reaching the castle's common area Lady Dhariya descended the sweeping staircase and paused at the final step. Her eyes fixed upon the drawing room's open doorway where a soft red glow spilled into the dimness of the great hall. She knew he was in there, though neither sound nor hint of movement betrayed him. Yet his powerful presence seemed to beckon unto her and she thus answered its call.

She approached slowly, cautiously, heart beating thunderously in her ears while inwardly she chided herself for such foolishness.

Suddenly a voice as deep as midnight commanded, "Who is there?"

Dhariya froze—unable to move, nor form a reply.

"Come forth where I can see you and state your purpose now!" The voice came again. The angry tone brooked no refusal.

Lifting her chin Dhariya steeled herself as she entered and silence held the room while her skirts whispered toward him. All at once she felt very odd, as if she moved in slow motion, yet in a strange state of heightened awareness she took in every detail.

The room about him was in darkness. He sat alone beside the hearth, crystal goblet in hand and resting against the burgundy velvet chair. *Always alone and in darkness*, the thought slipped unbidden into her mind as Dhariya watched the shadows and firelight play softly upon his handsome visage. The sight stole the very breath from her body.

Great velvet wings of the oversized chair spanned out behind him creating an ethereal, otherworldly façade. But not by any means a heavenly or angelic apparition. *No, more some dark-winged god of myth or legend*, Dhariya acknowledged to herself, as a peculiar sensation stole up her spine.

The power of his presence was undeniable as was his absolute maleness, swarthy of coloring, powerful of build—an echo of the ancient warrior race that went long ago from these lands. Dark unbound hair lay loose about an impressive breadth of shoulders; this made evident as both jacket and waistcoat hung draped over the sofa along with his cravat. Thus, his fitted shirt of crisp white lawn more than revealed the lines of a well-defined torso beneath.

The collar was open leaving his bare throat further exposed to her overtly avid gaze, which then took in the long legs stretched out before him, encased in dark breeches and high black leather boots. His feet crossed at the ankles.

The handsome face was solemn, Dhariya noted; it did not look to be a face that smiled often. And although he gave all the outward signs of being at his leisure she sensed something very different lurking beneath the surface, causing her to feel suddenly apprehensive, wondering what on earth she was doing here.

Belatedly she realized that time away had definitely altered her perceptions, she had somehow forgotten how frightening, how very dangerous he had seemed that night. Now it came flooding back as she experienced it all anew. Yet it was too late to retreat. She would not allow herself to cower before him. So she forced herself to keep moving toward him, while her heart continued to pound, hard and heavy against her ribs.

Llyr was angry and irritated with himself. He did not like being caught off guard, especially when feeling his most vulnerable. *Damnation!* He swore silently, *what the bloody hell was the matter with him? Hadn't he been warned about leaving himself so unprotected?*

Even as Llyr berated himself in thought his gaze never once left her—his intruder, for the dark silhouette approaching was most obviously of female gender and rather tall for a woman, while the sensuous slither of silken garments bespoke one of affluence. More than at little curious as to her purpose he intently watched her draw nearer. Primed and ready to take her to task, when she finally emerged into the circle of light however, the change to his entire demeanor was immediate.

He could not believe his eyes. She appeared like an apparition, this woman who had haunted his every waking moment since that one fleeting glimpse of her rare beauty so long ago.

He had seen her no more after that. Yet thoughts of her had brought him to the very brink of madness. He recalled his endless obsessing over how to find her again— this mystery woman—then that one eve he had strolled the gallery corridor for the first time and seen her portrait there, hanging amid the others. He had stood for a long time staring at her flawless image. It was obviously a recent painting, she looked much the same as the night she had come to Skara Brae. The artist had been skilled even capturing the untamed glint in her hazel eyes. How often he had returned there to gaze upon her.

Finally Llyr had been unable to endure it any longer, thus he turned on his heel, searched-out Tamas and all but demanded to know who she was, where she was, everything about her. Yet he had found no solace in the older man's reply. And she had not come back to the castle again—until now….

Hastily setting his goblet aside Llyr came to his feet at once, straightening his clothing as he did so.

Stopping before him, Dhariya addressed him sounding much more confident than she felt. "Good evening my lord. Pray I've not disturbed you overmuch."

Regaining his composure he captured her gloved hand and brought it to his lips.

Beneath the cloth Dhariya's flesh tingled wherever he touched. "We've not met before." She managed, still startled by his effect upon her. "I am Lady Dhariya Brae of Dreghorn. Lord Tamas is my uncle."

"Yes Lady Dhariya…" came his reply "I know who you are." His head suddenly filled with Tamas' voice, *Dhariya is my niece.*

Though the tie goes a long way back, we are indeed blooded relations. Llyr thrust the rest of the thought aside as well as the guilt that went along with it. "And my lady," he went on smoothly, "you may rest assured your unexpected arrival is most welcome, please come sit by the fire with me."

He motioned to the matching chair opposite his. Dhariya thanked him and accepted his offer, "perhaps a drink for my lady?"

"No thank you. I shant' stay long." She answered. Not wanting to overly impose.

Reclaiming his own seat then, Llyr sat at full attention his gaze never straying from the beautiful face before him.

As Dhariya looked back across the short distance between them she somehow knew instinctively that this was a man unlike all others. And the memory of him came nowhere close to the overwhelming reality before her.

"My lord" She began nervously feeling those dark endless eyes so intently upon her. "I came to you hoping to find out where my uncle has gone. He's never before left in such a way…" She paused averting her eyes. "…Without a word of where he planned to travel or—"

Stopping abruptly, Dhariya tried to get hold of her suddenly riotous emotions. Dear heaven what was happening to her? She wondered in a rush of tangled thoughts. Drawing a deep steadying breath she attempted to refocus. "Uncle Tamas is all I have left now you see, everyone else is gone and …I am alone."

Llyr felt the crushing weight of her words in his chest and all of the long denied sentiments he kept locked there seemed to stir. "My lady" He said with measured effort. "Would that I could tell you of Tamas' plans, but in truth they were not revealed to me either. I was told only, of a dire business emergency overseas that would keep him away indefinitely and any messages for him should be left with his solicitor in town." The lie came easily to his lips yet the discomfort he felt inside was something as unfamiliar as it was unwelcome and he was relieved that she was not looking at him just then.

"Yes, I was told that as well." Dhariya replied keeping her eyes lowered in an attempt to hide from his all-too penetrating gaze. Yet the sparkle of tears on her dark lashes betrayed her and to her further dismay they came spilling forth down her cheeks.

It was the feeling of utter abandonment and aloneness that overwhelmed her in that moment, and the sudden vivid memories of telling her uncle of her mother's death that triggered Dhariya's tears. Being at the castle now and missing him so had brought it all back without warning. She would never forget that last night she had been here. That night when she had just lost her mother and this loss was still a raw unhealed wound.

Dhariya was powerless against what was taking place within her. As if removing the lid off an overstuffed container the recollections spilled out, unfolding before her inner vision one upon another. Her pain—her uncle's pain—yet most of all his strength coming forth to fortify her when she had most needed it—needed him.

He had taken her into his arms, allowing her to be the child she so needed to be. To express the grief of the little girl who had lost her mother. To weep those child's tears as well as those of Dhariya the woman who had also lost both friend and confidant, qualities that were an integral part of the remarkable woman that was Lady Suriya and of the special bond that she, as mother, had always shared with her daughter. Dhariya had not allowed herself to cry since that night.

Now, unbidden it came pouring forth into Dhariya's mind in a series of images as all the emotions attached to them filled her heart, how Tamas had taken it upon himself to deal with all the arrangements sparing her as much of the arduous ordeal as possible. Although he had consulted his niece on every aspect of the funeral details for which Dhariya would always be grateful to him.

She no longer saw the room about her but gothic walls with stained glass windows. A white casket draped in white gardenias, Lady Suriya's favorite flower, from Lord Tamas' own conservatory at Skara Brae Castle, had been strewn together to form a thick blanket of blossoms—the air redolent with the fragrance from thousands of petals.

It had been a candlelight service in the early evening. St. Giles Cathedral had overflowed with the ranks of nobility who wished to honor a greatly respected lady. A crowd of much lesser status had gathered outside, along the Royal Mile, for the same reason for Lady Suriya was known as much for her kindness and charitable endeavors on behalf of the needy as she was for her legendary beauty, impeccable bloodlines and immense wealth. The beauty that remained unmarred by death, as the fatal injury had been a broken neck, the deep gash on her arm was the only visual evidence of the accident and it was hidden beneath the sleeve of her gown.

Those who attended had proclaimed it a glorious tribute befitting a glorious woman. To Dhariya however, it had been naught but a blur of people, words and haunting notes of choral requiems, the piper's laments echoing through the vaulted ceilings. All seen and heard from behind black veils and an overwhelming grief that made everything seem unreal and far away.

Yet much too reminiscent of the ceremony given years earlier for her father and brother, or so Dhariya was told as she herself had been in no condition to attend. Both Lord Darrien and his son had been mourned together as their identical coffins lay side by side in the very same Edinburgh cathedral; the magnitude of these losses was only compounded by she who now joined them, leaving her daughter all but alone in the world.

Lord above, thought Dhariya desperately, whatever was the matter with her? Was she truly going to completely fall apart after all this time? Right here before this stranger, this man who had so consumed her thoughts for well over a year? Dhariya strove to regain some semblance of composure. "Oh please forgive me my lord." She said. Her hand quickly dashing away the tracks of moisture from her cheeks, yet the tears kept coming.

What must he think of her? Dhariya wondered as she sought to try and explain herself. "I'm not one given to tears. Truly I'm not. But with my mother's recent passing …well it's more than a year now and yet—" her words halted at the feel of his strong hand upon her more delicate one.

Her huge doe eyes lifted to his and they shared a silent moment of oneness. Dhariya felt riveted, scarcely able to breathe, never in her life had she experienced anything close to the power emanating from this man before her.

Only a moment ago her emotions were spinning out of control—so unlike her. Now it was as if he claimed them and held them at his command as he did her eyes. A shiver of apprehension raced along her spinal column.

Then his eyes unlocked from hers and she noted his deep swallow.

Releasing her hand he offered forth his handkerchief. Accepting it, Dhariya was immediately enveloped by a heady wafting of sandalwood as she patted the pristine cloth to her face. Her mind seemed to swirl for a dizzying few seconds while her senses quickened into heightened response.

Llyr had been watching her carefully. It was clear to him that Dhariya was no weak sniveling miss. Nor was she the kind of woman to use tears as a weapon of manipulation as many others did. He knew only too well why Dhariya had wept when she had spoken of these painful wounds aloud. It was a natural response when such deep hurts were forced to surface to be laid open and exposed before another. It was something he himself had always avoided by never speaking of his own. He could see she was truly dismayed at having lost control so unexpectedly.

"My lady, you need not apologize for such understandable human emotion." He told her, the words tenderly suffused, "Know that I am here for you should you need comfort or a strong shoulder."

This last made her blush and coaxed a shy smile from her lips. She refolded Llyr's handkerchief and placed it on the side table while she sought to find her way through all of this peculiarity. Then Dhariya's gaze came to rest on his left hand and she thought no more of it. "Uncle Tamas told me he was giving you his ring" she said. The change of subject as unpredictable as her shifting thoughts, "This too seems so out of character. I've never known him to be without it."

Llyr made no reply, yet something had altered in the depths of his eyes as they rested upon her and Dhariya was feeling much more at ease suddenly. For some unknown reason she had a strong desire to share something of her past with this man. Perhaps it gave her an anchor of reality amid all the strangeness surrounding her.

Her voice became soft and reflective as she turned to gaze at a flame sparking to life in the hearth, "When I was small he used tell me it was a special ring." A hint of a smile touched her lips and inflected her tone as she continued, 'he'd sit me upon his knee spinning endless tales of the ring's powers and such, saying its symbols were magical and held secrets which could unlock the mystery of eternity."

Dhariya sighed as she came back to the present. "Uncle always did have an extraordinary imagination. Of course I now know none of it was truth, all the same it thrilled the little girl who listened so avidly and lived for a time within the world he created just for her…"Dhariya's eyes returned to the ring upon the Dark Lord's hand," I can't tell you how odd it seems to see you wearing it."

Llyr found this new aspect of Lord Tamas' character very interesting, an image quite unlike the man he himself had known. Then he too looked down at the topic of discussion.

Its polished surface and ornately carved silver setting gleamed as it caught the firelight.

"Yes. I'm sure it is strange for you." He concurred, still studying the object. "It's not something I'm comfortable with either. In fact I was thinking about that very thing just before you joined me."

His eyes came back to hers. *Dark piercing eyes* thought Dhariya, e*yes that could plunder in equal measure to their own fathomless depths.* She shivered.

"I did refuse to take it you know." Llyr was saying. "Tamas however, would have none of it. Insisting that if anyone should question my authority in his absence this ring would help my case. He can be very stubborn when he chooses to." Llyr's mouth curved wryly.

Dhariya could not help her own smile at that, nodding in complete understanding of her uncle's relentless nature. When he was set on some certain thing there was no altering his course.

At that point Llyr confessed to her how much he too missed Tamas' company. "I'm very glad you've come" he said with meaning, "this castle has felt far too empty of late.

Then as if in answer to Dhariya's unspoken wish he insisted that she stay and join him for a midnight supper. She would be delighted was her reply. She also accepted his second offer of refreshment. Thus it was that Llyr had left her there sipping from a glass of wine.

His reentry a short time later sent a strong rippling of unfamiliar impulses coursing through Dhariya and she found she could not take her eyes from him.

He had changed his clothing and now wore formal evening apparel; his hair neatly restored, drawn back at his nape with a sliver clip. Dressed from head to toe in the color of midnight and shadows, his presentation of himself was immaculate. *Magnificent,* thought Dhariya, it was the only word that came anywhere close to describing him. She realized then how much she must have unnerved him earlier by catching him in such disarray.

And of course he did not succumb to the fashion dictates of the masses she noted with approval. Instead setting his own unique standard of style, one of understated richness—an unmistakable statement of strength and self-assurance that Dhariya respected.

She and her brother had been encouraged by both parents never to fear being themselves even if it meant being different. Better to be proud to stand alone in their own truth rather than hide amongst the many in falseness. As a result she had always striven to be her own person, much to the disapproval of some of society's high and mighty and the admiration of others in that realm.

Lord Llyr obviously lived by a similar philosophy. He wore stark unrelieved black to perfection. Everything from breeches, jacket and waistcoat to shirt, cravat and polished boots, the only variation was in textures of silk and the leather, the well-cut lines fitting close to his body in a way that could not help but enhance his powerful form.

Essence of Sandalwood gently wafted from him, teasing the air with its seductive allure.

Llyr and Dhariya dined amid the opulent splendor of the formal salon. A room which had been uniquely redesigned years ago by Dhariya's uncle so that the whole outer wall and a major portion of the ceiling were now constructed entirely of leaded panes, with glass doors opening onto a terraced courtyard and manicured grounds.

Thus it was that in the darkness each small glass square reflected the candlelit ambiance and the room about them sparkled with the light of a million tiny flames.

As bespoke his position as Lord of Skara Brae, Llyr was seated at the head of the long linen draped table that could easily accommodate fifty people—up to three hundred guests with all the additional extension pieces. Tonight however, with only the two of them, Dhariya's place was to his right.

Sipping pale French wine from sterling goblets the formality between them soon faded. Dhariya found herself relaxing to a surprising degree, although by no means had Llyr's presence become less commanding, he still exuded a powerful aura unlike anything she had ever encountered. Even this huge cavernous room seemed filled by him Dhariya noted. Yet, as she removed her gloves, Dhariya realized that somehow he no longer seemed quite so fearsome to her and she was truly enjoying being in his company.

They talked easily and smiled often. Unaware of serving footman and scarcely tasting the feast artfully laid before them on silver servers. Yet try as he might Llyr could not ignore the constant intrusion of either—Ffyonna, Urien, or their far too good-looking son, Bryden—when one left another entered, clearing away a dish or stoking the fires which was unheard of behavior for their stations. Though Dhariya seemed oblivious, Llyr was becoming increasingly annoyed. Finally he summoned the houseman to his side and promptly dismissed the trio for the night.

Urien hesitated but knew better than to question his lord and employer. He looked toward Dhariya who merely smiled at him thinking Llyr was being kind to them, then with a stiff bow and a curt "as you wish my lord… Lady Dhariya." Urien turned, his heels loudly clicking his disapproval as he departed.

None of three was seen in the dining chamber again, although Llyr harbored little doubt that they were likely, in turn, peering in through some crack between the stones. At least now there would be no further interruptions and he could finally dedicate his full attentions to his beautiful companion.

Dhariya was finding it easier now to speak of those who had brought her to tears earlier. Being with Llyr seemed to soothe her in a way that was new and unexpected, for there was an element of excitement there as well. As a result she no longer felt so completely alone in the world. All the concerns and questions she had come here with somehow slipped away unnoticed, while the night wove its spell in and around them.

Soon she was telling him more and more of herself—her life. Of the close bond she had always shared with her uncle and how much more important he became to Dhariya the little girl, when at the tender age of nine years, her father and brother were both killed in a terrible accident. The impact of her loss resonated deep within Llyr as he mentally noted the eerie coincidence, having been the same age when similar tragedy had struck his own life. The more she spoke, the more his respect for Tamas steadily escalated, so too did the guilt that he tried hard to ignore.

Dhariya explained that with her aggrieved mother left to raise a small child alone, Tamas—being the only surviving sibling [already grown to manhood when Suriya was born]—he had basically raised his sister since she was six years of age and their parents drowned in a storm at sea while returning from France.

Tamas was there again for the young widow and for her daughter as well. He had stepped in as head of the family, becoming the stabilizing force and strong male figure for each of them in their own way. Not only had he taken on responsibilities in Dhariya's father's vast shipping enterprise, he had also seen to such details as Dhariya's extraordinary education, ensuring that she have the best tutors in her early years.

Once she became a young lady she had attended only the finest schools in various locations around the world, resulting in a wide range of knowledge on numerous topics. Everything from learning business and financial affairs to studies of philosophy, which was her favorite she confessed. This was over and above the standard scholarly subjects.

"I was kept so busy I hardly had time for mischief, except on holidays of course." She added with a teasing note and Llyr laughed. It was a sound he scarcely recognized and he found he could not remember the last time he had smiled without guile or spontaneously responded with anything close to genuine laughter.

Then Dhariya listened as Llyr spoke of his schooldays in London and his years of world travel. He told her that he himself was also quite alone in the world, though he did not elaborate, saying only that he had been without family from a very young age.

She noticed he offered no further personal details or family background as she had done. But she quickly dismissed this—loving the deep rich sound of his voice and the way the rhythmic pulse of his words seemed to enfold her. *I could listen to him forever,* thought Dhariya, *yet for all he's told me of himself, he's more a mystery to me now than before...And he draws me to him, somehow, without word or gesture...he draws me.*

Llyr was equally as fascinated by her. He found it impossible to define or categorize Dhariya in any way. She was unlike any woman he had ever known, especially beautiful young women of wealth and title, in fact nobility, as a rule, were known to be vain and small minded, unable to see past their own self-gain. Lord knows he himself had, up until recently, been that very same way. But Dhariya was indeed a rarity, she was a multifaceted unique individual, who was dedicated to helping those less fortunate than herself.

He well remembered Tamas proudly telling him that Dhariya had founded and headed up a very successful charitable organization, one that raised funds to better the lives of those without. Llyr himself had seen the sizable, monthly contributions from the estate in the account records.

What surprised and intrigued him most however, was her extreme sensuality, so naturally a part of her that she herself was not even unaware of it. He of course was more than aware. Recalling the first sight of her then, how he had been struck by the spark of unbridled passion flaring in the eyes of this well bred lady. It was there still flashing in velvet softness of those hazel depths.

Yet now, spending this time with her, as new and exciting aspects were revealed, there was so much more to this woman's enticing allure. Such a rare combination of innocence and sexuality was a sweetly potent seduction. And he was completely captivated, not only by the impossible beauty of her face and form, but of her spirit as well.

She is light within my darkness thought Llyr, as he savored each moment of this time with her. Yet the open trust and need he saw in her eyes dismayed him. He felt the ultimate betrayer, because he wanted her, despite all that was right and wrong. He wanted her more than any woman he had ever known. And not just her body—he wanted to possess all of her—completely and entirely.

And she wanted him too...his mind encouraged. How easy it would be to throw caution to the wind. To take what was so subtly offered, then as his thoughts began following that erotic trail along the forbidden—dark passions surged to life within him igniting a hunger he could not control—blood pounded through his veins in a violent fury of desire. He knew he must get away from her at once.

Using all the force of will he possessed, he clamped down on his rioting mind and gained a measure of dominance over his wayward emotions, though he knew it was only a temporary respite.

"Dhariya my dear," he managed to say with the utmost effort, "Surely you must be tiring by this late hour. Please don't let me keep you from your bed."

"I am rather sleepy now that you mention it." Dhariya replied, placing her white linen serviette atop the table. At that, the footman stepped up to pull back her chair. She and Llyr arose together and stood. Their faces now merely inches apart making his inner battle all the more arduous.

She looked up at him—into his eyes so deep—so black—*there seemed an eternal sadness welled within them* thought Dhariya. *As if some great dark sorrow shrouded his being and would not let him go.* And she so wished to reach him. To somehow cast out these demons he carried. How could she have known then as she gazed into those endless depths that she would never again be free?

Nor it seemed would he.

Llyr felt her soft gaze touch him—it seemed to penetrate to that hidden place at the very core of him and he could not bear what might be found there. For a silent moment expectation hovered in the air. Pulsing like a heartbeat between them.

Dhariya waited.

While Llyr—still fighting his own roiling desires managed to remember the likelihood of protective staff members covertly watching—quickly bent his head, pressing his lips to the silken flesh of her hand, which of course was only proper. Yet they both felt impact as their flesh met for the first time.

Though she had truly wished to feel his mouth upon hers, Dhariya knew it would be wrong, decorum never allowed for such scandalous behavior. Nor would any true gentlemen take such liberties with a lady. So she smiled at his gallantry, appreciating the level of respect he was imparting and said meaningfully, "Thank you Llyr for the happiness you've brought me this night."

With the beautiful smile still gracing her lips, Dhariya glided from the room and down the very same corridor by which, she had fled what seemed a lifetime ago. Her heart full to overflowing with feelings she had never known before. Still she did not look back—but straight ahead—to the future, wondering when she might see him again and hoping it would be soon.

And just as he had done once before, Llyr stared after her, watching until her slender form had faded into the shadows and vanished from sight. Leaving him to wonder if Dhariya was in fact truly real, the way she kept just appearing as if made manifest from the ether. *Perhaps this is all naught but the vain imaginings of a lonely man who has finally fallen into madness,* he cautioned himself.

Then turning about he faced the room they had shared and knew she was indeed real. For there, upon the table beside the goblet she had sipped from, lay her discarded gloves and the air still fragrant with the exquisite scent of her perfumed body. He pick up her gloves, drawing deep of her lingering essence, he closed his eyes against the torment. *Oh yes it was all far too real and far too much to bear.*

Though, back on that first night he had promised himself that he would have her, would take from her what he wanted and that would be that—just as he had always done with others in the past—he now knew that would not be possible with this woman. Even in this short time with her he knew she was something very precious indeed and deserving of so much more than he could ever offer.

Sudden thoughts of her nearness plagued him, burning like flames within his blood. Merely up those stone steps, through the maze of passages he now knew so well. Then down the long east wing corridor, not far from his own suite, were her tower rooms. With that came an image—that of her bedchamber, of her lying amid the soft folds of silken linens—her hair spilling its dark waves across the pillows…

Llyr felt the pulse of his dark passion again drawing him toward her, urging him to surrender to the wild impulses throbbing through his veins, begging him to take her. He was shaking, his entire body trembling with need. He could not risk being anywhere near her while such overwhelming desire claimed his being. He had to get away, it mattered not where.

Turning on his heel he strode purposefully toward the stable where Taranis awaited—this extraordinary horse that Llyr had paid a hefty price for a few years ago—had always been a source of pride for its owner. A source of salvation when the only way Llyr could to escape from himself was to ride wild and free across the moors.

Taranis seemed to have the same need burning in his fiery soul and from their very first ride they had formed a unique bond of unspoken understanding based on mutual respect. The fierce barely-tamed animal was the one thing Llyr had allowed himself to really care about and was now the only part of his past that yet remained—the massive black beast, equally as eager to be off as his master, danced beneath Llyr as he mounted.

Then together they set off into the night and rode out the remainder of its dark hours. Llyr, consumed by forbidden passion with Dhariya's beautiful face, a torturous image that never left him, his mind endlessly flooded over with thoughts of her—and only of her—yes he knew now there would never again be anyone but her. And he knew the memories of this night would haunt him unto eternity.

It was near dawn when Llyr finally deemed it safe enough to return to Skara Brae. Having given his shadows what they wanted they were at least satisfied for the time being, while he was exhausted both physically and emotionally.

The smell of cheap cologne still clung to him as he stumbled into his suite and abruptly dismissed his valet Dacron, much to the young man's injured pride. Then, purposefully turning the latch, Llyr locked out the day along with the rest of the castle.

Avoiding his reflection in the mirror as he passed he took himself deeper into the drape-drawn unlit regions of his chambers and threw himself down onto the feather-stuffed mattress.

Keenly aware of every ounce of his own depravity, Llyr could feel it taking further control of him as it seethed its way through his sated body and he hated himself for allowing it—hated his own inability to fight against these demons he carried inside of him. He closed his eyes to the world around him, trying to forget the truth—of who; of what; he really was, and of all its cursed repercussions—seeking respite within the oblivion of unconsciousness. Then as sleep began to claim him, he heard Tamas' voice echoing in his ears again…

"Dhariya is my niece, though the tie is a long way back, we are indeed blooded relations." This time there was no escaping the rest of the words that followed, nor the degree of desperation that had so infused their meaning…

"Nothing in this world means more to me than she does… I warn you now, stay away from her Llyr!!"

———

~ Llyr,

Thank you for such a wonderful night in the pleasure of your company. I've not felt such happiness in so long. I hope I may look forward to this again in the future. Please find my address below and should you come into town do not hesitate to call upon me.

Yours most sincerely,
Dhariya~

———

These were the words that greeted Llyr's arrival in the drawing room the next eve, beautifully scripted in an unmistakably feminine hand.

Of course she did not realize that he knew only too well where she lived or how many nights he stood there, hidden amid the shadows just to be near her. Nor did she realize so many other things about him that made their situation an impossible one.

How could she know that he yearned for her as he had for no other woman before? That every fiber of his being cried out for her and her alone? That she had become an obsession. The forbidden fruit ripe upon the vine and he the starving man whose hand ever reached to pluck it—to taste it—to devour it—and in doing so that he would destroy it...

All at once he felt the loss of her and all that would never be between them. It was too much to ask of any man. But he had made wrong choices in his past. Choices by which, he was now condemned to fate he did not want yet was powerless to change.

And worse, he had made promises he should never have given voice to. Promises that in the end meant they could never be together. These things he could not reveal to her nor could she ever know the truth of him—of what—he really was and the horrific task he had been burdened with—all that would ultimately keep them apart.

Yet how was he expected to exist in a world without her in it?

Anguish swept him, he stood alone now in the gaping expanse of the void, head bowed and eyes closed, her note crushed in his fisted hand.

Lord it was truly too, too much!

For Thou Art With Me

IV
~ And I shall fear not the darkness ~

…So strange ~ that amid shadows and silent suffering, I am thus, reborn ~ rising up out of the ashes of my former self…

Dreghorn Town-home ~ Edinburgh ~ June 1711

~ **D**eep in the night I awaken—choking… smoke thick and heavy… my lungs burn with pain…blinded by billowing haze and searing sting of tears. Then a starburst of pain explodes inside my head, leaving me helplessly aware, yet neither a part of the outer world nor apart from it. Drifting…in and out of semi-consciousness…Dear God what is happening? I'm so afraid.

I want to rise- to flee but cannot move. I try to cry out but find my voice locked in muted silence. Heat—unbearable heat—and a deafening roar—loud crackling sounds. Realization comes, all the more terrifying for its truth; my home is burning all around me and I can do nothing. Overwhelming panic grips me, threatening to strip me of these last moments… My life force is ebbing…I feel it fading away. Desperately I reach for it within me…trying to cling to it…as the reality of impending death comes upon me…I pray for my servants,

Lord…let them escape unharmed…and Lord help me…I'm so very frightened…please be with me now….

An answering calmness fills me, lifting me above the chaotic fear. I'm shown that the world I knew is only a dream in the mind of something greater—as am I too, it seems—much more than what I thought. In this wondrous moment of self-realization I know I am not my body…though its inert form yet imprisons me, I feel strangely separate from it. And I am no longer afraid. Flesh and bone will perish. Spirit will not. I shall indeed go on… O' what a glorious revelation, I am thus liberated and released from mortal bondage.

Then a loving presence enfolds me…taking me toward the light…

~ D ~

~ **Llyr** found these long months of solitude to be nothing short of torturous, seeming to stretch out, barren and endless, before him. Darkness had become the one essential—being both guardian and enemy—keeper of his secrets and betrayer of his soul; he did not know how he would survive it yet he could not survive without it.

For all that he was a completely different man and in many ways he was now a better man, this only served to make the truth of his altered existence and the magnitude of all that it entailed that much harder to bear. And as the shadows would gather to greet each coming night, so too, did the shadows within him stir to life. He had discovered that there was no way to fight against these dark passions that lived within him. This was merely one of the many things he had been forced to learn—for when one spends all of their time alone it becomes much more difficult to hide from one's self.

He had now also come to know Skara Brae Castle for the living thing it was. Thus with wisdom born of its long years, these aging stones kept watch upon him—this new Lord—who had come so suddenly to rule here had yet to earn their trust, therefore he would not be made welcome here.

And so this castle guarded her secrets well, whispering no tales to him on this night or any night since Lord Tamas had gone. Strangely this was something Llyr understood and respected, for he himself had never given trust easily and now with his world so devastatingly changed, trust was something he never gave at all.

But when the deafening silence of the castle proved beyond bearing, as it always did, his nightly rides had become his sole means of clinging to the fraying threads of sanity. Tossing back the last swallow of whiskey, the glass was set on hearth at his side. He stood, then reaching for the lightweight cloak he had left draped over the sofa, Llyr strode from the darkness of the drawing room out into the darkness of the waiting night.

It was time to ride…

Yes, he confirmed this to himself on a deep breath of fresh air, already he could sense Taranis stirring in his stall. Llyr knew this had become the animal's ritual just as it had his own and needed equally as much by them both. Sounds of neighs and snorts reached him as he approached the stables. Llyr's lips curved into a wry smile, he recognized the source only too well—it seemed Taranis had become quite vocal in his anticipation of their furious ride.

Opening the rough wooden door he stepped inside a world where strong scents of fresh hay, horseflesh and manure vied with those of tanned leather saddles and bridles, proclaiming this to be exactly what it was.

To Llyr, who always had a great love of horses and spent many hours of his early boyhood in a place much like this one, the odd mixture of smells immediately transported him back to that time before tragedy had come to painfully shatter his life, a time when the innocence of youthful dreams still lived in his boy's heart. He shook off the memories before they took hold, wanting to avoid touching all the raw emotions so tightly bound to them.

There was no one around at this late hour, only a quiet stillness and gentle sounds of resting animals, save one. The staff of grooms and underlings would all be slumbering in their quarters above stairs. Llyr had told them in the beginning that they need not leave their beds in the night to aide him. He was a skilled horseman and more than capable of readying his own mount. What he did not tell them or anyone else, however, was as much as the loneliness ached within him, he much preferred the solitude in these dark hours. Although he did appreciate their gesture of always leaving two or three safety lanterns lit as a courtesy since the braziers used for winter warmth were not needed at this time of year and offered no glowing light by which to see.

A few horses lifted their heads and nickered in greeting as he passed, Llyr whispered some soothing words in the old tongue to each along his way. He was headed to the largest stall at the farthest end, the one specially constructed to accommodate the size of its occupant—Taranis—who like Llyr himself—did not particularly care much for company and thus was kept on his own well away from the others that, despite their own fine breeding, were smaller and far less temperamental.

Llyr cast an admiring eye over his prized possession, never ceasing to marvel at the magnificence of such a massive creature—the warhorse, originally bred to bear the heavy weight of armor, yet still move with speed and precision on the battlefield. The ultimate combination of power and grace, Taranis embodied this and wore it proudly, it emanated from every fiber of his sleek form. His coat—neither black nor charcoal—but a darkness like the very breath of night, gleamed like polished silk in the lamplight, delineating the strong muscular lines of every thew.

He stroked the velvety muzzle affectionately. "Aren't you in fine form this night my ferocious beast?" The huge dark head nodded in reply. Llyr chuckled. He had always felt that he and Taranis were a true and accurate reflection of each other. He well knew the animal had a wild restless spirit that matched his own—like a storm that ever raged within, it was this that had prompted Llyr to name him Taranis, which means 'Thunderer' in the old tongue—a name he more than lived up to.

"Steady now!" Llyr commanded the restive horse, barely able to get the saddle secured for the animal's prodding at the ground with his hoof.

Then it was done and they were gone.

Many hours and many miles later Llyr found his way to the same place he always did. Reins in hand, he stood with his horse in the shadows, staring across a deserted Edinburgh street where a light glowed from the upper window of a tall narrow town home, "Dhariya" her name would come in a scant whisper from his lips.

This seemed to have become an integral part of his nightly ritual if not its very purpose. Here he would linger long until the candle finally went out, leaving only the darkness and its shadows. Always at that very moment he would feel the cruel hand of fate further tighten its merciless grip upon his heart.

Again Dhariya woke in a fit of coughing with her lungs aflame. She thought she was reliving her nightmare all over again. Gripped in fear, yet so exhausted she had not the strength to lift her heavy lids even as she gasped desperately for air. Then from somewhere across the dark chasm of her anguish Ffyonna's soothing voice reached her, speaking soft words of reassurance.

A gentle hand lifted Dhariya's head from the pillows. Prompting her to drink of the cup pressed to her parched lips. Dhariya complied, wincing at the taste of bitter herbal tincture and the pain of swallowing. However, at once she began to feel the powerful calming effects of the draught as it cooled her scorched throat before melting warmly through her limbs, enabling her to draw breath without choking.

Awareness came then, the distant crash of waves to shore, the wafting ocean breeze, all so familiar. Dhariya needed no visual confirmation to know she was in her own chambers at Skara Brae Castle—and Ffyonna was here with her—continuing the soothing litany as she eased Dhariya's back down onto the pillows

...*Yes* thought Dhariya dreamily *I am safe now.* And she slid into the soft comforting cloud of oblivion ...

———

It was the sound of Llyr's voice that pulled Dhariya from sleep. "How is she?" He was asking. And her consciousness began swimming upward seeking the source of the dark velvet tones. Her eyes fluttered open and there he was—standing at the foot of the bed looking back at her—impeccably groomed, all dressed in black, his tall imposing form and absolute maleness a stark contrast to whitewashed walls and pale earthy tones of the feminine decor. Her heart faltered at the sight he presented.

His eyes were linked with hers, although his question clearly addressed Ffyonna, his penetrating gaze remained upon Dhariya. And in the candlelight she could see the concern that etched his handsome features.

"Her ladyship's much improved today milord." Ffyonna was saying. Both Dhariya and Llyr turned in unison toward her. "Finally takin' a turn for the better she has. Aye, she'll be right as rain before long."

Even in her lucid state Dhariya could not miss the open admiration in the older woman's eyes as she answered him, and knowing this was not something easily earned, Dhariya wondered how the Dark Lord had won such favor.

Llyr nodded seeming satisfied with the reply, "Thanks to your wisdom and diligent care Ffyonna. Now you may go. I shall stay with lady Dhariya while you take your much needed rest."

"But milord I don't—"

"That will be all for tonight Ffyonna." He cut in, clearly dismissing her and any forthcoming protest for propriety.

"Aye thank you milord" She bobbed then turned toward her patient with a warning look and waving that cautioning finger Dhariya had seen so often during her childhood. "You'll behave yourself young lady and they'll be nay be so much as squeak from you now or you'll more than answer to me. Understood?"

Though the words held warning, as always, they were spoken with great affection. Dhariya obediently nodded her agreement. The ghost of a smile touching her lips as she watched Ffyonna's retreating form disappear down the stairwell.

Then Dhariya's eyes shifted back to Llyr, now they were alone and the air seemed suddenly charged. He came forth to the bedside and seated himself next to her. His sandalwood scented presence overwhelming, his nearness unsettling. She felt her body reacting in strange ways to the closeness of his.

Dhariya fought hard against the drowsiness assailing her, not wanting to sleep now. The drug however, was also causing her to feel languid and daring, being unable to hide her feelings. She very much liked that he was here with her and no one else —scandalous as it may be.

Wishing to convey so much to him, yet without the ability to voice herself, she stared wordlessly up into eyes as black as the onyx he wore upon his finger. So intense they seemed to trap her there within their endless depths.

Llyr took her small hand between his two, her flesh prickled sensuously beneath his touch. They were large hands she noted and she drew comfort from their strength as they enfolded hers.

"You gave us all quite a scare my lady..." He began saying. yet Dhariya's uncomprehending look gave him pause. Prompting him to ask "Don't you remember the fire in your town house Dhariya?"

Her eyes widened in alarm. She shook her head frantically and tried to rise.

"No-no it's alright." He soothed. "Everyone got out safely."

Relief flooded her. She sank back into the pillows weak and aching from the exertion. While silently thanking God that her loyal servants—all of whom she card a great deal for—had not been harmed.

"In fact," Llyr voice cut into her thoughts. "Not only have I hired on Josey and her husband Iain here at the castle, but Maybel is helping out in the kitchen even as we speak. Your personal groom Danvers is busy making himself useful in our stables. The majority of Dreghorn under-servants were able to find temporary positions with your Edinburgh neighbors, most of which generously offered to employ one or two in the interim.

"Of course" he went on "as you know your houseman Forbes is already on leave due to his sister's illness. However we'll find a place for him here as well should the need arise."

He could see his reassurances were having the desired effect. "So they'll not go hungry or want for employ while you're laid up… I've also been in touch with your family solicitor Jeremy Saunders, in Edinburgh. He's taking care of any details regarding the fire and he's hired someone to look into what caused it."

He paused for a breath, his emotions beginning to resurface—twisting and tangling inside him, as they so often did of late. "Saunders will be contacting you at some point with his findings. Everything is looked after. There's nothing at all to concern yourself about, you must rest and think only of getting well." Llyr drew in another long labored breath and she thought the shadows in his eyes seemed to suddenly deepen. He turned from her, looking toward the hearth fire. But in those flames he could see only the pictures of Dhariya's burning town home.

"I'm afraid you yourself took the worst of it Dhariya." He could feel the searing heat that threatened to melt the flesh from his bones, hear the deafening sound of roaring flames closing in. And the images kept coming—flashing through his mind in endless relentless sequence, then finally came the sight of her unconscious form lying defenseless amid the inferno's fatal fury. He had thought for certain that it was all over – that she was dead.

He managed to regain his composure and looked back to her "Though you're blessedly free of any burns, you did however take in a great deal of smoke. We're all grateful that you're still among us. And as you heard the all wise Ffyonna assures you'll make a full recovery."

Endeavoring to sound casual he went on. "Of course you shall remain here under Ffyonna's care for as long as you wish. This is where you belong after all Skara Brae Castle is more your rightful home than it is mine."

Even as he spoke the words Llyr knew he should not be saying them. All the same he was unable to stop them. Even in spite of what her nearness could bring. Thrusting that thought away. He did not want to think about the consequences just now. Telling himself that he was strong enough to bank the dark forbidden fires within him, because having her here was what he wanted above all things. And gazing down upon her at that moment God help him it was what he needed.

He wants me to stay, thought Dhariya. *How wonderful that he wants me here with him.* There was certainly nowhere on earth she would rather be. Nor any other she would rather be with. Momentarily forgetting her condition Dhariya opened her mouth to speak.

Llyr pressed a gentle finger to her lips. "Hush now or Ffyonna will have my hide as you well know," his voice becoming a deep caressing sound as he chided tenderly. Dhariya realized then she was incapable of speaking anyway and could only watch a softness transforming his expression as he continued to gaze upon her face. And the way he was looking at her now made her feel strange, as if warm honey flowed through her veins.

Lord God but she was beautiful thought Llyr. 'The Master' had truly done His finest work in creation of her. Each fine feature sculpted unto absolute perfection and bespoke the immeasurable love in the Creator's hand. Yet it was the radiance of her spirit that eclipsed all else, he admitted. Remembering it having been so from the very first time he had ever seen her.

That same radiance was shining through now, as she lay there drenched in a flickering halo of candles, hair loose, spilling over one bare shoulder and down to pool on the carpet at his feet. It took every ounce of control not to plunge his fingers deep into the dark silken cascade and lower his lips to hers.

Though he was powerless against a greater temptation unable to keep his eyes from wandering to where the coverlet had fallen away and the finely woven ivory bed-gown allowed an unimpeded view of her breasts. Their lush fullness strained the thin barrier, pressing taut pink crests up against transparent fibers. His breath caught, his hands tingled with thoughts of touching—of soft warm flesh filling his palms.

Abruptly raising his eyes he found her still watching him with such serene countenance. Though he knew it was the laudanum, her heavy lidded gaze seemed so sexual as if lustful and dreamy.

Dhariya *was* floating on a cloud ~ *with him…*

Unbidden her free hand slowly lifted to cradle his left cheek. Thumb gently tracing the small scar along the ridge of bone above. *Someone or something had hurt him,* she thought. *And it wasn't just this mark upon his face. No his deepest scars are within.* She knew it for she could feel the pain of his wounded soul …*Oh Llyr,* Dhariya begged silently—*let me love you— let me help to you heal— let us heal each other…*

Though her actions had clearly surprised him he made no move to stop her. Then her lips parted slightly as her eyes lowered, coming to rest upon the sensual fullness of his mouth. His blood stirred. His loins pulsed and Llyr knew the moment was ripe and dangerous.

Lord it was happening already, he was thinking, while the shadows within him danced in anticipation. He was an absolute fool to have asked her to stay. Yet it was far too late to reconsider. He could not take back the words. Nor did he truly wish to. The only thing he could do was exert a mastery of will over himself if that was indeed possible, and thus with a heroic force he drew-in harsh rein on his emotions.

She could not possibly know what she, in all her innocent sensuality, was doing to him. Nor could she comprehend how much he wanted to taste the sweetness of those full rose-petal lips. And that was just the beginning. For her eyes revealed many things to him this night–too many things. With her newly awakening desire so openly displayed within those hazel depths he fairly trembled with the effort to control his own response.

After a moment he curved his hand around hers and brought it from cheek to lips where he placed a kiss to the center of her palm. Shutting his eyes he continued to hold her palm to his lips, nothing else just that.

Taking a long indrawn breath he lifted his head to meet her gaze as he whispered, "sleep now sweet angel and dream wondrous dreams."

Then with the tingling memory of his lips imprinted upon her palm Dhariya's eyes drifted closed

Llyr sat unmoving for the longest time, savoring the sight of her slumbering form, unwilling to relinquish the soft trust of her hand still clutching his. Oh what a coil he had created by his earlier invitation, he thought, having her here was going be the ultimate test. At least she was sleeping peacefully now which, for the moment, set him somewhat at ease.

He turned his gaze to admiring the room about them.

The sheer lawn under-curtain danced as the night breathed in through the open casement, gentle with the summer's warmth, bringing the scent of the sea and the sound of waves crashing on the rocks far below and stirring to life the various fragrances from the box of herbals on the bedside table.

Ffyonna had proven herself a rare healer, he thought gratefully, as the wafting of her medicinal aids brought her skills to mind. Recalling how he had watched her diligently care for Dhariya. The older woman had shown a stamina that matched his own; staying beside her patient all through the day, then often, reappearing in the night hours as well.

He thought back on their conversations during those hours they had shared in bedside vigils. Sitting quietly on a night much like this one the older woman had smiled as she recollected various aspects of Dhariya's girlhood, back in those days when she, along with her brother, and Bryden had spent much time together making mischief at every turn.

Llyr found himself smiling too as he learned some of Dhariya's antics. "Ever tryin' to prove herself she was." Said Ffyonna, "always takin' risks the older boys would never have dared." Ffyonna had gone on to relay what had led to Dhariya's claiming of these rooms for herself when she was twelve years old. It seems at that point Dhariya no longer felt the need to sleep in her mother's suite.

Ffyonna had told him that Dhariya had sat her mother and uncle down together. Then calmly went about explaining how she was feeling to them, instantly recognizing the young girl's needs neither had made any objection. Both understanding that Dhariya was beginning to develop her own sense of independence, they had indeed encouraged her.

Tamas had then told Dhariya she could choose her own suite of rooms from any of those available at Skara Brae and he would ready it for her. He vowed to make it beautiful and that together they would decorate it in whatever colors and styles she preferred.

And Dhariya had chosen this tower. "Of course 'tis changed somewhat." Ffyonna added, "As she grew into womanhood the young girl's wants were replaced with the more sophisticated tastes she had acquired."

Llyr sat now admiring the finished result. The elegant beauty of the chamber and its fine furnishings gave testament to the depth of Tamas' love for his niece. Ffyonna had told Llyr that his lordship had ordered each piece specially crafted for Dhariya. The sitting room below was just as exquisitely done and followed through with the same theme of color and décor.

All creamy tones and complimentary earthy accents, a true reflection of the woman herself, open and light, with a rare balance of strength and softness. So completely female in every way, yet nothing flashy or frivolous, nothing overdone, for even here the measure of Dhariya's character remained undeniable. Everything from the pale washed stones of walls and floors to the plush eastern rugs was pure perfection.

On this bedchamber level the one straight wall partitioning off the small bathing-area and privy closet also served as backdrop for large bed that held dominion over the room. Its four-posted frame was the most unique Llyr had ever seen.

Crafted of light colored wood, perhaps birch or beech, its massive headboard skillfully carved into a filigree of lace work. With scalloped edging that curved high and crested into point at the center—this wavy border gave an eastern flavor to what was otherwise reminiscent of a gothic arch—a smaller version of the same design made-up the footboard.

His eye followed delicate patterns of ivy and trailing vines etched into the heavy posts, weaving their way up toward the canopy of heavy ivory damask overtop, where crisp pleated folds widened outward from a puckered circle. The soft tone matching the corded ivory window drapes, chaise lounge and winged chairs, as well as the creamy crewelwork bed hangings and coverlet.

The same damask covered the padded window seats below the casements, which he noted, had been widened from their original arrow slits into a series of long windows, complete with leaded glass to keep out the chill of winter, yet opened on a hinged frame to allow the warm summer breeze to filter through, as it was this night. No doubt another of Tamas innovative designs, thought Llyr with further admiration.

Several oversized damask pillows with their tasseled corners tossed purposefully here and there added to the relaxed, comfortable elegance that further complimented the eastern flavor lent by the thick Turkish carpets, whose dark earthy tones were as deep and luxuriant as the pale shades were delicate and pure.

Ornate brass candle stands and wall sconces added their own brand of warmth and uniqueness. For these were not polished to a glistening shine. But instead had a muted dark gold finish that gave a far richer ambiance.

The atmosphere was subtly sensual like a whispered invitation. And as the candles illuminated the exotic patterns carved into these brass holders, those that reflected the far eastern lands of their origins, Llyr was suddenly reminded of a Sultan's palace he had once visited many years ago during his travels.

What he found most impressive by far however, was the huge hearth made entirely of white jade and sculpted specifically to accommodate the dimensions of the curving tower wall. He had never seen anything like it and his eyes were intent upon their study of it when a soft whimper brought his attention back to the slender form in the bed, where Dhariya lay. She was still asleep although her brow was now deeply furrowed and she was becoming increasingly restless, clutching his hand tightly between her two.

It quickly became clear she that was not going settle. As her whimpers became moans of distress Llyr's concern escalated. He reached over and yanked the corded bell pull to summon help. Within minutes Dhariya's young maid Josey appeared and he sent her off to find Ffyonna at once.

It seemed an eternal wait for their return, while Dhariya's movements became more and more violent with arms flailing. Llyr thought it unwise to wake her in the midst of such obvious trauma. Yet he worried she may injure herself. So he lay himself down beside her and drew her into his embrace, while murmuring sweet words in a calming voice. "It's all right Dhariya…you're safe in my arms now. Can you hear me?"

She made no response yet started to ease somewhat, just as Ffyonna's voice broke harshly into the stillness, "Lord no—not the fits again!"

Llyr's gaze flew to the doorway. One look at the older woman and his initial relief dissipated. And Ffyonna's fearful expression was only mirrored in Josey's terrified face, hovering in the background. Llyr immediately took charge of the situation. With Dhariya still held in the safety of his arms he addressed Ffyonna in stark tones that brooked no argument. "Fits? What do you mean fits? Tell me what you're on about–now!"

That got her moving, coming directly to the bedside. "I'll explain all to you milord once we get her ladyship settled down," the look she gave him imploring his understanding.

"Very well Ffyonna. What can I do?"

"Just keep holdin' her steady as you are so I can see to the herbs and such."

Llyr complied while he observed Ffyonna's skills at work. First she reached into her box of herbals on the bedside table and selected some sort of dried leaves. These she crushed into her heavily creased palm then held her hand beneath Dhariya's nose allowing the unconscious patient to inhale the full strength of scented leaves. Llyr himself caught traces of the strangely potent aroma and he could feel Dhariya's body already beginning to relax within his embrace. Ffyonna's watchful gazed also noted this change. Only then did the older woman carefully administer the dose of laudanum. Within a matter of minutes the treatment had its desired affect and Dhariya became as limp as a rag doll. Yet Llyr continued holding her, not wanting to let her go. With his eyes still intently upon Dhariya's sleeping face—his voice was soft as he spoke to Ffyonna. "I wanted to wake her but thought better of it."

"Aye milord, there's always a risk of danger in wakin' one in such a state. Best that you hold her safe until it passes, just as you did."

Then Llyr's dark eyes lifted piercing Ffyonna where she stood. Instantly interpreting his meaning she flashed a quick glance over at Josey. Llyr also understood the unspoken gesture she had given him in reply.

He reluctantly released Dhariya as he arose and turned to the younger servant. "Josey you will remain with Lady Dhariya while Ffyonna and I discuss things in private. We'll be near enough for you call out if there's any further disturbance."

"Yes my lord. I surely will." She bobbed, then seated herself by the fire and took up some stitching from the basket at her feet.

No one spoke as Ffyonna went through the motions of lighting the oil lantern, adjusting its flame, and replacing the glass encasement. The room seemed veiled in a quiet sorrow, laden with all that was about to be revealed.

Then—lantern in hand—Ffyonna turned and walked away. Llyr followed the older woman and the undulating golden light she carried, through the narrow stairwell that spiraled its way upward, to the open battlements atop the east tower. Soft sounds of their booted feet brushing the stone steps echoed into the stillness.

Upon reaching the landing Ffyonna set the lantern down and they both stood silent. Each trying to gather inner strength and prepare for the words to come, while the brine scented wind whipped and whirred about them and waves crashed against the rocks far below —Llyr waited.

After a time Ffyonna, her gaze distant and solemn looking into the summer night, which never turned fully dark this time of year, finally began. "T'was many years ago now milord, Lady Dhariya was but a wee lass of nine, a most dreadful night in all our lives."

Though Ffyonna's voice sounded emotionless, Llyr knew that she was scarcely clinging to composure. He said nothing. Only listened to this tale he did not wish to hear.

"The family was stayin, at the Dreghorn townhouse in Edinburgh when word came that one of their biggest ships was just come in to port. T'was loaded full of spices and other riches from the Far East."

Ffyonna's eyes remained fixed and staring, her voice impassive, "Lady Dhariya... she went along to the docks with her father and brother as she'd often done. The men would oversee the unloadin'... t'wasn't really necessary, but somethin' they all enjoyed. Dharyia's mother, Lady Suriya bein' six months gone with child and havin' miscarried two of her babes in the past, stayed home."

She paused for a breath. "So off they went the three of them, Dhariya, her father Lord Darrien, her brother and only sibling the young fifteen year old lord and heir, who bore his father's name, but everyone called him DJ. Aye, there was always much excitement with every new shipment and the docks were abuzz with it as each huge create was lowered to the ground then hauled away into the storehouses."

Ffyonna's hands tightened the ramparts as her grasp on her emotions began to slip. "Then suddenly a rope snapped and one of them huge creates came down, crushin' Dhariya's father and brother beneath its heavy weight...the shouts of warnin' had come too late, and the both of them died instantly there that night."

"And Dhariya bore witness to this?"

"Aye she did...T'was only at the last second her father looked up, and seein' their fate, was able to push his daughter outta' harm's way, else we'd have lost her as well."

"My God," Llyr's words came out in a mere harsh whisper.

"There's more milord and t'is much worse I fear."

Llyr's insides knotted in apprehension as he stared straight ahead and endeavored to brace himself. While the wind keened around them, like a solemn wail of grief.

"T'was much later," Ffyonna was saying, "after all the panicked confusion began to settle that someone finally realized the wee lass was missin.'

Llyr turned haunted eyes to her. "You mean Lady Dhariya?"

"Aye milord, they started searchin' that very night but t'was for naught… A full four days she was gone. In the end t'was his Lordship Tamas who somehow managed to find her…" Ffyonna faltered and her body trembled as she recalled these agonizing memories.

"Ffyonna are you all right?"

"Aye," She replied. "T'is just…I've never spoken of this before, but you must know, so you can understand what the young lass is goin' through now… and t'is even more important if my instincts are right about the two of you." Ffyonna did not turn toward him, or even cast so much as a glance his way, yet she seemed to sense Llyr's startled response to her sudden change of topic and its obvious implications.

"Aucccc, I can nay stop you." She went on, "t'would bring only heartache to even try…and maybe t'will be a good thing for Dhariya, if you treat her right that is, Lord knows the lass needs love in her life now more than ever and t'is the kind of love only the right man can give. Pray God that t'is you."

Llyr, completely taken aback by this altered course and the woman's bluntness about it all, began to mount a defense. "Ffyonna I—"

"Aye," she cut in. While her gaze remained on the darkness stretching out before her, "these eyes may be gettin' old but they're nay blind."

"No. You're eyes see very well indeed." He concurred, purposely sidestepping the true meaning of her comments and of what those eyes had seen.

Then just as abruptly, Ffyonna returned to the previous topic once again and plunged on without pause. "I trust nothin' of this will ever stray from your lips. Only three of us ever knew the full truth of what happened to the wee lass— Dhariya's mother bless her soul, Lord Tamas and myself. Not one of us would ever speak of it aloud. Now I'll have your word on that as well milord"…This time she waited for his answer.

"Of course Ffyonna, I formally give you that pledge here and now."

With a nod of acknowledgement, she proceeded. She still had not looked at him, just continued to stare out into the night as if entranced. Though when she spoke now her voice shook with emotion. "His Lordship Tamas brought the child back here to Skara Brae…" she paused drawing a handkerchief from her pocket and pressing it to her mouth, seeking moment of composure. "I'll nay forget the sight of her wee body all battered and brutalized."

Llyr turned away in shocked disbelief. "Dear God Ffyonna." His words lost to the wind.

"Seems she'd fled the docks in a panicked state of grief," Ffyonna went on, "runnin' blindly through the streets and into a danger she could nay have imagined…and she met it in the worst way. With a beast of a man full of twisted thoughts and ill-bred passions…and he, upon seein' her impossible beauty—for she was even then—this monster took her for himself…and raped the child with his man's body."

Llyr closed his eyes against the words. As if the feeble gesture could make them stop or somehow undo the reality of the appalling tale they told.

Yet Ffyonna, seeming totally unaware of him now, only continued. "Aye," she was saying. "The bastard he took our wee Dhariya for his own sick pleasure…then when he'd sated his filthy lust and finished usin' her, he tossed her aside like trash and left her for dead inside an empty warehouse."

In a white knuckled grip of the parapet, Llyr's body wrenched and repulsed against the images this horror evoked, while he fought a rage such as he had never known.

"By grace Lord Tamas somehow found her barely clingin' to her last breath she was, when he brought her to me."

Llyr was still trying to gather his inner resources and somehow cope with what he was being told, while the older woman beside him just went on and on. He did not know how much more he could handle. Yet he must find a way, just as those who lived through it had had to do. *Face it.* He told himself, *for the first time in your life man, look this grotesque painful truth straight in the eyes it's the only way.*

"And t'was here," Ffyonna's weary voice cut into his thoughts, "within these same castle walls in which she was born that I tended the wounds of our wee Dhariya, along with the strength and stoic efforts of her grief stricken mother. "Lady Suriya, who'd just lost both husband and son, then, from the shock of it all lost the babe she'd bin' carryin' as well. Yet she rose from her sickbed and with a firm vow that she'd not lose her daughter too…she mounted her horse and rode the distance to Skara Brae alone—more alone than she'd ever bin' in her life.

"In the end Dhariya survived. Though her child's body was so damaged she'll never bear a child of her own. But she's a brave one our lass, just like her mother was. With strength of spirit such as I've never known in any other."

Ffyonna drew in a long labored breath…these painful emotional memories were wearing her down, *how tired I am,* she thought, grateful to be nearly done with the telling of it. "The healin' took many long months that's when these fits first started up, just like you saw tonight. You must know that our Dhariya is a rare and special soul. I don't just say that because I love her like my own. 'Tis because as she healed and regained some strength, Dhariya—child that she was of only nine years—began to think about helpin' others, wantin' to do somethin' so that those who are weakest and most vulnerable would never fall prey to such an evil.

"That's when she first came up with her idea for Harvest~House Foundation. 'Tis also when the fits suddenly stopped, though there were times as Dhariya grew older, that she'd turn a wee bit strange and suddenly rage, sayin' no one knows what they're truly askin' for when they pray for another's survival. Then she'd go off alone and not be seen for hours on end. Afterwards, when she came back she'd be all right, just like herself again…I'm thinkin' 'tis the fire's trauma bringin' em' back now."

With that the older woman turned away and left him, saying nothing more, she seemed to know that he needed time to absorb the impact of all that she had disclosed.

And she was right.

Llyr stood there alone on the windswept battlements shaken to the very core of his being. His mind and body roiling in a tangle of emotions he could not even name. Nothing could have prepared him for this. What hearing this story had brought forth within him astounded him. But then it was not just a story it was truth, Dhariya's truth. Beautiful sweet Dhariya, with her life of affluence and privilege, with her smiling face and radiant spirit, no one would ever think her life to be anything but perfect.

Well how little any of us know what another has endured or must face on a daily basis, he thought to himself. *Yet how easily we decide who and what another is or is not?—making our judgments and bold proclamations, and to what purpose?—so that we may justify our own behavior or view ourselves in a better light. And I am just as guilty of it as the rest if not more*, he silently confessed. He had had to face many things about himself in recent months, and tonight, new depths had opened up within him, forcing him to look further inside himself than ever before.

Just then the flame in the lantern gave its final flicker and died—leaving the world draped in a darker veil. *Yes, that's better*, he thought wryly, for tonight this lighter shade of darkness showed an accurate reflection of what he had found within the gapping core of his being. This darkness that refused to fully cover the all the lies and deceptions he tried to hide there. His hands clenched into fists as he fought his way through it all.

Dear God how could such a thing be true? How can people call themselves human and hurt one another so? Why must some suffer so much more than others? How can this be fair in the eyes of any merciful God? These were the same questions that had plagued Llyr since his own tragedy as a young lad. Yet no answers had ever come for him. Now there was a new question to add to these others. But it was one that only he himself could answer if he but dare. *What had he himself done in response to that little boy's pain? Had he not decided all those years ago that it was 'take or be taken' which is exactly what he had set about doing while giving no thought to anyone's feelings whatsoever?*

Although he had never done anything close to the atrocious acts this monster had inflicted upon Dhariya, defiling a mere child. The thought alone turned his insides into knots. Yet could he truly claim himself to be any better? Are one's sins rated? Or are they all the same in the eyes of that final judgment call?

These questions screamed out again and again in his mind, twisting and tangling with the thoughts of all that Dhariya had been forced to endure. The images of such sweet innocence debased and violated would not leave his mind. He could not purge himself of the vileness. He felt tainted in a way he never had before, in a way that would never be cleansed. He was a different man now than the one who had awoken only hours ago, than the one who had ascended the curving steps to this place where he now stood; this kind of knowledge never leaves a person. And he raged anew with these injustices and the harsh cruelty of this world about him.

He had always felt that life owed him a great deal for having taken so much away. Now he knew different, now he knew another who had suffered even more than he, yet had not sought to hurt back. Well he still wanted to hurt back. Yes he did, in a different and far more violent way than he could have ever believed himself to be capable of.

Despite his past and this fate that had been pressed upon him, he had never been comfortable with the idea of killing. That had all suddenly changed, in these last segments of time here atop this tower, he had become someone else. For another thought had come to displace all others and now burned continually in his mind…

If only I could find the beast that perpetrated such atrocities upon Dhariya's innocence, I would gladly see the last breath from his body, a slow and very painful death, Yes—and I would relish every drop of his blood, thusly spilled upon the earth. There, that was the truth of it, and it was merely the first of many startling revelations he had unearthed...

And now that pledge he had made so readily before ever knowing Dhariya, would prove next to impossible to fulfill, the only answer he could find was to try to keep himself separate from his feelings for her...but would he be strong enough? He did not know.

Bloody Hell! He raked his fingered through his already disheveled hair nearly tearing it out by its roots. The last thing he needed was to begin to feel, to care, to have his long dead conscience resurrected at this juncture. Well it was already too late. He could not stop what was happening any more than he could alter the twisted hand of his own fate. Lifting his gaze to the heavens above he beseeched whatever powers that be ... or might deign to listen to one such as he...

How could he now conceivably become so emotionally detached from Dhariya after all of this that he would be able to fulfill that long ago vow?

Closing his eyes against the darkness without only to be greeted by an equal darkness within...and he knew just as he had always known that for him there would be no escape. Nor would there be any forthcoming answers to these questions.

And when the first light of dawn came to grace the sky Llyr slowly descended the curve of stairs and stepped into Dhariya's bedchamber. The room was quiet. A boiling herb pot hung suspended from a chain above the fire, wafting its soothing scents into the air. Drawing the fragrant medicinal blend deep into his lungs Llyr summoned his inner fortitude and finally turned toward the bed.

...*There were times as Dhariya grew older,* Fyonna had told him, *that she'd turn a wee bit strange and suddenly rage, sayin' no one knows what they're truly askin' for when they pray for another's survival. Then she'd go off alone and not be seen for hours on end. Afterwards, when she came back, she'd be all right, just like herself again...*

Llyr understood this inner rage; he knew only too well the high price that certain survival demands. He felt his heart constrict within his chest as he looked upon Dhariya now—knowing what he knew—and he was grateful she was not awake. Selfish though it may be he knew he needed time to get hold of his emotions before he truly faced her and looked into the depths of those beautiful hazel eyes.

Josey and Ffyonna he noted both sat near to their patient. Josey stitching, Ffyonna sorting her herbal remedies, neither paid him any mind, they had become quite used to his presence in this chamber of late. Llyr stood and watched the scene a few moments. Then, satisfied that Dhariya rested without further disturbance, he left her in the women's capable care and sought his own much-needed rest.

V

~ And thus I wait, upon the edge of twilight's beckoning call ~

…He frightens me. He excites me. He makes my heart yearn for something, while my body aches with a woman's desires, for that which I have never known …

Skara Brae Castle ~ August ~ 1711

~ **Bed** rest was the major component of my recovery along with Ffyonna's herbal treatments. With each passing day my strength returned a little more. No longer in need of constant eyes upon me I filled the long lonely hours of solitude with memories of my family. My thoughts traveling back down the road of my life. Reliving special moments shared with those now gone, carefully preserving each precious recollection in ink upon the pages of my journal. This proved a form of healing in itself and helped ease the ache of loss that never truly left me.

I'd seen to the accounting ledgers of my foundation that arrived regularly by messenger. I'd written replies to those friends and *acquaintances who'd sent notes inquiring after my well being, I'd sorted endless stacks of forwarded invitations, sending regrets of non-attendance to all. I did not miss the city life of socials and galas, of gossip and falseness. I'd never truly felt a part of that world.*

But mostly I thought of him.

My mind seemed to become more and more consumed with him. I felt powerless against this ever-increasing intrusion. It frightened me. He frightened me, though not in that fearsome way as before. There is something about him—something indefinable like a beckoning invitation into mystery and the unknown. Intrigued in spite of myself, feeling drawn in a way I'd never experienced before, as a moth to flame.

~ D ~

~ **D**hariya had not seen Llyr for nearly three weeks. Not since the night he had come to her bedchamber. That night they had shared secret feelings–silently revealed with their eyes alone. It had been so wonderful to her. Yet now it seemed he purposely kept away.

To her mind, Llyr's actions bespoke one who did not care. In spite of the fact, Ffyonna and Josey both confided his constant need to know every detail of her progress. Even this did not relieve the hurt and disappointment she felt.

Nor did the fresh flowers that kept coming day after day, filling the vases in her chambers to overflowing, "Lord Llyr's orders" said Hannah, the shy under-maid who assisted Josey as she arranged them. The blush in Hannah's cheeks gave testament to the dark lord's effects upon the female gender. At first Llyr's thoughtfulness had touched Dhariya. Now, so many days later, she scarcely noticed the colorful bouquets or their fragrant offering.

She sat curled in the window seat of her bedchamber staring out from the tower like one held captive and awaiting rescue. For indeed that is just how she felt.

Watching the crash of waves to shore in an endless rhythmic motion, she cared not that the sun was streaming in through the opened casement and glinting off the ocean far below, or that the breeze was a caress—soft and warm—upon her cheeks. She was only aware that her heart lay heavy within her breast.

Why? Why does he resist me, and this, that is between us? I know he feels the pull just as I do, I've read that truth in his eyes more times than I could count. Yet just as we're about to move forward he steps back— shielding himself from me. Over and over again, I do not understand. Each questioning thought seemed to rise and fall with the incoming tide. Her mind and heart both yearned for the answers

She knew that Llyr now left the castle each night after taking his dram of whiskey in the drawing room and did not return until just before the first rays of dawn streaked the sky. Dhariya was more than aware of his comings and goings.

Having chanced to overhear Annie and another undermaid gossiping shamelessly about the 'Dark Lord' as they went about cleaning the sitting room, unaware that their voices clearly carried up the narrow stairwell to the occupant of the bedchamber on the floor above, amid giggles and bawdy suggestive remarks they discussed him in great detail. It was apparent the staff members, particularly the female variety, continued to take an avid interest in his Lordship.

Dhariya however, had already bore witness to his nightly departures. As her strength increased she often escaped the confines of her bedchamber by climbing the steps to the battlements seeking the freedom of the open air.

From there beneath the light summer sky and pale moonlight, one could see for miles in every direction and so she had stood and watched him ride from the castle. Mounted upon his huge black horse, disappearing into the forest, then once he emerged from the trees, he would rage across the moors. Looking like some unearthly beast in the night, his cloak flying out behind him like great dark wings, until he finally disappeared into the mist and vanish from sight ... *Whom does he ride so eagerly toward?* She wondered.

Hours later when sleep eluded her as it did so often now, she would find herself climbing those steps again looking for him to return. But she never saw him come back. The more Dhariya tried to understand the complexities of the man himself, and her feelings for him, the more confusing it all became. For there were the other times when she had awoken in the dead of night and felt his presence hiding in there within the shadows of her bedchamber.

She need not see him to know he was there, aside from faint traces sandalwood, the essence of power he exuded was unmistakable. She would lay there in the dark, feeling him near, feeling him yearning to reach for her, and she, yearning to reach out for him. Dhariya could not comprehend his strange behavior. The war he waged with himself and his obvious attraction to her was so far beyond reason.

She had to find out for certain where things stood between them before she went completely mad. Thus Dhariya determined, tonight would be different. For tonight she would escape from this a-cursed feather prison and seek him out then he would have to face her.

It was only after much pleading on Dhariya's part that Ffyonna finally relented, yet not before first imparting numerous threats and warnings upon her patient's head. But deep down Dhariya knew the older woman would never agree if she thought there any true risk in permitting a few hours respite from the endless hours of rest.

It had also become very evident that Ffyonna no longer opposed Llyr and Dhariya's feelings for one another, while Urien and Bryden were quite another matter, both men knew their stations, that they were powerlessness to interfere, and Ffyonna would always outmatch either of them.

And so it was, that amid much excitement, the preparations for the night ahead began. Ever faithful Josey helped Dhariya bathe and dress just as she had done so often in their shared past. Yet tonight the young maid was clucking and fussing about like a distressed hen, until Dhariya, though her naturally contralto voice was still hoarse and barely there, finally spoke out "Lord above Josey, listen to yourself. I do believe you've been far too long in Ffyonna's company."

Josey paused in thought, "Why my lady, I do believe you're quite right." Their eyes met in the mirror and two young women, who also shared a close friendship, burst into gales of laughter, echoing a sound reminiscent of their shared girlhood and one that was often heard in those early years.

They had in fact known each other practically their entire lives and had always talked easily in spite of the difference in their stations. Dhariya had been scarcely two years of age and Josey just three, when Dhariya's parents had taken the homeless child and her widowed mother, Maybel off the streets and into their home.

Lady Suriya had added Maybel to her kitchen staff, where she had trained diligently under the aging head cook Agnas and eventually took over the position, while Josey became playmate to Dhariya, and had also been tutored alongside the Dreghorn children. When the girls reached their early teens, Dhariya went off on her educational travels and Josey was sent to London to learn the role of 'Ladies maid.' Once Josey had successfully completed her training stint, she then traveled abroad to reunite with Dhariya and began her service to her dearest friend.

They had grown into lovely young women. Both of similar stature and taller than the average female, though Josey was slightly shorter than Dhariya's five foot six inches, the young maid was also pretty with dark hair and large black-brown eyes, she was always much sought after by footman and valets of her acquaintance.

Much to everyone's surprise, however, just over three years ago Josey had married beneath her, and wedded Iain, the stable hand of an Edinburgh neighbor. He too had then joined the Dreghorn town-home staff, which included stuffy yet loveable old Forbes as houseman, Ester the housekeeper and the ever-witty groom Danvers.

There had also been Alyce at one time. She had been Lady Suriya's personal maid, who had since found another posting after her employer's death. The household had been a happy one long ago and Dhariya longed for those days again—then Dhariya's laughter suddenly ceased in a fierce fit of coughing.

"Oh now look at you!" Josey near hollered. "Shall I fetch mistress Ffyonna then?"

Dhariya frantically shook her head in the negative. Then as her coughing fit subsided and she regained her breath she reinforced her answer. "Heavens no Josey, of course I love Ffyonna like my own blood relation, but pray don't get her all riled after it's taken me so long to win acquiesce for this night."

"As you wish my lady," Josey gave an uncertain look before turning her attentions to Dhariya's hair, which would be worn up in loose array. Never having cared for overly prim coiffures Dhariya preferred a barely contained appearance, which allowed for curls to spill out here and there. This in fact, had become Dhariya's own signature style of late, and one, which many of the more daring society ladies now mimicked.

Dhariya watched Josey's skilled hands at work magically transforming her tresses. On the odd occasion Dhariya had tried to see if she could duplicate this unique style. Yet no matter how many times she had seen Josey do it her own attempts always failed miserably and she inevitably gave up.

"I do hope you're sure about this Dhariya," Josey said a moment later, in the informal way they often adapted when alone. She loved Dhariya like a sister. Right from the beginning it had always been so. Josey felt beholding not only to Dhariya, but to her parents as well. Lord knew where she and her mother would be if not for their kindness and generosity.

Josey's mind was still haunted by fragments of the small frightened girl she had been, living in the streets with her equally frightened mother. How quickly things could change.

One day they had been a happy family of three, somehow managing to exist on the meager salary her father earned at the docks unloading cargo from ships.

The next day, two hours after Josey's father left for the docks word came that he had died on the job—his heart seemed to give out was the only explanation offered. Neither Josey nor her mother ever knew what had happened with the body, there had been no time for such detail or any grieving, the following morning the bill collectors had learned the news, they came in droves, and mere survival took all precedence.

The business proprietors had been generous enough when they knew there was a steady wage, small though it was, coming in. Once that financial promise no longer existed, their henchmen gathered at the door. Like vultures picking at the bones of a carcass, all of them demanding payment in full.

Of course there had been no money to pay them, thus by that very evening, Josey and her mother found themselves cast out from their home into the unforgiving streets of Edinburgh City with nothing but the clothes on their back. The few belongings they had were claimed as forfeit, to be sold off for whatever could be gotten for them.

Fortunately Josey's father had often worked for Dhariya's father, Lord Darrien who, unlike most others of his rank, always took time to speak with those in his hire, learning their names as well as their circumstances. When he heard of this tragedy he was genuinely concerned for the wife and child left behind. He told this news to his wife, Lady Suriya, she too shared her husband's caring ways and together they set out to find the homeless mother and daughter.

Unfortunately it had taken weeks to track them down. During those days and nights of utter desolation Josey would huddle deep in the shadows—watching her mother beg from strangers—witnessing her mother steal from merchants, an act which her God fearing mother had always taught her was a sin. Yet with the desperation of mere survival all morality and values were of necessity cast aside.

But no matter what, Josey had been fed first and her needs tended to, even if it meant her mother had to go without. Maybel would only allow herself enough sustenance to ensure she would be there to look after her daughter and somehow get them both out of this horrific nightmare they had been thrust into.

In the end it had been the beautiful Lady Suriya herself who, like an avenging angel of mercy, had finally found them. Accompanying her was a kindly looking man they later learned was her solicitor Jeremy Saunders, as Lord Darrien's business duties had kept him from the search. Josey had never forgotten that day and the depth of her gratitude to these people—her saviors—could never be fully expressed.

Never once had Lady Suriya, Lord Darrien or Jeremy Saunders ever talked down to them, nor caused them to feel shamed because of what the twisted hand that fate had bestowed upon them. Josey and Maybel had been welcomed into Dreghorn staff and the entire household with open arms and treated with as much respect as one of high birth. Josey had also found immediate acceptance from both Lady Dhariya and her brother the young Lord Darrien as well.

This type of charitable precedent was believed in and practiced by Dhariya's entire family. It had been the motivating factor for Lord Darrien starting his own shipping line. He wanted to create a place of employment for those who were willing yet unable to find work due to lack of education, lack of skills or lack of available jobs.

The company had served its purpose well and provided a better life for many Edinburgh residents of lower birth. Darrien & Co. Shipping Enterprises had also spared Lord Darrien the boredom of idleness as well as giving him a place to use his brilliant mind, all of which resulted in soaring profits.

She felt deeply indebted to this family. Since Lord Darrien and Lady Suriya were no longer here to protect their daughter

Josey felt she must try to do so by voicing her concerns if nothing else. The young maid truly feared this growing bond so obviously developing between Dhariya and his lordship.

Josey herself was more than aware of the pain that came from acting irrationally. Her own marriage to Iain was proof of that. What had at first seemed a fiery passion had quickly burned away leaving only ashes in its place—Josey did not want that for Dhariya.

Lord Llyr was without question the most handsome man any of them had ever seen, Josey admitted to herself. If this alone was not dangerous enough there were also other dangers about him, and these were more fearsome, yet indefinable beyond a sensing of some great darkness within his soul.

Who was he? What was he? No one knew. From all she had deduced he seemed to arrive out of nowhere and assumed the longstanding title of one of the most powerful lords in the realm, not to mention the wealthiest. In the young maid's mind there was no doubt as to what her duty was.

"I know it's not my place to speak so freely," Josey went on, determined to at least warn Dhariya against him. "But you were my friend before you were ever my employer…and…What I mean is…his Lordship's very handsome and all yet there's something about him that scares me I don't know what it is. Even Iain says he doesn't fully trust in this dark lord."

"Josey you are indeed my friend, first last and always, and as such you're permitted to speak freely at any time. You know that." Dhariya told her, meaning every word. "Believe me. I do thank you for your genuine concern. However your fears are unfounded Josey there is truly no reason to feel that way about Lord Llyr."

Josey seemed somewhat reassure by these words and said no more about it Dhariya had spoken her reply in a soothing manner, while purposely omitting the fact she herself was also a little afraid. She could not understand how it was that fear and desire could come together. She only knew that they indeed did. For as she had already inwardly acknowledged, she found that this sense of danger about him excited her.

Later Dhariya stood in the main entry hall beneath its high vaulted ceiling reaching ever skyward, she felt small and vulnerable amid the vast cavernous surroundings, but she held her ground with determined resolve. She would not let another day pass without seeing Llyr—she needed to see him—needed to come to some understanding of what his feelings were.

She waited in apprehension, her heart fluttering like a trapped bird inside her chest knowing at any moment he would descend the grand staircase en-route to the drawing room and his dram by firelight and being unsure of what the night ahead might hold. Just then without any pre-warning of approaching footsteps, Llyr emerged from the shadowy depths above, resplendent in his customary evening attire of unrelieved black, groomed without flaw to his usual impeccable standards—and Dhariya thought her heart would surely cease to beat at all.

At mid-point on the staircase he saw her, a vision gowned in emerald green velvet with dark curls trailing-down bare throat and shoulders, his steps halted…He was not prepared for this–for her. He had not yet dealt with the new dimensions their relationship had suddenly taken on. Something had shifted within him that night on the battlements, hearing what he had heard had stirred something—something he thought dead and buried long ago. Yet once uncovered it would no longer lay dormant nor stay hidden and silent in the darkness.

Although he had known he cared for Dhariya from the very beginning it was different now. It had become a primal, protective emotion that ran deeper than he dare dive to explore, he did however know its name—love. And it was a far more dangerous emotion in him than any other ever could be.

Love—the word itself seemed foreign to him, perhaps even more foreign than the prisoner it held within him, for it had been so long denied.

Caught unprepared, the full impact of her beauty startled him and stole all the breath from his lungs. He had not seen her since that night when everything changed between them. He knew he had been running from her—from this inevitable moment, even as he had once vowed never to run from anything again. Yet he had more than willingly broken this promise to himself because he had been incapable of doing anything else.

Oh yes he had been purposely avoiding her, not sure how he would react after all he had learned about her and learned about his own feelings for her. All he knew for certain was that he was not yet ready to face her. Except now here she was looking up at him with a radiant smile that nearly brought him to his knees.

And just for an instant he thought perhaps God had forgiven him something, that he should be permitted even a glimpse of one such as she—but then the torment it evoked within him proved a far greater punishment for his sins.

Llyr somehow managed to regain his composure, his booted feet now echoing loudly against the stones as he descended the remaining stairs and crossed the great hall to where she stood. "Lady Dhariya" he greeted her smiling, "how wonderful to see that you're well enough to be up and about" taking her gloved hands into his, he raised one then the other to his lips. "And may I say," his tone softening as he met her gaze evenly, "you, my lady, have never looked more beautiful."

Something shifted in the depths of his eyes and was gone. *He's different now,* thought Dhariya. *Like someone suddenly playing a role—the way he'd been looking only moments ago from the staircase—that had been real, then, all at once, he hides himself behind a cordial mask. Why?* She wondered for probably the thousandth time, *why does he run from me in his heart?*

"Thank you my lord" Dhariya replied in a husky-voiced whisper that was all she was capable of. "In truth," she continued, "I keep few things here, fortunately however, my favorite gown was among them."

"Fortunately indeed," Llyr concurred, his dark eyes making a slow perusal from her head…all…the…way… down…to the toes of her green velvet slippers.

Dhariya, suddenly self-conscious of the extremely low neckline and her body's heated response to his obvious appreciation, sought to distract him, "Seems most everything else was lost."

"Yes my lady." His gaze returning to hers, "And I'm very sorry for it."

He was being very formal with her tonight she noted. Feeling hurt all over again at this distance he insisted on putting between them, but she tried not to let it show as she replied "Please Llyr don't apologize." this so softly said, yet the impact of underlying emotion touched him. She went on— unaware of her effect upon him as her focus was to keep herself under control, "I'm told you risked your life to save me."

Dhariya now knew that this was reason for the admiration Llyr gained from Ffyonna. For it had sparkled in her pale blue eyes again the other day when the older woman relayed the tale of Llyr's heroics to her patient's disbelieving ears. Since Ffyonna always wanted every possible detail to aid in determining the best form of treatment for those in her care, she had insisted on hearing Llyr's description of events. This along with the gossip servants so willingly voiced, she had been able to piece together that Llyr had managed to gain entry into the fully engulfed town home, somehow finding his way through smoke and flames to Dhariya's bedchamber where she had lain defenseless amid the inferno. Then, he had lifted her unconscious body into his arms and somehow carried her to safety.

"I can never repay such a debt." Dhariya then told him, feeling overwhelmed by the danger he had willingly placed himself in for her sake. "And I fail so, even in my meager expression of gratitude. Truly there is naught to fully convey all I feel toward you." But her huge eyes spoke volumes as they held to his. Her words too held double meaning and they both knew it. Suddenly all the emotions she had been keeping inside began to surface. Tears glistened on her thick lashes and slowly began to slide down the pale perfection of her cheeks.

Without thought Llyr's hands lifted. Reaching out to cradle her face between is palms while his thumbs captured the moist, visible evidence of her feelings. Then, still holding her thus, he closed his eyes against the escalading emotional tumult that was threatening him as well.

A moment later he swallowed hard and released her. "Come my lady, you should not be on your feet so long," he said from behind the safety of his restored mask and shield. Then placing her hand upon his arm, he led her into the warmth of the drawing room where he seated her in one of the massive winged chairs beside the fire.

Once she was comfortably settled, Llyr went to the bell-cord hanging in the corner next the sideboard and gave it a tug. To the footman who instantly appeared he quietly gave revised instructions for the night, which unbeknownst to Dhariya, included the specific order that they were to be left undisturbed for the remainder of the night.

That done he proceeded to pour out a goblet of wine for Dhariya, a dram of whiskey for himself, then took his seat in the matching chair opposite her. For now nothing more was said nor needed to be said, as they both stared into the flames for a time sharing the stillness.

Something has definitely changed, thought Dhariya, though she did not know exactly what it was. She did however, know that whatever lay between them had deepened and taken on far greater proportions. She was also certain that for some strange reason Llyr continued to fight hard against it, with all the ferocity of the ancient seasoned warrior he so resemble. And in the silence of the darkened drawing room the magnitude of all that went unspoken hovered in the air around them.

She was still looking into the fire in contemplation of her thoughts, while Llyr's eyes were inevitably drawn to her—to watching the dancing of light and shadow caress the exposed flesh above her gown. The sinuous shoulders, the lush upper swell of breasts, the graceful curve of neck and throat, his body stirred more than a little in response, giving him further cause to wonder how he would endure all that lay ahead.

Things between them had a way of shifting like waves on a storm tossed sea and equally as unpredictable. Yet, as if some unseen force were directing the flow, this powerful tidal current appeared to be leading ever closer to one ultimate destination.

Suddenly feeling Llyr's gaze upon her Dhariya turned toward him. As their eyes met they seemed to lock with one another, neither being able to look way and neither wanting to—forging invisible fibers of increasing intensity, a bond uniting them across all distance for all time. And somehow they both understood this on some deep level in that moment.

Yet as always reality insisted upon intrusion into their private world and it came with the call to dine.

Much to Dhariya's surprise Llyr did not take her to the formal dining chamber as she expected. Instead he guided her in the opposite direction, toward the castle's conservatory and there beneath the domed ceiling of crystal panes, Dhariya found a candle lit façade of flowers and foliage.

The floral chaise-lounges were still arranged as usual amid the greenery in the outer circle. However the ironwork table and its four chairs had been removed, in their place, a white linen cloth with a simple meal for two had been laid out upon the large eastern carpet before the fountain at the room's center, the water trickling softly in the background. She turned to Llyr, wonder shining brightly in her hazel eyes.

With a mock bow he motioned toward the lush setting before them— "An informal moonlight supper for my lady, if she so desires?"

"How extraordinary," she whispered "yes, I would love it."

At that Llyr gave some signal and the footman departed, shutting out the rest of the world behind double doors of heavy oak. Placing a gloved hand to his proffered arm they descended the four terraced steps together, heels clicking against the tiles in unison and echoing through the cavernous glass chamber.

The numerous braziers needed for heat during long months of winter were unnecessary at this time of year and remained unlit. The sultry atmosphere had been gently tempered by twin sets of leaded doors now standing open at each end of the massive windowed wall, thus allowing the warmth of the summer eve to filter through.

The light humidity carried with it scents of rich soil, fragrant blossoms and the tangy-bite of countless leaves. Dhariya found this jungle like environment most inviting if not seductive. Slanting a quick covert glance at him, she was more intrigued than ever by this man, he who would think of such a thing.

He was so unexpected in every way. Mystery infused the powerful aura that surrounded him, dark and dangerous; his masterful presence commanded whatever space he occupied. She could feel the air pulse and stir as he moved through it, ushering her along with him. *Who is he? What is he?* She wondered one more time. The little she did know about him gave no real clues to this man at her side, he whose complexities only deepened the more they were probed.

Llyr handed her down onto the plush eastern carpet. Dhariya sank comfortably into the oversized silk-covered pillows. Settling her froth of skirts as Llyr stretched out beside her and began pouring the wine.

The air suddenly filled with sound, beautiful deep rich tones. *Music...* She looked askance at Llyr. He smiled at her obvious puzzlement. "Cello," he explained, "Turns out my valet Dacron has an unexpected gift for the instrument. Thus, I sent a servant and bade him practice in the corridor outside the conservatory doors this evening," offering her a silver goblet of pale French wine.

"Dacron—why who would have ever thought…"

"Indeed, seems the man who prefers to keep his voice silent chooses to express himself in other ways and has a few out of the ordinary interests." Pausing to sip his wine, "I made the discovery of his musical talents quite by accident myself late one night. I could hear this…" his hand motioning into the air "…wafting through my rooms, and intrigued, I followed the threads of sound, which led me from my own chambers to Dacron's quarters next to mine, and thus I found him bow in hand."

"Oh it's so lovely, you *do* think of everything."

"You've had far too much sorrow Dhariya. I only sought to bring you some joy." Then seeing her eyes brim with tears again, he leaned over and gently touched her cheek, "it would seem I've already failed miserably in my task." He quipped, attempting to lighten the mood.

She smiled at that. "You have brought me joy Llyr. I don't know why I've become so weepy of late."

"You have a right to each and every tear Dhariya. But just for tonight let us not dwell on such things. Agreed?"

"Agreed" and their goblets clinked, toasting their declaration.

Llyr took another sip of wine then leaned back. A million stars began to fill the darkening sky above. Gazing up at them he thought wistfully, *if only there was a way I could be absolved from a pledge once given, I would never ask for anything more than to be with her forever.* Something suddenly shifted in the silence. He turned to her, "What is it Dhariya? What's bothering you?"

Dhariya was startled buy his astute intuitiveness. However, she gathered her courage and seized the moment. "Well, being one who's always spoken my mind and heart, there's something I need to ask you…then I promise the remainder of this night shall be dedicated only to positives."

"Certainly Dhariya, you may ask anything and I'll tell you whatever I'm able."

"… To begin with I-I want you to know you've been on my mind a great deal since the night I first dined here…" their eyes met, "…with you."

"As you Dhariya have also captivated my thoughts."

"I have?" She softly asked.

"Yes my dear, you have." He answered just as softly.

"Oh…" That was not quite what Dhariya had expected to hear. She glanced away trying to realign her thoughts "…Well, I can't help wondering then, why you've stayed away from me."

Looking back at him now, no attempt to hide the hurt in her eyes, "you never once called upon me in Edinburgh… and you've not come to see me again, since the other night," she continued before he could venture an answer, "I-I hope my forwardness hasn't offended you Llyr. But I must know."

"Dhariya of course I'm not offended. In fact I appreciate your complete lack of guile. Now, please listen to me…I apologize on both counts. Really I do." This time it was Llyr who turned away, seeking the right words. "It's difficult to explain… I did want…"

Drawing a deep breath he began again. "There were reasons I was unable to attend you at your home in the city. I too have various business ventures I'm involved in and occasionally they put demands upon my time that cannot be put off … and these past few days I've been busy trying to catch up on your uncle's estate matters that I neglected while your life was hanging in the balance. Dhariya—"

He took hold of her hand, she was looking deeply into his eyes in that searching way she had. Llyr could feel her reaching into the darkest depth of his soul, where all his secrets lay. Guilt welled within him. He wished he could be completely honest for once and tell her of the danger his nearness could bring her, yet alas, he could not do it. "—I very much wanted to see you, please believe me."

These last words were absolute truth she could clearly see that.

"If you ask me to believe you Llyr, then I do and I shall say no more about it." She also knew he was not telling her the whole of it. All the same, she sensed the sincerity in every word that he had said. Thus, she smiled her beautiful smile at him and the tensions between them seemed to dissolve in that moment.

And the night became filled with only each other.

In keeping with the usual informality of Skara Brae, Dhariya removed her gloves, as she often did when not among the haughty social set. She and Llyr began to feast on an array of curries, dhals, chutneys and fresh chapatti breads. Followed by various cheeses and sliced fruits. Finger bowls of lemon scented water and small linen drying cloths had also, thoughtfully, been provided.

"I see that you share my uncle's appreciation of eastern flavors and meatless Indian cuisine," Dhariya was saying, "I'd noticed it the first night we dined together as well."

"Indeed I do. In fact it was Tamas who introduced me to the fare and I confess I now find other tastes pale by comparison… Your uncle mentioned that he and your mother's bloodlines descend from Indian royalty." Llyr said as he refilled their wine goblets.

"True, although it's a long way back."

"Perhaps, but you Dhariya, reflect the exotic beauty of the land to absolute perfection."

"My, that's quite a compliment, thank you Llyr." Dhariya replied feeling awed by the magnitude of his tribute. She met his gaze and their eyes seemed to embrace, while the deep luscious strains of cello floated hauntingly in the air, surrounding them in its dark melodious splendor.

As he looked upon the woman before him, Llyr knew his dark hours would not be so empty this night, for they would be filled with her. Somehow in the dream of her presence, he could forget the nightmare of his reality, if only for a while.

Because of the way she saw him he could almost fool himself into believing that things could be different—that he could be different.

She did not see him as the creature he was. In Dhariya's eyes he was merely a man. And at that moment he so longed to be the man that she saw, to take her unto him as wife, to care and provide for her, to be hero and protector from all of the world's harshness and pain, and from its cruel infliction upon both of their lives.

He wished to show her the glories of intimacy. His body yearned to enter her, to worship at the fiery altar of her temple, honor her body and serve her well with all the pleasures of the flesh, to feel her trembling release as he brought her across the sacred threshold into womanhood.

Without warning, Llyr could feel the shadows start to stir within him, the forbidden desire sparking to life ready to ignite the fire in his veins. Recognizing the danger of his volatile thoughts, he quickly quashed them, and with every ounce of will he possessed, he managed to drag himself back from the edge of that dark precipice.

Abruptly he arose and straightened his clothing. Bending toward her, he offered forth his hand, "Would my lady care to dance?"

Dhariya beamed up at him, clearly delighted with the idea. "Why, yes my lord, I would very much. But how does one dance to music such as this?"

"Trust me."

In answer, she placed her ungloved hand in his. Their flesh met with a heated tingle.

After helping her to her feet, Llyr took her swiftly into his arms and began moving them about the perimeter of the room in slow sweeping turns—keeping pace to the deep rhythmic pulse of the Cello—his movements, smooth and expertly executed. *He was nothing if not confident*, Dhariya thought, as the strong hand at her back guided her out one set of opened doors and into the night.

Gazing up at him, all the darkness and mystery swirled in his eyes, as she swirled in his arms. It was incredible, *he* was incredible and Dhariya made a silent wish that it would never end.

Her soft fragrance tickled across his senses with promises of Eden and paradise, a perfect temptation of spice and sweetness, just like the lady herself. He remembered it clearly from every time he had been with her, as if it remained indelibly imprinted upon his mind, his body, his soul. And each of her graceful movements brought forth a heady wafting.

Llyr breathed deeply of this intoxicating elixir that was Dhariya herself, drawing it right down into the very core of his being. O' how he yearned to taste it upon her silky golden skin—to tongue it from the depths of all her most secret places—and he wondered, not for the first time, how one woman of flesh and blood could be both angelic innocence and smoldering seductress at once?

They danced their way along the length of tiled courtyard, the sound of her laughter blending sweetly into the music. Upon reaching the far end, Llyr easily steered them back inside the second set of opened doors, and there, he slowed them to a stop.

Dhariya was breathless and radiant in her joy, looking up at him unaware that her eyes again revealed too much—far too much "Oh I've not danced in so very long. It was truly wonderful."

The summer breeze gently wafted in and around them, with it came the scents of the sea, of exotic blossoms from foreign lands, and the evocative fragrance of Dhariya herself. Llyr still held her in his arms, reluctant to let go. It was beyond anything he had ever felt before. The magnificence of her being, just the nearness of her was like a potent drug intoxicating him with heady waves of her essence.

Even as he knew she was forbidden fruit and Tamas had warned him to stay away from her. Yet here she was, her body pressed intimately against his and it was she who had come seeking him. How could it be wrong when such feelings existed between them? Dear God it could not be wrong.

Llyr stared intently into her upturned face, his thumb slowly tracing the potent pout of her bottom lip, while guilt and desire turned his body into a battleground. He realized then that he was indeed surrendering, that little by little more of him was giving up the fight.

In a strange way as he looked upon her, Dhariya began to feel that she no longer belonged to herself, as if somehow he now possessed her. And she did not care, for she knew he was going to kiss her, and at that moment, she wanted that kiss more than she had ever wanted anything in her entire life.

His eyes blazed with dark fire, scorching heat infused her body, the tension mounted, Dhariya's heart beat furiously, every fiber of her being seemed to pull toward him. She felt a strangeness low in her belly, as it were curling in upon itself, and a tugging sensation at the essence of her womanhood, as the melting heat coiled in her vitals.

She was finding it increasingly difficult to draw breath, suddenly, just as he was about to bend his lips to hers, Dhariya's brow furrowed, she closed her eyes and she pressed her fingers to her temples.

"What is it Dhariya?— What's wrong?"

"It's nothing," she managed to answer, "I feel a bit dizzy is all." In truth, the room about her was spinning in a wild blur, nausea gripped her stomach and she began to cough harshly, lungs heaving laboriously.

Llyr inwardly cursed himself. "I should never have had you up dancing so soon. What in the world was I thinking?"

Regaining some composure Dhariya shook her head against his words. "No," she whispered, as her body finally settled, "I loved it, this entire night has been as a dream. I'm a little tired that's all."

But her husky voice was now extremely weak and raspy. The next moment Dhariya felt herself being whisked up into the air and Llyr was striding toward the doors carrying her with him, hollering at Dacron to open them. The playing promptly ceased and the doors swung open on soundless hinges.

The young, blond, angelically handsome, valet silently bowed and stepped back into the shadows—where he seemingly preferred to stay—his expression was passive, revealing none of his thoughts. As his dreamy-eyed gaze watched the two of them exit the conservatory.

"Hunt down mistress Ffyonna Dacron and send her at once to Lady Dhariya's chambers." Llyr commanded without preamble as he passed by, sending the young valet off hastily in the other direction.

Dhariya was in fact exhausted. Her throat felt raw and her lungs hurt from the exertion of dancing. She knew she had been foolish to push herself so far. Yet she could not regret any of it. She cared not if she had to spend another week in bed due to her recklessness. It had all been worth it.

Her only regret was that the kiss he had come so near to bestowing had been interrupted and now his concerns were overriding all passion. She had been so close to experiencing her desire—to having him desire her—to know a lover's kiss—his kiss. She sighed. Her eyes drifted closed as her head came to rest comfortably against the solid strength of his shoulder, her senses greedily drinking in the feel of his powerful arms around her.

His face was so close. She could feel his breath flutter across her lips and she dare not open her eyes to look at him. It seemed her courage was faltering along with her bodily strength. She sensed his anger at himself. His intensity was always absolute whatever it was focused upon and she was unsure of what his reaction might be now.

Llyr effortlessly conveyed her up the grand staircase and along endless lengths of countless corridors leading to her tower chambers. He too, was acutely aware of the way she felt in his arms. But as Dhariya had divined, his concern for her and his vexation at himself far outweighed any such amorous inclinations.

Dhariya followed their progress by the sound of his boot heels clipping against the flagstones, broken intermittently by the procession of plush carpets in each passage-way, while the aromatic candles wafted their familiar scent into the air.

They came to a stop and Dhariya heard the distinct click of a latch and the creaking hinges of an opening door. Despite her discomfort and fatigue she was disappointed that this night was soon to end and they would part company. She could never be sure of him, of his moods or behavioral reactions to the bond so obviously developing between them. She may not see him again for days—for weeks.

Llyr strode across her sitting room. He held her securely, easily maneuvering their adjacent bodies this way and that, as he ascended the narrow curving steps to her bedchamber. Josey, who had been plying her mending-needle by candlelight waiting to help Dhariya prepare for bed, came to her feet at once, worry evident in her expression. Llyr also dispatched her to bring Ffyonna at once. *Surely two servants searching this maze of stone should find the woman quickly,* he was thinking.

The young maid immediately turned and ran to do his bidding. A similar scene to the one played out not so long ago, during the worst of Dhariya's recovery when the sleeping 'fits' had come upon her. Thankfully those traumatic nightmares were now subsiding.

Josey sped down the corridor as fast as her legs could mange, encumbered as she was by her long skirts. *Dhariya had looked so pale and weak,* she thought, it seems her earlier foreboding had indeed been a premonition. *Lord, what had happened?* Josey was desperate to know. But of course it was not her place to question his Lordship.

All she could do was pray that she would find Ffyonna in her usual place at this hour—in the kitchen sipping tea with her husband—and not already gone to their suite in servants wing at the opposite end of the castle. Or heaven forbid she was in one of her late night stints in the stillroom, that much further again.

Dhariya's lids fluttered open as he gently placed her on the bed. "Llyr I'm fine now. There was no need to fetch Ffyonna and get her all riled over nothing."

"*You* are not nothing" he replied rather more tersely than he intended, raking his hand through his hair in anxious agitation, unmindful of the tieback falling away and the dark silky locks tumbling down about his shoulders. "I should've taken better care of you." He was saying—his tone softening as his gaze met hers.

"As I told you I'm all right now… just a bit weary is all," she reassured, yet the ragged edge to her voice betrayed her efforts. She was smiling at him now in that disarming way she had. He felt his initial anger dissipating. Yet other emotions came quickly flooding in to replace it, "Llyr, thank you for making this night so special."

He said nothing to that as he stood looking down at her. *God in heaven, she was so lovely, so very beautiful,* he was thinking, lying there upon her bed, so willing to love him with her body as well as her heart. He felt something inside his chest squeeze and turned away from it, not wanting to examine the cause too closely, instead, fortifying his shields with every ounce of will he possessed.

She was watching him carefully, trying to decipher the cryptic messages in his eyes, but they were dark pools of hidden secrets, offering no clues. She felt no closer to understanding this man. All she knew is that his inner battles still raged. Again there was the sudden impulse to reach out to him. Wishing to somehow sooth the tempest she sensed in the depths of his soul.

Would he ever allow for such? She did not know, yet she suspected he would not. And so for now they would stay as they were, two lonely restless beings yearning for one another across the vast invisible barrier of their separation. Then Dhariya saw some other profound emotion come forth from the fray—unable to stop her self—she slipped her small hand into his. "Llyr, are you all right?" the question asked tenderly.

"Yes Dhariya… Just lay back now. I'll go see what's keeping Ffyonna." He tried to pull away. Dhariya only clung tighter to his hand and would not let go.

"I appreciate all you've done for me more than I can say." She told him from her heart. "You've treated me so well and I know Uncle Tamas would also be grateful."

Would he indeed? Llyr thought cynically, feeling his conscience probing at the worst parts of himself. Hearing Ffyonna and Josey's voices as they entered the sitting room below, he was grateful for the respite near at hand. He tuned fully toward Dhariya, "I am your servant my lady," he said while trying to appear light-hearted. *He had to get away from her at once.* "Now I bid you good night and rest well." She let go of his hand then.

While Llyr, with great deal of effort, sketched a gallant bow and swiftly departed her rooms. However much he did not wish to leave her, he forced himself to keep moving. He could not risk remaining in her presence even one moment longer.

Watching him go Dhariya saw the shadows close in around him once again, those same shadows that always came to steal him away from her.

As Llyr reached the lower level Josey swept by him heading directly for the stairwell, he paused a moment to explain to Ffyonna that he had been thinking only of giving Dhariya some happiness this night and how they had danced together. He went on to relay what had happened afterwards, taking full blame for Dhariya's set back.

The older woman appraised him with her shrewd piercing gaze as he spoke. "Doesn't sound serious" she answered honestly, "tis only to be expected under the circumstance, some herbal tonic and rest'll fix her right enough." Then, shaking her head she too swept passed him. Already on her way up to her patient, murmuring something about young people today and their lack of sense.

In truth Ffyonna was not angry. She knew Dhariya was passed the worst and in no danger of relapse or she would never have allowed her out of bed. She was annoyed, however, and most of it was directed toward her ladyship. *Auccc men, they'll always get carried away and act foolish*, she was thinking to herself during her ascension, *but Dhariya knows better. What's more, she'd been warned not to overextend herself.* Well, Ffyonna sighed again as she reached the top of the stairs, *that young lady now smilin' so dream-like from her bed, was indeed goin' to get a severe talkin' to after she'd been tended.*

Outside Dhariya's chamber door Llyr closed his eyes and leaned heavily against the stone wall trying to gain some semblance of composure. He was feeling overwhelmed by the tidal sway of his emotions that ever threatened to pull him under. Drawing deep calming breaths into his lungs, he became overtly aware of the cold, rough texture beneath his palm, of the silent corridor echoing around him, a harsh reminder of the bleak reality he must face.

There could be no more running. He could no longer hide from himself. He had learned that impossibility far too well. And then that other reality came forth to challenge him, to mock him—*Dhariya, Lord how he loved her.* The magnitude of the feeling would no longer be denied, nor the magnitude of all its consequences.

He felt the dangerous lure of the forbidden come again—the throbbing need of dark passions, rising up in him, like waves on a turbulent black sea, rushing over him, in him, through him, an endless rush of desire—leaving his scattered thoughts trailing in its wake. While his demons laughed at him and continued to mock his feelings as they danced in the shadows of his torment. *Of all the women in the world it could not be her. He had given his word to see his duty done. It could not be her.*

If only God could help him, but it was far too late for prayers now and no one in the heavenly realm was listening anymore—if ever. Thoughts of life's injustices and the excess sufferings heaped upon those already suffering came again into his mind. His body shaking, he desperately clung to this last fragile thread holding him together. Things were getting so far out of hand now and in ways he had never anticipated. His rational behavior and sanity melted away at the mere sight of her.

What a coil this had twisted into, like a vine ever tightening around him—suffocating him. He raked his fingers through his already disheveled hair, this was all his own fault, he admitted, he should never have placed temptation so close within reach.

Asking her to stay here had been beyond foolish, no matter how rightfully intended he tried to tell himself it was…it was in truth nothing less than pure idiocy.

Like a starving man with a feast laid before him, he knew better that to taunt himself so, yet his old ways still held him, he was used to having what he wanted, when he wanted it. Whatever caught his fancy of the moment he had always just reached out and taken—without thought—without guilt—indulgence had been the cornerstone of his previous existence.

Well, those days were over now and Dhariya was the forbidden. He had best learn to accept this; for there was no way around it. Had he not already drove himself to the brink of madness toiling ceaselessly in search of some resolution? Even as he knew there was none. And in the end it mattered not. For when all was said and done, the truth alone would destroy her, even if he himself did not.

Turning on his heel, he fled in haste to answer the whispering call of the night and lose himself for a time within its darkness.

VI

~ And the flames of desire arise, to meet the coming of the midnight hour ~

…With him I felt the strangest of ways. How can one be so completely at ease, yet restless and unsettled in the very same moment? I need not even see him to know when he was there, for like the gathering of a storm my body stirred in his presence, my passion came alive with his nearness and the inevitability of what was to be edged ever closer…

Skara Brae Castle ~ Mid September 1711

~ As if by summons of some silent voice, I was drawn from the depths of slumber into full awareness and knew that I was not alone.

The hour was late. The single bedside candle burned low. A smoldering pile of cinders in the hearth glowed red against black. The darkness of the chamber remained untouched.

I lay there, listening to the strange unearthly stillness, where only the sputtering flame dared whisper. It was him—he was here in the room with me—like so many other nights, I sensed his presence in the shadows. Easing up onto one elbow, I called softly into the unlit emptiness…

"Llyr, is it you?"

There came no answer. The silence lengthened.

Yet I knew he was there, just beyond the reaches of dying embers.

I could feel the magnitude of his need calling to me.

Unbidden my hand lifted—reaching out to him across the vast chasm of darkness separating us—an offer and a plea in the one wordless gesture, I waited....

Then suddenly he was there.

~ D ~

~ **Dhariya** watched as Llyr slipped out from the shadows. He seemed carved of their very essence, while they lingered upon him caressing his every hollowed feature and etching his handsome face into one of the starkest beauty. He had the look of a barely tamed beast about him, the aura of danger—feral and unpredictable. He even moved with the prowling grace of a predator. Approaching his quarry slowly, eyes wild and focused intently upon her.

With his hair spilling freely in a dark silky tangle of waves, the fastenings of his black silk shirt were undone. Its tails loosened from his breeches, it hung completely open down the front revealing a great deal to her questing gaze, which then traveled lower to where his desire for her was blatant and obvious—thrusting boldly against the straining confines of cloth. She was absolutely mesmerized by the lure of his sensual magnetism, unable to look away. *This is meant to be,* Dhariya inwardly acknowledged, *divined from that first meeting of our eyes, if not before.*

And somewhere just below the threshold of awareness, she realized she had always known they would come to this, no point in either of them denying it any longer. With that thought, Dhariya felt both fear and the thrill of anticipation coursing through her.

While Llyr felt as one entranced, everything seeming distant and surreal to him.

And Dhariya... the dream made flesh.

The air between them throbbed with intensity, pulsing like a beating heart as he came toward her. Oh yes, he knew he trod upon dangerous ground, could feel it tremble beneath his every step, yet still he took them, drawing ever nearer, powerless against a greater need.

What has she done to me? Thought Llyr, *I am bewitched by the purity and innocent sensuality of this woman—she, whose magnificence is beyond any measure of my expressive capability.* She was his strength—his weakness, his solace—his torment, both willing and forbidden. She was everything, without her there was nothing—he was nothing and this overwhelming need for her not merely one of body, but one of soul as well.

He had been coming here to her chamber for nights on end, even after she had fully recovered from all the complications of the fire he had kept coming, unable to stop himself. Because he craved her presence and had to be near her now as if her light could somehow dispel his shadows. Hovering there amid the unlit depths like some dark angel keeping guard, as if his own presence did not pose far greater danger than any outside force ever could.

Still he could not to stay away, spending endless hours watching her slumber with desire twisting his insides into chaos. And now there she lay in all her beauty—her hair a dark rippling mantle, draping the pillows with its silken splendor—and looking at him with dreamy eyes that offered welcome.

Temptation—the forbidden—the ultimate sin beckoning Eve in all her glory...

Reaching her bedside—his glazed eyes riveted upon her—he spoke for the first time. His words came slow; his voice strangely intoned "You do not fear me being here Dhariya?"

"I am not afraid of you Llyr." She lied, as fear and excitement merged into one indefinable. Suddenly a new and very real alarm struck. "But is something wrong? … Is- is it Uncle Tamas? … Has something happened?"

"No, everything's fine…I'm sorry to have woken you."

"Don't be sorry Llyr, for I'm not." This was the truth and the words slipped easily from her lips as desire returned in a hot flooding-tide. "In fact I'm glad you are here and we are alone like this. You know, away from the prying eyes and gossiping tongues of servants."

She was shocked by her own boldness. Although she had always been daring and never one to let fear or apprehension hold her back from what she wanted, this was completely out of her realm. Dhariya had very little experience with men. Despite her many suitors these past few years, she had never before cared enough for anyone to encourage their attentions. While a few brazen libertines had stolen a kiss here and there, she was always too busy with her foundation or other more meaningful pursuits for such dalliance.

Yet Dhariya loved Llyr. He was here with her now without his usual barriers and she knew that this was it, a defining moment upon which everything between them hinged. If he walled himself off and walked away from her tonight he would be out of reach forever, their chance would never come again.

She was not about to let that happen.

Endeavoring to hide her nervousness, she leaned back against the propped pillows and patted the edge of the bed, thankful her hand did not quaver. "Please sit."

Llyr took hold of that hand, his fingers twining with hers as he seated himself— hip to hip and face to face—alongside her. Dhariya made to pull him into an embrace, but he stayed her, while inwardly he fought for control, desperately trying to ignore the heavy ache in his loins and the dark passions pulsing in his veins.

Then, gaining some mastery, he cradled her face between his hands. His eyes glittering as they held her own, "Dhariya," his voice husky and imploring, "listen to me this is not right. We cannot—"

Dhariya pressed her fingertips to his soft lips, halting his words. "Please don't give me reasons why not, save one." his gaze now searched her face waiting. "Are you pledged to another?" She bravely asked.

"Not in the way that you think."

"There *is* someone else then." Dhariya's stoic statement made from the depths of a sinking heart.

"No Dhariya, there's absolutely no one else, only you." His hands still framing her face as his eyes beseeched her understanding. "My heart—my love are yours and yours alone you have owned them from the very first moment I saw you and thus shall never belong to any other."

He drew a deep steadying breath. "All the same I can never marry nor live a normal existence."

Dhariya felt her heart sink a little further while she strove not to show it outwardly. Of course she had always thought that finding love would mean marriage, as it had for her parents and her uncle. She now knew that this would not happen for her. Yet was she going to throw love away because it had not come the way she had planned? She could not imagine loving another the way she loved this man. Was she about to settle for lesser emotions with one who was able to make her promises? She must now choose.

"My life is not my own." He was saying, clearly anguished by his circumstances. "I'm bound by mistakes of the past in ways beyond belief. I cannot explain the impossible complexities of my situation…there are reasons…things I cannot tell you or anyone, yet they're real nonetheless and thus, I'm held in a vice-like grip from which I'll never be free."

Watching her carefully, he responded to the unspoken question in her searching expression…"I don't expect you to understand Dhariya but that is all I can say," closing his eyes against the torment his hands dropping in utter defeat.

Dear God how could I ever possibly explain? He wondered in vain desperation. This was the worst possible situation—the two of them here like this—it was absolute madness. Yet was it not what he had wanted? Had he not been baiting the odds of this very thing by coming here night after night, hour upon hour, knowing it would eventually lead to this? Of course he had, if he were at all truthful with himself. Well here it was. So now what would he do with this wish come true?

Dhariya was doing her best to comprehend what he was trying to tell her, she could not imagine who or what could have such a hold upon another. He said he could not reveal anything more, so to love him was to accept him as he was.

"This is the secret you bear and why you've run from me inside your heart?" She softly asked.

"Yes."

Llyr felt her small palm touch his cheek—the warm flesh infused with tenderness. And he knew he would never forget that touch, for he had not been touched in such a way in so very long. *Was it a thousand years? Perhaps a million?* He did not know, only that it seemed as though it were—for the touch was a touch of love, pure and untainted, he knew it without either of them speaking, because the touch itself told him so, thus leaving nothing to wonder—and he could have wept at the feeling.

How strange, thought Llyr, *that amid all of this I should suddenly think of my mother, yet it had been she who had last touched me with such love—it was ever there the boyhood memories of her smiling face, in the comforting warmth of her maternal embrace, in the way she lightly stroked my cheek before kissing me goodnight—mother,* he silently called to her, *so long gone from me now and o' how I still miss you so.*

Then Dhariya's words found him, drawing him back to the present—to her—to the potent promise hovering in the air. "Then I'll question you no more," she was saying, her voice gentle yet resolute. "Llyr, look at me." He did so and the torment in his eyes pierced her unto her soul. "Of course I'd rather that we could wed and build a future together, with family— children. But we don't often get exactly what we want in this world; I've known for a many years…that I…I'm unable bear children… so my life was not meant to follow a standard path either. However, I do believe that you and I have been given something special and rare, perhaps to make up for the losses.

Taking hold of his hand once more, she said "You've been forthright in telling me how things stand Llyr…and I trust in your word to me." Her voice now becoming a mere whisper of sound as she continued, "So if your love and heart are indeed mine as I believe, then I shall claim them as thus. What I'm asking of you this night is to lend unto me your flesh as well."

She slid herself up in the bed, the pale pink wisp of cloth that barely covered her further taunting him; he tore his lingering gaze away and raked his hair with desperate fingers. "Dear God woman! I cannot slake my lust within your beautiful body take from you your innocence, offering you nothing more!" His tone suddenly softening, "What I feel goes so much deeper. Yet I am unable to—"

This time Dhariya stopped his words with her own confession, "but I am no longer innocent…you see, that was violently taken from me when I was yet a child." A shadow of pain clouded her eyes then was gone.

Llyr could not believe his own lapse. Had she not only a moment ago spoken of her inability to bear children? Bloody hell! What was the matter with him? To be so insensitive with her of people—but he was having trouble thinking straight, being so caught in the moment—and she seemed so untouched, "Dhariya …I-I'm sorry I—"

"Llyr." she broke in once again. "I know that you too bear deep scars of a painful past…yet perhaps we are meant to heal one another…Perhaps through our love we can find solace for our souls. You see, although my innocence was viciously stolen away, I know you can give it back to me."

His eyes now held the unspoken question and, sensing his weakening resolve, she pressed her point. "You can teach me Llyr. You can show me what it means to join our bodies in love and mutual desire. I ask no more of you than the sharing of this time together. Must I beg of you to take what I offer, my love, my heart, my flesh and must I beg yours in return? Teach me Llyr. Teach me of passion. I wish to know what it is my body feels for you."

Dhariya paused to allow him to respond. Llyr however, was incapable forming any answer. When she realized this she proceeded. "The way we feel for each other is a most precious gift. One not easily found in this world. I know I shall never find what we have again. Are you willing to just toss this all away because it cannot be as we would wish it?"

"You deserve better Dhariya...you deserve to have it all."

"What I deserve is to make my own choices, which is what I'm doing now. If I've learned anything it's that life is unpredictable and none of us are guaranteed even the next breath. Let us not waste another moment."

Dhariya knew she would have to deal with Ffyonna's disapproval once it became obvious there would be no marriage between she and Llyr, not to mention her uncle's, well she would handle that when the time came. She was an adult and it was time she was treated like one. It was far too easy for others to make judgments when they were not the ones who were so alone.

How could Ffyonna ever understand? She and Urien had met and fallen in love when they were both very young, and despite the vast difference it their stations in life, they had married shortly thereafter and lived long years together. They had even been granted the added blessing of a son. Ffyonna would have long forgotten how it feels to lie alone in a cold empty bed night after night. Dhariya did not want to think anymore about that just now. For here, tonight, this was all that mattered.

"You must be absolutely certain Dhariya." Llyr's velvet voice cut into her thoughts. His eyes probing deeply into her own "No matter what the future may bring I would never have you regret this night. You must try to understand that what we begin here and now cannot be undone, ever. And not just our physical joining, but the ties we'll forge in doing so, will bind us eternally."

Dhariya no longer had any doubt that she wanted him and had from the very beginning—it seemed to her that every preceding moment of her life had been only to bring her to this one—that every breath drawn had merely been to keep her alive until this time had come and they were brought together.

And she could easily see that his own body continued to betray all his valiant efforts—sliding long slender fingers into the dark midnight of his hair, she drew him closer saying softly, "My only regret—my lord—would be to wonder what might have been, if we allow it all to slip away."

She watched and waited…

For an instant the flickering candle revealed disquiet eyes yet this was quickly displaced by desire—pulsing hot and dark—within their endless depths … "Dhariya-a-ah" he breathed, finally pulling her into his embrace, "Elysi-a-a-an" he whispered against her lips.

And then his kiss, not gentle but potently seductive as his mouth claimed hers, his tongue dipping-in, tasting of her sweetness, hunger and fierce longing swept him, its raw undiluted waves flooding the very core of his desolate soul.

The darkness — the danger—the forbidden

A sudden crack of thunder jolted the heavens above the castle, though the lover's gave no notice to it nor to the white flash of lightening that had preceded it. They were cast away upon their own raging sea of heightening desire.

And Dhariya—caught in the powerful currents of this drowning tide—was sundered beneath the onslaught of sensation after sensation—while the heat of his mouth further enslaved her unto him.

He made a sound between a hum and a growl as he filled his hands with the lushness of her breasts, feeling them swell against his palms. A deft movement had him slipping the straps of her bed gown from her shoulders—baring her to the waist. Breaking the kiss, he looked down at the newly uncovered splendor. Her golden hued flesh, her full round breasts luminous in the candlelight their ripe puckering crests beckoning, lowering his head, he brushed his lips over one taut yearning peak.

Dhariya gasped as he suckled. Drawing her deeper into the moist interior of his mouth, her spine curving upward in response, lifting toward him in offering as he turned his attentions to the other.

Llyr had expected Dhariya to be somewhat timid after the violence of her childhood. Thus, he could not believe her melting surrender or his own lack of control. He felt like an untried lad with his first woman, when in fact he had had more than his share of willing females in the past. They had been literally throwing themselves at him since he could remember. Always he prided himself on his calculated seductions, an unemotional enlisting of technique artfully applied unto the ultimate fulfillment for his partner as well as himself.

But this—this was primal, a rampant torrent of need beyond all thought, beyond all reason. In Dhariya too there seemed a desperate force propelling her and its impact upon him stunned him. He stopped rather abruptly. His breath labored. His voiced strained. "I'm trying to go slow with you Dhariya, yet I—"

"Oh but you mustn't." She broke in, her voice as breathless and ragged as his-own. "I'll not have you hold back from me Llyr. Not now when I've waited so long for you, for this...I don't want to be afraid anymore. I want to be freed from the horrors of the past... let me feel all the wildness my darling, let me feel the full unbridled glory of your passion. Love me Llyr—love me."

"I do Dhariya," the words feathering across her ear as he embraced her once again, "my God, if you only knew how much."

"Then show me Llyr, show me how much you love me," her voice now a mere breath of sound.

This uninhibited statement rekindled the sparks inside of him and fire leapt to life in his veins, its pulsing heat burning through his body rendering the last of his resistance unto ashes. She never ceased to do the unexpected. She amazed him with her openness. Yet when he recalled what had flared in her eyes the first time he had seen her, he should not be at all surprised now that this wild untamed passion had finally been unleashed.

With a muffled groan Llyr's mouth came down upon hers in a thoroughly drugging kiss, primitive in its fervor, desperate in its consummation—his tongue thrusting inside —tasting, savoring, drinking deep of her. In one swift motion the meager confines of her bed-gown was swept away exposing all of her luscious feminine flesh to him.

Llyr released her and stood back, while his reverent gaze took her in by slow deliberate increments. How many times he had thought of her this way? Imagined baring her thus? Yet as she lay there before him now—the flush of her blood heated skin, her glorious hair spilling over pillows, eyes dreamy with desire—she was truly a vision beyond anything his mind could have ever dared depict.

The masterful perfection of beauty he had once praised was now completed in the rounded curves, slender waist, long shapely legs and the dark erotic promise hidden between. How he yearned to pay homage to each and every one with mouth and hands. Silently vowing to himself that he would do just that—oh yes, before the pink of dawn's first light—he would indeed know every inch of her and all of those hidden secret places would be thus revealed unto him.

At first Dhariya felt a little shy when he had stripped her to the flesh and she had lain beneath his languid perusal—for he stood over her a long time looking his fill. Then he moved to her—his hands following the path his eyes had just taken—and all thought disappeared.

"My God Dhariya, your body feels like satin beneath my palms," he said huskily after a few moments, "it's absolutely incredible."{Dhariya was instantly grateful her mother had taught her the special waxing technique used by many French and Eastern women to remove body hair, followed by daily massage with scented oils after bathing, these rituals kept the skin soft and radiant.} She smiled a secret smile, whispering her thanks to him for his praise.

Llyr's clothing soon joined the scant remains of hers upon the carpet and it was Dhariya's turn to stare appreciatively. The honed perfection of his swarthy nakedness held her in thrall. Despite her mind having long-since blocked out all details of her childhood trauma, Dhariya was aware of how a man's body was formed. Her mother had explained this and certain other facts to her. But never would she have dreamed that all the parts came together like this. Her heart tripped over itself—then resumed, each beat thudding slow and heavy against her ribs.

The broad sweep of his shoulders, the smooth planes of his bare chest, the narrow tapering of his muscled midriff and lean hips, she had already known his legs were impossibly long, had in fact endeavored to envision how well developed they indeed proved to be. And although Dhariya had no past recollections, nor any prior knowledge for comparisons, when her eyes encountered his fully aroused manhood, she somehow knew instinctively that he could never be found lacking in any manner whatsoever.

The warm glow of candlelight kissed a seductive path over him, as he came toward her in all his masculine glory. Dhariya swallowed hard as her nerves were beginning to threaten her composure. Without taking her eyes from him, she grasped two handfuls of the coverlet beneath her to dry her suddenly damp palms. Then he was lowering himself upon her and

Dhariya could only marvel at the sensation of their meeting flesh.

He captured her mouth with such possessive command that Dhariya—his willing prisoner—opened completely unto him. His kiss was passion without mercy, his tongue sweeping inside—demanding, devouring—mating with hers in a parody of bodily intimacies soon to follow.

Dhariya, though inexperienced and unsure, was also curious and exhilarated, and she had no wish to be passive. She wanted their joining to be mutually pleasurable. To give unto him as well as receive. Thus, she began tentatively exploring his body, learning its responses and reactions to her curiosity.

Llyr felt her feathered touch—like that of an angel's wings, his angel's wings—and a strange sensation stirred in the center of his chest. At first she merely followed his lead, but Dhariya was soon matching the full ferocity of his passion as her own came to life, responding in-kind to the fierce demand of his need. With his each and every caress she offered forth her own, and she soared anew upon the unspoken promise of ecstasy.

Her senses were swirling to the sensual rhythm he played, to the intimate chords he plucked. As his hands traced the terrain of each curve and every furrow, seeking the sacred petals, the hidden bud of desire, which bloomed beneath his touch, beneath his kiss—his mouth skillfully unlocking all the secrets of her womanhood—elevating her unto further and further heights. Dhariya moaned her soft feminine sounds into the night, and then suddenly she flew apart in a sweet melodious crescendo, like a starburst in the heavens, soaring, exploding, and dissolving into trembling wonderment.

With the taste of her desire melting upon his tongue—delving deep, seeking its source—Llyr savored each honeyed droplet of her fulfillment, until she floated back to him languid and limp. He lifted his head and rose above her. Dhariya smiled up at him. Her eyes heavy lidded, laden with newly awakened sensuality.

Perched at the entrance to her body Llyr looked down at her, open in offering. His words came out forced and hoarse, "my Elysian, you taste of paradise" he whispered, "will you take me inside you now—will you let me enter your temple?"

Dhariya nodded her head in answer and he slipped inside her, telling her "don't be afraid my darling." —groaning as moist velvet heat clung to him in a scorching grip of ecstasy, and he knew he had indeed entered the gates of heaven— trying to ease his way slowly—shaking in effort to control his own burgeoning need as he pressed deeper. "God you're so tight." He breathed. "I don't want to hurt you…" He felt her body tense beneath him. "Are you all right love?" He asked on a tremulous exhalation, "Dhariya?" He called out louder.

But Dhariya was incapable of answering, feeling the fullness of him inside of her, pulsing and hot—so strange— yet familiar—instant terror. All the past's trauma rose up like a haunting specter.

The horrific nightmare had come to life again—it was here and now—it was no longer Llyr atop her, inside her, it was that horrible monster—a dark hulking shadow looming over her, invading her body, violating her, tearing her in two— oh God she was being raped again. Panic seized her. She was writhing trying to get away. Her chest constricted. She could not breathe.

"Dhariya!" Llyr's near-shout finally pierced through the hallucination and brought her back to him. Wanting to free her from all distress he was easing out of her body.

"No Llyr" the sorrowful cry spilled from her lips, "don't you see? If we stop now I'll never be free. Let our bodies stay as they are at least for now. Please. Just hold me. I must face this in order to overcome it. I'll not allow the past to destroy me or destroy the passions that lay between us…But I'm afraid… Oh God I'm so afraid of the closeness…. you cannot know or understand that this closeness—this intimacy means only pain to me Llyr for I've known nothing else… Nor do I know what to do or how to stop it. Yet—"

"Hush love." He told her softly. The emotion in her voice tore at him. She sounded like that frightened little girl she had been, which was no doubt just how she felt. "It will be all right love. We'll find a way through it all." Then he carefully rolled onto his side taking her with him.

For a time they did not speak just lay holding each other closely. Dhariya nestled deeper into him needing both his strength and his gentleness, which he knew instinctively and gave willingly. Llyr did not know what else to do. He felt as helpless as she but in a much different way. This was something he had never come anywhere close to dealing with before and he desperately wanted to give her everything that she needed, if only he knew what that was. All he could do was hope that her Creator would heed the call of her sweet voice.

He was still within her as she wanted him to be. His manhood remained semi-hard and ready to resume whenever she was. Yet his mind was far more concerned with the woman he loved than his own bodily pleasures. He stroked her back in a soothing motion. The tenderness between them in those silent moments needed no words, for nothing could convey the full magnitude of what they were sharing—but they both felt it and knew it for what it was.

Through this wordless exchange Dhariya was being fortified and beginning to feel safe again; her mind calming, regaining clarity while her body became accustomed to him, so large and full, inside of her. What affected her most, however, was the immensity of the love she felt flowing out from him and enfolding her and it was this that gave her the courage she was so desperate for. She lifted her head from his chest and met his concerned gaze evenly. "I will be all right now." She softly told him.

He leaned up onto one elbow. His eyes searched the depths of hers. "Are you sure my darling?"

"Yes."

"Very well, but you must promise you'll tell me if you cannot go on," Dhariya nodded once again. Then reaching up with both hands she drew his face down to hers and began kissing him hungrily. Llyr felt the overwhelming measure of her new need for him and he began to move. As his exceptional skill as a lover came to the fore, the power of mounting desire soon displaced any of Dhariya's lingering fears. A sudden rapturous longing overtook her, she began to shift restlessly beneath him and Llyr was lost.

He took her—both mouth and body—with a potent fury, seeking the full measure of Eden's splendor and of its sin—and knew she would fulfill both. His long held ardor exploded, melding in with his desperate love for this woman. Now she was his and she denied him nothing, offering forth all that she was, in the sweetest gift he had ever been given. And never in his life, had he wanted anything more than this most precious time with her—these moments stolen from the dead of night.

"Give me all Llyr," came her seductive plea "let me share everything with you…only with you," the words a mere wisp of sound, sending him beyond the brink. While her lithe body enforced her plea, gracefully arching up to meet his every thrust, they moved as one in a rhythmic cadence, in a dance as old as time itself. Yet this was a dance unlike any other—for this was the dance of darkness and light becoming one—uniting together in a sensually erotic twilight that could never be eclipsed by neither sun nor moon alone.

Suddenly in a wondrous revelation, Llyr knew what it was to completely merge with another, soul to soul, to think only of giving without measure to one who gave the same in return.

Yes now he finally knew the true meaning of paradise—knew that this ultimate fulfillment, which so many {that he-himself had once} sought through variety, debauchery and all manner of empty sensual gratification, would never be found there. Yet, even more importantly, he now also knew why—and this frightened him almost as much as it thrilled him.

He drew her gasping breaths from her mouth into his own. Then he sent them soaring together beyond earthly bounds, with her name spilling forth from his lips over and over, like an incantation or fervent prayer—his body shuddering, spilling forth his essence into the very depths of her.

At that same moment, a lightning bolt catapulted Dhariya into the farthest reaches of space and time—where one world ends and another begins, where one dies, only to be born anew—which she was.

And thus when her eyes finally fluttered open, she found him hovering above her, his heavy lidded gaze intently watchful. Dhariya knew for certain that through their joining she had indeed become a different woman—now a complete woman—in all its full and glorious meaning. "Oh Llyr I never imagined it could be so wonderful," Dhariya sighed, her small hand lazily tracing the damp, sleek muscles of his back.

"Nor did I my love" he said honestly "nor did I. For though there have been others, none my darling have been you. Thus for me there has truly never been anyone else, nor shall there ever be…there is only you," his tone laden with tenderness.

Her soft words held the same tender emotions as she told him, "do you know how many times I've stood on the battlements atop these chambers and there, beneath the full moonlight, I've watched you ride like a wild thing across the misty moors beyond the forest?" He smiled and shook his head in answer, somewhat surprised by this revelation.

"With your cloak flying out behind you like great black wings," she went on; her voice a husky whisper. "Even from that far away place I could sense the passion flooding through you, pulsing in your veins and felt my own rise response. How I longed to share that passion with you Llyr. Thank you for allowing me to do so. And for helping me to overcome the ghosts of the past, I know it wasn't easy for you either my love. Yet once I was able to face the fear and move passed it into the glory of our joining, it was beyond anything I could've wished for. I feel so …so…I don't know. I can't find the words."

Her face was radiant and her eyes shone with the light of her beautiful soul. And he thought as he looked upon her that she was absolutely breathtaking. "I'm so proud of you darling." He told her, feeling a sudden wave of intense emotion that made his chest weighted and heavy. He swallowed hard against the threat. "Your courage and strength are truly an inspiration to me, in ways you could never imagine. Don't give a thought to any difficulties I might have had. All that matters is that you came through and you are free." He kissed her on the tip of her nose and then his eyes sparked with mischief. So I take it you were not disappointed?" He teased.

She smiled. "No. I most definitely was not disappointed."

Seeing the seductive glint in her eyes as she spoke, Llyr felt his is own passion rising to life again. "Good." He replied, smiling back down at her. "Because that my love was merely the beginning." His words brushed gently against her lips before he reclaimed them. Then he proceeded to prove to her that he had without a doubt, spoken the truth.

In the hushed predawn stillness the lovers lay in each other's arms, both naked spent and replete. She—draped atop him, facing him, her two legs between his, her head resting against his chest as she slept—her dark tresses spilling all around them.

Llyr stroked the silken texture beneath his palm, drawing deep of their heady fragrance while staring up at the ivory damask canopy above them, listening to the soft sounds of her breath fluttering across his skin, and he was awed. He felt as if a legion of angels had suddenly descended and clasped him unto their merciful breasts.

Yet it was but one lone angel, though both halo and wings remained unseen, that they indeed existed could never be denied. For naught but a heavenly host could storm the gates of his hell—could lift him up from the dregs—and into Elysian Fields. Allowing him to glimpse a place so far beyond his endless pain, that every fiber of his being had been sated.

And even as he knew it was all to be savagely torn away—for now—he clung to it with the greedy hands of one too long forsaken.

Revelations

VII
~ And the dark velvet passions pulse to life ~

...How often my body would quicken with thoughts of him, of how he would kiss me, how he would touched me, how he would love me. And how I would surrender unto him—all, willingly open my body for his entry; feel him filling me with the powerful potency of his passion, his hot seed spilling forth into my depths, and thus, we become one within the trembling embrace of our flesh...

Skara Brae Castle ~ Autumn ~ 1711

~ *From that first night forth I adapted my life to his nocturnal habits. I did of course, wonder at his strange and cryptic ways—yet these thoughts I kept to myself. Somehow knowing whatever was hidden there, so deep within him, he would never willingly reveal unto anyone—and I accepted this.*

We were left to ourselves for the most part, no longer plagued by certain, well-meaning overprotective staff members. In fact even Urien and Bryden were far less bothersome of late. Whether this was due to Ffyonna's stamp of approval, to Llyr's position as overlord, or to my own obvious happiness, was never disclosed. Nor did it really matter.

For I was feeling quite contented within this idyllic setting, surrounded by the man I loved, in whom love was returned unto me, not only with fierce passion but also in sweet tenderness. I gloried in every aspect of our togetherness—in each new experience we share—the gift of love beyond price.

Yet it proved impossible to keep the outside world at bay, for reality eventually found its way to Skara Brae and its intrusion could no longer be ignored.

~ D ~

~ It all began with the arrival of Dhariya's dressmaker, Madame Thérèse's top assistant Mistress Louise and her team of six seamstresses that Llyr—having gleaned the information from Josey—had summoned from London. The procession of carriages came, one upon the other, laden with trunks of fabrics in textures and colors Dhariya was known to favor. Since both Dhariya and her mother had been long time patrons of the Madame's exclusive establishment, the woman knew exactly what to send along.

The usually quiet castle soon became a hubbub of activity, spilling over with giggling young females all of whom openly ogled the handsome dark lord. It seemed he held quite a fascination for women of all types and of all ages, their eyes were constantly drawn to him, yet most were too in awe of his powerful countenance to actually flirt with him, his very demeanor bespoke he was not one to ever play such foolish games.

Llyr for his part paid no heed to any of them, not that he was unaware of the blatant ogling however, but it was a common enough occurrence to have become a fact of life to him. And as always his own attentions were solely devoted to the woman he loved, to his mind she was the only woman who existed.

While he, self-proclaimed recluse that he was, surprised Dhariya by taking an avid interest in all the designs and choices of fabrics, seeming to derive pleasure in doing so. His taste proved equally as exceptional with regard to women's clothing as with his own.

Thus within a matter of days Dhariya had a selection of gowns and two velvet riding habits, both with specially designed divided-skirts which allowed for riding astride, a scandalous freedom that Dhariya heartily enjoyed whenever she was out of public viewing. Each riding ensembles also included a matching fur-lined cloak, with fur-trimmed hood for the cold winter weather soon to be upon them.

Llyr had arranged for a cobbler and milliner to accompany the entourage, therefore appropriate footwear and necessary accessories were ordered to compliment each new outfit as well. With these preliminaries seen to, the remainder of Dhariya's wardrobe was to be made in London town and sent on at its completion.

Since she had been making do with the few things she kept on hand at the castle, Dhariya was grateful to have the lovely selection of fresh garments to chose from, yet she was not sorry to see the caravan of carriages driving away one week later. She was relieved that Skara Brae would now return to the peaceful place it usually was—which meant that she and Llyr could spend all of their time together once again.

The very next day however, another unexpected visitor came to call…

Dhariya made her way into the brightness of the morning chamber looking the epitome of decorum and modesty in her new deep lavender, high-necked day gown. Her mass of hair had been hastily forced into obedience {in a rarely worn style} *neatly* pinned atop her head.

The room she entered was aptly named, having been refurbished with a series of long casement windows that looked out onto the back gardens, while allowing the early hours of daylight to come flooding in. Lively colored tapestries draped the walls and thick rugs of complimentary tones adorned the flagstones. A cheery place even on the grayest of days as this one was.

It was here that Dhariya found the family solicitor awaiting her. He was standing before the fire gazing into the dancing flames. He turned as she entered. Having been called from her bed at such an early hour with her skin still flush from a night spent in Llyr's arms exploring the world of sensual pleasures, dare she hope her demure presentation would prevail and the evidence of her most unladylike behavior and indiscretions go unnoticed? Apparently not...

"Lady Dhariya." The ever-cordial Jeremy Saunders greeted as he came forth and bowed over her hand. "How relieved I am to see you well and recovered of your recent trauma." The smallish man eyeing her closely from behind his spectacles was now well into middle age, yet he had always been a trusted associate who had served her family faithfully for many long year, "and if I may say so, you are indeed looking exceptionally radiant my dear."

"Why-thank you Mr. Saunders, please do come and sit." Dhariya replied, feeling precariously close to a guilty blush as she motioned toward two winged chairs by the window where the servant was setting a tray of tea and cakes onto the low table between them. They moved to the setting of refreshments.

Once seated with cups in hand Dhariya inquired. "What business is it that brings you all the way out here?"

"Edinburgh isn't so far my lady. Does me good to get out of the city every so often, aside from wanting to visually confirm your state of health and well being, I've also brought along the latest financial figures from Darrien & Co. Shipping Enterprises' Edinburgh offices. Paid a visit to the docks to see your late father's partner Dexter Dreshem the other day and requested the account books."

Saunders set his cup down. He retrieved a file from his leather case and handed it to her then picked his cup up once again, "Told him I'd pass them along to you once I'd reviewed them." He went on. "Dreshem seemed rather reluctant to give them over, saying he intended to bring them out to you himself but in the end he finally relented, odd thing about that, him coming all the way out here on a meager errand."

"Yes it surely is. I can't imagine why he'd take such an absurd notion. Besides, he knows very well they always go to you first."

Dhariya took the file and placed it on the table. She was glad Dreshem had not come. For some unknown reason she had never really liked her father's partner. Her father had been seventeen and newly come into the title of Lord Darrien when he had happened upon an eight year old homeless boy, it had been Dreshem and the young lad was being bought like a prostitute by a grown man in the Edinburgh streets.

Lord Darrien had been sickened by what he saw, although he knew of such things, to witness it first hand was something else again. Thus he had stepped up, interrupted negotiation and then taken the filthy lad to the home of his widowed Aunt, Lady Lieghton. She was a kind-hearted woman who had lost her own two children to fever when they were small.

Lady Lieghton agreed to Lord Darrien's proposal that she see to the boys care while he assumed the financial responsibility for the young Dexter Dreshem, whose mother had been a whore and had no idea who had fathered him. The arrangement seemed to work out well for all concerned and the orphan thrived on the maternal attentions the older woman bestowed upon him. He received a nurtured upbringing in the Lieghton home. He was provided with tutors and given an education equivalent to any highborn child while being taught the all the mannerly ways of a gentleman.

Lord Darrien, who had been an only child, felt a protective brotherly affection toward the lad, so much so, that once Dreshem had grown to manhood Dhariya's father made him a full partner in his new company Darrien & Co. Shipping Enterprises.

Dhariya could never pinpoint what it was that so unnerved her about Dreshem. Yet there was a definite prickle of warning whenever she was in that man's presence and she sought to avoid him whenever possible. Just hearing his name now made her shudder.

"I agree that it makes no sense. Especially since everything seems to be in order." Saunders explained. "In fact the company is doing exceptionally well as you'll see for yourself. The profits are quite impressive. But then he's always been an odd one that Dreshem."

"I can't tell you how much I appreciate you stepping in to oversee the numerous family ventures and company operations Mr. Saunders." Dhariya told him as she refilled their cups.

"More so now than ever, with Uncle Tamas being away indefinitely, he always kept a diligent eye on papa's company and with my own foundation to run I'm afraid it's far more than I could handle alone. Yet I know you're also a very busy man."

"Think nothing of it. Since I employ a large staff now it allows for a great deal of flexibility and numbers have always been a hobby of mine you might say." This was just one of the areas Jeremy Saunders ventured into.

Dhariya had sometimes wondered if the man ever slept. The schedule he kept was astounding, even more so after his wife died last year. Being so much more than just a solicitor, he had a brilliant mind that he put to use in a variety of ways. His large city offices encompassed three entire floors. With his own team of skilled investigators, who helped aide his clients interests if ever there were allegations against them or threats to their businesses or any other number of things.

"I'm only too happy to help you wherever I can Lady Dhariya," he was saying between sips of tea. "And your financial recompense is far more than generous. After all your family's done for me over the years, beginning with giving me my start so long ago. If they hadn't taken their chances on a wide eyed lad straight off the graduate line, why, I may never have made a success of it."

She smiled. He was such a kind man. "And you sir have never failed us."

"But I have in a way miss" came his unexpected reply, "which brings me to my main reason for being here."

"Do go on." Dhariya prompted, sudden apprehension inflecting her words. She could not imagine what he could mean; this man never did anything less than two hundred percent. Yet her instincts were on high alert telling her all was not well.

"I feel it's my duty to inform you, that you may well be in grave danger my lady."

"What on earth do you mean Mr. Saunders?"

"Lady Dhariya it seems the fire in your town home was deliberately set"... All at once her mind was reeling. She was desperately to keep hold of herself lest she fly apart into a million pieces, her mind reaching out for his every word trying very hard to follow them...

"And along with these," he was saying, once again he reached into case. This time he produced a small bundle that he placed on the table before her.

"Letters," he was saying, "which your late mother entrusted into my keeping…you see my dear, her death was no accident either. This here," pointing a thin bony finger at the folded pages, "is the proof she was indeed being threatened."

Dhariya sat in stunned silence. Unable to form coherent word or thought, she simply stared at the offending pile of parchment, strangely aware of the bright red cord binding it all together. The world seemed to have suddenly shifted beneath her, becoming a different place entirely and she now felt as though she were observing everything from very far away.

Setting the china cup down with a clatter, she took up the evidence and studied it closely, noting the heavy black ink, which boldly scrawled out her mother's name. "What did this person want from my mother?" She finally managed. Her voice seemed to come from far away.

"That's just it my lady. The letters make no demands, only warnings to beware at first, becoming progressively worse, then finally that her life was soon to end."

"H-how long had this been going on?"

"The letters started arriving six months prior to your mother's death."

"But who…who would do such a thing and why?"

"That's exactly what we intend to find out, a thorough investigation is currently underway, at my order. We hope to soon have the culprit in hand. Meanwhile, I must caution you to take great care my lady and I feel remiss that I'd not done so earlier, thus, sparing you the fire ordeal and your all too narrow escape." He looked away unable to meet her gaze. "If anything had happened to you I—"

"Mr. Saunders." Dhariya cut in. "Please let us not dwell on such things. What I cannot understand is how mother could've kept this from me. Why did she not tell me someone was doing this?"

It was Dhariya who now fell-prey to painful speculation, "Perhaps if I'd known I might have…" Her voice trailed off, unable to complete the thought let alone speak it aloud. Suddenly fighting back tears, she drew a lace handkerchief from her pocket, lifting it to dampen her eyes with a trembling hand.

"My dear," Saunders said—his voice gentle. "Your mother was only trying to protect you. She came to me because I have the means and staff to conduct a proper investigation, which was launched right away unfortunately it was not soon enough."

The room then fell into utter quietness. Minutes seemed to lengthen as the solicitor allowed Dhariya to absorb the impact of his disclosures.

She turned and stared out the window where raindrops were beginning to tap against the leaded panes blurring the image of the gardens beyond. But Dhariya did not see anything that lay before her now, for her eyes were looking into the past.

That explains why mother seemed so agitated and so unlike herself some months before her death, thought Dhariya, *and why when I'd questioned her about it she'd said she just had a lot on her mind with organizing such a grandiose charity ball.*

Suddenly Dhariya recalled her mother's word with heart-shattering clarity, *"nothing for you to worry about darling,"* Lady Suriya had said with a beautiful smile, her lovely musical voice soothing to the ear. She then lovingly bestowed a reassuring kiss to her daughter's cheek—the open gesture of affection so often displayed between them—and they had never spoke of it again.

Oh God-oh God Dhariya felt a panicked sort of desolation rising within her. *Oh mama how could you have not told me? Why mama? Why did you keep all of this from me?* She felt the grief inside her anew, as she thought of what her mother must have been going through and she ached to think her mother had kept it from her.

The strong stoic Lady Suriya, whose generosity and charitable nature were as legendary as her breathtaking beauty, of course she would never have wanted such worry placed upon her daughter's shoulders. Dhariya knew it was done out of love and as a measure of protection, yet it did not ease the pain it wrought within her. She felt such a sense of betrayal and then overwhelming guilt because of it.

Jeremy Saunders' gaze was full of concern as it rested upon Dhariya. He was filled with his own anguish at that moment. Never could he have imagined a day such as this. Having to speak of these things to this sweet girl he had know all her life—whom his own arms had held when she was a mere infant—who now sat there bravely trying to face such horrid truths, and to watch the pain it so clearly caused in her young heart was more than his own could take.

He had no choice however; she had a right to know the truth. Even more pertinent was that to keep silent would not only to risk far greater suffering, but quite possibly result in

Dhariya's own death, which was beginning to appear to be the case.

But Lady Dhariya was always a spirited one, he thought, right from the time she was a wee lass. Now she had grown into a lovely young woman and that spirit would see her through all of this—it would have to. *So sad that she's already had so much tragedy in her short life.* He felt a heavy ache in his own chest for all that she had suffered.

Clearing his throat, he then proceeded. "Lady Dhariya I don't wish to overburden or unduly frighten you my dear, but there is something else you need to be aware of…" She slowly turned back to face him, her huge eyes seemed to widen further and he hesitated feeling all the more uncomfortable.

"Pray continue." Dhariya heard herself say. Yet her voice sounded faint and foreign to her own ears.

"My investigators have been working with 'The High Constables of Edinburgh' and together they've been diligently considering every piece of this puzzle. From the most recent townhouse fire right back to the incident on the docks all those years ago, which ultimately claimed the lives of both your father and brother, and well…there's some thought now in light of everything else that this too was no accident."

Dhariya felt as if the walls were suddenly pressing in upon her making it difficult to draw breath. The solicitor accurately read her pained expression.

"I'm very sorry to recall this to you my lady. I know you were there and bore witness to their deaths. The thing is we now have cause to believe this tragedy was also intentional …I understand that were it not for your father's swift action in the final moment you too would have perished beneath the falling crate that same night."

Once again Dhariya felt the burning sting of tears and her throat ached with the effort to swallow them. Thus she could only manage to incline her head in answer. It seemed her mind was ready to snap like a twig at any moment. She scarcely clung to the fraying threads of sanity.

"All things considered in retrospect," he was saying, "it grieves me to tell you that someone out there is bent on destroying your family Lady Dhariya, like some sort of vendetta. I vow to you, whoever it is that's doing this, we shall find him and put an end to it. On that you have my word."

She could not speak—was in fact incapable of uttering so much as a sound at that moment—yet she somehow managed another nod acknowledgement of the solicitor's words, which had begun spinning like a whirlwind inside of her head, making it pound with a throbbing pain that matched the one inside of her heart.

She watched as Jeremy Saunders rose to his feet and said. "There's no need to see me out my lady" his voice sounded grave and strained. But only he noticed. "I'll keep you informed on any new developments … and please lady Dhariya, heed my warning for your safety." With that he reached over to pat her ice-cold hand and turned toward the door.

Dhariya eyes followed him as he walked across the room. His movements seemed unnaturally slow—like when she was small and Ffyonna had insisted all the children learn to swim. They had been in the deepest of Skara Brae's ponds where one of the servant's was teaching them, and as usual Dhariya had not been paying enough attention, so she had opened her eyes under the water to watch what Bryden and DJ were doing—*how strange* she thought, *that that long ago memory should find its way through all of this.*

"Mr. Saunders." Dhariya heard her voice call out from that strange far off place.

He turned back toward her. "Yes my lady?"

She looked at the older man as he waited. Kind, reliable Jeremy Saunders his hair white now, his face creased by time and circumstance, she mustered enough momentary rationality to speak these final words to him, "I'd appreciate it if no one else was told about this at least for the time being."

"I agree my lady. It's wise to keep it quiet until we know more of the facts. Although Lord Llyr may inquire about the fire since he was the one who spoke to me about looking into it initially."

"Yes I understand."

He bowed respectfully, picked up his leather carrying case that he had left by the door, then turned about and hastily departed. Heaving a sigh of relief as he closed the door, he drew his crisp white handkerchief from his pocket and mopped his damp brow, dearly hoping he never had to go through anything like that again.

Just then Urien approached, a footman following in his wake carrying the solicitor's cloak and hat, "Are you feeling quite well sir?" The houseman inquired.

"Yes thank you. Just a little warm is all" Saunders replied, taking his belongings in hand. Accompanied by the two servants he crossed the expanse of the great hall, yet the solicitor took none of the usual pleasure in these beautiful surroundings; the silk hangings, plush carpets and richly carved wood furnishing that he had always admired went unnoticed this day.

Just then, Lyos and Ellyon loped out of the drawing room. Having served his Lordship Tamas these many long years Saunders was as well acquainted with this pair of deerhounds as they were with him. He knew these dogs must be missing their master—the former Lord of Skara Brae—even more than he himself did. They came with tails wagging, being familiar with Saunders they were eager for his attentions, which he bestowed by petting each of their large heads affectionately.

Urien and the footman stood aside courteously, until the solicitor was ready to proceed. Then they escorted him out to his waiting equipage and bid him good day.

The footman closed the door and the carriage pulled away from the castle. Loosening his cravat Saunders sagged against the swabs. He was suddenly very weary, the years weighing heavily upon him and he wondered for the first time if he was getting too old for this, his life's work.

Dhariya remained where she was for the longest time. Numbed by the horrific possibility of Jeremy Saunders words, the idea that someone could have purposely set this cruel fate upon them—upon her—was beyond bearing.

She sat unmoving, like one of the stone statues in the gardens, feeling every bit as void of spirit and heavy laden. Frozen in place by the icy chill that gripped her, a numbing coldness both inside of her and around her at once—as cold as those loved ones now below the hard ground, she thought—feeling as though she would never be warm again.

It was as if her entire being had suddenly shrunken inside the empty hollow shell of her body, leaving the outer world even more distant and surreal. Time moved in a different place than the one in which she dwelt. She had no concept of it. No way of measuring how many moments or hours passed as she sat there trying to sort through the tangles of thought and emotion that were hopelessly knotted together.

How could so much have changed since she had awoken with a smile—since she had walked through those doors and greeted the solicitor—earlier this very day? She had only just begun to find some happiness once again…and now this. Her eyes fell to the letters still upon the table.

The harsh reality sat there before her, bold black lettering and red binding cord vivid against the white parchment. A bundle tied with a bow that looked more and more like a gift-wrapped package as the defining edges blurred in the fading light.

Dhariya shivered beneath another cold wave of fear and renewed grief. This evil person was out to harm her too she reminded herself. Thank God she was safe and protected here at Skara Brae. But then again was she?

Shadows were lengthening into dusk when the same servant that had come for the tray and built up the fire earlier, returned to enquire if her Ladyship wished to have the lamps lit. It took a moment for the words to penetrate and register with any sort of meaning. "No thank you, Alastair." Dhariya managed to reply, somehow putting a name to the servant's face.

Strange were the things that came clear to mind while all else remained out of reach behind an impenetrable watery barrier; to be viewed only in a slow moving distorted way.

Before the young footman departed again Dhariya forced herself and a portion of her mind into some semblance of functioning. "Please inform Lord Llyr's valet that due to Mr. Saunders' unexpected visit today I'll be very late in joining his Lordship tonight."

"Right away my lady," The young footman bowed and went at once to do her bidding.

With a vast amount of effort Dhariya gathered enough will to veil-over the devastation inside of her with a determinedly detached air, which was so unlike her natural demeanor. Yet it was the only way she could possibly propel herself to action.

She could not allow herself to succumb to what was threatening to rip her apart. If she had any hope of surviving all that was pressing in against her at this moment, she must find whatever way she could to get through it. She vowed there and then that those whom she loved would have justice.

Thus with that silent promise she arose stiffly from her chair—her movements like one in a laudanum-induced stupor as she picked up the stack of letters in one hand, the account ledger in the other and left the morning room.

Llyr stepped from bathing tub, droplets glistening golden in the firelight against the natural swarthy tone of his skin. He made regular use of the convenient bathing chamber within his suite. Having always been particular about his grooming and wardrobe he had no qualms about bodily cleanliness, the way so many others did, in fact he found it to be quite relaxing and an all round pleasant experience.

On cue his valet Dacron approached with a warm drying towel in one hand and the missive bearing Lady Dhariya's message on a silver salver in the other. The young valet's gaze raked over Llyr's body appreciatively then came to rest on his flaccid manhood, as it always did each time his master was undressed before him.

Llyr just smiled. He was well aware of Dacron's sexual preference and not in the least uncomfortable about the lad's obvious feelings for him, nor was he the least uncomfortable in the company of those who preferred their own gender. In fact on many occasion he had bore witness to men making love to men at the more exclusive private clubs. These establishments could be found in every large city, they catered to varied tastes and preferences of the titled and affluent, where the main drawing rooms became a scene of every type of gender-coupling imaginable—with intertwined bodies in every conceivable intimate act—in every available space.

Llyr himself however, had never been uncertain of where his own interests lay. Those of the fairer sex were all he had ever desired, although he had often indulged his excessive appetites with more than one willing woman at a time, yet despite the dark perversions that ever plagued him, he now desired one woman above all others.

Dacron was far more discreet in his amorous pursuits and he rarely spoke a word, Llyr highly valued these unobtrusive qualities. Moreover the valet's work ethic was impeccable. Llyr could not imagine anyone else who could match his own exacting standards or take such fastidious care of him and his wardrobe. Thus he overlooked the valet's unspoken envy of Dhariya's presence in both his heart and his bed.

Besides Dacron was much sought after, his pale-blond-blue-eyed good looks gave him an angelic quality. In fact a likeness of his image could easily be found painted upon many a church ceiling. With that kind of pretty-boy baby face, he was not lacking for partners, especially amongst such a large castle staff and the team of equerry in the stables.

Llyr had often overheard servants talk of the valet's managing to convert numerous heterosexual men to his ways with his seductive lure, dreamy long lashed gaze and a beautiful face most women would die for. As long as the male lovers were willing and of a decent age Llyr had no objection, after all, he himself was the last one to stand in judgment of another.

"Thank you Dacron." He said as he unfolded the parchment and scanned its contents, while the valet waited patiently, toweling in hand. Then Llyr tossed the note into the fire. He stood uncaring of his nakedness; as with staring eyes he watched the edges of the parchment darken, the corners curling in, the fiery red embers sparking into flames, flames that consumed greedily until they had devoured completely leaving nothing of what had once been.

Despite wondering what Dhariya was about, Llyr was in fact relieved that she would be unavailable until later, he had his own secret need to see to, a desire that took him like the flame had taken the note. Beginning gradually, gaining ground and then finally raging into an uncontrollable force that would not be stopped until it was satisfied, uncaring of consequences or aftermath.

He was finding it increasingly difficult to get away of late. Thus, the dark fire within him was becoming increasingly intolerant of his denial—this was also very dangerous. Such a path led too close to the edge until one became careless and lost their footing, plummeting into the waiting depths, from which there was no ascension.

Finally taking the towel, Llyr informed his valet, "I'll be going out for a few hours. You'll see that my evening cloak is laid out along with my clothing. Oh, and summon Iain from the stables, I'll see him briefly in the drawing room at fifteen to the hour."

Silent as usual the valet bowed his acquiesce and exited the bathing chamber.

With thoughts of the fulfillment soon to come, Llyr's hands trembled as he toweled his body dry. His manhood no longer flaccid but hard and pulsing as the shadows moved inside him, sliding themselves seductively along the sensitive nerve endings just beneath his skin.

He had ignored them for too long now they would have their vengeance.

VIII

~ And what be this place, where darkness touches light, where neither is, yet each exists, one within the other? ~

―――― ‒ ――――

...I'd never known the meaning of passion, before him—never known the meaning of longing, of hunger, of desire, until him. No other could evoke such feelings. No other could whisper into my heart, as does he...

―――― ‒ ――――

~ I spoke not of these things, which now haunted my mind and ached within my breast. For it would become far too real if voiced aloud and I could not yet face the magnitude of all that it entailed. Instead, I chose to seek solace within the arms of my beloved dark lord.

He exuded an aura of strength. Like a silent command of authority both subtle and overwhelming at once, so much conveyed by mere presence alone and the potent power of his embrace, swept all else away.

We seemed to exist in our own private world—out of time—out of place with everything on the other side of the forest. As if its trees marked the boundary between dream and reality.

Our nights—the nights of lovers—of moonlight rides and midnight strolls and the untold ecstasy of our union, yet always even amid the fiercest, the wildest moments of our joining there remains an underlying tenderness.

No thoughts of taking exist between us only a ceaseless desire to give all unto the other. And even as we sip passion's sweet nectar from the most erotic of cups, the act is one of beauty, a physical expression of love for every part of each other. The endeavor to convey depth of feeling, for which, words have never been crafted.

~ D ~

~ **Dhariya** had indeed known the wonder of sensual pleasures with Llyr but she had also sensed the vastness of his dark pain as he loved her, though it lay far beneath the glorious splendor of their oneness. As their souls touched she felt a sorrow so deep it seemed to consume his very being within its lightless prison, which was as roiling and tumultuous as the passions between them. Except this other was a destructive force within him.

She admitted to herself that this frightened her, as did he at times. Yet over and above all else there was ever a truer substance of his spirit that spoke to hers, and she thus heeded its plea with an indefinable knowingness—beyond all reason or logical explanation for nothing else mattered.

And when twilight came to call her back from her dreams, he would be gone. Yet his pillow was never empty, for always within the imprint of where his head had lain, she would find two perfect roses—stripped of their thorns—one the purest white, the other blood red. Always upon finding them, Dhariya would lift the delicate velvet blooms, her eyes closing as she brought them to her face. Then, drinking deep of their subtle fragrance she recalled certain moments of their most recent intimacy. Moments she would keep forever safely stored within her. Moments she would bring forth and relive whenever she wished.

This eve as she performed this ritual all pleasure vanished into the sudden unbidden thoughts of waking to an empty bed, to a time when no roses adorn his pillow. When not a faint reminiscence of sandalwood would linger, nor musky scent of spilled passion would tease the air—for he too would be gone, leaving only the void of his going and the ache of his loss. As the pain of this pending reality proved too much to bear, Dhariya swiftly pushed the lonely future aside, re-immersing herself in the moment, allowing for only thoughts of their night ahead—and she found she was able to smile after all.

The hour was late. All was dark and still when Llyr finally returned to Skara Brae. He had found his needs driving him from the castle with greater and greater frequency of late.

He knew Dhariya would be waiting for him and he hoped she would not question him on his whereabouts. How he hated lying to her. It ate away at him each time he was forced to do so. But God knows he could never tell her the truth.

As expected, he found her sitting before a crackling fire in the library's massive hearth, how well he knew her he thought. The warm comfort of the cozy low-ceilinged, wood paneled room was enveloping. It was a place both Llyr and Dhariya loved and were often found together, each immersed in their own book or one reading aloud to the other, the perfect setting on a stormy autumn night such as this.

Wind gusted and raindrops tapped against the large outward curving window, another of Tamas' revisions, which spanned one wall of the reading area. A tufted sofa and two winged chairs sat neatly arranged around the fire and thick eastern carpets covered the cold flagstones.

Oil lamps burned brightly atop corner tables and the ornately carved mahogany desk that dominated the other side of the room. To its left, an open archway accessed the adjoining tower, which housed the impressive collection of rare books. They rose upward alphabetically—row upon row—in specially designed galleries, each row having a built in brazier to keep the dampness at bay. In the air the scent of polished wood, vied with that of tanned leather from the hundreds of bound volumes and leather furnishings.

Dhariya was curled into the far corner of the sofa, her legs tucked up beneath her. She was absorbed in the book she was reading and had not noticed him standing in the doorway. So he leaned his shoulder against the frame, savoring the moment as he gazed his fill.

His breath caught at her absolute beauty. Beautiful, it was such an overused word, tossed about without thought to its meaning. How often he himself had used it in empty flattery plied upon a potential conquest. Well he had been brought to his knees by the reality of it and had learned that true beauty was the 'rarest' of things, a blessing bestowed upon the eyes if its beholder—as of this moment he experienced it anew looking at her now—it was the only word that came close to capturing all that was Dhariya. She could be described as nothing less, yet so much more, with the radiance of her spirit always shinning through.

How untouched she still seemed, he thought. *Even after the immensity of their shared passion her purity remained untainted. For how much longer could it possibly remain thus?* He did not have the answer he only knew he could he not bear to see her light diminish knowing himself to be the cause.

The time for difficult choices was pressing in upon him. But he would not think of that now, so he brought his attentions back to this night—to this room—to this woman.

She had removed her heeled slippers, which sat neatly next to a stack of legers and various files upon the carpet below her. She had obviously spent some time reviewing the accounts of her foundation and more than likely those of her late father's shipping company as well.

Dhariya was a responsible, bright-minded woman who always oversaw important matters such as accuracy of financial records and the like. Llyr deeply admired these aspects of her character and he was proud of her, of the woman she was.

That she could love one such as he, never ceased to astound him—never ceased to prod at the scarlet stains upon his conscience—upon his very soul.

How lovely she looked, he was thinking, *grand enough for any ballroom*. Yet he was glad he did not have to share her with any others, did not have to witness the desire in other men's eyes as they gazed upon her. She was his. She had dressed solely for him, but then she always did.

Tonight she wore bronze silk; one of the gowns he himself had designed for her and it was also one of his favorites. Though Dhariya herself had exquisite taste in fashion as in many other things, she knew how much pleasure he took in choosing clothing for her and indulged him in this.

The low cut of the bodice displayed the fullness of her breasts temptingly, while still sufficiently retaining her modesty. The shade suited her natural golden skin tone to perfection, accentuating the fiery lights in her dark tresses, which were unbound and flowing freely—as was his preference.

He felt the twinge of guilt once again at having kept her waiting so long. "Somehow I knew you'd be here." He finally said, assuming a casual tone as he eased away from the arch and stepped inside, closing the door behind him.

Dhariya looked up slightly startled. "You're quite late tonight. I was worried …you hadn't mentioned you'd be out this evening… and with the storm." She motioned toward the window. She did not smile he noticed.

Crossing the room he bent and kissed her cheek. "Something came up unexpectedly and I had to make a trip into town to take care of it." He answered noncommittally avoiding her gaze. Then he proceeded to the small heavily carved sideboard of dark wood, nestled in the corner, where he poured them each a goblet of wine.

"I see." Dhariya replied, watching the tension in his body as he moved. The exaggerated set of his broad shoulder—the right held slightly higher than the left—was always a sure sign. He was so walled off from her at that moment they might as well be in different rooms, she thought. She did not like it when he kept things from her, as he was doing now, as he had done so often of late.

Into her mind came recollections of this past week or so, of the several times she had inadvertently interrupted Llyr speaking in hushed tones with Iain. Highly unusual for the lord of a castle to have a lowly stable worker called into his presence and address him directly; whatever need be said would customarily be passed down through a succession of servants.

The behavior of both men when she happened upon them had been that of 'being caught out' with far too much effort put into acting as if nothing was amiss. Yet Dhariya was also certain that on one of these occasions she had seen Llyr slip Iain a piece of paper with something written on it, she knew Iain could read and write because Josey had taught him.

Iain had given her a curt bow and hurried off pocketing the note as he did so. Dhariya determined she would not force the issue, hoping that given the chance Llyr might decide confide in her. And having to admit that she herself was not being completely forthright with him either, *perhaps some things were best left alone.*

Returning with goblets in hand—the finely cut crystal surrounding the blood red contents glinting off the firelight as he approached—and placed them within easy reach on the nearby table.

After seating himself on the sofa next to her he reached over wordlessly drawing her into his arms, he nuzzled her neck, the scent of her intoxicating him as always. And Dhariya, as always, responded instantly to his touch, as the tension between them melted in the heat of their passion, which was ever waiting there, just waiting to burn.

Her head resting on his shoulder, his arms encircling her, his palm gliding slowly over warm silk, as he stroked her spine in that familiar soothing motion Dhariya now knew so well.

The two lovers sipped wine and watched the dance of flames together for a time, while the unspoken promises gathered in the quietness and hovered in the shadows until the hour of fulfillment came.

When Llyr arose to refill their goblets Dhariya began telling him of interesting ideas in the book she had been reading and for a time their conversation turned philosophical as it often did. A sharing of thoughts, of questions and doubts, as they both quested to uncover the ultimate truths that were hidden.

"I believe there is a definite purpose for everything that exists." Dhariya was saying in a confident proclamation. The book she had been reading now forgotten in her lap.

"Perhaps" Llyr allowed, "however, if that is indeed true, then what be the purpose for evil Dhariya?" He gently challenged. Dark eyes glittering as he desperately sought solace for his own existence.

Though Dhariya felt the question an uncomfortable one and the look in his eyes disturbing and unreadable, she made no mention of it but instead addressed his question, "Evil." she replied evenly, refusing to spoil the moment with thoughts of the malevolent force shrouding her own life. "Why, evil has no place but that which it's given, just as the 'Holy Scripture' says."

Her large expressive eyes giving emphasis to her earnest explanation, as she inwardly clung to its comfort. "Yet if that place be taken away, then there's nowhere it can hide. Thus, we are not at its mercy but the reverse."

She continued on in the same manner "Of course this doesn't mean that bad things don't happen to good people." She knew that reality too painfully well. "However, I think true power lies within our own mind and thoughts. In the end it's up to each of us to choose. If through our bad experiences we allow evil to claim us then it has won yet another place on earth and another willing hand to do its bidding."

While Llyr was enjoying the absolute sincerity in which Dhariya relayed her beliefs, his was also reflecting back on his life. Recalling far too clearly how he had come to learn the ultimate truth of her words.

"How could we recognize light if we had never known darkness?" she was saying, "in the end perhaps evil exists to challenge us in offering a choice; when bad things happen how shall we react, by turning the other cheek or by raising our own hand in violence?" He felt suddenly humbled. Knowing she now referred to her own life experience. As he had reminded himself so often she had not become bitter and vengeful, as he had done, instead she had transformed the negative into positive action.

Though Dhariya herself never really spoke of these things to him or anyone else, the brutally taught lesson of life's cruelty had forged a will in her. Knowing firsthand what fate befalls the weakest and most vulnerable of society when left to the mercy of others, she had thus, vowed to save as many as she possibly could, from the horrors she herself had suffered.

He remembered Ffyonna's boastful telling of Dhariya's charity work and the Harvest~House Foundation' she had created for this purpose—Being unable to bear children of her own, Dhariya dedicated herself to caring for those without, to seeing the homeless sheltered in manors, sponsored by those with means.

These large homes were shared and maintained by poor families, widowed women, orphaned children and the like, upon lands the foundation purchased with money raised. Various lands in the countryside that were worked by the residents, a place where they were educated, taught to grow their own food and eventually became self-sufficient within their shared community.

Llyr could only marvel at the woman before him and again felt himself to be so unworthy of her.

Dhariya watched the shadows shift and deepen in his eyes. As if he continued to fight some intense inner battle with himself. She wondered what it was that troubled him so, yet said nothing. For in that moment he seemed black as a moonless midnight sky and every bit as unreachable—so she waited.

Finally after a few quiet moments he seemed to master his demons and said, "I hear the echo of Tamas' wisdom in your words my lady. You are indeed a very intelligent woman Dhariya I only hope your faith is as well placed."

She smiled, "As do I."

Llyr turned fully toward her. "Now there is something else I'd like to address," He said while drawing a black velvet box from his pocket and holding it out to her, "this gift in fact."

Dhariya set her book aside, surprise evident in her expression, "for me?"

"Yes." Placing it into her hands he then sat back thoroughly enjoying her childlike exuberance.

"What have you done?" She chided sweetly, eyes sparkling. Lifting the lid she drew a sharp breath. A large oval locket ornately crafted in silver lay nestled amid the dark fabric. "Oh Llyr it's beautiful!"

"Happy nineteenth birthday my love"

"But that's not for another two weeks."

"I know. However, I couldn't wait."—*For I may no longer be here*—he silently acknowledged the all too real possibility, then savagely thrust the thought away.

"My lord, you're worse than I for patience."

"I am and I fully admit this flaw in my character." He agreed in a light tone.

Dhariya suddenly lowered the locket into her lap, looking at him in all seriousness. "Oh no, that reminds me—I've never even asked your age Llyr—and when is your birthday? With everything I hadn't thought. Surely I've missed it?"

"I am eight and twenty, born near the beginning of May. You and I were not even in contact at that point in the spring so you need not distress yourself over it."

"Next year then—which date?"

"The tenth"

"The tenth of May, I shall mark it on my monthly chart and we'll make it a special celebration."

"Indeed." Llyr answered, avoiding any further address to this future commitment, "however, as for special occasions, each and every moment with you is special Dhariya."

She smiled again. "But how did you know my birthday was coming, I'd quite forgotten it myself?"

"I have my ways—my secret ways." He teased. Then swiftly drew her attention back to the moment at hand. Pointing to the swirling pattern engraved upon the locket's surface. "This design is known as 'the ancient Celtic symbol of eternity.'"

"Yes, I recall hearing of it."

"There are countless variations of the pattern and this particular one is a replica of the silver setting in your Uncle's ring, which I now wear, called eternal because it has no beginning and no end." Llyr explained.

It was then Dhariya realized the castle's front gates also depicted this symbol in its black wrought iron design. Then she thought no more of the odd coincidence as her attention was quickly drawn again to her gift. "If you look closely," Llyr was saying, "you'll notice two letters worked into the center of the design."

"Yes, our initials, D and L intertwined together"

"So that you'll always remember me and our time together… " he said meeting her gaze"

"Llyr, you know that I'll never forget you. Good Lord how could I" Dhariya's whispered reply was filled with emotion and unspoken meaning.

Her declaration brought a smile to his lips and an ache to his heart— "The same pattern is repeated on the back," he quickly went on while removing the locket from the confines of its case and handing it to her, "Now, open it and see what's written inside."

Dhariya did so, reading aloud she cited the first half; *'Elysian ~ ever yours'*…then the other…*'unto evermore.'* Oh Llyr I love it and shall wear it always … thank you."

"You're welcome my love…Here, let me put it on for you." The feel of cool metal came to rest between her breasts as he fastened the heavy chain at her nape.

"Elysian?" She questioned somewhat shyly, "That's what you call me when… when we make love, I've wondered about it but I've always been far too occupied to inquire what it means." She added with a coy, teasing spark of her own. "Please tell me now."

"Elysian is from Greek mythology meaning; place of ideal happiness, Eden, paradise"—*blessed abode after death*, he thought but did not say—"all of those things…

And all of those things are what you've been to me Dhariya…'only in thy light shall be my salvation'" he quoted from his own writings… "for 'thou who hath placed no burden upon me—while thy love hath freed me from beneath sorrow's darkened wing, where shelter doth not lie.'"

He meant each of those words he had written for his beloved Dhariya. She was balm to his every wound. Yet he bled anew at the thought that he must leave her—She whose passion spoke to his very soul, in a language of spirit where only the depth of feeling exists and thus further unified them as one.

She was looking at him in wonder unable to find the words to adequately reply to all he had just said to her, about her.

Just let me live in the dream a while longer, he silently begged whatever unseen power might be listening. Then he reached for her and continued to act out his role in the dream, while the nightmare's reality ever hovered just behind it.

Pulling her to him he brushed his lips across hers in the gentlest of kisses and the rest of the world fell away, taking with it the last of her thoughts, leaving only him in all his potent maleness and that sacred place that they alone shared.

Somehow, Dhariya realized, they were now both stretched out atop the thick carpet before the fire and she was in Llyr's arms, while his hot mouth blazed its fiery trail along her neck where he bit ever so gently. He felt her quavering response as well as his own, before proceeding to the enticing swell of breast above the bronze silk.

An expert touch loosened the garment at back and the gown soon slid from her body followed by her lacy undergarments. Stripped bare—mind—body—and soul Dhariya, as always, offered all to him freely and completely.

Llyr looked down upon the glory of her naked perfection, running his hands over the luscious terrain. The silver locket gleamed and winked, catching the firelight as it lay between her breasts.

By taste and touch Llyr worshiped each and every inch of her in a reverent anointing of the flesh. Knowing and infinitely skilled were the hands upon her bared body, the mouth exploring the mysteries of her womanhood and solving them, one by one.

Exquisite sensations danced along the edges of Dhariya's consciousness, swirling seductively as she sank deeper into the hot whirlpool of desire, melting under his masterful command of her passions.

His clothing also soon disappeared and she in turn attended him most assiduously. His skin sleek and glowing in the candlelight claimed her immediate interest—her palms stroking, tracing the hills and vales of this erotic playground.

Finding desire peaked for further exploration—she bent closer to intensify her study. Her hair becoming a rich sable cloud—floating over him—as she pressed kisses along her pathway of discovery—her tongue darting out to seduce him into madness.

Llyr was fully in her command. Her mouth hot, wet, persistent—taut with promise—sleek against sleek—she drew him further—luring him onward—drawing him, further and further into ecstasy—unto the pinnacle of culmination.

"Enough!" Llyr finally managed in a strangled sounding voice. "Lest you unman me before we've yet begun."

Dhariya ignored the plea this night, reveling in her own feminine ascendancy, feeling his powerful body shuddering beneath her lips—her tongue as she took him fully over the threshold. Dhariya lifted her head feeling triumphant and waited for him to recover.

Bloody hell! He had no idea how astute his lovely student would become in the sensual arts, thought Llyr as he drew her up and rolled her beneath him in one smooth motion. With each movement his muscles rippled in the play of firelight and shadow.

Dhariya welcomed the weight of his strong body atop hers. He eased up onto his elbows staring at her with sated appreciation. She drank in the sight of his powerful chest and wide breadth of shoulders and raw primeval maleness.

His dark midnight hair falling in loose disarray, the ends curling to tease the nape of his neck and base of his throat as it fell forward. Framing the ruggedly handsome face that looked down upon her, eyes heavy lidded with the renewed desire already rising to life suddenly held hers imprisoned within their beckoning black depth, while his palm came up to cup her cheek, thumb sensuously stroking the delicate curve of her jaw.

The silence crackled with all that passed between them. Unspoken emotions flooding forth like the hot molten waves of their passion. His need pulsed hard and insistent against her. Her own answered as she opened to him willingly and completely.

Her breathy voice whispering provocatively, "Give me all of your wild reckless fury my love…fill me with it…I want to feel you inside me, feel you surging through me like the blood in my veins, I want to feel your pulse beating within my own heart."

Dark fire blazed to life in his eyes. Sparking them like millions of tiny embers as he lifted his head and torso to gaze down at all the splendor of her pale golden flesh, the breathtaking offering of heaven, at the gates of which he was perched. His hand tightened against her jaw.

"El-y-s-i-a-n…" The air hissed from his lungs as he lowered his mouth to hers, his kiss no longer gentle but fierce and demanding. He entered her welcoming body with a matching thrust, the heated sanctuary of bliss tightening around him.

"Yes-s-s-s…" He breathed against her lips. Moving inside her, gliding now with slow rhythmic cadence, "Take me…deeper and deeper into you…yes-s-s-s…into the sweet paradise that you are…"

Uniting with him, Dhariya—her spine arching beautifully—rose up to meet him. Her fingers curled, clawing into the flesh of his back. And the knowledge that it would not be forever only drove them on—to seek all within the limited span of moments they had been given.

Every emotion she had ever evoked in him came forth as he loved her, from passions primal fervor unto its unspeakable tenderness

And once they finally surrendered there was indeed no going back. Everything held in check for so long now came rushing forth, in a hot, fiery torrent. Each time they came together the intensity of passion escalated as the level of love became more and more profound. "Come…come with me, my darling" She softly called to him "…Come with me…"

He did. And Eden—again—fulfilled its promise.

Languid and weak limbed Dhariya returned to awareness.

Her dark lashes lifted, the huge hazel eyes luminous in the flickering light of flames, still awed by the splendor of fulfillment.

Hours later, Llyr and Dhariya lay together in the sated aftermath of their passion. They had dressed hastily and slipped away from the library.

Laughing like mischievous children they had raided the kitchen, now empty and shut down for the night, packing themselves a basket of various cheeses, breads and wine.

Hurrying upstairs amid clandestine whisperings to each other, hoping none of the servants would come upon them in such dishabille. Such visual evidence of their previous activities would leave little to question.

Thankfully they were unobserved as they stole through the long lengths of corridor and twisting passages along the way to Dhariya's chambers, where they had laughingly tumbled in the door like guilty children.

Josey was off this night so they stretched out together on the wide chaise in the bedchamber secure in their knowledge that they would be undisturbed.

The warmth from the hearth fire cast its glow as they shared their pilfered repast and sipped their wine. Afterward she turned to him with her palm beneath the locket saying, "My lord, I don't believe I've thanked you properly for this beautiful gift."

"Is that so my lady? To my recollection you showed your gratitude exceptionally well." His eyes glinted with the same spark of sensual teasing that hers held.

"Not nearly well enough." She whispered. Her hands already busy at the fastenings of his breeches. They languidly undressed each other and moved to the bed.

They were both more than ready.

Dhariya was asserting herself again now pressing him down onto the coverlet. Llyr lay back enjoying her tactics as she straddled him and took him fully into her, her body gripping his with liquid fire as she moved over him, finding the rhythm and motion of heightening desire.

Then she made love to him in a slow tender joining, which encompassed their new level of profound emotions and culminated in the ultimate oneness.

She was resting quietly beside him now while Llyr traced back over the events of this night. He couldn't help but smile as he recounted the expression on her face when he had given her the locket.

The open unguarded love shinning in her eyes each time his body had melded with hers, when she had taken him to the heights and they had reached the pinnacle of their passions.

How he relished in these moments of respite. Moments of pretence to a life he could only wish for.

As the night moved into the darkness of predawn, however, Llyr found he was not so easy of mind or spirit. The way he felt about Dhariya, the way in which he loved her he would give his very life for her without hesitation.

His life, however, had already been given elsewhere and he could offer her nothing.

He had been battling hard against the ever-increasing guilt within him—against the lie that would not be covered over—against the choices closing in upon him and now he found he could no longer escape the torment of his conscience…

How wrenching to watch the dreams of innocence die and remember only the ghostly-echo of your own? Yet how much worse to know you shall be the cause of such loss to one so beloved? Well that is what lay before us in the future; there can be no other way. I knew it. She did not.

And how selfish am I? How cowardly? Not to have walked away in the very beginning. For her own good by far…but I could not do it. He admitted this all to himself as he gazed upon her in her slumber and felt that strange fluttering in his chest once again.

No—He was the worst of the worst for staying and all the more undeserving of her because of it. Yet her open innocence still seduced him, indeed as much as the first time her beauty had ever graced his vision.

And even now she slept the sleep of the unburdened soul. Lord—had he ever been that? He could not remember a time when he was free of darkness and its heavy weighted encumbrance.

He drew her gently into his embrace, careful not to wake her. She nestled against him with a soft sigh, her flesh warm against his own. He could not look upon her any more just now. Lest he go mad, screaming out at both heaven and hell for what they demanded of him. Could God truly be as cruel as Lucifer? He no longer knew—only that at this moment it seemed so.

He swallowed past the tightness in his throat. Closing his eyes, he kissed the dark silk of her hair. Perhaps tomorrow—yes—maybe tomorrow he would have the strength to leave her. It still may not be too late.

IX

~ And what doth one truly seek within the other? Could it be fulfillment of one's own self promise? Yet perhaps it's more an opposite reflection, a hope of balancing some perceived weakness with naught but an overpowering extreme ~

…I too, have now become haunted by the secrets—hidden there—within the darkness of his eyes. I feel the torment of his soul as if it were my own, yet still; I remain a prisoner of my own passion…and prey to an unknown predator…

~ I smiled upon awakening and with eyes still closed I reached for the roses I knew would adorn the pillow next to mine. My hand recoiled with a gasp of pain. My lids flew open. Turning, I looked over at the white and the red roses, their petals were shriven and dried, their stems covered with sharp prickly thorns. They were dead. And beside them, three distinct droplets of my blood stained the pristine linen.

Pressing a handkerchief to my injured finger, I stared with disbelieving eyes at the disturbing display trying to comprehend its meaning. I arose and dressed. Eager to speak with Llyr of this and have him set my fears to rest.

"His lordship will not be joining you this night, my lady. Called away on some unexpected business in town…asked me to tell you" Urien had this message as I'd entered the drawing room four evenings ago. Llyr still hadn't returned to the castle—to me. Nor had he sent any further word. I had noticed how often he'd become restless of late. I'd sensed a different wildness in his spirit, a deep yearning of sorts for that which I could not fulfill.

My heart ached at his leaving me. My thoughts swirled round in my mind, in an endless painful turning—why—why—why?

~ D ~

~ **D**hariya had not slept at all well since Llyr had been gone. She tossed and turned in the grip of restless frustration, her body crying-out for a touch that would not come, her lips hungering for a kiss that was forsaken.

Of course there were no more roses, living or otherwise, to adorn his empty pillow. While the image of those dead ones ever haunted the back of her mind, pricking their sharp thorns into her thoughts when she least expected. While Dhariya refused to believe that Llyr would do such a thing, *yet who else could it be*—would come the unwelcome query over and over again—a*nd where was he when she needed him so?* This was another of those questions that endlessly plagued her within the unspoken realms of her mind and heart.

Whatever else Dhariya might try to reason away, she could not deny the fact that in Llyr's absence strange things had begun occurring at the castle with greater and greater frequency. Whenever Dhariya chanced to walk the corridors alone, she would hear someone following from some unseen place behind her. Pacing her steps—stopping as she did. The sequence was always the same…she would turn and see nothing, then call out, who is there? But only the sound of an echoing silence answered. Before she knew it, she would be running through the endless passageways in a panic, seeking the security of other's company.

Meanwhile, her every unguarded moment brought forth an echo of Jeremy Saunders words, conjuring unwanted images or sudden recollections, which were becoming increasingly difficult to thrust aside. And although she had purposely locked those letters away without reading any of them, it was not so easy to forget them. Nor everything that they represented for it seemed to be closing in all around her.

She was becoming increasingly aware that someone also frequented her chambers while she was occupied elsewhere. It was evident that her things had been deliberately disturbed, she had spoken with Josey of this being concerned that perhaps her maid was unwell, thus causing an unusual inattentiveness in her duties.

Josey had sworn that she had tended to the rooms as always and left them exactly so. She also assured Dhariya that she was fine—Dhariya had, in fact, noticed how extraordinarily fine Josey seemed to become recently, happier and more radiant than she had ever known her to be. Yet in other ways she had become somewhat reserved with Dhariya, and as a result, their friendship was now a more distant one.

Whispering voices echoed in the passageway. The sound seemed to come from somewhere up ahead. Dhariya's step slowed, her heart began to beat heavily. Slipping into the shadows, she quietly edged her way forward. One of the sconces had burned out leaving a large portion of the corridor completely unlit.

Dhariya could not make out what was being said, nor could she see who it was sharing secrets in the darkness. She was, however, determined to find out. With the element of surprise weighing in her favor, she moved closer on silent feet, now she could see two barely discernable figures in the shadows, a male and a female. When she was nearly upon them, she emerged from hiding and purposely startled them.

The woman screeched, and Dhariya, playing the role of innocent intruder also gasped in alarm. "My lady... you frightened me near to death." Josey's voice said as she came forward into the torchlight clearly shaken—hand pressed to heart. The figure following behind was then illuminated. Dhariya instantly recognized Bryden handsome features.

"We didn't hear you coming Lady Dhariya" he said, all calmness and eloquence.

"So it would seem." Dhariya replied, looking from one to the other, still disbelieving of what she was seeing. Could these two seemingly loyal employees, whom she also loved as her own family, possibly be plotting against her?—and to what purpose?

Clenching her fists into the silk folds of her skirts, Dhariya gathered herself and faced the situation at hand. "What is going on here?" She asked bluntly, assuming the uncharacteristically cool manner of Lady of the Castle. After all, she thought, these were her servants be they friends or no. She had to remember that someone was a threat to her and it was obviously someone she had misguidedly trusted. Her nerves were so frazzled and she was exhausted from lack of sleep, until she found out who it was, everyone was suspect.

"Aahh... n-nothing my lady ...aahh," Josey floundered.

"Actually" Bryden stepped smoothly into the fray. "Not but a few moments before you came, your maid and I had a similar collision in the shadows here. I was heading one way, she the other, and well...I'm afraid I knocked her down and was just helping her to her feet when you happened along."

Nicely done thought Dhariya, but she was not buying it for a second. She felt a stab of deep emotional pain knowing they were lying to her. Knowing they were up to something. Yet she could not very well just come out and accuse them. So she would have to let it go for now and watch them carefully. It hurt to think of it. She abhorred the mistrust; the suspicions of those who were so dear to her heart. All the same, the ache of betrayal was equally as painful. "Very well, on your way then Josey." she replied. Josey flashed an odd look at Bryden, bobbed toward her and hurried off.

Dhariya turned to Bryden. "Have a servant see to these sconces at once, before any other mishaps occur." She order, then turned and walked away.

Dhariya awoke to a strange unearthly moaning. It seemed to reverberate eerily between the stones of the castle's walls. For a moment she blinked into the darkness listening, trying to decipher the sound, but to no avail.

Instantly frightened, her thoughts at once returned to the terrible discovery she had made earlier that evening. Having just finished bathing, she entered the bedchamber, her attention still occupied with wrapping the length of toweling around her nakedness. Then she heard the definite sounds of someone hastily fleeing down the stairwell that led to her sitting room. Too startled and afraid to cry out, she followed as quickly as possible—she heard the crash of the door being flung open below as she descended the steps.

Reaching the sitting room, the heavy door stood open rocking on its hinges, beyond it, the fading echo of fleeing footsteps in the outer corridor. Running to the entryway she stood looking this way and that. Clutching the linen toweling around her, her breath labored with fear and her exertions. From this corner vantage point, Dhariya could see nothing but ever deepening shadows in either direction. All was silent now. She stood a moment, shivering in the cool draft seeping through the cracks in the ancient stones.

Turning back she bolted the door behind her and leaned against it, feeling disoriented by the strangeness of what had just occurred. After a few moments she slowly made her way up to the bedchamber. Her thoughts chased each other trying to sort through the tangle of confusion as she climbed the steps.

Then Dhariya sat there on the edge of her bed surveying the room for any clue to the intruder's identity or purpose. How disturbing that someone was in here while she bathed in the next room. And that someone was most obviously a man she realized now, seeing the large muddy boot-prints on the carpet. Then her eyes lifted to dressing table above and she froze.

Her heart began to thud heavy against her ribs. The drawer in which she had locked her mother's threatening letters was open. She stood and started to walk toward it—her movements felt slow. The room seemed to stretch out and lengthen before her—then she was there looking down at the dresser's surface. The letters were scattered in disarray, the red binding ribbon discarded alongside them.

A single sheet of parchment lay on top. The toweling slid from her limp fingers onto the carpet as Dhariya recognized the same bold hand scrawling out her own name. With a shaking hand she lifted the sheet and read what was written below, *'Beware. Someone watches. Someone waits'*.

As she put it down, she saw another unfolded note, obviously left deliberately beneath her own warning. It read; *'Suriya, Beware. Someone watches. Someone waits'* the omission of both their titles was obviously intended to further offend.

With that memory still vivid in her mind and the haunting moans still wafting into her chambers, Dhariya arose. Without a thought to robe and slippers, she grasped the candlestick from her bedside table and exited the chamber. She refused to lie there cowering in her bed. No, she would seek out this evil and meet it face to face.

Shivering in the cold damp air, Dhariya—clad only in her white French-silk bed gown— looked like a wraith in the night as she descended the narrow curving steps, the stones icy blocks beneath her bare feet. The moaning became louder as she crossed her sitting room to the gothic-curved wooden-door, creaking it open—heart pounding like a drum, she stepped into the darkened passageway, the moaning even louder here, echoing through the corridor, seeming to fill it with layers of mournful tones.

The walls sconces, once again, had not been replenished Dhariya noted. Someone was being lax in his or her duties; most of the flames had burned themselves out. The scant light ahead tunneled its way into complete blackness at the farthest reaches—the same blackness at her back.

Shadows seemed to shift, crowding in on her as she crept along the passageway. While the single flame candle she carried only enhanced the surrounding darkness.

Suddenly she stopped dead—her heart still thudding madly.

The sound was coming from the servant's chamber next to hers. Josey's chamber—Dhariya knew that Iain was still in town purchasing castle supplies. Dear God Josey! She thought in renewed alarm.

Without hesitation Dhariya opened the door and stepped inside, ready to defend or aid her servant. Then she halted, gaping in absolute shock at the sight before her.

Numerous candles burned throughout the small room. Revealing a very naked Josey sprawled across the coverlet—her head arched back—dark brown tresses tossed about in wild dishabille. An equally naked Bryden lay atop her. They were deep in throws of passion, both loudly moaning their pleasure to the other and to everyone else in the castle as well.

For a moment Dhariya could not move, only stared in stunned disbelief. *So this is the cause of Josey's newfound exuberance.* That thought came floating unbidden into Dhariya's mind. Then mentally shaking her head she wondered, *Lord what was happening to this place*—while Bryden continued thrusting madly into Josey's eager body, to the young maid's obvious enjoyment. So involved were they with one another, neither knew Dhariya was there. For which she was most thankful.

Quietly tiptoeing out, she closed the door. Pressing her free hand to her racing heart Dhariya leaned against the wall of the passageway trying to catch her breath after the shock and preceding tensions of these past moments. The coldness of the stones at her back seeped through the thin lacy fibers of her bed-gown, hastened the sobering of her mind and body.

She turned about and left them to their pleasure quietly clicking the door shut after her. As she hurried back toward her own chambers, Dhariya was filled with concern for Josey. Few things could be kept hidden amongst such a large staff, especially with the volume of their lovemaking. Josey knew this as well as anyone. Did she care nothing for her own self? Dhariya wondered.

Lord! What if Iain were to find out? He was not a man to be crossed let alone cuckolded and he had such a volatile temper. Shuddering from that thought as much or more than the chilled air, Dhariya knew she would have to caution Josey, which meant of course, she would have to confess to her own unintentional observation of their tryst.

Well so be it. However uncomfortable it may prove, she would somehow find the right words to broach this delicate subject. Josey's safety was far more important than the inevitable embarrassment they all would face. In the meantime Dhariya could only pray that her two dear friends would take greater care for themselves.

With her mind still twisting in the same circle Dhariya reached the open doorway to her tower chambers. As she stepped over the threshold she heard the definite scraping of boots at her back—sudden pain burst inside her head, sparking stars behind her eyes—she felt herself falling helplessly into oblivion, her body hitting the cold hard flagstones. And everything went utterly black….

The afternoon was cool, only a light mist hovered just above the castle grounds and thus the spectacular view of the surroundings was not impaired. The bracing breeze wafting in off the North Sea was invigorating. After being abed recuperating for two entire days, Dhariya relished the freedom of being out of doors despite a lingering headache. The blow to her skull had left a deep contusion but had not broken through the skin so there was no stitching required.

She had been fortunate this time. If not for Josey and Bryden hearing the thud from her chambers—as her unconscious body hit the heavy door, slamming it shut with force—and come so quickly to investigate, who knows what might have happened.

Not only had they found Dhariya lying there just inside her entryway, they also must have unknowingly interrupted the predator's plot before any further harm was done. For Dhariya was absolutely certain that someone had hit her and that same someone intended to dispose of her one way or another.

Yes she had been fortunate, but what of the next time, or the time after that? How long could this go on? How much more could she endure of the anguish—the torment? She wondered. There had been no more word from Jeremy Saunders. His investigation obviously had not turned up anything yet. How much longer could she survive?

These thoughts plagued her continuously. Ever hovering at the edges of her consciousness, waiting to come flooding in and consume her in her weaker moments or when she least expected. It was always an effort to keep them at bay and she welcomed every opportunity to apply her attentions elsewhere.

Arms laden with flowers—collected in the conservatory along the way—Dhariya walked directly over to the large section of land dedicated to the family plot. The fragrance wafting off the petals floated around her as she moved.

Creaking open the iron-gate entry Dhariya stepped inside. The change of mood was immediate, as if the very air had shifted and quieted, defining this to be a separate world from the one outside its stone wall enclosure. The strange sense of stillness here enfolded her; it was not the soundlessness of death, but the silent peace of resting souls.

Her sapphire velvet skirts and cloak rustling softly, stirring the low hanging threads of mist, as Dhariya made her way through rows of Celtic crosses and headstones marking where each ancestor lay beneath the hard ground. Most dated back hundreds of years and were so aged they were no longer legible.

Everywhere she looked life size figures of angels met her gaze—sculpted of marble and stone, wings unfurled, offering shelter to those whose earthly shell lay eternally reposed here, and solace to those who came to mourn them—gracing the burial grounds with their sublime presence, a gentle reminder of the heavenly reward for a life well lived.

Her uncle had created this to be the beautiful place it now was.

Even Dhariya's father had been caught in the spell that was Skara Brae Castle. Lord Darrien—being last in line and sole heir to his family's aging legacy—had possessed many estates that went along with his own prestigious linage and numerous titles—yet he too had had to admit that none could compare this castle.

Yes he had also grown to love Skara Brae in the same way they all did and had agreed early on that they would all be buried here, the true home of their hearts—and so they were. Dhariya herself would lay alongside them some day, she now hoped it would be later rather than sooner. But she had become too afraid to be certain of anything.

Gathering handfuls of flowers from the larger bouquet she carried, Dhariya whispered a special prayer as she placed the colorful offering at the base of each of the newest headstones—Father—Brother—Mother—their absence from her life so suddenly and completely, so absolutely gone—was such an overwhelming emptiness. The staggering impact of such loss could never be measured, performing this weekly ritual that her uncle had had first begun, at least helped to ease a little of the grief.

One last posy was offered with equal reverence at the grave of Lady Chondra, beloved wife of Lord Tamas—oddly this severely weathered stone bore no dates to indicate the span of her lifetime.

Dhariya had never known her aunt; she had died so long ago. In fact, with the vast age difference between Dhariya's mother and uncle, the twelve-year-old Suriya had still been away at school when the newly wedded couple arrived in Scotland. She had been thrilled when the letter came bearing her brother's news and telling her they would all gather at Skara Brae to celebrate the upcoming Christmastide and even more excited with the prospect of having a sister. Unfortunately however, Lady Chondra died a week before the holidays and Suriya never got to meet her brother's wife.

But they had all seen the portrait of the beautiful woman hanging in the gallery alongside countless other relations both past and present. Yet Lady Chondra's image had always drawn her niece's admiring attention, it was so very different than all the others.

She had been depicted with her long black hair flowing freely, the ebony eyes shone with all the majesty and mystery of her exotic origins. Her slender body draped in a saffron-colored silk 'sari'—the traditional costume of her homeland. She stood with all the regal poise of the Indian Princess that she was, and since Dhariya's own maternal ancestors had also been of ancient Indian royalty, it was an interesting coincidence, one which further linked the family blood ties to that mystical far eastern country

Perhaps this accounted for the eerie resemblance of Lady Chondra to both Dhariya and Lady Suriya. Dhariya herself had noticed it though neither she, nor anyone else had ever spoken of it, and it had only been covertly whispered about in society's circles—first by the few who had actually seen the portrait, later by others whose own lives so lacked excitement they were left with only the speculation and intrigue of gossip.

It seemed Princess Chondra had purposely left her royal title behind along with the members of her family, when she defied them and fled with her new husband to this part of the world. She was finally beginning a life she had chosen for herself and from that point on, she insisted upon being addressed only as Lady Chondra or my lady.

Outsiders never knew the full story, in fact even Dhariya herself did not, yet what she did know of it, she had heard many times and always thought it so romantic. Tamas had been in India on one of his many world ventures, while there, he had met the exotically beautiful Princess Chondra during a gala at the royal palace. They had fallen instantly and madly in love. Her powerful family however, had already prearranged Chondra's betrothal to another and forbid any contact between she and Tamas.

But the heart is oblivious to protocol, and Chondra and her beloved knew it would be impossible to live without each other. Sending messages back and forth through their servants, they arranged to meet in the dead of night and ran away to a nearby town where they were secretly married. Tamas had then taken his young bride aboard his ship—since Lord Tamas dabbled in the import-export business, he had two ships of his own, which served to transport him, and all the worldly treasures that he purchased, to and fro. Fortunately the tides were with them, they set sail at once, bound for Scotland and Skara Brae Castle.

They arrived safely and all was well. They soon learned that Lady Chondra was with child and were elated. Everything was perfect. Then tragedy had struck with a vengeance; Lady Chondra died during a difficult labor birthing twin boys.

However, no one really knew the true fate of the infants. Though it was said they were stillborn and the gravestone bore the names of both sons—Sattva and Ragas—they were said to have been laid together within their mother's arms before the casket was sealed and lowered into the ground. Perhaps that naming had been a bad omen, for the babies had been called after Tamas' and Suriya's twin brothers, who had also died as infants years before Tamas' own conception.

Yet there had always been a persistent rumor that one of Tamas and Chondra's sons had lived only to be stolen away in the night and taken back to India by a servant of Chondra's royal family. It was also said that Tamas still searches for his son to this day, which is why he continues to travel the world and is always gone for so long each time—was that where he was now? She wondered.

For as far back as Dhariya could remember there had always been strange rumors about her uncle, although she had forgotten most of them by now. People seemed to consider him mysterious, perhaps because he never remarried and lived such a solitary existence afterward.

Whatever the truth, it was all so terribly sad. Of course Tamas was the only one who knew what really happened. But he would never speak of it, would never even speak the name Chondra again, so deep was his pain at losing her.

Only in these last few years had Dhariya learned the sorrowful end to this bittersweet romantic tale from her mother. Tamas had been inconsolable and locked himself away for months.

It was during this deep mourning that he himself had painted the portrait of his wife—displaying an exceptional artistic skill—yet he had never painted anything before or since. It was done from memory as a tribute to the woman he loved, a creative expression of the face that ever haunted his mind. He would never get over the loss of her or that of his sons.

But then, whoever got over death? Dhariya wondered. And multiple deaths rend one's being unto the very core. She knew that reality too painfully well. Each loss carved its own hollow deep inside the heart, an empty aching void that could never be filled. Each loss made all of the others that much more vivid, that much harder to bear.

Dhariya's parents story had not been nearly so dramatic—they were both darlings of society, no one opposed the union between them, in fact it had been much celebrated by most. Right up until Lord Darrien's death they were the still envy of all who saw them together—for their love and passion for each other had been equally as powerful as that of Tamas and Chondra.

Dhariya herself now understood that kind of all consuming intensity as well the heartache that went along with it—which was why a part of her mother had never ceased to grieve for her husband, while a different part grieved for her son and the miscarried babes she had buried, until the day she'd finally joined them. Here too, were those small crosses, one for each of the tiny bodies that now lay near their mother. Dhariya said a blessing and laid a single flower for each sibling she never had the chance to know.

The burials always took place here on the evening following the funeral services, and they were always private. It was tradition that only the remaining family members would stand with the clergyman to pray over the lowering casket.

Who would stand to mourn her? Dhariya wondered, she being the last of the bloodlines for either side of her family. If her time came soon her uncle would still be far away; if she lived on for many years to come, then he more than likely would have predeceased her.

Staring down at the names of those she loved, those she missed so terribly. Her finger tracing the letters etched into the cold-rough stone with such finality—Father— Brother— Mother. That someone had deliberately set out to end their lives stabbed at those raw empty places within her—and the knowledge that this same someone was now trying to harm her hammered in Dhariya's head along with the throbbing reminder of just how close he had come to succeeding.

She was feeling like that lost and frightened little girl once more, only this time there was no Uncle Tamas coming to her rescue. Even if she sent off a summons to him this very moment, he would never get back in time to help her—to save her. Dhariya felt completely alone and vulnerable in a way she had never known before, no longer was she able to hide from the horrific truth of what was happening.

How could she ever have guessed when Jeremy Saunders placed the folded stack of parchment into her hands, that this one simple act would mark the end of her safe haven at Skara Brae? That this beloved castle in which she was born would suddenly become unknown and threatening, as if the very walls had eyes that ever watched and ears that ever listened.

Even now out here in the open, Dhariya could those feel eyes upon her. She looked around for any sign of another person nearby. Yet she saw no one. Making her way out of the burial grounds she walked back toward Skara Brae. However, the sense of being watched would not leave her.

She stopped just outside the perimeter of Ffyonna's herb garden. From there Dhariya slowly surveyed the surroundings. The head groundskeeper's cottage nestled at the edge of the far trees appeared normal, though neither he nor his wife, were visible. The stable yard and paddock were empty as the grooms and underlings would be busy about their duties inside at this hour—at this time of year—and it was too cool to leave the horses out to graze after their morning paces.

As her gaze turned to appraise the castle beyond the barren rose-trellises and vine-encumbered arbors, her eyes were drawn to the crumbling ruin of the North tower. Where the ivy stirred and shimmered in the brine-scented breeze.

Suddenly her breath froze in her lungs. Everything stilled. Even the cawing birds silenced. Dhariya was sure someone was standing at the embrasure opening on the top level—just for a fleeting instant—then the shadow was gone, allowing the filtering rays of light through once again. A shiver crept up her spine; she drew her fur-lined cloak more tightly around her as she stood—watching and waiting—but the there was nothing more and she began to have doubts about it.

Impossible she chided herself. That tower was completely sealed off. Although it had been part of the original structure and historically valued by her uncle, it was extremely hazardous. No one had been permitted in there for years. *It must have been the momentary darkening of a passing cloud*, thought Dhariya, *yes that—or an illusion caused by the shifting ivy*, she told herself as the world resumed its normal pace all around her. Thus, she determinedly put it from her mind as she carried on her way. She would not cower nor turn and flee back inside.

This was the one place on earth she had never thought to feel fear. Yet now it crowded in on her continuously. And each eerie incident, real or imagined, only increased her paranoia that much more. This suspicion had finally begun encroaching upon all rationality until she was no longer sure whom she could trust, which is why she told no one the truth of what really happened to her the other night—saying only, that she stumbled in the dark and hit her head.

Her heart hurt, felt bruised and battered, with an aching pain for the sweetness of days gone by. Before long it would be Christmastide, what a joyous holiday season it once had been, the excitement of preparations, the gathering of holly and ivy for indoor decorations, the yearly ritual of choosing Yule logs from the surrounding forest here, the wassails and celebrations. Yet above all it was a time of sharing and giving. Her family had always made a tradition of charitable offerings, they set up soup kitchens to feed the hungry and shelters for the homeless to sleep, and these would be full to overflowing during Christmastide.

She and her brother had been taught from the cradle that theirs was a life of privilege, one to be respected and never taken for granted—they had also been shown the other side of life, the lesser world where people barely survived living in squalor without a glimmer of hope or so much as a promise for tomorrow.

A world where children were born, lived out their short lives, and died in the city streets never having known a full belly or the safety of four walls and roof overhead. Dhariya and her brother had been taught that it was their moral duty to help others less fortunate—those who were unable to do for themselves.

DJ never had his chance to make a difference. But Dhariya had and she had taken the initial idea that much further with her own foundation. She had soon discovered that those who were taught the skills to do for themselves were much happier and far more grateful than those who were only given hand outs and thus grew ever more bitter and resentful of life's injustices—seeming to expect more and more—their anger directed toward those who sought to help.

As she approached the back gardens, her eyes were drawn to the stone bench near the well. Once upon a time she had sat there and dreamed a vision to life. Into her mind came that memory now, during those long months of recovery after her attack. Still a child—but not, changed forever by horrors of which no child should ever know. Fortunately her young mind had blotted out the savage details and only the time following, the time spent at Skara Brae with her mother and Ffyonna tending her, remained clear.

Once she had finally begun to grow stronger, so too were the spring days growing warmer. Thus, at Ffyonna's behest, a footman would routinely carry Dhariya out into these gardens, setting her and her pile of books down in on the stone bench for a few hours of fresh air and sunshine. That spring a bird had nested in a nearby tree; both nest and bird were visible to the young girl who, day by day, watched a miracle taking form, an affirmation of life's continuance in the face of all that was lost to her.

The mother bird sat attending to her eggs by the hour, leaving them only briefly to nourish her own body from the supply within the rich garden soil. Before long three tiny featherless beings had hatched, their mother regularly brought food to their endlessly open beaks lifting above the nest in a nattering of baby-bird chirping.

They grew quickly and after only ten days or so, when Dhariya was brought to the garden, she saw that two of the babies had already flown from the nest, the third however, was afraid. For hours it sat perched beside the nest that had been its home, while the mother bird hovered nearby, making little sounds of encouragement.

Dhariya's heart ached for the young bird, forced to face the harshness of the world before it was ready, she understood the fear and shared all the emotions of the small creature, it seemed too cruel to her own young eyes. Yet she also knew it was nature's way of calling for a degree of strength that lest it be called upon, would otherwise always remain dormant within.

Finally a short time later the baby bird bravely spread its little wings for the first time and tempted fate by thrusting itself away from the safety of the branch. It flew a short distance to a tree on the other side of the garden. She knew everything that bird was going through. She understood its fears and its pain, its need to try despite the threat of the big intimidating world around it.

With confidence gained from the initial trial run, the bird again ventured forth, becoming bolder with every try. The bird soon began to soar. The wind lifting it higher as it swooped, riding the currents in glorious freedom across the sky. Dhariya felt the tears run down her cheeks at the sight. It was the first time she had cried since her attack.

As she watched this little bird flying on that warm spring afternoon, wings outstretched in newly discovered triumph, an idea was born in Dhariya's young mind. Overcoming is the key, thought the nine-year-old girl. And for the first time in so very long she felt a sense of power flutter to life inside of her.

Feeling vulnerable and powerless was the worst experience imaginable; she had come to this harsh understanding in the most painful of ways. The homeless women and children of the city streets were easy prey for depraved predators such as she had encountered. She had a fierce need to spare others from the same. There had to be a way to help these others help themselves, it was an essential element of any human being's self worth to feel purposeful.

Sometimes one only needed to be shown how or encouraged by another to find their own way, their own freedom, thought Dhariya. What if people could be given the tools to build a better life? Thus it was that the 'Harvest~House Foundation' first began to take form. It had given Dhariya a place to put her own pain, turning it into positive action which had also given her incentive.

It served as an explanation for what had happened to her, why she had been made to suffer such an atrocity. There has to be a reason she had told herself, she refuse to believe it was all for nothing, that indeed would be the ultimate betrayal of the faith placed in a loving God. And she clung to this purpose like a lifeline, pouring every ounce of herself into it. She felt a fierce pride in the successful enterprise that she had created.

I shall have to be sure something special is planned for the holiday at each of the foundation homes, thought Dhariya returning to the present. It was the most enjoyable part of her yearly devising for the Harvest~House locations at Christmastide, much more important now with all that was happening in her personal life. She could not fall under the burdens and thus neglect those with greater needs.

She thanked God for her two reliable assistants. Dellis and Leanna both were dedicated women who, despite being educated and of good breeding, had once known the utter desolation of homelessness through circumstances beyond their control.

Dhariya's keen intuitive sense had recognized something in them and she had taken them aside and trained them in the necessary office skills. Paying them a good salary from her own personal account to enable them to live independently, while ensuring that all the funds they raised for Harvest~House remained untouched and that the full sum went only where it was suppose to.

The two women proved a great team; working together they oversaw the foundations daily operations, seeing that all ran smoothly and efficiently. They kept Dhariya informed on a weekly basis and anything out of the ordinary that came up could usually be handled through messengers. Dhariya's instincts had proved right and she knew she had chosen well. As a result the foundation was far more successful than she had ever dreamed possible, if only she could be as intuitively insightful in the matters of her own heart and the terrible threat that hovered over her life, she thought with a sorrowful sigh.

Suddenly she felt a prickle of apprehension. If something were to happen to her what then would become of Dellis and Leanna? Of Harvest~House Foundation and all those whose survival depend upon it? She had been so caught up in her own troubles she had given no thought to that. She would be wise to have legal documents drawn up to secure the future of the foundation at once, clearly defining that her personal wealth was to be held in trust for Harvest~House, then further specifying that Dellis and Leanna were to continue on as its overseers, and naming Jeremy Saunders as executor for dispensing any money from the trust funds.

Yes, Dhariya told herself, *I must begin preparations for any possible outcome. The holiday celebrations must be organized very soon as well.* This would also keep her occupied with purposeful activity. 'Helping another was the best way to help one's self' she could hear her mother's voice ringing through her mind. She remembered these words and had learned their truth so well. There was a comfort in familiarity, in the memories that kept a deceased loved one alive inside those that were left behind and she often sought solace in these recollections.

Drawing her attention back to the stark beauty before her, Dhariya's thoughts turned to her uncle, remembering how he had always taken as great an interest in Skara Brae's outside world as he did its inner, always having specific instructions for the gardens as to their design, as well as intricate detailing of all the plants and flowers that would fill them.

It gave him such pleasure but he drove the groundskeepers mad, thought Dhariya with a wistful smile. Although his hands had never touched the soil, these gardens were as much a part of him as if his own fingers had sifted the earth and laid each leaf and every petal in its place.

Strolling through the endless, brooding sprawl of castle grounds, Dhariya could not fight the grayness within her. She realized how withdrawn and isolated she had allowed herself to become. She had a wide circle of friendly acquaintances but few select friends that she would call close—this by choice—amongst a high society whose values differed greatly from her own.

She kept in touch through written correspondence, yet she had no wish to see any of them, not with her life in such shambles. Nor had she ever shared Llyr with any of them, even those with whom she was closest. Whatever it was she had with him, it was theirs alone. What was there to say? No one else could possibly understand what even she herself could not.

She felt as colorless and void of bloom as the winter gardens surrounding her—*though their life force merely sleeps, awaiting its Spring of reawakening* …She thought sadly, then as one sorrow displaced another, Llyr's image suddenly filled her mind… *but for myself, I know not when my spirit shall rise again, nor when 'he' might return…if ever.*

"My Lady!" the male voice came from behind her. The call startled Dhariya from her musing, her nerves ever on edge of late—she spun about in fear and agitation, to find Bryden's smiling face greeting her warmly. "I saw you from a Castle window and… well, you looked so alone… I thought perhaps you might like some company."

The shadow in the north tower flitted through her mind again. Dhariya mentally shook her head, dismissing the absurd notion for the second time. "Thank you Bryden," she replied, trying to collect her widely scattered wits, "Y-yes I would like that very much." Then, unbidden, the vision of he and Josey suddenly sprung to mind and Dhariya felt her cheeks flush at the memory.

To look at him now, this smiling handsome man, this very same Bryden whom she had known since he was a young boy and who had shared so much of her own childhood. *How long ago those days*, she thought with a stab of pain in her heart, *when he, DJ, and I ran and played all over these grounds. Ever causing mischief, much to Ffyonna's loudly voiced disapproval. The three of us had been reckless and inquisitive in the way that only children can be. O' the innocence of youth, how could we have guessed what fate lay ahead or that one of us would soon be gone?*

"That was a nasty tumble you took my lady," he was saying… "I do hope you're feeling better now."

"Yes. I'm much better today Bryden. I appreciate your concern as well as your timely arrival on the scene the other night. Lord knows I could have taken ill from lying on those cold stones until morning." She told him. "And please, when we're not in company do call me Dhariya. Heavens, we've known each other far too long to be so formal."

"As you wish…Dhariya," he replied with that charming smile she remembered so well. As his familiar face touched that long ago place within her, that place where no sorrow or grief had yet tainted. Where that wide-eyed curious girl lived; always trying to prove she was as capable as he and her brother DJ were, so that they would include her in their games and antics. Both Bryden and DJ were older than she, Bryden by two years, DJ by six years and Dhariya always sought to make up for her lack of years.

How many times, 'Dhariya the little girl', had hidden her fear from them when they had dared her to do this or that. Things she realized now, the boys themselves were too angst-ridden to do; stealing cook's fresh scones and oatcakes from the cooling trays, opening the paddock gates and letting the horses tramp through Ffyonna's herb gardens, pouring the laundresses soap into the conservatory fountain. But she would have braved almost anything just so she would not be left out.

Yet they had also protected her and when it came time for punishment, they never let her take the blame alone. They always stood together, one on either side of her, and bore out whatever doom lay in store. Dhariya had the sudden urge to thrust herself into Bryden's arms, to seek safe haven within the shelter of his strength. Then perhaps she would have the courage to tell him everything and beg him to help see her through this endless nightmare.

However, Dhariya knew she could not afford to take such a risk. Nor would it be fair to involve him in this danger, if he was indeed as innocent as he seemed. So instead she gathered herself together as best she could and on they went from there, laughing as one unto another, they recounted some of their many shared memories.

And at each turn, pictures of the past rose up to greet her. These were only enhanced by Bryden's own colorful recollections, which he relayed in such vivid detail, that Dhariya relived them all over again with him. *How lucky they had been to know such happiness.*

It seemed there was not a place here that did not hold some treasured moment of days gone by. Of endless carefree hours in the warm summer sun, playing Robin Hood or hider and hunter games in the forest. The three of them sneaking away with their horses to race each other across the moors, this of course was forbidden because of the dangers, thank God they were never caught and no harm had ever befallen them.

Dhariya had to admit she was truly enjoying herself. Listening to Bryden as he went on to tell her of his life in these more recent years when he had been away at one school or another—it was a welcome diversion from her own problems— his fine speech revealing the high level of education that Ffyonna and Urien had striven so hard to provide for him.

He had also learned all the charms and manners of a titled gentleman she noticed.

She supposed she could not blame Josey for falling under the seductive spell of one such as Bryden. Iain was not a handsome man. He was coarse, crude and even violent at times. Although Josey had refused to talk of it, Dhariya had seen the bruises and knew that Iain did not treat his wife as a loving husband should. No, she could not blame her friend for seeking comfort elsewhere. Besides, thought Dhariya, who was she to judge another especially in the ways of loving or in matters of the heart?

Witnessing the passionate display with Bryden the other night had certainly been a startling way for Dhariya to discover her young maid's indiscretion. There was once a time when she and Josey kept nothing from each other. Now it seemed they both had their secrets.

Bryden's eyes were intently upon Dhariya, though she was lost in her own thoughts and completely unaware of his scrutiny. *Lord how utterly beautiful she is*, he was thinking. Then again, she always had been and he had always been a little in love with her.

He could still recall when he had first learned the meaning of such love. And it was Dhariya herself who had—unknowingly—taught him the difference between love of family and friends and this deeper emotion that a man felt for one special woman, her mere existence alone had been enough for that lesson.

He had never spoken of these feelings to her or anyone else. What would be the point? Still there had been a time when he was young and foolish enough to believe that one day she would be his. Now of course he knew different, yet a large part of his heart would always belong to her and her alone.

Bryden was well aware of how things stood between Dhariya and Llyr, despite their efforts to be discreet. Over and above his own feelings for Dhariya, Bryden had been concerned about that situation from the beginning, he felt very dubious of the man that had taken over ruler-ship here at Skara Brae, and he did not like the relationship this dark lord had developed with Dhariya.

Looking at her now did not ease his mind. She seemed so unhappy beneath the surface of her smiles and laughter at some of their childhood antics. This was not the true Dhariya whom he had known so long and always felt such closeness. It made him angry to stand aside and watch her suffering.

Although the pure light of her soul could never be fully extinguished, Bryden's own eyes had seen how Dhariya's former radiance had faded away into a pale imitation of something unknown and unreal.

He knew of course, she was still grieving for her mother, which was understandable. He too felt deep sorrow over the death of Lady Suriya, that beautiful lady had always taken time to speak to him whenever she had seen him—always being genuinely interested in his life and had never been anything but kind to him.

Yet he was sure of late, that it was Lord Llyr who troubled Dhariya so deeply. *Yes*, he thought to himself, *she'd been positively glowing when she'd first begun spending time with the dark lord. Now look at her. And where was he? Didn't the man know how fortunate he was to have the love of such a woman?* Bryden shouted out in his mind.

His thoughts ranted at the injustices of affairs of the heart, *and how could she still want him, which she so obviously did, when he'd caused her this much distress? What would it take to for her to see this dark lord for the bastard that he truly was?* These thoughts were abruptly interrupted as the two deerhounds suddenly made an appearance—both came bounding up from behind, then went running ahead and came circling back repeatedly, in the thickening mist.

Bryden found a dead branch on the forest edge which he broke it two, then handing a piece to Dhariya, they proceed to toss them for the dogs to fetch, until the animals finally tired of this game and raced each other up toward the gatehouse, where—more often than not of late—they bunked in with old Crowley, who spoiled the gray furry pair shamelessly.

With their canine entertainers having thus departed, Bryden and Dhariya resumed their reminiscing, neither taking notice of the time nor the gathering dusk around them.

Suddenly the mist parted and the large dark figure of a man seemed to manifest right there before them. His face masked in shadow. He stood motionless surrounded by a small cluster of trees that sighed in the wind and whispered to each other amid rustling leaves and swaying branches.

An imposing force was this black silhouette; the twilight sky bleeding crimson behind him, while the setting sun seemed to have all at once ignited into a living flame. Then Llyr's voice broke into the stillness, "I believe your presence is required inside the castle Bryden."

For all that Bryden was tall and amply built, not a small man by any means, yet he appeared so now compared to Llyr's size and overwhelming presence. Despite the younger man's momentary hesitation there was no question of refusing his lord's order.

"Yes my lord, a good eve to you…and to you my lady." Bryden replied with a stiff bow and quickly strode away.

Llyr fixed his eyes on the other man's retreating form as it faded into the misty veil wreathing Skara Brae; he was feeling very dangerous at that moment. He was not accustomed to all these rioting emotions within him and sought some way to control them before he faced her.

Although he had been away from the castle it was still his responsibility, he had left Dacron behind to keep an eye on things and given him an address in the city where he could be contacted. Llyr trusted him as much as he could trust anyone—he had to— as valet; Dacron would be privy to Llyr's personal habits and thus, see into some of the darkest corners of his existence

Llyr had accepted Dacron's services when he had come to the castle, his own personal servant having recently married and given up his posting, while Tamas' valet, Dacron Sr. had served his lordship for many years. His son, of the same name, had just finished his training and was ready to take over for his aging father, as is often the way with these high-level positions.

But then Tamas had left and where he was going he had no need of a personal servant. So the new lord took him on.

This son has since proved himself to be worthy of his position and the confidences that were given unto him. Llyr had never had cause to question the young man's loyalty. In fact he noticed that the valet seemed to have become fiercely protective of him.

When the message came informing Llyr of Dhariya's accident he had been fraught with worry. At the time it was not yet known if there would be any lingering effects from the trauma to her head. So Dacron could offer nothing more.

Llyr had raced back to Skara Brae, guts twisting with anxiety, his mind filled with images of the woman he loved. He knew head injuries could be serious; he had no idea what condition he might find her in.

Then he had arrived only to discover her out strolling the grounds 'as pretty as ye please' with the likes of young Bryden, talking and laughing together like carefree lovers. He had there stood amid the trees watching them, burning up inside. The magnitude of his own jealousy shocked him. It was a totally new experience, one that he did not relish in the least. He had never cared enough for anyone in his past to warrant such proprietary fervor as he had felt watching the two of them. He had wanted to tear Bryden from limb to limb—he still did.

Somehow he must calm himself before he spoke to her and said things he would later regret. Thus he called forth the full magnitude of his will to fight down the demons.

Dhariya's heart had begun to pound—waiting—all of her senses heightened—watching him. For long moments he just stood there utterly still, staring into the middle distance. This was a different Llyr than the man she had known, the man she loved. She was unsure of this person before her now—this person who had vanished without a trace for days on end.

Then he turned and stepped purposely toward her. "I'd heard that you were injured" he said evenly, trying to mask-over his true feelings, yet he could not help the words that came spilling out nor the accusing tone that accompanied them, "so what were you doing out here *with him* Dhariya?"

Dhariya's eyes flashed fire at him, "well that's a fine greeting after disappearing without so much as a word for seven entire days" she retorted hotly—anger flooding her, "while I hear no apologies, no reasons being offered to me, yet now I must explain myself to you? I think not my lord!" She gathered her skirts and made to sweep past him but he grasped hold of her arm.

"Dhariya please"

In a dizzying flurry of sapphire velvet and white fur she, shook her arm free then whirled on him, "Dhariya please what Llyr?! Please what?! Please understand?! Please forgive me?! Just what is it you want from me Llyr?!"

"Everything…" He answered so softly, this time reaching out to gently pull her against him. Too startled to hold back—and not really wanting to—she went easily into his embrace with a muffled so. As their bodies met Llyr felt the hard angry emotions that protected his heart, crack like a shell inside of him—and a rush of tender-vulnerability swept through him like an unfamiliar tide.

She was clinging to him now. Her every cell cried out for his touch—bereft of it for so many days. The yearning to join was an ache, the need for his presence within her painful and unceasing, while his whispered words were feathering her ear…

"I want everything from you Dhariya and I've no right to any of it. But God help me I cannot stay away, Tell me my darling, are you all right?" easing his hold, his eyes searching her face. "Are you hurt?—I should never have left you," drawing her close to him once again.

"I'm fine now…now that you're here… Oh Llyr what is happening? I'm afraid, but don't know what it is I fear… Yet when you're with me, the fear flees and the nightmare is no more—there is only you."

Llyr suddenly wanted to shake her *'Can you not see the truth?'* His thoughts cried out *'that **I am** the fear…of course the reflection pales amid the looming shadow of its reality! … Dear-God in heaven Dhariya, **I am** the nightmare!'* He wanted to yell this at her, to warn her against the danger that he was. Yet he remained silent—his voice locked deep within him along with all his demons—leaving only desire in all its potent fury.

"This that is between us" she was saying, "it's so intense, so confusing sometimes it scares me as well, yet I too am unable to resist it" she breathed, "nor can I resist you my love."

Llyr still said nothing, no longer trusting himself to speak. Thus, in wordless response, his one hand slipped inside her cloak and tightened around her slender waist, the other laced into her hair—sending pins flying everywhere, as its heavy length came tumbling down to her knees.

Then, as the last remnants of day surrendered itself—he cradled the crown of her head in his palm—and claimed her mouth with all the savage passion that was pulsing through him.

And Dhariya answered the harsh beauty of such desperate need, with that of her own. While the night deepened around them, shielding them within the dark embrace of its shadows. Her back against a tree, his body pressed into hers. She thought he might rip her bodice in his haste to free her breasts. But then she did not care, for he had done so and his touch—his mouth upon her flesh was all that mattered.

Dhariya was reeling beneath the overwhelming magnitude of his seductive prowess, as one hand had found its way under her skirts, caressing the soft bare flesh of inner thigh above her lace garter, on an upward seeking path.

Her breath caught as knowing fingers reached their destination and slipped between the petals to find the very heart of her desire, the scorching pulse melting into liquid heat at his touch. He moaned into her mouth feeling the readiness of her body, flowing fervid and freely, his own body throbbed with the urgent yearning to take her. Then her hands were on him, tearing at the straining buttons of his breeches, palming the turgid flesh. Groaning he pressed harder against the tight grip of her stroking hand, which was skillfully working him into aching madness.

Her soft gasp fluttered hotly across his cheek as he entered her—filling her. They were both trembling as he began to move within her, with fierce, deep, strokes, each movement propelling them further, unto the ultimate oneness each vehemently sought.

A distinct crack of thunder sounded in the distance, melding into the primeval sounds of their joining—the air, moist and heavy with the promise of the storm soon to be upon them—yet they were unaware as their own passionate storm consumed them completely.

There was no gentleness between them this night—only starving mouths devouring, only frantic hands caressing, only the desperate thrust of his body into hers and her's responding with her own rampant urgency—both seeking to bridge the distance of days parted and nights spent alone—straining to move closer to that unifying moment, that absolute oneness.

There was that same sense of wildness to the night, to the whipping wind, to the raging storm—the entire world about them as unleashed and untamed as the lovers mating beneath the trees in the rain—and these lovers were even further fueled by the danger of their daring.

Even as lightening forked the sky overhead, glinting off the raindrops that dotted her naked torso and the polished silver locket between her bared breasts, the two were still lost to all but each other.

From that night forth Llyr only left Skara Brae for a few hours at a time. But he did so frequently. The physical expenditures of such intense sexual activity caused his other needs to be tended to far more often.

Both passions it seemed were intimately intertwined, one feeding the other in an endless, merciless cycle of burning desire that seemed to be escalating. He did not know how to stop it—he only knew how to temporarily pacify the savage beast that shared his body—this beast that seemed to grow ever more demanding and tenacious.

He took his opportunities as they presented themselves, escaping from the castle whenever he could. Usually in the dark predawn hours—after he had loved Dhariya most thoroughly and she had fallen into a deep sated sleep—only then Llyr would slip away.

X

~ And the brighter the light, the darker the shadow ~

…Thus comes the ultimate moment of reckoning ~ to stand face to face with the truth and bear the stark reality of its unrelenting reflection …

Skara Brae Castle ~ Early December 1711

~ **U**pon his return our relationship resumed, yet all was not as it had once been. We were reserved and somewhat distant in each other's presence now. It was more than that we both held something back, it was as if the element of secrecy separating us had grown so vast during our time apart that we could no longer reach fully across it.

While our lovemaking became all the wilder for it—infused with unspoken desperation and overwhelming need—our passion seemed the only truth left between us. Yet perhaps it had always been so and I was just now seeing it for what it was. This thought frightened me, but then I was becoming increasing uncertain of everything. As strange things continued to happen around me, I was feeling more and more frightened with each passing day.

Jeremy Saunders was too far away to be of any help to me here. Nor could he do anything until we had identified the perpetrator. Without a name or a face to go by, the solicitor would be just as powerless as I—fighting against an invisible foe. Thus, having nowhere else to turn with the ever-increasing panic, I kept it all inside and this was proving to be as much a threat to my well being, as the one who wished to harm me.

It was like chasing shadows in the dark, equally as futile as it was exhausting.

I had to unmask the evil and I had to do it soon.

I could not go on this way much longer. Whether I broke from the constant strain or fell into the hands of this killer, one way or another, I knew my time was running out.

~ D ~

~ **D**hariya stopped in the corridor.

So too did the footsteps that were following.

She was always alone when this happened, just as she was now. She turned about, as usual she saw no one behind her. But this time she waited. Her voice quavering slightly as she called out, "Who is there?"...

Only silence answered—a silence that defied the large staff—as if the very world had halted its course and baited its breath. Her heart began thudding loudly. Cold fingers of fear traced a path along her spine.

Her flesh prickled with the absolute certainty that someone was there. Still she waited, watching carefully. Then a shadow shifted in the dimness beyond the arch, though it was impossible to see the figure clearly, the movement itself had been unmistakable.

At once she was running…

Running blindly, as fast as her skirt encumbered legs could take her.

Heedless of her direction, moving without thought. The very passageways seemed to propel her forward. Leading her deeper into the dark unused neither-regions of the castle. Graceful curves and smooth archways soon became twisted and ugly, filled with eerily moving shadows.

The footsteps were coming behind her again, pacing her every step.

Dhariya no longer had any idea where she was or where she was going.

The black opening of a narrow unlit stairwell loomed ahead, nearly stumbling over her skirts in hast she ran into it. Her boots slipping on damp crumbling steps—she managed to right herself using the wall to guide her—palms slithering over the slimy surface of dank musty stones, their heavy odor filling her nostrils as she descended further and further into the increasing darkness.

Sticky veils of cobwebs clung to her as she plunged through their feeble barriers—lungs burning with every labored breath—heartbeat roaring in her ears—mind racing with her steps.

Then she was falling, falling into blackness—only blackness in the waiting depths below, a blackness that seemed to swallow her...

Pain shot through her left hip as it met the hard unyielding ground with force. The impact jolted through her with sickening finality. Her chest heaved in effort to gain breath and endure the agonizing throb resonating throughout her body. The pain so intense she could not move. Her head swam dizzyingly but she fought to remain conscious as nausea gripped her belly and terror gripped her soul.

The footsteps kept on coming. Slowly now, as if her pursuer knew she was trapped, louder and louder came the sound of boots scraping against the stones—closer and closer. Injured and helpless Dhariya lay knowing just how a hunted animal feels when it has been run to ground and knows that death is inevitable.

Everything slowed as she awaited her fate. Like a never-ending nightmare the moments stretched out. While her heart thudded hard and heavy against her ribs.

Finally the undulating glow of a flame appeared on the curving steps above. Dhariya watched it brighten as it drew nearer, she could not yet see who bore it. Then a face emerged from the shadows of the stairwell. It was Llyr's face hovering above the flame he carried—his eyes searching the darkness for her.

Dear God no! Not Llyr! I cannot bear that he is the one who will harm me. Thought Dhariya, as she lay upon the dank stones at the bottom of the moldering tower, helplessly watching him descended the remaining steps. Knowing at any second he would find her there. "Dhariya!" he called out anxiously.

When she did not answer he called again "Dhariya!" Then he saw her. "Dear God! Are you hurt?" He said more quietly upon reaching her. Setting the candlestick down as he knelt beside her.

She still said nothing only stared up at him with huge frightened eyes.

"Why did you run from me?" He questioned in that gentle voice she knew so well, "I was calling your name, but you wouldn't stop, nor answer, Dhariya?"

"It w-was you? … B-but why were you chasing a-after me?"

"I saw you running and tried to catch up to find out why. I was calling out to you, did you not hear me?"

"No I…I —"

"Never mind now, we'll talk of it later. Are you hurt my darling?"

"Y-yes my left hip"

"All right, don't move. I'll carry you back to your chambers. Ffyonna can assess the damage and treat your injury." He picked up the candlestick, "Can you take this?" Dhariya nodded and grasped the ornate silver holder—the single flame sputtered madly and threatened to expire in the cold draft seeping in between the ancient stones—she cupped her free hand protectively around it while Llyr scooped her easily up into his strong arms.

As he carried her up the curving steps, Dhariya had a reminiscent flash of her Uncle Tamas' rescues years ago. Yet it was all so different. For the first time she realized she did not feel the safety in this embrace as she once had and this knowledge was every bit as frightening as anything else could be.

Llyr eased the limp female body to the ground in the shadows, where the darkness would hide his sin. The streets were empty but for he and his prey. Not a sound disturbed those slumbering innocently nearby.

Wiping any traces blood from his mouth with the back of his hand, he turned and staggered like a drunkard into the woods a short distance away. Flopping himself down onto a mossy knoll he waited for the pain to subside.

His body ached from the incompletion—it was the price he paid for not taking all of the life from his victims. Yet how close he had come this time, it seemed to get more and more difficult to pull back. Only at the last possible second had he managed to gain enough control—so she lived, though just barely. She would awaken sometime later, weak and disoriented, her thoughts hazy, having no memory of what had happened to her. He hoped he had hidden her well enough that she would be safe until then.

More long agonizing minutes ensued before he felt any relief. Only then could he surrender and allow the full force of the feeding high to envelope him. Closing his eyes, diving deeper into sensations that were strangely erotic, reveling in the hot blood coursing through him, like waves of passion. For what else could the life force itself be, if not passion in its most primal form? Yet this life force within him now was not his own, and thus it soon began to fade, leaving Llyr with just the cold harsh reality of what he truly was.

It was always the same, the mortification that followed this elemental necessity of his existence. He loathed himself. Then there was the other anguish, as much as he did not wish to face it, something had to be done about Dhariya and soon. The chances of her learning the truth were becoming increasingly likely.

Tonight was a perfect example. Thankfully he had not been recognized. He was hunting far too close to home of late. The risk of discovery was all too real, looming ever nearer with each chance he took. He could not allow that to happen. There was more at stake here than just himself and far greater dangers.

More distraught than ever, Llyr finally returned to a tethered and restless Taranis—the huge animal's breath misting in the cool moist air—dark liquid eyes watching his master's approach.

"What are you looking at?" Llyr snapped, feeling both judged and condemned in his own guilt. The stallion snorted his indignant reply and danced beneath Llyr as he mounted.

"All right then, 'Thunderer' make good your name" was the command, "for now we shall ride. Yes, let us ride far and fast until this world is naught but a blur about us and we topple over its edge into nothingness."

With these words he gave the magnificent beast free rein and they headed out of town, to race across the barren moors beyond.

"Bless you child." Ffyonna was saying in response to another of Dhariya's altered explanations of her own negligence. The older woman clucked and fussed as she tended her far too frequent patient of late. "I've never known you to be so careless Dhariya, even as a wee lass with all the mischief and rough play. Perhaps your thoughts are too much on his lordship to mind where you're goin?'"

"Perhaps," Dhariya managed to agree noncommittally, wincing as Ffyonna poked and prodded her. She offered no further comment. Despite the pain, her thoughts were indeed focused upon 'His Lordship' who had disappeared after depositing her in the bedchamber and leaving her to Ffyonna's skilled hands.

"Nothin's broken, but the tissue's bruised deep, already turnin' black n'blue and swellin' up." she was saying as she went to her herbal box. But Dhariya was only half listening, unable to keep from replaying the events over and over in her mind. She felt more confused than ever. She suddenly wanted to throw herself into the sturdy comfort of the older woman's arms and cry her heart out like she used to when she was small. She could not allow herself to fall apart, however. Hysterics would solve nothing. She needed clear thinking above all things, so she prayed for help to keep herself strong.

Having concluded her examination and treatment, Ffyonna pulled the covers over her patient and handed her a goblet of laudanum laced wine to ease the pain. Dhariya winced at the familiar bitter taste, but did what she was asked then laid back against the pillows. Unbidden, Llyr's distraught facial expression—when he had found her at the bottom of the stairwell—came clear to mind and she relived those terrifying moments. *We'll talk of it later,* he had said, yet it never would be talked of for other concerns would soon come to sweep all else away.

"Josey is missing."

"What!" Both Dhariya and Ffyonna said as one, turning toward the bedchamber entryway where Bryden stood in obvious distress. If anyone noticed that he had breached all propriety by barging into Dhariya's bedchamber unannounced and spoken to her so informally, no one spoke of it.

"Josey, nobody's seen her since suppertime last night."

"Today is her day off." Dhariya replied. "She was supposed to go into town."

"Yes my lady," Bryden, recovered enough to address her properly. "Josey mentioned this. But she was only going to buy thread. She's been sewing a special quilt for her mother's birthday next week. She'd said she wouldn't be gone for long since she needed every spare minute for sewing to have it finished time. Her chamber is empty, yet her hat and cloak are still hanging on the peg next to the door."

"Have all the staff been spoken to?" Dhariya asked, her mind immediately going to Bryden and Josey's secret, wondering if any others had found them out and perhaps confronted her or worse told Iain and he had confronted her.

"Yes milady." Bryden was saying, "Nobody has seen her", his blue eyes full of worry, his face pale and drawn.

"And what has Iain to say?" Dhariya pressed.

Bryden's hands fisted at his sides, yet he was thankful his voice betrayed none of his anger. "He has just come back from errands in town. He says she didn't tell him anything about going anywhere, says he hasn't seen her since he left the castle at dawn this morning and she was still sleeping."

"Then Iain *did* see her earlier today." Ffyonna questioned.

"So he says." Bryden's reply conveyed his doubt.

Dhariya frowned, "Strange…everyone else knew her plans surely her own husband would've been told. And why would she not have gone in the wagon with him. None of it makes any sense."

"Don't the two of you be gettin' yourselves all riled up now," Ffyonna told them. Dhariya was sure the older woman had no idea about Bryden and Josey. This was just Ffyonna's way of trying to keep everyone calm. "Surely she'll turn up soon, you'll see, likely she just forgot to say she'd be away for a while is all."

This explanation sounded convincing enough, but the furrow in Ffyonna's brow betrayed her own concern. And Dhariya knew that Josey was not the sort to forget such a thing.

Bryden's initial message had been given late in the evening. It was now well past midnight and there was still no sign of the missing woman. Of course Josey often ran errands or saw to outside tasks on her free time when Dhariya was not in need of her. Especially with a castle full of servants only a bell-pull away, it was not necessary that Josey remain constantly close at hand. Yet despite all of these rational musings Dhariya knew deep down that something was indeed very, very wrong.

Not only was she frantic with worry for her friend, she was also guilt ridden. Amid all the turmoil that was consuming her, Dhariya had not yet had a chance to speak to Josey about her liaison with Bryden and the need to take greater care against discovery by any others. Now it was quite possible that her oversight had cause the young maid harm.

Making his way back toward the castle, Llyr was in a quandary of his own. Had he remembered to seal the wound after? He could not be certain. It was a relatively new skill that he had only recently developed enough strength to perform—one which sealed the twin incisor entry points and served as a protective measure for the highest ranking of their kind, for they were the guardians of all the others. Yet he could not recall if he had done this.

It would not have mattered if he were Edinburgh where he had always sought his prey until recently, or any other large city, but he was not. He was only a short distance from Skara Brae Castle in the nearby town. In this town most known for the countless witch trials they had held—dating back for two hundred years—if anyone here ever suspected 'what truly dwelt amongst them' …he shook his head against the thought.

Yes, he was becoming far too reckless. This was an endangerment not only to Llyr himself but also, because of the enormous responsibility he carried upon his shoulders, there were far reaching consequences that could prove devastating to others of his kind, as well as to the innocent whose lives so closely intertwined with his own. He could not allow himself continue on in this way. The degree of potential damage was far too frightening to even contemplate.

Before he and Dhariya had become lovers, Llyr would resist this baser bodily hunger to the point of near starvation. This of course had its own dangers, causing the beast in him to rear its head and rage in fury, yet even so, he had managed enough clear headedness to cover his tracks—now however, his tight grasp of the reins was slipping.

The 'Ancient One' who sired him to darkness had promised severe reprisal if this should occur. Llyr had made a binding vow to prevent this at all costs. Of late he was failing miserably at keeping it and many others it seemed. It all related back to what he and Dhariya now shared between them and the depth of what they felt for one another, for this had become all that matter in the world to him—*if only we had not come to be involved so intimately—to love each other so completely*

Well it was too late now. They had both been unable to fight the pull of passion and finally given in to desire. Llyr knew he should have been stronger, yet in the end he had taken what he wanted and damn the consequences. Foolishly believing he could somehow have it all and protect Dhariya as well, only to learn the folly of his own arrogance once again.

Now Dhariya had become the priority, taking precedence over and above all else. Thus, as much as he detested it, the need to hunt and feed was imperative as he tried to avoid the risk to the woman he loved and the far too real possibility that he would harm her while lost in the haze of passion—where all desire merged into one with increasing intensity—and one primal hunger also melded with the other.

On more occasions than he dare admit, he had come oh so close to taking her in that way, and each time recalled to mind the warning he had received from the 'Ancient One' who had sired him into darkness…

...Times of passion are the most dangerous for our kind," the ancient vampyre had said, *'the more you care for your lover, the more lost you become in the act of loving the and the more difficult the ability to keep control upon the darkest urges...keep this in mind and choose wisely Llyr...*

Well, Llyr had come to know the harsh truth of this statement in his love affair with Dhariya. While, at the same time, he had learned that he would never again feel pleasure without also feeling pain. For though the pleasure was highly intensified as a result of the dark curse, it was all too fleeting as well, offering only a brutal reminder of how much was lost to him now and the lingering torment of its passing.

How could he have so casually cast aside the fact that he no longer belonged to himself? That he was as a slave to the dark forces that ruled his existence, those that demanded and reacted—his own feelings notwithstanding. Yet he had done just that. Now he was being shown in no uncertain terms, that far more drastic measures would definitely have to be considered.

———

As the hours wore on there was still no sign of the pretty young maid. While everyone in the castle was anxious and quietly going about, consumed in their own troubled thoughts, Dhariya was sick with worry.

Ffyonna had suggested promoting Annie to temporarily fill Josey's position, though not formerly trained in the refinements of Ladies maid. Annie had stepped in before on Josey's days off, she was capable enough to see to the basic tasks and more than willing to take instruction and helpful suggestions when they were offered.

Dhariya had agreed that until they had determined exactly what had happened to her dear friend and employee, it was wise not to bring an outsider into the castle. Nor was it fair to hire someone for such a prestigious position, while they were all still praying for Josey's safe return.

Of course Dhariya also had her own private reasons for not wanting a stranger as her most personal of servants. She was having enough trouble trying to sort out who of those she knew and trusted was out to harm her.

Upon his return to Skara Brae, Llyr had been informed of Josey's disappearance and the few related details that were known. He had immediately gathered a crew of stable hands and footman together and had them organize into groups, each taking shifts to scour the entire forest and surrounding areas, with lanterns in hand, for hours on end. While another grouping of under-maids had gone through Josey's things and reported back to him, that it seemed nothing was missing from the chamber nor out of place.

Later when Llyr came into Dhariya's chamber—his large elegant black-clad form moving with his usual powerful grace—as he came to the bedside to report. Dhariya could tell by the expression on his face and the way he held his shoulders that the news was not good.

Drawing her into his arms, "I'm sorry my darling" his voice soft, feathering across her ear, "no one has been able to find any trace of her, no footprint in the dirt paths nor any clue as to what might have happened. I'm so very sorry my love."

At least there was still hope then, thought Dhariya, feeling a glimmer of relief.

Llyr eased her away and looked intently into her eyes. "Saunders should know about this." He said. Llyr had recently asked her about Saunders' investigation into the fire and they had discussed the solicitor's suspicions, but that was all. Dhariya would not speak of the rest to him or to anyone else.

"I'll send a missive to him at once," Llyr was saying. "He can start looking into things from that end. Is there anything else you can think of that I should know about? Any other information I should include in my note?"

He was still looking at her, waiting for an answer. Dhariya suddenly felt that strange uncertainty about the man before her again. Wanting with all her heart to dismiss it and confess all to him here and now—to have him take her in his arms and reassure her—to prove the trust she had once had in him was well founded, yet she could not make herself speak a single word.

Llyr was very concerned about Dhariya. He knew she was deeply troubled lately, yet even before Josey's disappearance she had not been herself and he had no idea why. Though he had not dared to ask her what was troubling her so, lest she have a few questions of her own in return. Leave it alone he had decided and done just that. Then he brought his thoughts back to the present matter.

"Can you think of anything else Dhariya?" He prompted.

She shook her head in answer.

"I know how difficult this is for you my love." He drew her back into his arms, palm stroking her hair. "Josey is your friend as well as your closest personal servant. We'll find her" he told her. Although Dhariya was desperately trying to believe him, she was not unable to do so, any more than she was able to gain the comfort he was offering.

Later however, when he came to her and loved her gently, Dhariya was indeed able to lose herself and all her fears in the passionate joining of their bodies. Between the laudanum and his skill she even managed forget the pain of her bruised hip for a time.

And yet when exhaustion finally claimed her, she could find neither rest nor comfort in her slumber.

…*Help me my lady*…Josey's voice continuously called to her in the dark void behind her closed lids—not that of sleep—but a strange restless state of tormented slumber—a place of shadows—of endless corridors lined with countless open doorways, whose thresholds dropped-off into black pits of nothingness. And the only thing to be heard was the resounding echo of her dear friend's fearful pleas...*Oh Dhariya; I beg you, help me! Please help me! ...*

Dawn's pink fingers streaked across the sky, Llyr stood amid the rosin hues spilling into Dhariya's bedchamber, staring down at her limp form in the bed. She looked so small and childlike at that moment and equally as helpless.

The memory of her fall down the dark twisting stairwell would never leave him. He kept seeing her lying there starring up at him with fear, raw and real, in the depths of her eyes. Her fear of him had sliced him unto his very soul.

Bending down he lay the roses in place upon his pillow and then he put his lips to the softness of her soft cheek in the most tender of kisses. A slight smiled briefly curved her mouth, but she did not wake. Just as well, he thought, feeling his heart lighten a little that she had smiled, however slightly, in response to his touch.

Tearing himself away, he strode the lengths of corridor to his own suite. Seeking the windowless confines of the dressing room, squatting down, he drew back the area carpet, grasping hold of the metal ringed handle set into the flags, he lifted portion of the floor and lowered himself into the hollow storage area below, which served him well as a sleeping chamber.

Then easing the thick wooden square back into its place within the stones, he laid down, closed his eyes and surrendered to the blackness within himself where the cold arms of death awaited.

Footsteps were following...
Stopping, spinning about, the footsteps also stopped. Seeing nothing I waited. A shadow moved.
"Who is there?"
Only silence.

Fear—suddenly I was running, deeper and deeper into darkness. And the footsteps kept coming behind, pacing my every step. I no longer knew where I was or where I was going.

The odor of dank musty stones filled my nostrils. Sticky veils of cobwebs clung to me—my lungs burned—my heart thundered. Terror— I must get away.

My foot slipped.

I'm falling, nothing but blackness below, hitting the hard ground—pain, I'm unable to move, my chest heaves seeking air.

And still the footsteps kept coming—louder and louder. The glow of a flame

Then, Llyr's face, hovering above the flame, coming after me...

Dhariya sat bolt upright in the bed, heart still racing, breath coming short, her body damp with perspiration—the nightmare again.

All during her recuperation she had found suspicion seeping its way into every corner of her life. Even though her 'fits' as Ffyonna called them, had finally ceased, now it seemed her ever increasing paranoia was invading her sleep. She could not stop having this horrible nightmare.

Fortunately the injury proved to be no more than a badly bruised hip for which Ffyonna's poultices and potions proved, once again, that infinite wisdom infused the woman's wondrous healing gift. Yet it seemed other things could not be so easily treated.

Shivering in a sudden chill, Dhariya sank back heavily against the pillows and pulled the bed-clothes tightly around her. She looked over to Llyr's place next to hers—it was empty of course, as it always was when she woke. Yes, the roses were there, the ritual had resumed upon his return.

Absently she reached for them—these ones were still vivid and fragrant—only that one time had they been dead and their sharp thorns drawn her blood. She had not questioned Llyr about those dead roses. If fact she had not mentioned them at all to anyone.

Dhariya cradled the blooms tenderly as she inhaled their delicate perfume. She knew she would not be able to go back to sleep now. Her mind was overflowing with too much turmoil—too many questions. *Dear God in heaven where was Josey?* This nightmare was real, far too real and there was no waking from it. Dhariya felt there was some connection between Josey's disappearance and her own crisis. If she could only just figure out what it was, perhaps then she might actually be of help to her friend. And not be so powerless against it all.

Dhariya was feeling frightened, helpless, and completely undone—not knowing which face her enemy bore—suspecting everyone—suspecting Llyr… *What be the purpose for evil Dhariya?* …Llyr's own words suddenly thrust through the swirling cacophony of her thoughts.

She shivered again. Perhaps she should suspect Llyr most of all if she dare be honest about it. Her heart was sinking, aching with the far too real possibility. Perhaps the only one that made any sense. For though she loved him, she could no longer deny that he might truly wish her harm.

As she was continually discovering, he was a mass of contradictions. Powerful and all commanding, yet she had witnessed the magnitude of his need, caught fleeting glimpses of his vulnerability, like the night they had first made love. He had come to her then with no guards in place, no shields, no barriers to keep her and the rest of the world at bay—such a rare moment to find him thus revealed before her. So she had relentlessly pursued her own aims and taken advantage of the opportunity—but she did not want to think about that now.

Bringing her mind back to the issue at hand, Dhariya continued with her unsettling recounting. She had always known that Llyr hid a great many things behind the numerous masks he wore, this was nothing new, she suddenly recalled how afraid of him she had been at first and how very fierce his strength had seemed at that time. Yet she herself had known only tenderness from him. Dhariya shook her head she could make no sense of it.

Then again, nothing made sense anymore.

His enigmatic ways had always puzzled as much as intrigued her and those mysterious dark secrets lurking in his depths that enticed, beckoning discovery, had only excited her. Dhariya had to face the fact he was not the man she had believed him to be.

Heaven help her, she was shaking. Trembling with the sudden turn her thoughts were taking, filling her mind with all she had been hiding from herself. She could not stop them now. They kept coming and coming—of their own accord—one upon the other.

Strangest of all, the more she knew him, the less she knew of him. He had a way of both concealing and revealing at once.

Having been educated in the finest London boarding schools and they spending many years traveling the world, very little was actually known of him in local society. When he returned he had taken the London social scene by storm. No one, however, could say that they really knew him.

Lord knows she had made enough enquiries about him after their initial encounter. Dark, mysterious, brooding, were the words most used to describe him and of course, tall, impressively built and impossibly handsome, all of which Dhariya could easily decipher for herself. But he was only newly returned to town and having left as a child to attend a prestigious school in London, some rumors about a family tragedy leaving him an orphan.

And dangerous, yes, she now recollected dangerous had also been used rather often and she even used the term herself… yet the word that had once meant exciting and alluring had now suddenly taken on a totally different and very disturbing meaning.

So many questions suddenly surfaced. Dhariya stood and began pacing the length of her chambers—though limping with the pain of her still tender hip—she could no longer remain seated as she tried to think clearly with her mind, instead of her breaking heart.

The truth was she knew nothing about him. He was secretive, reclusive, disappeared for days on end with no explanation. Dhariya felt sick, her insides churning with the horrors in her mind.

Her uncle's ring that had always struck her as strange—what if Llyr had actually harmed Tamas? But no, Tamas himself had come to her, telling her he would be away indefinitely and also mentioned he was giving his ring to Llyr. Could it have been blackmail or coercion of some sort? Dhariya immediately dismissed that notion, her uncle was far too powerful a man, no one would dare risk his wrath not even Llyr.

Yet Perhaps Llyr had somehow arranged for Tamas' trip to become a permanent one? Could that be it? Dhariya fought the urge to weep. It was just too horrible to contemplate. She must keep her wits about her now more than ever.

And what of the dead rose who but Llyr could've he done this—even the chosen colors had been accurate and that very incident had marked the beginning of his disappearance. Gone for all those days without so much as a word nor had he ever offered any explanation upon his return.

Yet what if he had never truly left?—but merely staged the entire scene and kept out of sight, in order to avoid suspicion—easy enough in a castle this size—and all these odd occurrences had increased during that time as well.

Dhariya chewed at her lip in dismay as these thoughts whirled in an endless tangle. Up until now, no matter how incriminating the evidence against him, the moment she saw Llyr all doubt melted away. She could not allow that anymore, she must look at the facts honestly regardless of how difficult it may prove to be.

Then there was the fire, Dhariya had begun having vague recollections of that night…nothing concrete, just quick flashes of memory. *And how was it that Llyr happened to be there, close enough to rescue me from the townhouse fire?*

Suddenly she remembered…yes, someone had indeed been there that night, she had woken to the rustling sounds of movement in the darkness, the explosion of pain in her head, as she was knocked into semi-consciousness. An ache filled her chest. She could not truly believe him capable… *What be the purpose for evil Dhariya?* …Llyr's words forced themselves into her mind again.

Next came the haunting recollection of Josey's warning… *I hope you're sure about this Dhariya…"* the rest of her words followed"…*His Lordship is very handsome and all, but something about him scares me. Even Iain has said he doesn't fully trust in this dark lord…Oh dear Josey should I have listened to you?* Dhariya silently called, *"Might you have been safe if I had done so? Where are you?"*

Not a single clue had surfaced, and thus, they were no closer to finding the young missing maid. Poor Maybel had taken to her bed since her daughter's disappearance; she was being kept calm by Ffyonna's regular laudanum ministrations, lest her weak and aging heart give out under the strain.

Jeremy Saunders had started his own search in Edinburgh on the chance that someone in the city might have seen or heard something. So far, however, neither he nor his contacts within the Society of High Constables had been able to turn up anything at all—vanished without a trace is what was both being said aloud and whispered about by everyone—but Dhariya would not accept this and kept the searches going, even funding them from her own pocket.

Dhariya had found the opportunity to speak to Bryden alone, telling him that she knew of his relationship with Josey. He had flushed at this revelation. He was, however, clearly distraught over the missing girl. All the same, it had been a strange conversation and one which continued to trouble Dhariya, for she had a strong feeling that not only was Bryden keeping something from her, but she had also sensed that he wanted to tell her whatever it was, yet could not—perhaps because he had been pledged not to.

"You're quite sure then Bryden?" She had asked, "There's nothing else you can remember that might be helpful?"

"Nothing my lady" he had answered definitely. Yet despite his reluctance to reveal anything further, Dhariya could see how much he cared for Josey, his handsome features etched with concern and fatigue. Nor had she ever seriously suspected Bryden.

She had only thought if he knew Dhariya was aware of his and Josey's intimacy, perhaps he would be able to disclose anything Josey might have confided to him, which in turn could offer some sort of clue. Unfortunately, all he had said was he could not recall anything of relevance.

Iain seemed to display his own brand of worry at his wife being so suddenly gone. Dhariya had also questioned him at length about the matter, yet this too was for naught. Although Dhariya had never really liked the man, and she knew he treated Josey roughly at times, there was nothing to indicate he would go so far as to do her severe harm. And Bryden was absolutely certain that Iain had no idea of the relations between himself and Josey.

Dhariya further reasoned to herself that there was a great deal more going on than just Josey's disappearance. Perhaps it was a case of mistaken identity. After all, she and Josey were of a similar height and weight. Both dark haired, though Dhariya's was darker and much longer, she frequently wore it up concealing its length and in candlelight the true color could easily be mistaken.

Josey was often in Dhariya's chambers alone. It was entirely possible whoever took Josey had, in fact, been seeking Dhariya. This scenario seemed to make the most sense all things considered. Right then and there, Dhariya made a silent pledge to Josey, just as she had to her own family that she would indeed get to the bottom of it all and find out the truth no matter what might befall her. Thus her mind returned, once more, to the other remaining evidence.

The threatening letters, anyone else would have sought some financial gain from such a wealthy family. Since there had been no demands made and no orders for ransom monies, it must be that Llyr wanted clear access to all that Tamas had left him.

Did he think she would try to usurp his position as overseer of her uncle's estate, while he was away? Although Dhariya was sole heir to Skara Brae, she had more than enough wealth of her own, the last thing she needed was the burdens of running the castle, Tamas' vast business empire, as well as her own foundation, and all of her late father's affairs. Her uncle had known this and told her as much when he had come to see her about his upcoming trip and said that he had asked Llyr to assume these responsibilities in his place.

Now she questioned whether any of it was even true?

Could it be mere coincidence that the first time she had ever seen Llyr was here, when her mother had died only hours before? *Thinking on it now, how odd I'd never seen him, never even heard tell of his name before that night. He was supposedly the son of a dearly departed friend of uncle Tamas'.*

But who— what friend? No name had ever been given, nor did Dhariya ever recall any previous mention of such a friend.

Whoever was doing this also had to be someone with regular access not just to the castle but to Dhariya's own chambers as well—and she could no longer quell the mounting doubts.

Everything seemed to point toward him. He must truly think her a threat to him and his quest for power. Dhariya's heart was breaking as each piece of evidence fell into place. What did not make sense however, was the dock accident so many years ago. Then again, her father and brother's deaths could well have been unintentional, yet, everything else certainly was not and it all seemed to coincide with the arrival of one Lord Llyr.

If only I could speak to Jeremy Saunders, thought Dhariya, but it would take too long to send a messenger to summon him. She was already in danger and could not wait. Nevertheless she decided she would write the solicitor a missive, it made her feel better to have someone to call to her aid. Even if something happened to her before he got here, still he might be able to catch this killer and then at least justice would be done.

With a shaking hand Dhariya penned her note, sanded the parchment and sealed it by pressing the hot wax with her family crest. Then pulling the bell cord, she summoned a servant and gave the necessary instruction. That done, Dhariya returned to her bedchamber to try and decide what to do next…

What be the purpose for evil Dhariya-a-a-? …
I hope you're sure about this Dhariya-a-a-a…
Even Iain has said he doesn't fully trust in this dark lord-d-d-d…
Something about him scares me-e-e-e…
What be the purpose for evil Dhariya-a-a-? …
What be the purpose for evil Dhariya-a-a-? …
What be the purpose for evil Dhariya-a-a-? ….

Everything was closing in upon her now.

She could no long sit back and do nothing, waiting for this killer's next strike.

She had to do something. First she must confront Llyr, refusing to contemplate the potential danger in doing so, instead she turned her thoughts toward the need to avenge her family and Josey, whom she was now sure had fallen prey to him as well. Dhariya's heart clung to this purpose, even as it thudded anxiously against her ribs.

She could not go on this way. Pressing trembling fingertips to her pounding temples—the cruelty, the torment, the anguish, it was more than anyone could possibly bear. Yet no matter what happened to her she would see this done in loving memory of those who could no longer do it for themselves.

It was near dusk and as usual he remained, sight unseen, within his rooms. Lord only knew what he was about, hour upon hour, thought Dhariya. For her own safety and sanity she knew she must determine the truth, discover whatever dark secrets he kept hidden from the light of day. Thus decided, she turned about and made for his chambers.

In the dim lamp lit corridor Dhariya stood staring at his door, eyes fixed upon the iron latch, heart thudding within her breast. She certainly was not going to knock and give him any forewarning. Finally swallowing down fear, she drew a deep breath and reached out her hand. Clasping cold metal to moist palm, she pressed downward and—s-l-o-w-l-y—it clicked open. The creak of ancient hinges echoed loudly into taut silence as she entered and closed the door behind her.

Darkness draped the chamber—the walls steeped in shadow—as if the night gathered here awaiting its time. Unmoving, she listened nervously yet there came no response to her intrusion. As her eyes adjusted to tenebrous surroundings, Dhariya realized the sitting room was not only vacant but bore no signs of recent stirring. Not so much as a single ember of fire burned to relieve the chill dampness.

The scent of his sandalwood lingered like a ghostly presence haunting the air. And in spite of herself, Dhariya felt her senses stir in response. Barely risking a shallow breath, she ignored her aching hip and stepped lightly across flagstones and Persian rugs toward his bedchamber where twin doors lay open as if offering an invitation to inspection.

This room also appeared uninhabited with drapes drawn and hearth cold. Striking tinder to wick, a soft golden glow suffused the chamber. Then taking the brass candleholder in hand she proceeded through the entire suite.

As with most of the guest's accommodations, Dhariya had never occasioned to enter these rooms before, though she knew each suite bore its own theme of décor and colors. Here she noted the deep burgundy tones and the richness of the furnishings with dark heavily carved wood, all of which flowed from room to room.

Finally re-entering the bedchamber she confirmed that the entire suite was indeed empty. There was no sign of Dacron either. *How odd, wherever could Llyr have gotten to?* Dhariya wondered.

Turning to leave, just then, she noticed the dressing room door stood slightly ajar, and though no light shone from within, for some indefinable reason she was drawn. Stepping into the vast dressing salon, the lone flame she carried cast ghostly tenure upon the scene, giving illusions of shifting shadows, as if hidden figures moved amid endless racks of dark clothing.

Surveying the eerie facade, apprehension prickling her flesh, Dhariya quickly decided there was naught to be found here. Taking a step toward the door she stumbled over something. It was the area rug—someone had rolled it back and left it so—annoyed, she made a mental note to speak to the staff of such lax.

But then her boot brushed across something else—a large metal ringed handle set right into the flooring—most curious this. *Perhaps it's a secret passageway by which he comes and goes*, she thought to herself, knowing that Skara Brae had a great many of them.

Kneeling down, she set candle aside and grasped the ring firmly with both hands. Though it required every ounce of strength, she managed to lift what seemed to be a thick wooden insert from its place. Then, setting it aside, she lowered the flame into the sea of blackness within, and thus, to her shocked amazement she found him there.

He lay upon his back. Eyes closed. His hands—open palmed and crossed over his chest—the death pose—she heard herself gasp into the unholy stillness. All at once, taking in details of the small airless cubicle, reality struck full-force…

"V-Vampyre"

She shook her head against the site displayed before her. His words again came echoing into her mind…

What be the purpose for evil Dhariya-a-a-a-? …

What be the purpose for evil Dhariya-a-a-a-? …

At that very moment Llyr's eyes opened and looked into hers, "Dhariya." He whispered, seeming nearly as startled as she.

Her hand shook so, that the candle expired. Everything plunged into sudden blackness. Tossing the brass holder aside, she scrambled to her feet in the darkness and somehow managed to run from the room.

Her hip throbbed in protest as she fled through the endless corridors—hearing the echoing sound of his booted feet against the flags, drawing ever nearer as he pursued her.

Dhariya," Llyr called in soft tones, as he stood before the barred entryway to her chambers, it was the first time she had ever locked her door against him. He had no need to try the latch—he had heard the unmistakable sound of scraping metal as he approached—the bolt was firmly in place.

"Dhariya," He spoke her name again gently, seeming to know she was just on the other side of the wooden barrier listening, needing to hear the words he offered. "Dhariya, you know I would never harm you… I can't help being this creature, yet I'm still the same man I was yesterday… can you not see that?"

He waited, but when she made no reply he continued. "It's only your knowledge of me that's changed it alters nothing between us unless we allow it to. *Please* my love, talk to me." Again he waited. There came no reply from within.

How easily he could have slipped past this or any other locked door. Now that Dhariya had uncovered the dark truth of him he no longer need hide this ability. But he refused to countenance such an unfair breech of her defenses.

Hearing the sounds of her weeping tore at him, knowing he was the cause of her grief was more than he could bear. Yet had he not always known it would finally come down to this if he stayed with her, that she would eventually come to learn the dark truth of what he was? Of course he had. However, standing there now—amid its reality—he felt a depth of such excruciating emotion that had him bordering on the brink of a madness he could never have imagined possible.

He was desperate to make her understand, if that was at all possible, yet he firmly rejected the use of hypnotic vocal cadence to influence her will. He respected Dhariya's feelings and would allow her time to come to terms with the shock of her discovery, while inwardly he held fast to the depth of love between them, to the belief that once the haze of shock lifted, she too would clearly recall what they shared—and that she would also come to realize why he had hidden this truth from her.

At this point nothing could be gained by a forced confrontation. He wanted her to come to him freely and if she did not, he would then have to consider more drastic measures. So he turned on his heel and retraced his steps back through the labyrinth of candle lit corridors.

While Dhariya—ear pressed against the heavy wooden door—listened to him striding away, feeling the frailty of each passing moment as it crumbled to dust before her, then was gone—a was he—from her life forever.

She slowly climbed the first set of stairs to her bedchamber. Crossing the room, Dhariya then ascended the second set of curving steps leading to the battlements above, as she had often done of late. She arrived just in time to see the dark cloaked figure ride from Skara Brae into the forest and emerge, only vanish a moment later, into the misty moors beyond. She had known instinctively that Llyr would leave the castle to seek his solace this night.

But alas, there was nowhere she could go to seek her own.

In the still darkness just before daybreak—after a long sleepless night of tears and pain—Dhariya arose. She lit a fresh candle and, moving in the same slow methodical way as the previous night, she dressed herself in the amethyst-velvet riding habit and fur-lined cloak she had laid out the night before. Taking the brush from the bedside table, Dhariya drew it through her long dark tresses to remove the tangles, then she left it flowing freely, not wanting to take any more time to fuss with it.

As she crossed the chamber her eye was suddenly drawn to her mirrored dressing table and what lay atop it. Stepping closer, she gaped at the sight of her mother's blood splattered white-leather gloves. The very ones she had been wearing when she died.

Lady Suriya always wore this exact type of glove during the months of cold weather, their fur-lining served to keep out the damp as well as the chill—having a new pair made in the current color for each and every new season.

That year's color had been white; the new pair had only just been delivered before Lady Suriya's departure to the Chattan Estate. Dhariya all too clearly recalled her mother drawing them on as she bent and placed her soft lips to her daughter's cheek in a parting kiss—one last time—both of them being unaware they would never see each other again. How could they have ever known then that it truly was goodbye? Grief, sharp and merciless, speared through her—tears flooded her eyes at the vivid memory.

Even now the scent of her mother's perfume still clung to the gloves—the exclusive scent that had been blended specifically for her, just as Dhariya's had been crafted for her alone, and each as uniquely unmistakable as the women it reflected. Now Lady Suriya's fragrance seemed to suddenly fill Dhariya's chamber.

All at once Dhariya remembered when she had enquired as to why her mother's body had arrived at their town home without the gloves; she had been told that there had been no gloves found at the accident scene. Dhariya knew her mother always wore her gloves, so she knew that they were missing—only the killer could have accessed them. Dhariya could not help envisioning the wretched beast sifting through the rubble and tearing them from her mother's lifeless hands, yet the image in her mind's eye was but a man's shadow.

A folded sheet of parchment sat beside the blood-stained gloves and next to that were two dead roses, one white the other blood red. Swallowing hard Dhariya opened the message, which merely served to confirm what the dead roses meant.

And she knew then without a doubt, who had done this, knew with all the pain suddenly flooding into her heart. The now familiar bold lettering scrawled its usual warning, but the name at the top was not Dhariya nor was it Suriya, it was Elysian.

No other knew of this name he called her only in their most intimate moments. She had never removed the locket, it had stayed around her neck since the moment he had fastened it there nor had she revealed the written words within to another living soul. Her throat constricted. She could barely breathe. Dear God it was true, she thought she might be sick. Stumbling over to the bed, she sank down heavily. Drawing in deep breaths of air she tried to calm herself.

Her mind was racing out of control, thoughts echoing, overlapping one upon the other. She felt on the verge of madness. She could no longer reason the doubt away by Llyr's kindness and loving ways toward her, the overwhelming truth sat plainly before her eyes in bold black letters…

Elysian…

Her hands trembled as she pressed them to her skull, trying to stop the echoing of his words inside her head …
What be the purpose for evil Dhariya-a-a-a-? …
What be the purpose for evil Dhariya-a-a-a-? ….
Dear God she must get away. Clasping the brass candle-stand from her bedside she silently exited her chambers. Hastening through castle corridors praying she would not encounter anyone on her path to the stable.

Sweeping down the long gallery lined with her ancestor's portraits, all at once Dhariya came to an abrupt halt and looked closely at the canvases mounted on either side. As each image began to clarify—she gasped at the horrific realization—they had all been slashed to ribbons.

Her eyes crept over the terrifying scene of destruction, Dhariya shivered as a cold current of air swirled through the dark corridor. The tattered ribbons of shredded canvas swayed gently in a slow foreboding dance, while shadows seemed to shift all around her. The lone flame she carried flickered wildly, glinting off something just ahead to her right.

Dhariya stepped forward—her gaze then fell upon her own portrait—it too was slashed through like the others—but the knife was still there protruding from the wall... moving closer...

Silent waves of shock reverberated through her entire being. She began to tremble uncontrollably, for the blade had been plunged into the heart of her painted image. There was fresh blood on the blade and crimson droplets dripped from it—glistening wetly on the stone flags below.

The echo came again in her mind and brought the image of him in the death pose lying in that airless tomb.

What be the purpose for evil Dhariya-a-a-a-? ...

What be the purpose for evil Dhariya-a-a-a-? ....

"My God," her words whispered on a halting breath. Suddenly, the candle flame expired—at that same moment—came a ghostly echo of footsteps from behind her.

Dhariya turned in frenzied swirl of amethyst velvet and fled as fast as her shaky legs and tender hip would allow.

———

XI
~ And o' the night where be thy mercy? ~

...For I have known sadness at its greatest triumph ~ that of a heart which yet beats though it is battered and torn unto its last fiber. What crueler fate be there than this?...

*~ **B**etrayal and aloneness hung like a dark heavy shroud upon my spirit—while my body, so frail beneath this burden—found that even the drawing of breath had become a laborious task.*

Inside the stable only neighs and soft snorts of greeting fluttered in the stillness. Grooms and underlings would still be slumbering peacefully in their quarters above, though the braziers they'd lit hours ago continued to glow in the darkness, offering warmth and meager light in the chill-darkness of the early morn.

Fighting against weariness, I somehow saddled my horse and rode the winding length of the carriage path. Thankfully the hounds, being spoilt and pampered, were not left to roam about the grounds at night and therefore could not raise any barking alert.

Easing down from Andromeda's back I creaked the gates open hoping Crowley had imbibed his usual nightly quantity of whiskey—then I led the mare out, creaked the gate closed and remounted.

Every moment, every movement challenged the depth of my fortitude and these last efforts stripped me bare. I cared not where we went only that we were quickly away. Thus, amid the first faint light of dawn, horse and rider departed the slumbering castle.

And yet long after Skara Brae's gates had faded into the past, the echo of their closing still remained. For all that lay therein would not be so easily left behind.

~ D ~

~ The mare settled into a strong rhythmic stride, stirring lazy tendrils of mist throughout the waking forest. While Dhariya remained oblivious to the scenic beauty around her, seeing naught but a distant blur of green and shadow.

Even the painful throb of her hip seemed to be far away from her now. Her only awareness was that with every graceful glide of hoofs, the silver locket—his gift bearing their entwined initials—pounded against her heart, a constant reminder of its engraved words *'Elysian ~ ever yours, unto evermore.'*

Elysian…the word savagely tore her unto her very core, this word that once represented only joy in the intimate joining of their bodies, had now come to mean the condemnation of the man she loved, proving him to be both killer and destroyer of all that she held dear. How had the dream so suddenly become a nightmare? Fresh tears spilled unheeded down her cheeks as each memory of him came forth in endless inner visions of shared moments, precious beyond speaking. Yet she could not forget the way he had looked the last time she had seen him, lying there like a dead man.

And within her the torn jagged edges of her being lay open, revealing the place where such passionate love had surged with life—that place was now a gaping chasm where only the ceaseless ache of its loss remained.

Somewhere well into the deep woods, Dhariya began hearing a second set of hoofs beats distantly following.

Drawing rein, she turned in the saddle, carefully surveying her surroundings from all sides.

Dappled morning light filtered through the branches, revealing only the languid sway of leaves in the whispering breeze. All else was hidden. All else was silent—save for Andromeda's restless snorts and the occasional impatient clomp of her hoof against ground—yet fear still gripped Dhariya's mind and turned it fiercely upon her once more …

*What be the purpose for evil Dhariya-a-a-a-? … What be the purpose for evil Dhariya-a-a-a-? … Dhariya-a-a-a…Dhariya-a-a-a…Dhariya-a-a-a…*Came the echoing memory of his words, these words that never seemed to leave her now. Coming over and over again, even as she waited helplessly—her heart beating hard and heavy against her ribs—thundering in her ears, these relentless thoughts came again and again.

I should not be riding alone Dhariya inwardly chided herself, as Mr. Saunders warning found its way into her mind to tangled with the memory of Llyr's ever-haunting question, sweeping aside all other emotions. *But the sun is high*, she thought in unspoken answer, *surely that means I'm safe from him for hours yet. Why then did the eerie pickle of warning refuse to cede?*

Then came the sound of snapping twigs and Dhariya had no more time to think, she spun about to see a man mounted upon a dark horse emerging from between the trees. Her heart continued to pound as she watched him approach. At first it was impossible to see who it was clearly yet the voice that now hailed to her was familiar, one she knew well enough to recognize. All the same, it took Dhariya's confused mind a moment to register that it was in fact Josey's husband Iain who was riding toward and her doffing his cap respectfully.

Relief flooded her in a dizzying rush. The intense fright she just experienced had shaken her back into alert awareness, forcing her to inwardly acknowledge the very real danger she was in and her vulnerability, as nothing else could. Now she welcomed the intrusion of his companionship despite her aversion to this particular man.

"Iain thank God." She said—one gloved hand lifting to press against her racing heart. "You frightened me half to death."

He made a quick apology, all courtesy and manners that were so unlike his customary curtness. Iain then went on to explain how he had seen her ride out alone and followed out of concern. Dhariya did not give Iain's odd behavior much credence, he had never been comfortable around her, nor she him, so she merely sketched a weary smile and thanked him.

Although there was no need for her to explain her actions—strange or otherwise—to a servant, Dhariya still had enough sense in her scrambled wits to try to avoid as much gossip as possible. She hastily offered a feeble tale of feeling hemmed in and being too far away from the city for too long.

Iain in turn offered her his escort since—as he told her—he himself was headed that way to pick up some supplies on back order. Dhariya then willingly placed herself in his hands and allowed him to lead her toward Edinburgh.

There was no further conversation between them during the remainder of the journey, which more than suited Dhariya. She had nothing to say to this man, nor anyone else for that matter—Iain was taking charge and that was fine with her. All that mattered was getting away from the person who was such a threat to her, the thought of whom sliced through her like a blade once again.

The anguish came again in a tidal flow of sorrow and Dhariya, no longer able to fight against it, fell back into herself, merely following along with Iain's direction, becoming oblivious to the world around her once more. Thus she took no notice of his cunning smile, that of a cat having finally cornered its prey. She also did not notice his bandaged hand, or the fresh blood staining the cloth binding.

Despite the pain of his injured hand, Iain was indeed feeling extremely smug, *Aye the big man'll be pleased*, he was thinking. While his body stirred with pleasure at his coming rewards, *I'll send word to 'em once I've got 'er somewhere secure…won't e' be surprised…e'll surely pay extra coin fer gettin' the job done so fast.* His self-satisfaction only intensified as he mentally reviewed his future plans and imagined that special one he so desired to share that future with.

Once inside the city, Iain proceeded along the narrow cobbled streets until they reached a small Wynd on the furthest outskirts, here he brought them to a stop outside a decent looking Inn. He said something to Dhariya about always staying here whenever castle business brought him to Edinburgh. When he suggested taking a second room for her, Dhariya agreed without hesitation. She was beyond exhausted and the throbbing in her hip was excruciating from the relentless pounding against the hard leather saddle.

After securing separate lodgings for each of them, Iain had seen Dhariya safely up to her room, which he insisted was the finest to be had and then he went off about his city business. She felt a measure of relief at the sound of the closing door and sank down into the chair.

Dhariya did not know how long she had been sitting there staring into the flames, but the shadows were beginning to lengthen and gather. The small rustic room about her was clean and warm, but she felt none of its comfort. The tray of food that had been brought sat cold and untouched upon the table behind her, though she had made good use of the wine which had accompanied it.

As darkness began to fully descend Dhariya fairly stumbled from the hearthside chair to the bed and promptly fell into exhausted slumber. Only to be awoken what seems mere moments later by a loud thud in the hallway followed by a rattling of her latched door. *Was someone trying to get into her room?*

Easing up in the bed, Dhariya groggy and disoriented, could not seem to grasp any coherent thought, they kept sliding away on what she now realized was a laudanum induced stupor.

The wine she managed to decipher, though it had not been enough to taste, and she could not comprehend why someone wished to drug her. But she could see the door now slowly opening, the sound of its hinges creaking seemed to echo in the stillness. Dhariya assumed it was Iain coming to check on her, or perhaps the maidservant returning for the tray. However, as the person stepped inside she knew instantly this was no woman, nor was it Iain.

Dhariya watched as the dark figure, that was large though not tall enough to be Iain, came toward her—then, stepping into the firelight the bulky form of Dexter Dreshem—her late father's partner at Darrien & Co. Shipping Enterprises—became recognizable.

"Mr. D-Dreshem?" Dhariya's unease and confusion evident in her voice as she sat up in the bed, "W-Whatever brings you here?"

"Why, you of course, Lady Dhariya." He replied with an odd smugness, as he locked the door behind him and lit a taper.

The mild mannered man she had always been acquainted with had suddenly become someone quite different, she realized. Now fearful, Dhariya swallowed hard and forced a calm even tone, "I-I don't understand Mr. Dreshem."

"No, although you will soon enough my dear," his inappropriate familiarity further disturbed her, yet she tried to hide her rapidly growing panic.

Then Dhariya's heart leapt to her throat as he moved toward her with a stalking gait, his voice softening to a provocative whisper that made her skin crawl. "So beautiful Dhariya, though I never imagined another being even more beautiful than your mother, whom I coveted from the first moment I saw her."

Dhariya sat huge eyed in shocked disbelief, as she pressed herself deeper into the propped pillows at her back.

"But," he placed the candlestick on the bedside table then began pacing back and forth across the floor as he went on, "of course the exotic 'Lady Suriya' was already betrothed to your father 'Lord Darrien of Dreghorn.'" He spoke the title with such scorn and his eyes turned hard with hatred. "The greedy man had to have it all," he spat out each word with such unconcealed venom.

"How dare you speak so of my father?" Dhariya challenged, anger quickly displacing fear and pushing aside some of the drugging fog.

"If not for his generosity, you would have lived out your childhood as an orphan on the street—that is if you even survived the deplorable conditions of such a life. Yet my father took you in and saw to your excellent education, offering opportunities most only dream of. Not only did he treat you as a younger brother, he made you an equal partner in Darrien & Co. Shipping—"

"Oh yes," Dreshem cut in, "I admit I endured my brutal beginnings and rose well above my station with Darrien's aid of course," waving his hand as if it were nothing. "Yet that bloody man—your father—had to be everything I wanted to be and have everything I longed to have. And as time wore on such injustice became more and more intolerable!"

Dreshem's pacing step increased in degree with the anger in his malevolent diatribe. "He, your father, was far too handsome, far too rich, a titled gent of course, and then he married the most beautiful woman any of us had ever seen, the most beautiful that is, until you—Dhariya."

He came to her then, sitting himself down alongside her. "Even when you were but a mere infant," he continued, staring at her now with undisguised awe, "your beauty out shone all others—the combined perfection of both mother and father culminated in you, of course he'd already had his son and heir which then guaranteed that I never would attain anything more or rise into the lofty realm of high society."

He stood abruptly and resumed pacing the length of floor beside the bed, sweeping thick fingers through the clumps of his muddy brown hair. "but when I looked at you all those years ago, so proudly displayed in your father's arms—I knew then why I'd been forced to endure all the painful years of watching the two of them together, their eyes only for each other, then came the son they'd created from their carnal lust—oh yes, in that instant when I first laid eyes on you I knew you were the one meant for me."

Dhariya was so stunned and frightened at his proclamations, she was scarcely able to draw breath let alone utter one word. While she silently wondered if he could have been the one who had raped her as a child, she had managed to somehow block-out those details, and could no longer recall the face of her attacker. Yet perhaps that's why she always felt such an aversion to his presence.

…"Finally, after years of torment," he was saying, "I decided I'd show 'the hallowed 'Lord Darrien' and all the rest." Dreshem's average looking face became an ugly mask of envy. "I would take whatever I wanted. I need only eliminate the obstacles; your father and brother were the first, although it all nearly went awry when you came close to perishing that night as well. Of course your father, the great Lord Darrien, had to play the hero even unto his final breath and saved you at the very last moment… yet at least it served my purposes well that time. After that, in order to avoid suspicion, I had to wait and bide my time before I killed your mother. But I'm a very patient man when I wish to be."

He stopped and looked toward her on the bed, his voice turning soft and beseeching. "They had to go surely you see that, don't you Dhariya?" His beady light brown eyes piercing hers, seeking answer, Dhariya managed an abrupt nod of her head in desperate attempt to placate him, though her heart clenched in pain at his every word.

Then gathering her nerve she spoke. "You'll not get away with this. I'm not alone here, my servant Iain is with me and he'll be back from his errands any moment now."

"Iain?" He asked incredulously, "You lady, are really quite a fool. Iain has been working with me for a number of years now." Waving his hand in dismissal, "He purposely courted and married that pretty little maid of yours just to have access to your household. He was naught but a willing pawn and proved himself a greedy one who'd do anything for money."

Dhariya bit back a bitter retort lest she further fuel Dreshem's anger and he continued without pause, "For a hefty price he was only too eager to rig carriages, set fires, slash paintings and generally wreak havoc in your life." Dreshem said with a cruel smile. At that he turned, walked to the fire, bent low to add some peat and wood splinters, and then stood silent for a time watching the flames spark to life.

What a stroke of luck Iain had been, Dreshem was thinking. *Having an accomplice right inside the home had proved nothing short of brilliant. As a result, it hadn't taken nearly as long as he'd figured to have this beautiful young woman lured away from the protective confines of Skara Brae Castle. She was the only one left—the only remaining barrier between him and the entire vast fortune that was Darrien & Co. Shipping Enterprises—his plan had worked perfectly.*

Good thing he'd instructed Iain to keep watch on her and to follow her if she ever rode out alone. Why, he could scarcely believe his eyes when the crudely scrawled message had arrived at his office earlier, informing him where Lady Dhariya could be found.

Upon receiving the missive Dreshem headed for the Inn post haste. Iain had been waiting for him by the stables out back looking for his rewards. *Well he'd gotten it too, that low born cur had served his purpose and indeed gotten just what he deserved,* Thought Dreshem, who had then spent an hour or more in the Inn's taproom before he summoned the courage to mount the steps and enter this room—this room where Dhariya had been lured, drugged and laid-out waiting for him.

Yes here she was Darrien's daughter—just thinking of His 'high and mighty' Lordship's reaction—he was surely turning over and over in his grave right about now, thought Dreshem, his own body already responding to this idea and this final vengeance he was about to take, as well as certain images of what he would to do to her and to have her do to him. Oh yes thinking how 'His Lordship' would feel seeing his daughter used so. These were the same thoughts he had harbored and envisioned countless times a day for more years than he could recall. Every lover he had ever taken had, at least in his mind, always bore the face and body of the one he truly desired.

Then he turned to look at her and said in a strange sounding voice, "I long ago vowed to myself, I'd either possess all that was Lord Darrien's or else it would cease to exist and I've nearly accomplished this. But tonight, tonight is my ultimate victory," his eyes gleamed, anticipating some obscene intensions, "for I shall taste all the sweetness of your fully ripened body."

Upon hearing these words all the horror of Dhariya's past came flooding into the present like a drowning pool. She shuddered in revulsion as he came toward her. Firelight gleaming off the silver blade he carried, the bed sank beneath his generous weight. His free hand took hold of her bodice, while the other lifted the knife. Dhariya's heart faltered, thudding in slow, thickening beats that reverberated throughout her entire being.

The knife lowered and began slicing its way through the front of Dhariya's clothing. She stayed absolutely still, daring not a breath, fearing even one slip of the gleaming honed-blade.

Heavy Amethyst velvet fell away as the blade progressed down the length of her, and following in its path, Dreshem's eyes glittered with an unholy light, the evidence of his lust becoming increasingly visible beneath his woolen trousers.

At the completion of the knife's journey, Dhariya took advantage of his distraction and quickly rolled to the opposite side of the bed, attempting escape, only to let out a screech as he grasped hold of her hair and yanked her back.

His pudgy fingers clamped hard over her mouth, Dhariya felt the prick of the knifepoint at her throat, followed by a warm trickle of blood that spilled down her neck and into her hair.

"I'd hoped you'd be reasonable Dhariya," his face scarcely inches from hers; sweat beading his brow as he breathed the words on a wafting of brandy fumes… "We could get along very well together you and me, if you'd but only co-operate."

Drawing a length of rope from his pocket he tied her wrists tightly together and secured them to the heavy wooden headboard. Then, Dreshem hastily loosened his cravat and gagged her. All the while, Dhariya squirmed, trying to kick at him, the coarse fibrous rope painfully biting into her delicate flesh.

"But you seem to want the rough stuff instead—" His meaty fist slammed hard against the side of her temple. Pain surged through Dhariya's skull, sending a spray of stars across her line of vision.

The room swam before her eyes. She struggled against fading consciousness, yet terror proved an unexpected ally as the heightening rush of adrenaline thrust its way through the effects of the blow and the laudanum's drugging lull.

"Is that what you like?" He was ranting at her. "Is it…you beautiful little bitch? Believe me I'll give you all that and more." Suddenly he remembered another weapon, one that would be much more threatening, Iain's wife was her maid and Dreshem knew only too well that she was still missing.

"I have your pretty little maid tucked safely too," at Dhariya's obvious shock he smiled, "yes, that's right, and if you fight me anymore—she dies." With that he savagely tore the thin chemise down the front, and, using the tip of the blade, he peeled back the layers of clothing.

At his words she was consumed with panic. Had Josey been powerless like this in Dreshem's clutches all this time? Had she been forced to endure this horror of horrors ever since? Oh, Lord in heaven no! Her mind could not possibly contend with such a concept.

Thoughts spinning out of control now, Dhariya lay there helpless, virtually naked but for her heeled riding boots and gartered hose. All her womanly endowments exposed to his gluttonous gaze. His anger seemed to melt into some sort of reverent hypnotic state. And the silver locket between her breasts gleamed in the candlelight.

"Dear God but you're lush." With a deep swallow, his quavering hands reached out and touched her bare breasts, which he fondled at his leisure.

Lord-God, this cannot be happening all over again, thought Dhariya, and she was suddenly that defenseless child once more, unable to protect herself from such an appalling defilement.

Uttering some grotesque sounds his one hand slid down her midriff. Cruel fingers began their invasion, roughly prodding into the delicate softness between her legs. His other hand worked madly to unfasten his breeches.

Dhariya tried with all her remaining strength to squirm away, her muffed voice crying out in protest beneath the gag. Only the thought of Josey's safety kept her from fiercely wrenching away from him with every ounce of strength she possessed. While the horror of past and present melded into one living nightmare.

He opened his breeches releasing his flaccid manhood, angry now at the loss of his erection, stroking himself madly. Moving away from her, he closed his eyes and turned his back. He was becoming more and more desperate to arouse himself. The efforts were obviously failing; the only thing that was increasing was his rage.

Dhariya's fogged mind was trying to make some sense of Dreshem. He sounded more like a spurned suitor than anything else. Then a sudden realization came piercing through the drugged haze and, all at once, Dhariya recognized the lie hidden in his words.

Dreshem had not hated her father at all. Whether the man himself understood the distortions of his own emotions or not, he was actuality in love with Lord Darrien and the real source of his anger stemmed from knowing he would never have his desires fulfilled.

Of course her female body did not arouse him, nor would any other woman's. That is why Dreshem had to turn away to try and excite himself by thinking of something quite different. Although she herself did not fully understand his type, nor was she wise in the ways of such matters, however she was quite aware that such preferences existed.

She did not doubt that these feelings were any less intense than what she felt for Llyr. Nor did she believe the man before her now felt any less betrayed in his distorted perceptions.

Dreshem had never shared intimacies with her father, of this Dhariya was absolutely certain, yet she was also sure that in Dreshem's sadly confused mind they had been destined to know each other thus. For a second Dhariya almost felt sorry for him. At that moment Dreshem threw himself into the nearby chair and re-buttoned the front of his breeches. Leaving her lying with her body exposed to him.

He was not able to take her just yet, but he decided to unnerve her by looking at her and touching her as he would. Yes, he thought, feeling his sense of power and dominance restored, he would show her one way or the other that she was his, to do with as he willed.

Thus, did the next hours play-out. Dhariya was freezing, her exposed flesh prickling as the embers in the hearth finally burned themselves into ash. It was late she knew. Noise from the taproom below had long since faded into quietness.

Dreshem was now passed out in the chair. He had left the room earlier only to return some moments later, with a bottle of whiskey in each hand. He had placed these on the table. After that he had gone around and lit every candle in the room, then proceeded to drink himself into a stupor. All the while he had been talking to her, using profanity and vulgarity in his descriptive dialogue of what she would endure as his captive.

Yet there was somewhere Dhariya could go—deep inside herself —where she would be safe. *Do what you will*, she told him in thought, *but you shall never own me nor take my soul, it is mine to give. I am a survivor. My strength has already proven itself. I know how to hide from the likes of you in a place where you can never truly reach me.* She had found it once a long time ago. She knew how to find it again and went there now, to lock herself away.

Every now and then he would stagger over and start touching her again, his hands always cruel and hurtful, fingers prodding and violating in the manner that his manhood had failed to. Replacing candles as they burned down he kept the room brightly lit so no part of her body would be hidden from his eyes. The threat of the knife was silent yet ever present ever within his reach, the blade gleaming in the candlelight.

And as the night wore on the worse it got. Dreshem was determined to degrade and humiliate her, forcing her legs wide apart so she was fully open to his gaze, would look at her there in her most intimate place. Pressing his face close against her inner thigh, hands touching as he made his thorough study. She had lost consciousness a number of times during the many vile acts he forced upon her.

Finally when he was done with her he staggered back to his chair and proceeded to pour more whiskey down his throat. At one point he folded his arms on the table and laid his head upon them.

His shoulders began to shake, he was weeping Dhariya realized, then his slurred voice came between the sobs, "If only *s-she* hadn't come and s-stolen him a-away," he was saying, "I might have been able to …to show him how I truly felt… h-how wonderful it c-could have been b-between us…he and I … the way of men together."

Her suspicions of his sexual preference had been correct. The drink was obviously bringing the truth out of him. "I showed Iain the way of it." He said. Then, as if he sensed Dhariya's shock at these words, he looked up at her. He was quite composed now and seemed to see a new way to torment her. Thus, he proceeded to describe these sexual encounters that he and Iain had shared.

"It's always better when they're new to it," he explained with a gleam in his eye. "Especially if they have a wife as Iain did, pretty young thing too," Dreshem laughed, "Iain was quite insulted by my advances in the beginning, saying he was a real man and not that way inclined. He had no choice, however, and he knew it. If he wanted to keep working for me—to keep that extra coin coming in—he would have to give me free rein and he did."

Dreshem sat back in his chair. "They don't think they want it at first, struggling against it. Yet if one doesn't take them by force and is careful, soon they start to rouse." He was watching her for any reaction to what he said "they can't help responding to a knowing touch, an experienced mouth. Iain was no different, even in spite of himself he was hardening beneath my hands and tongue, thrusting his hips moaning his pleasure. Mmm such a big man too." He said as his hand slid down front of his breeches.

"Next thing he was eagerly kissing my mouth like lover." He went on, closing his eyes, his voice turning dreamy as his hand worked. "Iain was no longer insulted by any means. By then he was only too willing to fall on his knees and return the favor, which to my delight he proved incredibly adept.

Dhariya did not want to see these images Dreshem so clearly painted for her, yet she could not help it, her mind fatigued and fogged as it was, still had the ability to create pictures of its own accord.

She was stunned to think that Iain, such a big burly Scotsman, had not only done these things with another man, but had also enjoyed it to the point of seeking Dreshem out often afterward, as Dreshem told her. Choosing his words carefully he went on and on with his graphic depictions, bombarding her with all the facets of their extremely shocking behavior.

Finally the alcohol took its toll, Dreshem's words trailed away and he began to snore very loudly.

Daylight had come hours ago. Dhariya arms ached from their straining sockets to the wrists rubbed raw beneath the rope. She had barely risked closing her eyes, and she was so thirsty, the cloth in her mouth sticking to her tongue. Dreshem stirred in the chair. She held herself perfectly still scarcely chancing a breath.

Groaning, he lifted his head from where it had lulled onto his chest. His eyes opened, blood shot and squinting against the brightness, they fixed on her once again.

He said nothing just reached for the half full whiskey on the table beside him, bringing it to his lips and tipping it back, he took a long pull—eyes returning to rest on her, as he set the bottle on the table and dragged the back of his sleeve across his mouth.

He stood abruptly and a little unsteadily, then walked to the door and left the room. Dhariya let out the breath she had been holding—listening to the slide of the bolt locking her in.

Dusk shadows were gathering into night when Dhariya was roused to full awareness by the sound of the key in the lock. She was so cold. There had been no fire in the room since the night before.

Though the pain in her body had become oddly separate from her, it was still there, yet she had found a way to adapt her mind, making it bearable as well as everything else she was being forced to endure. It was the fear that was all consuming now as she saw Dreshem enter the room and relock the door behind him.

He went to the hearth. She could hear him fumbling about for a few minutes before the stick of flint caught to flame. He made the rounds then, lighting all the candles until the room was aglow, as it had been the night before.

Flopping himself down with two full bottles of whiskey. He had said nothing yet, but there was no need to, he had been slow and purposeful in his little ritual to be sure that Dhariya knew exactly how the hours ahead would unfold. And so they did.

Yet there were differences this night. He remained silent. He came to her again pressing her legs wide, head resting against her inner thigh, he would not let her close her own eyes to escape. He forced her to look at him, and he even placed a pillow under her hips to make sure she could clearly see him. See that she was completely open to his gaze—see that his eyes were watching his own fingers prodding her, sliding deeply into her then out.

Suddenly he stopped. "Yes." He breathed, eyes still fixed and staring seeming to glaze over, "Beautiful" He whispered—Dhariya felt his hand slide further along, fingers began touching her bottom.

He raised himself up onto his knees and started unfastening the front of his breeches. Dhariya could see the unmistakable bulge. Releasing his manhood from its confines there was no question of his readiness, or of his intent. He pressed her knees against her chest with his own. Dhariya was trying to kick him away. Then she saw the glimmer of the knife blade in his hand as he put it to her throat again.

His other hand went to his arousal he leaned-in, she could feel him against her bottom, trying to force himself into her. Then Dhariya felt her mind giving way and she fell into a gaping black void.

A deafening explosion thrust Dhariya back to awareness, where she was being suffocating beneath the weight of Dreshem's sweating body. Both her and her attacker's heads turned as the heavy door flew from its hinges in a showering spray of wood splinters then crashed loudly to the floor.

Most of the candles extinguished in the sudden burst of air. Even in her present state Dhariya could never have mistaken the identity of the powerful black clad form framed in the open entryway. For there stood Llyr, his body pulsing with murderous rage.

Lifting himself on his straightened arms Dreshem demanded, "Who in God's name are you?"

"Wrong appellation I'm afraid" came Llyr's cold retort, "though you'd best begin to pray." The warning in a voice so icy calm it seemed to freeze the very air around them.

Three strides brought Llyr across the room, where he loomed over a cowering Dreshem. Dhariya lay there utterly helpless staring up at Llyr—she had never seen such raw undiluted anger, it fairly thrummed through the room as it radiated out from him, the sight was beyond frightening.

Llyr grasped Dreshem by his shirtfront, and with the force of one arm alone, lifted the hulking figure off Dhariya and tossed him, like a wet rag across the breadth of the room, Dreshem hit hard against the stonewall and lay unmoving, the knife fell from his limp hand onto the floor beside him.

Llyr stared a long moment at despicable excuse for humanity heaped in the corner, breeches still down around his ankles. Reaching up Llyr easily tore a dusty curtain from its valance and covered the offensive display, while his own body continued to quaver with the force of his fury, only his concern for Dhariya overrode his baser instincts and his need to tear the appalling beast apart from limb to limb.

Finally sure that he was under control Llyr stepped closer and squatted next to this pile of rubbish and lifted the edge of the curtain to check for any signs of life. One look at the unnatural angle of the neck, the wide staring eyes and Llyr knew the man would never torture or harm any another. Saying nothing, he let the fabric fall from his fingers and calmly stood.

To Dhariya, peeping out from the depths of her internal hiding place, everything was unreal and far away, as she watched Llyr come to the bed and sit at her side facing her. He began carefully removing the gag and wrist bindings, the tenderness of his touch a stark contrast to the violence she had just witnessed. As the rope fell away the sight of her delicate flesh left raw and bleeding by the course fibers, further sickened him.

Now freed, Dhariya began to gulp air into her lungs with a panicked desperation that was more from shock than lack of oxygen. She found could not move her arms; they felt painfully frozen in place after being held so long in such an unnatural position.

Llyr tried to help by massaging the circulation back into the trembling muscles, after a moment, his ministrations began to work. Finally Dhariya could lower her aching limbs, hugging them around herself. Her jaw was also throbbing, from the force of the gag and days of immobility.

Her entire body had begun convulsing now, and she was making little sobbing sounds, yet there were no tears. Llyr pulled her to him and held her close until she regained some semblance of composure. Then he shrugged out of his cloak and wrapped it around her shoulders, drawing the edges together in front to cover her nakedness.

Her one hand was motioning wildly toward the side table, where the water jug was. Understanding at once, Llyr poured a cup and held it to her lips, pressing her palms against his hand Dhariya forced the cup upwards, gulping and choking in her desperation. "Easy love" he cautioned.

This was repeated three more times before Dhariya had had enough. He gathered her into his arms again. Her breathing was steadier yet she was still trembling. "Did he hurt you very badly Dhariya?" The question gently asked.

She wanted to scream *yes—yes he did in unspeakable ways!* What she and Llyr had explored together in their sensual ventures, Dhariya felt had been beautiful expressions of their love for each other, but this, this violation degraded all that had once been, and it *was* unspeakable. So horribly unspeakable, she could not tell him of the kind of pain a man like that inflicts— the unseen wounds that never heal and must be borne alone. She was raging, raging and frantic inside. Curling into herself she shook her head—no—against the strong breadth of his chest.

"Thank God." He said. And she closed her eyes at his words, feeling the magnitude of her lie. She could not speak of it—she could not speak of it. Her mind kept saying over and over, swirling around and around making her dizzy. Suddenly she pushed herself out of his arms, threw her body toward the edge of the bed and vomited violently.

Llyr held her hair back and supported her, while she emptied the scant liquid contents of her stomach and bile onto the floorboards. Then wetting his handkerchief he bathed her face and gave her a few small sips of water. "Are you all right now? Well enough to ride at least?" He softly asked.

Dhariya nodded and Llyr carefully lifted her into his arms. Suddenly, she clutched at him with desperate clawing fingers. He looked down at her.

"J-Josey," Dhariya scarcely managed to whisper, "He s-said—he-said—h-he had J-Josey." Her eyes were fierce and imploring, piercing him to his soul.

"I'll send word to Jeremy Saunders and have the Inn searched as soon as I get you to safety. We must be quickly away now." He replied as gently as his urgency allowed. "Before this body and the one behind the stables are discovered, the magistrate and his authorities will soon be swarming all over this place. The last thing we need is to be held for questioning," he told this to her while striding to the gaping doorway carrying her with him.

She could but stare up at him—still frightened and unsure of the man that held her, yet oddly comforted by his presence in spite of it—the question asked with her eyes.

"I'm sorry Dhariya... the other one... is Iain," he answered. Then Llyr lapsed into silence as he hurried along the hallway to the rear exit and they emerged out into the chilled night.

Dhariya too remained silent, numbed with shock, leaning heavily against the stable wall for support. She could only watch as Llyr readied their horses, securing Andromeda's reins to the back of his saddle.

Everything seemed to be so far away, she felt strangely detached from the world around her. The night was so cold yet she barely noticed—only the steaming breath of the horses and humans registered the temperature. Llyr's huge black destrier 'Taranis' snorted and danced as Llyr—holding Dhariya in his arms once again—mounted, then settled her sideways before him.

And so it was, amid the thickening mist they rode away from the Inn—yet even in this altered state Dhariya still had enough sense to realize that they did not turned toward Skara Brae, but in the opposite direction, into the heart of Edinburgh City—with her little silver mare trailing in their wake.

XII

~ And o' the darkness where be thy solace? ~

...Standing on the edge of a disappearing shore, with the cold gray void of desolation washing over me, ever threatening to pull me under like a drowning tide...

~ *All was hushed and still behind the white murky veils that swathed the city. Our own procession was slow—laden by the weighted silence between us—and thus, only the rhythmic clatter of hoofs against the cobbles marked our passing.*

The narrow streets were unlit, although every now and then a lamp burned in a window or corridor—the small golden spheres casting an eerie glow against the mist's ghostly paleness—but the meager light could not push back the shadows. For night had come full upon us now, I could feel its cold darkness creeping over me, while its unknown yet awaited.

Llyr easily wound his way through the blinding haze and utter darkness as if guided by some extraordinary sensing ability. He seemed to know just where he was going. "Where are you taking me?" *I managed on a whispered breath.*

He said nothing in answer, only pulled me closer into him— though it seemed a gesture of affection—it was also one of complete possession. I kept my eyes fixed straight ahead, no longer knowing how to interpret anything. Although he was treating me as always, everything had changed now and there was a new kind of intensity about him.

I remained unsure of him—of his intentions. And these powerful arms that held me firmly yet gently were as much a threat as they were a comfort. Having now witnessed their extreme capabilities—from absolute tenderness to extreme violence—I was left to wonder, which of the two might surface next. For all that we had once been together; he had suddenly become a stranger to me.

~ D ~

~ **D**hariya so wanted— needed—to sink back against the solid wall of his chest, to seek refuge within the haven of his embrace. How she longed to reach out for the man she had known—had loved. Then again, had she ever really known him? Was anything they had shared truly real? Perhaps it was all just a false façade of things only wished for?

She was so lost inside herself, deep inside where everything was twisted into a hopeless tangle. All she knew was that her heart ached with lonely pain and she could not bear it.

Llyr finally drew rein before one of the tall narrow town homes which lined most of the city streets. Its dark stone frontage loomed mysteriously behind the mist, allowing for only a veiled impression and glimpses of a single burning lantern.

"What is this place?" she managed to ask.

"It's my own private residence I keep here in town," he replied as he dismounted.

This too was another secret. He had never told her of this home. "W-why have you brought me here?"

He paused and turned to her then, looking directly into her eyes, into her soul. His own expression unreadable—

indefinable—interminable, his gaze as dark and unfathomable as always, yet there was something else there now, something that had never been there before—hidden in black core of their depths. Whatever it was made him seem completely unknown to her and that frightened her more that Dexter Dreshem ever could have. So too did the realization that no one would have any way of knowing that he had brought her here, unless he himself chose to reveal it, and Dhariya was no longer certain that he would do so. "I brought you here because it's nearby and you're much in need of quiet rest" he spoke softly and calmly then lifted her into his arms saying nothing more."

Llyr had been as silent as Dhariya during the ride. In truth, he did not trust himself to speak. His entire being had been rocked in a way he had never experienced before. His insides were in chaos. He had killed a man this night, something he had sworn never to do. Yet he had indeed done this and now it seemed his only regret was that it was done far too swiftly and far too painlessly.

The full magnitude of what had transpired in these last days was still crashing around within him. He had been so desperate with worry when he awoke to learn that Dhariya was missing from the castle and had been gone the entire day. Then after he was shown the ravaged portrait gallery, he had ordered the staff gathered in the main foyer. He was in the middle of grilling the servants when Jeremy Saunders, having received the note from Dhariya requesting that he come to Skara Brae as soon as possible, arrived on the scene.

When the solicitor was told of her disappearance, he immediately drew Llyr aside and quickly explained the facts of his investigation and the very real threat to Dhariya's life. As Llyr and the older man ended their conversation, Annie, the servant who had been filling in for Josey as Dhariya's personal maid, approached.

She told them that she had been unable to sleep over her continued worry for Josey, so she had been sitting in her window and seen Dhariya ride out at dawn, with Iain following closely behind. The maidservant had said she then went to tidy her Ladyship's rooms.

This at least was a place to start. Iain was likely on his regular supply pick up, since he had not yet returned, it was surmised to be his monthly visit to Edinburgh for the items he could not purchase in the nearby town, there was a chance he had seen something, if Llyr could find him.

"There's more milord," Annie had said, then led him and Jeremy Saunders up to Dhariya's chambers where she showed them the eerie display on the dressing table. Explaining that this is what she found when she had come in early that morning. Annie had told them she thought it all far too eerie too touch, so she had left it be, and had turned then fled in fear to fetch Ffyonna.

Llyr and the solicitor both stared down at the blood stained gloves—the two dead roses in stunned horror. Saunders instantly recognized the gloves as being Dhariya's mothers, the ones that had gone missing from the accident scene.

"And this," Annie pointed to the folded sheet of parchment which was lying on the carpet next to the dresser. Llyr had felt a strange prickle along his spine at the sight of the roses. Then picked up the paper, unfolded it and froze. He did not even see the written warning. His eyes were locked on the name at the top...

Elysian, the word fairly screamed from the page. Yes, this more than confirmed his earlier suspicion. There was only one person who could have written it. "Dear God!" He whispered in a scant breath of sound.

"What is it?" Saunders' concerned voice broke through the icy fear encasing Llyr.

He turned to the older man. "Iain," he said by way of explanation, "Iain's the one that wrote this and he's also the one who rode out after Dhariya all those hours ago. I can't take the time now to tell you how I know this Saunders'. You'll just have to trust me."

Saunders nodded. "I'll send a footman with a message to my lead investigator and get him and his team searching in the city immediately. Once I take a closer look at everything here, I'll head back to Edinburgh and join in the hunt. We'll have to keep each other updated regularly through my assistant, that way we'll be sure not to overlap our search areas."

"Yes." Llyr agreed.

With that he turned and made for the stables at a run—once he was mounted upon Taranis—he fled the castle in frantic haste. Yet his vampyre tracking abilities were proving useless. {Normally, these were used for hunting nearby prey and also served as a safety measure for his own person} yet this skill was only newly just developed, thus had not fully strengthened, if it had been he could have found her instantly by focusing-in upon her mind and following her thoughts to their source.

Never in the past had he tried to purposely probe into Dhariya's mind, out of respect for her and her privacy. He felt it would be an unfair breech of her trust. It had, however, happened once quite by accident. And a few times, during the hours he had sat in her bedchamber watching her slumber, he had somehow slipped past their mental barriers to share her dreams with her. Such moments were among a vampyre's greatest treasures, for a vampyre could no longer dream.

But why could he not reach into her mind when it was so vital? All that he could pick up on was her fear. Stranger still was that he could get not the faintest reading of Iain's thoughts whatsoever—of course he had since learned that was because Iain had been dead.

Even now with Dhariya cradled in his arms, Llyr's insides were still twisted in a hopeless tangle. He did not know what would happen if he eased his hold on them, all of his control might suddenly slip his white knuckled grasp. The thought of this possibility frightened him.

With all that had transpired in the hours since they had been amicable, there was so much that needed to be said, yet neither one of them was in any condition to confront it. Dhariya was far beyond his reach at this moment and he needed to channel his entire being on keeping himself together, which left him incapable of speaking more than a word or two words when necessary.

And so for now it all would remain, as the massive barrier it was, standing between them.

Besides Llyr consoled himself; she would be going nowhere until things were settled. One way or another he had to make her understand. So much was at stake, not only the fact that her knowledge of him proved a dangerous thing, but having just come so close to losing her, he was no longer certain he would be capable of letting her go.

Dhariya's heart began to thunder as he climbed the fifteen steps—for some unknown reason she counted each one that curved its way from the street to the front landing—ending beneath an alcove which appeared to be roughly-chiseled right from the very stones. Here is where the lone lantern flickered, its meager light revealing it to be the entryway.

He found the latch easily. The solid oaken door opened smoothly on soundless hinges then closed with a heavy thud. And the scrape of the lock sliding into place echoed loudly into the stillness.

Dhariya blinked looking around her; she was unable to see details clearly in the dimly lit interior and the haze of her own mind, only the panels of dark wood-wainscoting upon the surrounding walls. The waxy scent of their highly polished surfaces still hung in the air and this—for some unknown reason—Dhariya seemed to find strangely comforting, like a stirring of some long lost memory.

Suddenly without warning, a thin, black-garbed man of undeterminable years slipped out from the distant shadows. "My lord," he acknowledged with a slight bow, while he expressed not the least surprise at Llyr's abrupt arrival, nor at the woman he carried with him.

"Veldon—have Fairfax see to the horses out front." Llyr instructed the houseman "And send food and wine to my chambers at once—if there's any of cook's broth to be had send that as well, if not rouse her and have her prepare some."

"Yes my lord, right away." Came the obedient reply as Llyr began ascending the staircase, which then twisted itself into another, and another, and yet another. Upon reaching the uppermost landing he proceeded down a short scantly lit hallway where he entered twin doors standing open at the farthest end.

He carried her through an anti-chamber or sitting room from the little she could determine, all the torch flames burned tiny and intensely golden behind what appeared to be thick amber-glass fittings in the wall sconces. The effect was soft dim lighting, oddly warm and inviting amid the darkened wood surfaces, which also seemed to be a running theme throughout.

Inside the second room a single candle burned in a similar fashion, casting its golden glow while retaining the hidden mysteries within the chambers. Llyr gently placed Dhariya upon the huge canopied bed. Saying nothing, he adjusted his cloak more snugly around her before turning to light the hearth fire, which soon blazed to life, illuminating more details of the large bedchamber.

Dhariya's wide-eyed gaze circled her surroundings, noting the opulent richness of the sparse furnishings. Thick bedposts spiraled their way up to the canopied top, crafted of the same heavily carved wood and all bearing the same strangely intricate design, as did the high curving headboard.

The softness beneath her palm was a heavy cut velvet coverlet, in the deepest shade of midnight blue, which matched the corded bed curtains and the drapes drawn over a single narrow window. Dark mahogany paneled these walls as well, it reached three quarters of the way up where it met with midnight blue embossed-damask, which covered the remainder of the wall and the entire ceiling, as well as the four oversized winged chairs set in pairs near the hearth and by the window.

Thick eastern carpets with exotic patterns in shades of blues and black covered the polished wood floors. Sandalwood lingered in the air, which merely confirmed this to be Llyr's own bedchamber—all as unrelenting and unmistakably masculine as he, who was its inhabitant.

Filled with dark shadows and mystery; the essence of his powerful presence was everywhere, emanating from each piece of furniture, from the empty spaces between and from the very walls themselves. Dhariya shivered, she remembered that same feeling when she had first returned to Skara Brae after her uncle had gone. She supposed she understood something of what this was now—of what he was. She shivered again.

Llyr rose from the tending the fire and turned to her; everything was there in her face, he thought, every feeling, every emotion—as if scripted to be read in detail, but only by one whose eyes could truly see—well his eyes could indeed see, and the worst of what he saw there now was her fear of him.

The other concern for him was that she had not yet cried, though he knew this was to be expected after such a horrific ordeal, everything would still be buried within in that place of refuge where she herself was hiding now. Emotional release would come in its own time. Nevertheless he hoped it would come soon. For he could feel the heavy weight of her pain and the deep well of tears she kept locked away.

"Dhariya," he spoke softly as he started toward her, not knowing how she would react to him anymore. "You must rest now… first, you'll need to get out of those ruined garments and beneath the warm blankets."

She still said nothing, only watched him as he came to stand before her. His face, always beyond handsome, was nothing if not breathtaking when sculpted by shadows and glowing flames, she thought to herself in that detached manner her mind had shifted to, since she had locked herself far away inside.

A knock interrupted the stillness.

Llyr went to the door.

Dhariya could hear whispered voices, though she was unable to make out the words. He returned a moment later carrying a large silver tray bearing the items he had requested. Dhariya felt an overwhelming sense of weariness overtaking her. Strange black spots danced before her eyes. The room swam, his image becoming a distorted dark shape as she watched him, he seemed to be moving in slow motion now. The silver tray shimmered brightly amid the room's wavering shadows, as he came toward her and placed it on bedside table.

She looked up at him helplessly. Then with a gasp, her eyes closed and she fell back against the pillows, as white-hot pain suddenly exploded inside her left shoulder. Her right hand weakly lifted to it, feeling a warm stickiness seeping through the black woolen cloak

"What is it Dhariya?" came Llyr's voice from somewhere far, far away, "Dhariya!"

She felt him draw her hand away and then fumble with her clothing. "Good God you're bleeding!" More fumbling with her clothing… then cool air skimmed across the fiery pain. "Why didn't you tell me that bastard stabbed you?"

I did not know she wanted to say and indeed tried to tell him so. But she could not get the words out before the welcoming darkness came and swallowed her up.

Llyr had given instructions—to the footman who had brought the tray—for a missive to be dispatched to Jeremy Saunders home address, which the solicitor had given him should this very need arise, and Llyr could thus inform him that he had found Dhariya alive. A second missive was to be sent to Skara Brae summoning Ffyonna and her herbals to his Edinburgh residence post haste.

Llyr remembered far too well the disturbing effect of severe trauma upon Dhariya. He could not venture to imagine, nor did he particularly want to conceive of, what she might be facing now with multiple shocks piled one upon another. He would only fully entrust Dhariya's care into Ffyonna's loving hands.

Once he discovered the knife wound, he was more than grateful that he had had the foresight to send for the wise old woman. It was a feeling that would only intensify in the hours to come.

In the interim Llyr called upon the services of a physician. There was one he had heard of living conveniently across from him. Fortunately Dhariya remained unconscious during the physician's examination and stitching of wound, which turned out to be minor, tearing only muscle tissue. Llyr had given the explanation of an attack in the street. Since this was a common enough occurrence, it was accepted without question or suspicion.

After seeing the older man to the door with as much politeness as possible, Llyr immediately returned to his bedchamber. Where he sat anxiously by Dhariya's bedside, mentally chastising himself, he should have been more aware as he rode with her here—if his thoughts and emotions had not been so knotted, he would have sense her wound, scented the raw blood seeping from her body.

Not that he could have done much about it, yet at least he could have bound it and hurried them along, as it was he had taken it slow, wanting to be gentle with Dhariya and keep her from being roughly jostle about by the horse's canter.

By the time Ffyonna arrived, herb box in hand, just before dawn he nearly collapsed with relief at the sight of her. Dhariya was unconscious and burning up with fever and had been for the past two hours. In helpless desperation he had been continually bathing her body with a cloth dipped in cool water, not knowing what else to do.

Ffyonna—as was her way—sailed into the room and immediately took things in hand. Though never disrespectful, she ruled her own domain with no apologies, no matter that this domain actually belonged to her lord and employer, it had heretofore become the sick room of her patient.

Llyr drew the woman aside and quietly whispered the little he knew and a lot of what he suspected had happened to Dhariya. Ffyonna's eyes closed as he spoke and drew in deep breath as if gathering herself for the task at hand. Then with a quick nod of her head she set to it.

"First I'll need plenty of candles to work, can nay see a thing in these shadows, and some strong alcohol." She answered his uncomprehending look, "T'is for cleanin' the wound. Aye, 'tis not always common practice but should be, 'tis a secret I learned early on, said to date back to the Holy Isle of Avalon if one believes in such things." This said as a matter of fact, no indication what Ffyonna herself believed.

Waving Llyr aside, she walked directly to the door adjoining the sitting room, creaking it open he heard her say, "ask the houseman to bring all the candles and holders he can spare, also lots of water both hot and cold, then you come on in here and we'll get started."

Llyr went to the wooden cabinet from which he procured a crystal decanter full of amber liquid. After passing this to Ffyonna, he then poured a large measure for himself from another and, bowing to her bidding more than willingly stepped back out of the way. Sipping from his glass, his gaze fixed on Dhariya, he was not even aware that he still wore the shirt liberally covered with Dhariya's blood.

Ffyonna placed the decanter of spirits he had given her on the bedside table as a line of servants entered laden with the requested items, lighting branches of candles and placing them where Ffyonna directed.

As soon the room was suitably aglow, the older woman washed her hands and proceeded to the bed where Dhariya lay. A plump red head of perhaps twenty came into the room, washed her own hands and moved to the bedside, Llyr vaguely recalled having seen her about the castle of late, as an apprentice of sorts in the lore of herbs.

"This is my niece Katie," Ffyonna informed him, "She's come to help. Has a fair gift for healin' does Katie—" she went on, eyes and hands quickly assessing the most obvious concerns, *damage to the shoulder minor, inflamed tissue and hot fevered flesh extremely serious, often fatal,* she sighed "—and Lord bless us I dare say we'll need it."

Llyr did not welcome this news, although he was not surprised by it. He trusted the word of this woman implicitly, which was a very rare thing for him. He never ceased to marvel as he watched Ffyonna at work. In her element as a healer, her movements seemed to alter like she was following a rhythmic pattern, which had an almost hypnotic appearance to the viewer.

As she went about carefully removing the physician's stitching, her hands were indeed her instruments in the truest sense of the word and she clearly used them in just this manner.

He also thought it strange that although clearly well into late middle age, Ffyonna's hands bore no signs of the thin frailty of years but retained the fleshiness and strength of youth. He had occasioned to see her palms during her ministrations in the past, noting the unusual number of lines and strange webbing of creases; he had never seen anything like it. He was not sure why, yet he sensed this had some connection to her extraordinary skill.

Llyr was unused to having his most private chambers invaded by outsiders. At that moment, however, feeling near the limits of his endurance, he more than welcomed the intrusion. Ffyonna, standing at the head of the bed, turned and motioned him forward, "I'm goin' to cleanse the wound now and need you to hold her down. She may start to fight but it must be done."

Llyr positioned himself with care at Dhariya's hip level, where he sat facing her, her body was loosely covered with a sheet from her breasts down, he leaned his upper body down over top hers, he brought his arms around and under her waist drawing the sheet in around her and securing Dhariya's arms at her sides as he did so. Katie stood at the foot of the bed holding the patients ankles against the mattress with the weight of her own ample body.

He noted how Ffyonna drew a deep breath and seemed to brace herself before taking up her task. As the older woman poured the alcohol directly into the raw gaping wound Dhariya winced and gasped—Llyr could feel his own insides clench in response.

Dhariya's eyes shot open, huge and frightened, they also appeared glassy and unseeing, while her body writhed from the agonizing ministrations—twisting and thrashing with surprising force, struggling with all the power in her slight frame, as she sought in vain to fight the assault.

Llyr had to turn away. He could not bear to witness this deliberate infliction of pain on the woman he loved, however necessary it might be. He was also amazed by the strength that Dhariya managed to muster especially after enduring days of being starved and assaulted by a madman and even now, fevered with the poison of her blood, she was not easily subdued. He hated using such force against her especially after all she had just endured during her captivity, it made his stomach clench, giving him an overall sickened feeling. Fortunately however, the tortuous procedure was over with quickly and the entire room seemed to breathe a sigh of relief that it was done.

Dhariya's body went limp at once and they all relaxed their hold. Her eyes were closed again; she was moaning and whimpering softly. Llyr wanted to gather her gently into him, to offer comfort in the only way he knew but what she needed most was Ffyonna now. Thus, he reluctantly stood and stepped back out of the way allowing the older woman to do her work.

Ffyonna took his place, sitting herself down on the bed beside her patient and began stroking Dhariya's damp hair in a comforting rhythmic motion, speaking softly, "there-there luv… that's the worst of it now…" the older woman crooned, singing softly an ancient song in the old tongue.

Katie had busied herself with the tearing of white linen sheets into strips that would be used to bind the wound once it was properly tended. Llyr noted that the young woman was quiet and diligent in her duties; he appreciated the fact that her presence was a non-intrusive one. All the same, he suddenly felt like an outsider here and very much in the way.

While beyond the stone walls the sun starting to rise, the burn of its rays already reaching for him through the heavy velvet drapes—beginning to kindle its fire within his body. His limbs were suddenly weighted and heavy, warning that he must seek out his dark place lest the sleep claim him where he stood. Loath as he was to allow Dhariya out of his sight, he knew she was in far more capable hands than his, so he turned away and left her there.

He could hear Ffyonna continuing her soothing litany as he closed the bedchamber door, "You're a strong lass, always were, even as a wee one…and what a sight you were then little lassie…"

Dhariya was too close to the flames. Someone had fanned the fire too high and left it so. She wanted to move away from the heat and was trying to get away, but the flames would not let her…yet it was not like before when everything was burning around her and she was afraid…This fire was of inside her and seemed to want her to become one with it…she wondered if she gave in and allowed it to consume her, perhaps she would no longer feel the unbearable heat… Suddenly she felt a cool wet cloth wiping her down… Voices were floating around her …

O' someone was singing now… the words were of the old tongue… it was Ffyonna singing in that soothing way she had, stroking her hair…yes, it was nice, then the words changed to English…

'Hish-y-o-o-u, hish-y-o-o-u, hish-y-o-o-u-by' …Dhariya recognized this song from when she was a little girl, 'Hish-y-o-u-lassie don't you cry' she had heard it many times, Ffyonna would always 'Hish-you-by' all of her hurts away … Dhariya could even hum along…if she were not still so sleepy—if she were not so very hot…

…Ffyonna somehow knew that a strange fire burned inside of her and was trying to help…soon she would be cool … then she would get up and play with Bryden and DJ. She did not like being the littlest, always made to nap while they kept on playing without her…it was not fair…she wanted to say so too, but first she must sleep, she was so tired…

———

When Llyr re-entered the master's chambers hours later, he found Fyonna still sitting at her patient's side, brushing Dhariya's long hair with loving strokes. While Dhariya lay there looking much the same as when he had left her. And he was afraid, Dear God how he was afraid. It was not a feeling he was accustomed to nor was the utter powerlessness that accompanied it.

Bracing himself he listened to Ffyonna's recounting of the hours passed and her words offered no succor. Though the knife wound itself was not life threatening she explained, it had putrefied and was poisoning the blood, which was extremely serious. Not only was it imperative to eliminate the poison, the body also must be kept cool and not become dehydrated, as any one of the three could kill her and she was a hairs breadth away from succumbing to all three.

Fyonna had reopened the wound for cleansing purposes, but had not re-stitched it as she needed to re-examine the internal tissue and cleanse it regularly and often. She had however, applied a specially blended herbal poultice, which Dhariya still wore under the linen binding. This was to draw the poison out from her if they were lucky. It did not look hopeful for even Llyr could see the angry redness of inflammation around the edges of pristine bandage.

This, Ffyonna stressed, pointing at the visible evidence of infected flesh, must be watched carefully. If any red lines appeared he was to call her at once, not that she could do much at that juncture. Dhariya had lost a great deal of blood and the poison was near enough to the heart as it was; she went on, busying herself folding strips of bandage, unable to meet his eyes.

He was told that Dhariya would go from burning with fever to violent shivering with cold. When this happened; he was to wrap her in blankets and place the bricks, which were kept heating by the fire in readiness, around her. He was also to be sure she did not bite her tongue during these fierce convulsions.

Her body was now wrapped in wet sheets in an attempt to lower the temperature. When she was overheated like this, Llyr was to sponge her down with cool water at regular intervals, then lift her head and encourage Dhariya to drink as much of the herbal tonic as possible.

He did not feel at all comfortable with the idea of pouring liquids down the throat of someone who was not fully conscious and said so, "'Tis all right, she'll do it if you help her," Ffyonna told him, "Though she's nay keepin' much down poor wee lass." Gesturing to the chamber pot, "best have that nearby."

Ffyonna went on from there, warning him not to be surprised if Dhariya suddenly started shivering, with her teeth chattering and body convulsing uncontrollably as if she were frozen to the bone in an ice storm, she had said. That's when he was to change the wet bedclothes and wrap her up in the dry warmth of wools and blankets.

While the older woman continued instructing Llyr on what he was to do, Katie, who, unused to being in his presence nor the magnitude of the power he exuded, stood quietly by, studying the 'Dark Lord' with flushed cheeks and an expression of wide-eyed awe on her round face. It was not an uncommon reaction, but one that Llyr would not have noticed even if his mind had not been totally consumed by concern for Dhariya.

With his dark handsomeness and tall well-formed body he had always had an effect on women, at least since he came of an age to recognize it for what it was. Yet oddly enough among the multitude of his sins, being egotistical about himself in that fashion was not one of them.

Although he would certainly admit that during his years of self-gratification and indulgence he had partaken freely, often and without restraint in the array of feminine charms so readily offered. His personal view of himself however, was always one of being passable and still remained so; he simply could not understand what all the fuss was about.

And now that the dark change had come upon him, the effects {in this manner} had seemed to have only intensified. He was never without blatant advances from any number of females, regardless of age or status, from castle servants to high society, the offers were there and so too were the eager women if he deigned to seek their company—yet more often now, what he experienced was that people in general had a fear of him or at least he seemed to emit an unapproachable air—that nonetheless, left him isolated and alone.

The two exhausted women finally headed off to take their well earned rest. Katie had already left the room when Ffyonna stopped suddenly and turned to him saying, "I'll be just on the other side of that door on the sittin' room sofa if you need me. Else I'll wake in two hours time to cleanse and repack the wound with fresh extracts."

Then, as her pale blue eyes met his dark gaze evenly, she said, "Sometimes it helps to talk to them," seeing his questioning expression the older woman elaborated, "talk to her as if you knew she was listenin', 'tis all we can do now but wait and pray." And she was gone. The door softly clicking closed after her.

Llyr took his place in one of the two winged-chairs drawn up close to the bed and began his vigil. He had sat with her thus often before, after the town house fire that had nearly claimed her. What if he had not been nearby that night? He would have lost her then and never have known what loving her would bring.

Seeing her lying there now brought it all flooding back to him. It had only been the fact that his obsession with her always led him to her in the darkness of predawn. He had been just about to turn Taranis and head for her town-home after his hours of carousing.

They were still some distance away when Llyr had a sudden overwhelming sense that Dhariya was in danger. It was the first time he had had that feeling; it was one of the few abilities of his kind, one that, like most of the others only developed with time and use. He had turned Taranis in the direction of the Dreghorn city residence and pressed his heels to command the stallion to racing speed.

As he approached his worst fears were confirmed. A red glow lit up the dark sky above the billowing clouds of black smoke. "Dear God!!" He whispered as the horrifying reality gripped him. Tethering Taranis a safe distance away, he then ran toward the scene.

People wearing night robes and slippers had gathered in the close. Standing among the crowd of solemn faces, with staring eyes fixed on the fiery display of destruction, he spotted the small grouping of Dhariya's servants—whom he recognize from the many nights he had stood in the shadows and silently observed the household, he had often seen one or another of them coming or going—one look at their faces told him that Dhariya was still trapped inside.

Clamping down his instant panic, he focused his awareness and concentrated on scanning the situation inside. This was another of the few other worldly abilities he possessed. Great tongues of hungry flame, red, gold, and orange, licked along gray stones, consuming any combustible substance within their path.

The ground floor was already fully engulfed while Dhariya lay unconscious in her bedchamber above. Fighting the inclination to reckless action he took hold of his emotions and forced himself to try and think clearly.

Suddenly he remembered there was back lane that would give him the access he needed with less chance of being witnessed. Quickly finding his way around to the other side of the building, he saw windows along the top floor, but the internal glow and smoke seeping out between the chinks in the stones, told him he did not have much time.

Using the most powerful of vampyre abilities, which also demanded the most of him, he took to the air and soared up to the second story window ledge. He was not yet strong enough to cloak himself from mortal eyes while he did this, thus risking the danger of being seen, he had no choice however, it was the only way to get Dhariya out of there.

It was impossible to see anything inside through the thick black smoke. He savagely tore his cravat from his neck and used it to cover his nose and mouth and tying it in place. Then, arms up protecting his face, he thrust himself through the glass, the air fed the flames with a deafening roar and intense heat came fast upon him.

Smoke stung his eyes and the back of his throat. His vision blurred by the streaming tears, he crawled on hands and knees, feeling his way along. Of course he knew full well that fire could harm him and if enough of his body were to be destroyed, it would be beyond repair—thus, leaving his dark soul forever bodiless and stranded within the dark realms. But he tried not to think about that just then.

Without the ability to see, he managed to find his way to her bedchamber and reach her bed where she lay overcome by smoke. Draping her limp form across his back, he took to his hands and knees once again. Coughing and gasping beneath the fabric mask, he retraced his path toward the back window.

Heat grew more and more intense. Flames were burning through large areas of the wooden floor. The metal studding of what was left was red hot, searing flesh from his palms and knees. Finally reaching the window, he stepped out onto the ledge with her. He had just pulled her around in front of him as the entire floor inside gave way, in a thundering roar of timber and stone and shattering glass.

Llyr felt the slicing pain of exploding window glass at his back, as its shards and splinters pierced through his clothing and embedded into his flesh. He launched himself into the air, descending safely with her in his arms.

Trying to balance her against him in one arm, he used his free hand to tear the cravat away and took a moment to drag gasps of air into his charred lungs. He knew he was too depleted now to use the flying technique to speed them the full distance to the castle.

Hurrying to Taranis, whose eyes were terror filled and showing white, while his sleek black coat trembled in fear from the smell of smoke permeating the air "it's all right boy," Llyr tried to soothe even as he himself coughed and sputtered the reassuring words. His chest felt heavy and weighted each breath laborious, as he wheezed air in and out of his lungs. Each breath was shallow, irritating the tissue inside.

He mounted the horse while still holding Dhariya tight to him, which was no easy feat at the best of times. Settling her securely in front of him, he whipped the reins, pressed his heels and Taranis, who being every bit as eager to be away from the source of his fright, was instantly off and rode like lightening in the direction of the castle.

About halfway to Skara Brae Llyr dismounted and drew Dhariya's unconscious body down and into his arms once again. With one hand he tethered an exhausted Taranis in a wooded area out of sight, "I'll send one of the grooms to bring you back boy." He told the huge stallion and took to the air again holding Dhariya close to his body.

Then, Llyr was running through the east wing corridors with her still in his arms, his lungs hurting, rasping harshly as he coughed and shouted out orders to Bryden, who was on night watch and following at his heels. Entering her suite, Llyr laid Dhariya body on the bed. She appeared unscathed, but he knew she had inhaled a great deal of smoke.

It was then that Bryden came striding into the bedchamber, "Dogull has ridden out to seen to Taranis as you requested my lord, and my mother will be here without delay." Though the younger man had been speaking to Llyr, his wide eyes roamed slowly and freely over Dhariya. Llyr turned to follow his gaze and for the first time realized her near naked state, lying sprawled in the charred shredded remnants of her lacy nightdress.

"Thank you Bryden that will be all for now" Llyr told him curtly, pressing her legs together and pulling the quilts over her exposed flesh.

Ffyonna and her herb box came next.

"Most of the staff are awake now and runnin' about in a tither." She announced as she entered. Then placing herself and herbals at Dhariya's side, she turned to Llyr, her sharp eyes piercing him, as she asked him to relay all he knew of what happened.

Llyr sputtered out his altered story as best he could between fits of coughing. Thankfully the older woman was too concerned about her patient and never thought to question how he had managed it. As he spoke she mixed some sort of herbal potion that she handed to him and commanded him to drink. He had done so rather than draw any further attention to himself and his own injuries, wincing slightly at the bitter taste but it helped right away he noted.

Outside, the dawn was about to break, Llyr could feel its burning rays cresting the horizon, further igniting the fiery pain of his burned flesh. What little strength he had left was waning by the moment; he knew he could no longer delay. He had to seek his rest.

At least he was leaving Dhariya in good hands. Even then, Llyr had known Ffyonna to be a wise woman, renown for her skill in the healing arts. *Just as long as that son of hers kept his eyes and his hands to himself,* Llyr thought as walked the distance his own suite.

He found Dacron anxiously awaiting him inside his chambers. The valet had obviously heard something of the traumatic event. His angelic face wretched with unspoken concern as Llyr collapsed face down on the huge feather bed. Llyr realized then how much the young man truly cared for him and he was grateful, for such devotion was a rare thing. Dacron proceeded to cut away Llyr's clothing and then began tending the injuries. The removal of the glass shards from his back was done swiftly though not painlessly by any means.

Llyr was relieved that Ffyonna had not had time to notice the state of his back nor any of the burns he sustained. He had no wish to take the older woman's attention from Dhariya's greater needs, nor did he wish to draw the inevitable questions as to his unnatural rate of healing. How could he possibly tell her that he was a vampyre and as such his blood was infused with an agent of sorts that preserves him, that this element returns their bodies to the exact outer image, age, hair length, etc, at the time of their making, and any changes that occur would only last until they next rested—thus they never appear any older or indeed altered in any way for all eternity.

When Llyr woke he would be restored once again. That is, unless his burns had consumed more than ninety percent of his body. Then with no hope of healing, the outer shell would turn to ash, while the dammed soul it had carried would remain trapped between life and death—an even worse fate that did not bear contemplating.

Once inside the dark quietness of the sleeping chamber, Llyr realized he had been singed and scorched in more places than he thought, though not nearly enough to destroy his physical form, the pain was still excruciating, as were the lacerations in his back. He knew he would be healed by the next eve, Dhariya however would not. She had taken in a lot of smoke and they would have to wait for some time to know for sure how she would fare.

His mind returned to the present and the new fears he was facing. Although he had been fraught with concern and caring for Dhariya at that time of the fire, they had hardly known each other then—beyond the awareness of the undeniable attraction for one another—they had shared very little. It had been merely the beginning for them.

Now they had shared everything and as a result everything had altered in the most profound of ways. Following the fire's trauma she had succumbed to wild fits in her sleep. This fevered state however, produced only a slight stir and incoherent murmuring every so often. Yet it was the hours that her unconscious body lay in absolute stillness, which frightened him more than anything. He could never before have imagined caring in this way or that such a depth of feeling for another was even possible.

For the first time, since Llyr had witnessed the slaughter of his family at nine years of age, someone mattered to him, mattered more to him even than his own breath. It was just one of a thousand startling self-realizations that were suddenly crashing like cannon fire through the thick walls he had built to contain them. Of course he had known he loved her, had known it for some time, yet the full magnitude of what that love meant was only now making itself known to him.

Loving her had touched some elemental core within him, enlivening primordial characteristics and moral fiber that were a long denied, yet an integral part of the man he truly was. He realized in that moment that not only did he despise himself for not being able to stop the slaughter of his family, but he also harbored an angry resentment toward them for dying and leaving him alone.

Those long buried memories floated to the surface now, his family had come south for a clan gathering months earlier and knowing they would never make it back to the Highlands before winter—they stayed on with his mother's sister and the clan of her husband who was the clan's laird—until the spring weather came.

Llyr's family rarely ventured far from their lands where his father was laird of their own clan. But the political situation, always tedious, had become tumultuous. There were decisions to be made and oaths to be sworn. Thus, the importance of this gathering was of the utmost to all of them. His father, not wanting to be away from his family for so long a time, had brought Llyr, his Mother, and Llyr's two older brothers along—of them all, only Llyr had survived.

He had never returned to those lands that he inherited on that fateful morning and he doubted he ever would. He had a capable overseer who ran things well in his absence, while his man of business here in the city dealt with all the other the details. Llyr himself wanted nothing to do with it, for it only served to remind him of all he sought to keep locked safely away.

It suddenly came clear as crystal to him, that through this horrific experience of his family members' deaths, he had learned to view any kindness as weakness. After witnessing firsthand how his father and uncle's generosity in offering hospitality to those that had come to murder their unsuspecting hosts was a fatal and irreversible mistake, one which he vowed he would never make. Thus it was that the first shadows had come to find a home within his cold and embittered heart—thus the initial steps along the dark path—towards the blackness in which he now existed—had been taken.

His demons had begun to stir with his retrospection of their birth and they were now taunting that he could save this woman he loved, that he could take her in the way he had always truly desired to. He knew the poisoned blood would have no effect upon him. Yet the other part of himself—that part he had just uncovered after all these years—gave him a strength he did not know he possessed. Thus fortified, he turned purposefully away from these tempting thoughts and from the darkness that bore them.

Never! Never would he consider such desecration! Even if it meant he must lose her. For things being what they were, the harsh truth was he would have to let her go someday. But not yet, his mind silently cried out! Let our time of parting not have come so suddenly upon us now!

His heart constricted in his chest. He had failed her, Bloody Hell and all of its damnation, how he had failed her, just as he had failed his family. He truly did not know what he could have done differently, but there must have been something, some way he could have spared them their suffering and her all of this that she must now endure. When he had kicked down the door of the room and seen her lying beneath the sweating body of that bastard, he thought he had experienced the worst of the worst, he could never have imagined there was still more to come.

He raked his hair with his fingers. He felt as helpless as that nine-year-old boy again, hiding in terror within the shadows of that small cupboard where he had managed to flee unnoticed as the horror began. Still able to see through the cracks in the wood and the faint glow of the dying hearth fire---still able to clearly hear the savage attack upon the sleeping members of his family and his uncle's clan in the early pre-dawn.

His mother, having recently lost the babe she carried, was still in her sickbed at the time, her final words still haunted him as she begged for the lives of her family. By the time the light of full day had come, it was over and the snow ran red with the blood of those he loved.

The utter powerlessness was as unbearable now as it had been then—perhaps more so. Because then, he had felt the powerlessness of being a child, but to know that same sense of powerlessness as a man, was to know utter defeat. It crumbled one from the inside out—revealing all the futility of one's own vain perceptions.

Yet the need to do something—anything—was overwhelming. Not knowing where else to turn he looked within again, for another of those doors he had sealed shut on that cold winter morning long ago. And he fell upon his knees there, at the bedside. Head bowed, eyes closed, hands pressed together in supplication.

"Dear God." His voice came, a ragged beseeching whisper. "Though I've no right to thusly call upon You ... still I beg You hear me." He could feel the wetness spilling down his cheeks. "Bring not my sins upon this woman, beloved of my soul that she is. I beg You see Your daughter healed. Spare her life and I shall let her go freely if that is what she truly wishes."

Llyr remained as he was, upon his knees at Dhariya's bedside, shoulders shaking, body trembling, weeping the tears the nine year old boy never cried and all the tears he had never cried since, while his heart continued its own silent prayer.

———

Ffyonna and young Katie continued to keep the day vigils while Llyr kept the night. Twenty-four hours passed without change in either direction. All of them knew Dhariya could not possibly continue on this way, though none would dare speak the words aloud.

Dhariya could hear a voice again... that man's lovely voice ... she had heard it often... she knew it too...maybe he could help her put out the fire that was consuming her ...she liked the sound of his voice...she must try to think who it was...

O' but here was papa standing before her now...and mama was with him, DJ was but a step behind... they were calling to her... oh she had missed them all so ...

———

"Llyr..." His head shot up. He stared at the figure in the bed afraid to blink. Dhariya had often spoken in her fevered state, mostly soft incoherent murmuring or whimpering. Was he imagining things? He wondered. Or were her eyes truly open? Had he actually heard her breath his name?

Yes. Her eyes were indeed open and staring back at him. "Dhariya... Dear sweet God Dhariya." She smiled dreamily then closed her lids again. Llyr did not know what to do, he did not want her to close her eyes and go away from him again. With his gaze still riveted on the patient, he strode to the door adjoining the sitting room and cracked it open.

"Ffyonna," he called into the darkness beyond, unable to conceal the note of excitement and fear inflecting his tone.

Llyr hovered anxiously in the background while Ffyonna assessed her patient's present condition. Dhariya had not regained consciousness again since she had woken and smiled at him a short time ago. He was already beginning to doubt what he had seen.

The older woman's face offered no clues as she went about her task with diligent tender care. "Every body tells its own tale, a tale as unique as the person it carries around within it." Ffyonna had once told him, "If you know where to look and what to look for, you can read what's goin' on inside by sight and touch mostly," she had said. "But some illnesses can be scented in the air around the body it inhabits. Aye a body will always tell you what it needs and try as you may to give what's needed, in the end 'tis the soul within that decides to live or no." Llyr recalled the words clearly now as he watched Ffyonna.

She routinely ran her hands along Dhariya's body, as she was doing now. Stopping at certain precise points where she would lightly place her fingertips just so, then closing her eyes she stilled and waited.

Llyr had to admit he found this all rather fascinating and held no doubt that Ffyonna was hearing this language of the body that only she could understand. Yet all the while as he waited, he could barely suppress his own growing impatience at the lengthy drawn out ritual.

Once this was finally done Ffyonna then sought confirmation of the internal messages by touching Dhariya's forehead damp but cool beneath her palm, cool—yes the fever had broken, Ffyonna sent a silent thank you heavenward, as she proceeded to examine the wound. The livid redness of inflammation and infection was now paling into the blush of healthy tissue. Feeling satisfied with what she saw, she at last tuned to him. "The worst has passed milord."

"Thank God!" He said with a wealth of meaning. The flood of relief took him to the other bedside chair where he sank down into it with sudden overwhelming weariness, He silently offered another thank you heavenward.

"Amen." Ffyonna agreed then began the painstaking process of re-closing the raw edges of flesh, which in the end had required fifteen of the small neat stitches. Afterwards, she applied a fresh herbal poultice and wrapped the wound in clean strips of cloth. She worked deftly and efficiently as always.

Finally she rose with a weary sigh. "She'll sleep a great deal now, don't worry over it, 'tis what her body most needs to strengthen. And don't be alarmed if when she wakes, she's quiet and withdrawn, 'tis the way of this kind of trauma the shock 'twill stay with her a while yet, and the scars both visible and invisible, will always be with her."

Llyr drew Ffyonna away from the bed. Raking his hands through his hair he sought the right words, "You remember what I told you... about the way I found Dhariya with him? Well..."

Then he gave up and spoke bluntly in hushed tones, "Do you think she'll be all right?" Llyr recalled only too well how many hours Dhariya had been missing and what could have taken place during that time. He did not hold out any hope that she might have been further spared from lust's vile side, not after the way in which he found her, lying beneath that thrusting, sweating animal.

"Tis too soon to say for certain milord," She answered with an unusual curtness, her shrewd gaze piercing him where he stood.

"It's not an issue with me if that's what you're thinking?" He said with absolute honesty, meeting her eye to eye with his own challenge. "Bloody hell!" came his whispered shout of frustration, "I'll tell you straight out, nothing could change the way I feel about that woman." Motioning to the sleeping figure in the bed, "it's what all of this might do to Dhariya that worries me out of my own mind… and I feel as helpless in knowing what to do for her now as I did when she lay near death." His voice shook with emotion.

"Aye," Ffyonna replied, as if he had passed some kind of test, "As I said 'tis too soon to know the effects milord," her voice gentled, "I checked Dhariya over thoroughly just after I first arrived, she was used harshly to be sure and t'was not in the usual way that he used her, not as man to woman."

Llyr stared blankly at the older woman for a moment. Then realization hit him like a hard fist to midsection. He was still reeling amid this latest revelation when a tapping at the door interrupted them. It was Katie who had come to inform her Aunt that a messenger was waiting in the lower hall to speak with her.

Ffyonna excused herself and followed her niece from the room. Llyr walked to the bed where Dhariya lay resting peacefully, placing his palm to her cool forehead just to reassure himself before taking his seat beside her.

Looking at her now thinking of all she had endured—was he being selfish wanting her to survive because 'he' needed her so? Yet that very desire meant she would have to live with the consequences, the torment of all she had borne. These things would not heal as flesh and bone did, the memories of horror would never leave her mind.

Was it fair of him to beg that she stay because he was not ready to let her go? Well he had vowed to let her go and walk out of her life if God saved her. Yet was it fair that he had prayed for her survival when it might mean life long suffering for her? Suddenly he remembered something else Ffyonna once told him…

There were times as Dhariya grew older, the older woman had said, *that she'd turn a wee bit strange and suddenly rage, sayin' no one knows what they're truly askin' for when they pray for another's survival. Then she'd go off alone and not be seen for hours on end. Afterwards, when she came back, she'd be all right, just like herself again.*

His heart clenched in his chest as he thought of the hours she spent trapped in that room and what she had to endure there. He raged anew at his own incompetence, stumbling over his feet and mind as he had tried to track her. There came another light tap at the door that interrupted his chastising thoughts and preceded Ffyonna's swift entry. "Milord, a word if you please"

"Certainly" Llyr replied, immediately aware that something was wrong. *Bloody hell what now* he thought.

Ffyonna turned to her niece, who was trailing behind her, "Katie, you'll mind her Ladyship."

"Aye Auntie"

Llyr followed the older woman into the sitting room and closed the door.

"The messenger is from Mr. Saunders' office," Ffyonna said without pause or preamble "he's here with one of them 'high constables'. They say Josey's been found alive milord, though not by much. They've come to take me to her. I must leave at once."

"Where?" Llyr asked—feeling like he had been tossed into the middle of the sea amid a savage storm with no end in sight—no anchor within grasp.

"Another Inn they said, not far from the one that Iain took her Ladyship. Seems he'd been keepin' Josey trussed up in his room there. She's in a bad way they're sayin' milord, bloody, beaten, half starved and all. A physician is with her now but he can't help her in the way she most needs, I must go to her."

"I understand," he said and he did, all too well, reluctant though he was to let her go. He knew as much or more than anyone that Ffyonna was indeed a rare and true healer, her gifts were many and beyond price, as he was coming to realize more and more. "I can arrange to have Josey brought here," he offered, "that way my staff can help, I know you're exhausted."

"Aye milord that I am," She paused for a weary breath, "but I don't think t'is wise to move the lass yet. Not if she's as bad as it sounds."

"Of course, whatever you think is best. I'll have my carriage brought around for you and send along two of the maidservants to assist you. Keep me updated on how she's doing and if there's anything you need Ffyonna, I'll see that you get it."

"Thank you sir, I'll be needin' lots of clean linens, sure as anythin' as much as you can spare and alcohol." While Ffyonna went to gather her things, Llyr summoned Veldon and instructed the houseman to see to her needs and have the carriage readied. He dearly wished Ffyonna did not have to leave with Dhariya just barely out of danger.

And he did not know what would happen when Dhariya woke—then as if in answer to his thoughts, he turned to find the older woman standing there again, this time in her cloak and hat. She came toward him.

"I'll leave you with this milord." She said handing him a bottle of what looked like yet another herbal extract. "'Tis this that her ladyship'll be needin' for the emotional trauma. Give her half an ounce in water every twelve hours. "I want you to be the one to do it. 'Tis a special blend, 'twill help her release all the pain she'll be holdin' on to. If she keeps it inside it'll surely destroy her."

And how well did he know it. His own cursed existence was proof of that fact. Though he had never heard of any such treatment for emotions, however he would never question this woman's competence, "certainly Ffyonna. You may rest assured I'll see it done."

"One last thing milord, 'tis best to say nothin' to Lady Dhariya about her young maid. Close like sisters the two of them, always were…no sense riskin' another shock to her Ladyship this early on. No tellin' what it might do."

Llyr could not have agreed more. He only hoped Dhariya would not remember and ask him about all of that just yet. The last thing he wanted to do was lie to her now. "Yes, that's wise." He said trying to hide his concerns, which was futile with Ffyonna's uncanny ability to see beyond.

The older woman was a fierce fortress, yet once you had won her; she was on your side until the end, lest you betray that trust. For it was only given once. There was a new closeness, forged through long anxious hours of waiting, of shared fears that went unvoiced yet had filled these days and nights in Edinburgh. Now there was also the silent jubilation that Dhariya had come though the worst of her physical challenges.

Yet Llyr did not feel he would ever truly know the wise old healing woman, but then again he supposed it did not really matter. On some deep level he sensed that she was the essence of all that was good and her skill and wisdom as a healer could never be questioned. What more did one need to know?

"Katie's to stay on. She'll help see to her Ladyship's care till she's up and about. Dhariya has no more need of me."

The words sounded oddly final to him. Then Ffyonna looked directly into his eyes, "'tis the wounds of her soul that need healin' now," she said. "Her mother and I helped do it once when she was small, but she's a woman grown and you're the only one who can help her with what needs be done."

If the woman was attempting to make him feel better, she was failing miserably. He thought to himself but remained silent.

"Aye while she was fevered I'd feared her spirit was too wounded and she'd nay have the will to fight her way back. 'Tis why I told you to talk to her as though you knew she could hear you and 'twas your voice that she roused to milord—"

"But—" Llyr interjected, trying to divert the direction of the conversation, before he could utter another word however, Ffyonna had cut in again…

"Some things are unalterable." She was saying, looking at him with that strange piercing gaze that she had. "Like what's happened to you, it cannot be changed. You know that, yet it brought you from the falseness of the man you were, to the truer man you are now and 'tis all for the better. You love her and she loves you," She went on without mercy, "'tis plain as day to anyone with eyes. Dhariya heard your voice; she wanted to come back for you. She'll likely not even know it herself in her mind. But Dhariya's soul knows and her heart knows …so does yours… just listen to what they're tellin' you and 'twill be fine."

With that Ffyonna turned and was gone.

Llyr could but stare after her. Did she know the truth of what he was? Was that what she had meant by the changes in him and the reference to it being unalterable? He was not exactly sure what had just happened here. He shook his head in disbelief. The old woman never ceased to amaze him and sometimes she was downright frightening in her depth of perception.

Her words, however intended, had indeed found their mark, as they were meant to he did not doubt. Yet he could not help but feel the burden of having that much faith placed upon him, especially now when there was still so much standing between he and Dhariya.

XIII
~ And o' the dream, why doth thy vision lie? ~

...This empty colorlessness is all that keeps me from fragmenting, as fear ever hovers nearby. Will I ever be free from this prison? Will I ever wish to be? For the fear of leaving this barrenness is by far the greater terror...

Edinburgh City ~ Scotland ~ Mid-December 1711

~ The strange realm of mind I'd come to know so well—that distant place which kept me safe from all I was not yet ready to face—it was a place where everything comes and goes—passing before me—where my eyes bear witness. Like an observer staring out through a pane of glass, I cannot touch or be touched, cannot feel or be felt. There is nothing. Yet what lies beyond is much worse.

For reality is waiting there. Just on the other side. Its threat draws closer. Clawing at the cold stonewalls of my cell. Dear God help me I'm so close to the edge and the thought of just letting myself slip over it—gets easier and easier to imagine.

What was 'out there' has found the cracks within me. I cannot hold back the flow of wrenching emotions seeping in. I'm beginning to feel. The sorrows come now, one upon the other. Crowding in upon me, like desperate writhing creatures, slithering against me, pawing at me with razor sharp talons in their fury to be acknowledged.

All the pain held too long in silence starts to scream inside of me, like a thousand shrill voices, tearing at my ears with a deafening pitch, tearing at my soul with the shards of my shattered world—my violated body.

I'm raging—raging inside—bleeding—torn to ribbons—flayed to the bone.

Dear God…Help me…Help me…Help me….

~ D ~

~ Llyr turned toward the sound of rustling in the bed and found Dhariya awake. She said nothing only stared at him and her surroundings with wide uncertain eyes. She looked so small, so like a frightened child in the massive bed. No doubt exactly how she was feeling inside, thought Llyr.

He could tell she was still under the effects of the various medicinals. He recognized the laudanum glazed-over look. She was trembling and needed comfort he could read that plainly enough. He was the only one there to offer it to her and at that moment her need was all that mattered.

Acting purely on instinct he went to her. Without speaking, lest he say the wrong thing, if she did not want him near her she would let him know. He sat down on the bed behind her. Since she made no sign of protest, he drew her shivering form into him, her back nestled against his chest, mindful of the wounded shoulder he cradled her between his arms and legs—enfolding her within his own body—he began rocking her in a slow gentle rhythm.

He had never before done such a thing, but with her he was different, with her everything was different. It had always been thus, from that first moment he had ever seen her when he felt something inside him shift, knowing even then, it would never be moved back to where it once had been.

She offered no resistance. Strangely, for the moment Dhariya felt safe. With eyes closed, her cheek resting against the softness of his shirt—the solid strength of the body beneath it— and sandalwood—yes sandalwood—so much a part of him—of all that was him…nothing has changed, she thought…*though I still fear him in my mind, my heart does not, yet in truth, it has always been thus…*God how she needed him. She did not want to but she could not help it.

"I'm afraid of you yet I s-still love you." she said suddenly, startling him. "How can that be?" These were the first words she spoke to him, asked in total honestly —her voice sounding small—her hands clutching to him desperately, needing him in spite of it all else… "I don't understand any of this."

Nor did he, he wanted to tell her but did not. "Easy love," he whispered this altered reply. "We'll talk all of this through later when you're stronger. All you need know right now is that I love you more than myself. More than anything and that I would never harm you," he promised, his own voice wavering with emotion…. "You must believe me."

She nodded her head in answer. Then pulling from his embrace with a strength that again surprised him, she abruptly declared, "I must have a hot bath…" her eyes huge and luminous in the flickering candlelight, a strange sort of wildness lurking in their depths.

"You're wounded and far too weak for that now Dhariya. Besides you've been bathed countless time from head to toe while you were fevered."

"No! Shaking her head with frenetic motions, "No it's not the same thing! … You-you cannot know the things h-he … what he forced upon m-me … I-I must scrub the memory of *his* vileness from my flesh." She was beginning to gasp for air.

Llyr could sense her rising panic. "All right, all right,' he stated calmly. "As you wish Dhariya, however, I shall bathe you myself."

She looked up at him then and Llyr, seeing the emotion so openly revealed there in her expression—desperation—a silent almost frantic plea—her need so much greater than he ever imagined, it very nearly undid him.

She was like finely spun glass that had shattered but not yet broken, while the fragile webbing of shards barely held together along veined cracks and frail seams. How easily she could crumble away into an irreparable fragmenting of the person she had once been, he realized. Suddenly fearing he had said the wrong thing, perhaps the thought of him touching her now would bring about the worst.

"Yes." the word a pitiful breath of sound from her lips, "I must—I-I must feel your touch upon me once again …Llyr?—Please?"

"Yes." He reaffirmed his voice softening further, "Just keep calm. Let me look after everything. I'll take care of you Dhariya." He pledged and went about the summoning of his houseman to impart the instructions while Dhariya quietly watched the proceedings from the bed.

Since Llyr himself had become quite accustomed to the luxury of bathing each evening at Skara Brae, he had incorporated all the necessities into his own household here in the city. Although not nearly such an elaborate offering as the castle afforded, the preparations were nevertheless soon underway.

Nothing was said as the water arrived and each steaming bucket emptied into the large brass tub, which had been dragged from its storage place in the large closet and set before the fire. To this Llyr added a liberal measure of fragrant oil from his own costly collection and the scented aroma wafted-up invitingly into the air.

The silence only deepened as Dhariya watched Llyr pull back the bedcovers, revealing her unclothed body. Then he carefully gathered her in his arms and carried her over to the tub. His hands gentle as they helped her ease into the soothing liquid warmth.

And in that hushed unspoken, a slow rhythmic beat began pulsing through the room with an intensity neither had known before. It was both sensual and seductive, yet on a level far more profound than mere passion alone.

Closing her eyes, Dhariya sank back against the sloping metal support, her head resting atop its wide rolled rim.

Llyr looked down at her laying there, her long hair flowing like a dark river of waves onto the carpet. All her bared beauty displayed before him—she was trusting in him at this moment; even after all she had been through and all that stood between the two of them—she was trusting him in ways far beyond measure. She still wore the locket he had given her, it lay between her breasts right over her heart.

His own heart clenched inside his chest. He did not deserve her. He knew that more than any other soul in existence. While he recalled only too well his vow to God that he would let her go once she was strong again and he had see her safely home to Skara Brae or wherever she wanted to go, then he would indeed fulfill that vow and offer her, her freedom.

At the sight of the small knife puncture healing on her neck, the bruise darkening her temple and the stark white binding of the shoulder wound that had nearly taken her from this world, from him, Llyr could feel his rage resurfacing—the mere thought of that lewd beast marring her, striking her, touching her, using her so brutally. He wished the bastard still lived only so he could kill him over again, very, very slowly this time—He closed his eyes forcing the fury aside.

He turned his focus to the fact that Dhariya needed him now more than ever, needed him in a way he was not sure he would be capable of fulfilling. Yet he must somehow find within him the means to help her through it—no matter what the ultimate cost might be to himself, heaving a sigh of resolution—he rolled up his shirtsleeves and he knelt down beside the tub.

Tiny splashing sounds spilled into the quietness as he dipped the soft linen square into the water and with gentle benevolent hands began to slowly bathe her body. His eyes watching the firelight glisten across the beauty of her wet nakedness, further gilding the naturally golden skin. And with every passing of cloth, his lingering gaze followed the trail of droplets trickling their way over the rounded curves of succulent female flesh and down into the hallowed folds, where the purest sweetness lay buried.

His hand trembled as he washed traces of dried blood from her throat—he had only managed to slip away once, to see to his baser need since they had come here—yet the strength of his newly recovered self helped fight against the other. And it was by this means that he savagely ignored the dark passions pulsing through his body at the sight of the small wound and he tore his eyes and thoughts away.

With the all the power he possessed, he returned his mind purposely to thoughts of Dhariya's needs only. He could feel her entire being immediately begin responding to his attentive ministrations, her body stirring to life beneath his touch, as it always had.

He would make her forget he vowed silently. She would remember no other man but him. No other touch but his. The linen slipped from his fingers and his palm began gliding over the lightly oiled sleekness of her glowing skin.

The heat, his touch—melting the cold grayness inside of her—penetrating through the numb void at her core and finding her where she had herself hidden away, yet he did not demand that she leave her haven, nor bring her out to him, but instead came to where she was and joined her within that safety—where all thought took on a distant air—until only their feelings and the exquisite power of sensation remained.

The undercurrent of subtleties was not lost on either of them—perhaps it was this that flowed so heavily between them, from one to the other and back again, further intensifying with each passing—bringing such wondrous heightened awareness, even unto each breath taken by the other.

The splashing of droplets and the soft sputter of flames were the only sounds as Llyr lifted Dhariya from the tub, setting her feet on the plush carpet. He wrapped her in the length of toweling then carried her back to the bed, laying her gently down upon the velvet coverlet.

Suddenly her eyes opened wide she looked up at him.

She pulled at his shirt and he sat. Grasping again at his shirtfront she drew him close, her lips sought his. Llyr resisted and eased back to look at her. The message in her eyes was undeniable. "Make love to me Llyr."

Then she held her fingers against his lips to prevent the protest she knew would come. His gaze delved deeply into hers, "Are you sure?" was the unspoken question.

"Yes." She replied in the same language, "I need you... to feel you inside of me," was also conveyed, with no less clarity for its having been wordless.

It was their souls that always communicated so fully and freely and they did so now. Her eyes held to his—beseeching. He saw and understood her vulnerability at that moment. She needed to be loved, needed her own sensuality renewed—the sweet yearnings of passion revived—which far outweighed exhaustion and even any remaining fear of him.

Hours later they lay in the bed, still wrapped in the sanctity of the yet unbroken silence and the soft safety it gave them to seek refuge in each other. They were both awake, naked bodies entwined. The depths of all they felt conveyed by touch and the joining of their flesh.

They had both been unsure in the beginning, not knowing if Dhariya might, at any moment, suddenly splinter and break apart. Llyr had first taken her mouth in a kiss of such absolute tenderness that Dhariya nearly wept.

Then, loosening the toweling from her body his lips traveled lower, his tongue licking glistening droplets that remained from her silken flesh. As he moved along her torso, Dhariya parted her legs, opening herself completely to him; he looked down at her there—at the sacred threshold of her body, and the other—the place of her violation—she was letting him see everything, hiding nothing, allowing neither of them to hide from the truth of what she had endured.

This new level of trust she was offering frightened him, and then he heard Ffyonna's words echo in his memory."*Dhariya's soul knows and her heart knows …so does yours… just listen to what they're tellin' ye and t'will be fine."*

Thus he followed this advice and bent his head, Dhariya responded, giving her body without hesitation, without restraint, welcoming his mouth, his touch upon all of her sacred places. Llyr savored the precious gift of her sweetness—that she allowed herself to surrender all to him once again.

When the time came to enter, again she opened wide to him and he had again been riveted upon the sight, looking in wonder at the soft pink vulnerability, watching himself disappear into the delicate petal-ed entry to Eden's garden, feeling the melting fire of paradise, then sliding out, gauging her response to his presence within her. And as the heat of her body further welcomed him he lifted his eyes to meet hers.

He loved her slowly.

Looking into each other's eyes, as he moved inside of her, pressing deep, pulling back, the strong rhythmic cadence—gazes locked holding the image of the other and the knowledge that this was theirs, shared only together, no other could take it away or tarnish this communion of their two souls. It was beyond physical, beyond sexual, beyond all earthly limitations.

He felt their union and knew that she felt it too—those silken cords that bound them—in both body and spirit. Eyes still locked as he moved deep within her, each movement erasing all else—linking them further—lifting them higher—until they soared together unto the heavens once more.

Despite everything that had happened since they had last made love together surprisingly there had been no demons haunting Dhariya this time, perhaps because she now knew what to expect from their intimacy.

She was curled against his side now, head resting on his chest over the place where his heart beat. While his hand stroked her hair, feeling at once, the silky texture and curving bone of her skull beneath his palm. Neither willing to risk what the moment held.

The time for talking would come, but where words would only separate them now, the silence had brought them together. Eventually, he felt the subtle changes in her body as she relaxed further into sleep, leaving him alone with the sad regret that these hours of trust and silent communion were now over.

Could they ever staunch the bleeding wounds of betrayal? He wondered. Was there any way to mend the raw torn edges of all that had been viciously torn away, leaving only the vast emptiness that now gapped between them? The obstacles were great, but he had to believe in all that bound them, that what they shared would prove to be greater, if he did not hold fast to this, then there was indeed nothing

Is this our punishment for loving? He silently asked God, in case He might deign to listen. *Are we such terrible sinners then, because we love? Did not Christ Himself give a commandment greater than those henceforth given and proclaim 'love for one another be above and beyond all else?*

How could they be condemned for what they felt for each other? His plaguing thoughts were relentless in their quest for some kind of understanding. After all, they had not chosen to feel this way for one another, they had been virtually powerless against the will of their hearts. How could they possibly have changed anything then, any more than they could change it now? Why was this cruelty so ceaseless in its savagery?

Had his caring brought this upon her? Llyr wondered. He sighed heavily at this far too real possibility as he continued his internal litany. *No, I have not forgotten my avowed pledge to You in return for her recovery. And I will indeed keep it once she and I*

have spoken and everything has finally been laid to rest. I will indeed walk away from her and never return, which is surely what she would wish.

All at once he felt as old as the eternity stretching out before him and as dark as the lightless promise it held.

———

As Ffyonna had predicted Dhariya slept a great deal, though Llyr sensed she was aware of his presence even while she did so. He found this to be a great relief, not just because he knew rest was what she most needed, but also because it afforded time with themselves and each other without any demands. They would be forced to face everything soon enough. Somehow they must find a way through it all, somehow staunch the flow of invisible wounds that were all too real nonetheless. Was it possible he kept wondering?

If only she could have trusted him enough, thought Llyr for at least the thousandth time as he sat watching Dhariya's sleeping face, she would never have had to go through all of this. But then he was no less guilty of keeping his own secrets.

The stringent instructions Ffyonna left behind for herbal strengthening tonics and the special tincture he had been given to administer, were diligently followed to the letter.

True to her word the older woman sent regular updates on Josey, which unfortunately were not terribly encouraging. Between these missives and Jeremy Saunders' visits Llyr learned the details surrounding the young maid's disappearance.

Josey had been relaying bits of information as her strength allowed and little by little the story of what happened began to unfold. It seems that Josey had somehow discovered her husband was up to something sinister and had threatened to tell Llyr and Dhariya.

Iain did not care what his wife thought, he was planning to leave her anyway and flee to France with his lover and the large sum of money Dreshem promised as payment. Yet Josey could easily thwart all of this if she spoke out. So Iain knocked her unconscious and smuggled her out of the castle in the supply wagon.

As it turned out Josey was with child. She had kept it a secret and been able to conceal it, though she was nearly six months along. Iain had known nothing about it since he was so often away these past months and their intimacy had become a thing of the past. He found out at the Inn however, when he had stripped her bare intending to make good use of her.

Upon seeing her swelling belly, Iain had become enraged knowing she had taken a lover, even though he had many of his own. His wife had no right to seek her pleasure elsewhere. He proceeded to beat her to within an inch of her life as retribution for being unfaithful.

The beating caused Josey to miscarry the babe and she herself nearly bled to death in the process. Iain had apparently stayed for a while, watching his wife writhing in the pain of premature labor. Then he had stifled her cries with a gag, bound her hands to the bedposts and left her there alone and helpless without even the use of her arms to aid the child's birth.

The babe was born and died. The tiny corpse lying still on the bed between her legs where she had managed to push it from her body—while Josey, scarcely conscious from blood loss, grieved for the tiny soul's passing.

Many hours went by before she heard Iain come back, cursing her and the child as he moved about the cold dark room. She had lain unmoving with closed eyes, fearing what he might do next. Then she felt what she imagined to be the cutting of the umbilical cord. One of her last recollections was Iain exiting the room a short time later and locking the door behind him. Leaving Josey there alone again with the lifeblood seeping from her body, he had never come back. It was assumed Iain had disposed of the tiny corpse because it had never been discovered; only the evidence of its birth had remained.

Iain had never paid the for the room either it seems, so when the Innkeeper finally broke down the door, he had found Josey unconscious and barely clinging to her last breath, she had no idea how long she had been there. Llyr had listened to Jeremy Saunders' recounting of events with sick horror and dreading the moment he would have to tell Dhariya any of this.

He and the solicitor, whom Llyr learned had become a widower some eight months passed after twenty-plus happily wedded years, had come to form an interesting relationship during Dhariya's stay in Llyr's Edinburgh town home. The location of which, it turned out, happened to be somewhere between the lonely solicitor's office and his own home. Thus it was that Saunders appeared in Llyr's drawing room in the evenings with increasing regularity.

Llyr for his part did not mind—being more than aware of his growing need to share in things of Dhariya's past, of which this man surely was no less relevant, and with his own acute understanding of the effects aloneness had upon ones spirit. He had also discovered that he genuinely enjoyed the older man's intelligent-unassuming company and surprised himself by extending further invitations to stop by for a dram as the whim might take him, whether Llyr be in or not, his home would be at Saunders' disposal.

Each time Dhariya would awaken, she continued to remain in the same stupor-like trance she had been in when he freed her from Dreshem. Her first reaction was initial confusion at being in these strange surrounding, then all at once realizing her circumstances with sudden recollections of what had happened to her and why. Though she did not speak, Llyr could read her expressions. He knew none of this served to ease either her conscience or troubled mind.

He supposed it was a natural state of shock, one that she would need to diligently work through in her own time, though he wished Ffyonna were here to confirm his deductions and reassure him.

He recalled the older woman's caution—both verbally before she had left and in her missives afterward—that this was to be expected. She also told him to be patient in allowing her to remember only what could be managed at any given moment, which he was doing. Yet he continued to worry nonetheless.

During the brief periods of waking she was quiet and withdrawn. Her tendency was to stare wide-eyed and mostly at him.

Unbeknownst to Llyr, she was also watching covertly and very carefully. Something she had often done during these past few days. Watching as he moved about the room—tending the hearth fire, lighting lamps, drawing drapes—ensuring that his home offered its utmost comfort, caring for her in these small yet telling ways that spoke so much truer than mere words ever could. But words must soon be spoken.

Never once has his demeanor changed toward me, thought Dhariya, she had to admit to this—for he had continued to treat her with the same loving tenderness that he had always shown, perhaps even more so now. And he had been infinitely patient, she could not deny that either.

Never once had he forced her to talk of what had happened or pressured her in any way. In fact he had actually cautioned her against too much too soon. Insisting she allow herself whatever time necessary to recover from all she had endured. "I'm not going anywhere," he had said softly. "You have all the time you need, and when you're ready we'll talk everything through, and then decided how we go from here."

She was trying desperately to define a single thread of clarity in the multitude of tangled emotions within her. *Was it truth that only her knowledge of him was different?* Yet that knowledge plagued her now, how could it not? There still were so many questions she wanted to ask, but feared the answers.

He stood now with his back to her staring into the hearth, as if watching pictures in the fire or perhaps seeking his own answers therein, his black clad form casually, yet impeccably attired. The set of his shoulders was one she well recognized, the right slightly higher than the left, meant he was either extremely tense or extremely angry. Which was it at this moment? She wondered.

"Llyr"

He turned to her, feeling a bit startled at suddenly hearing her voice after so long. It sounded weak which of course was to be expected. "Yes darling."

Dhariya's heart clenched at the endearment. She swallowed hard and asked the question that had been most plaguing her sanity. "Who are you?"

So here it was, he thought. Initially, his main concern was her health and state of mind following her ordeal. Then as her recovery became more and more apparent, he knew their attentions would naturally shift and finally addressed this topic, which had been lurking in both of their minds, since the night Dhariya had discovered his darkest secret. He had waited for her to initiate this discussion when she felt ready to face it. Now she had done so. *Who are you? Three whispered words, simple enough,* thought Llyr, *yet the magnitude of what they asked—unanswerable.*

He could not possibly tell her the full truth for her own safety first and foremost. Nor did he, selfishly, wish to further tarnish her image of him, however undeserving he was of her. But she also deserved to know.

He came forward and sat on the bed facing her, taking her hand, small and warm, into his. "Dhariya, I promise to answer all of your questions and explain everything about myself to you, as best I can. There are many things standing between us at the moment, whatever happens from this point onward, you must know. Over and above all else, I am the man who loves you. I would never harm you I promise, will you please trust me?"

A frisson of guilt crept over her.

As if sensing something of her thoughts he looked deep into her eyes and smiled at her—it was a sad almost helpless smile.

Looking up into his handsome face Dhariya thought again of his gentle manner, of how his love was always there so openly displayed in every gesture, every word—His eyes held hers. She, once again, felt herself falling into the dark fathomless gaze that was his, and from which, there was no protection. Thus, one by one, she was aware of each of her defenses melting away, as they always did—leaving her bared and naked before him, on every level.

With their eyes still locked, Dhariya then watched as his own barriers began to fall. She knew he was allowing her to see things in him that he would never reveal to any other. Only to her did he yield these deeper truths—his longing—his vulnerability—his pain—and the full magnitude of his love for her.

This was Dhariya's undoing—something suddenly cleared inside her, and enough of the numbing fog lifted to let her strong intuitive sense to come flooding forth, sweet relief following in its wake. In that instant Dhariya realized how completely she had been duped by circumstance and she knew she had been so very wrong about him. There were still a great many questions she needed to ask and he needed to answer, and they would do so in time. But for now she knew it would be all right and that was enough.

Her eyes welled with tears. "Llyr, I'm s-so s-sorry..." He rose and reseated himself behind her. Her tears began spilling freely down her cheeks; falling onto his hands as he drew her between his open legs and into the sheltering embrace of his body. Wishing he could take the pain from her, he would willingly have borne it himself if it meant that she would be spared this suffering.

With her back against his chest, Llyr held her close against his heart, "It's all right love," He said, closing his eyes against the anguish, his insides clenching and twisting in painful knots. Dhariya then turned, her hands grasping onto his shirt as she buried her face into his chest and wept to the depths of her soul. He again, began to rock her in a soothing rhythmic motion, stroking her back as she clutched him in tightly. "That-t man at t-the Inn," she finally managed a long while later, between sobs. "H-he killed my f-family…H-his name is Dexter D-Dreshem… m-my father's shipping partner."

Llyr had since learned some of these facts from Jeremy Saunders during his visits to the town house during Dhariya's recovery; he always relayed any news or latest developments in his investigation. Of course Saunders was not aware of the worst details of her ordeal, and at that moment with Dhariya weeping in his arm, Llyr knew himself to be the ultimate coward because he did not want to know them, did not want to hear them—Dhariya had had to live through this horror and he was afraid to even hear of it—God help him but it was true.

What he must focus on is that Dhariya needed him now in a way that was more important than anything they had ever shared together. She needed to tell him about what happened in those hours with the man called Dreshem. Thus, he swallowed hard then braced himself mentally, physically, emotionally and spiritually, for it was going to require the combined strength of them all to get through this and help her heal.

"Yes darling." He said encouragingly. She was not looking at him, which helped. Her head was resting against his chest, her hands still clutching his shirt.

She dragged a labored breath into her lungs and continued "H-he thought to h-have it all f-for himself, the entire shipping enterprise and pocket all the profits …but that was only a part of it."

Her voice suddenly sounded far away, Llyr thought, almost as if she were recounting something that happened to someone else. "B-but it was Iain who b-brought me there, to the Inn."

She was saying, "Iain worked for Dreshem, y-you see. I can't b-believe we w-were deceived b-by so many w-we trusted."

"Dhariya love, I'm so sorry for it. For all the pain and loss you've suffered at the hands of this Dreshem. If I could, I'd gladly give my last breath to return your family to you."

"Please." Her head lifted from his chest, tears still streaking her beautiful face, as her eyes beseeched his. "Do not say such things Llyr. As much as I would wish them back I couldn't bear losing you, I… I still love you so." She reburied her face in his chest and her weeping began anew. "C-can you ever f-forgive me? I've b-been such a f-fool."

Llyr pressed soft kisses to the crown of her head and rubbed his cheek against her silken hair. "Hush love. It is I who must beg your forgiveness, which I humbly do on bended knee if necessary."

"No Llyr. I should not have left" Dhariya stated, her voice shaky and tear laden.

"On that we agree. You should not have left as you did, without giving me a chance to explain, although I understand your reasons."

"I've never before r-run from anything…W-well once a long time ago. The consequences w-were much the s-same. I should've learned that l-lesson."

"With such a shocking truth as the one I laid before you, anyone would've reacted as you did." Llyr replied, continuing to hold her, attempting to sooth her with his touch and his words. He was relieved when she finally began calming down, though she still clung to him like a small child desperately needing comfort.

"Yes but, I only made things worse by not facing you. I should've at least listened when you wished to talk." Pausing to draw another deep shuddering breath, "least of all I should've believed in the love we've shared."

"Hush now and let yourself rest." Llyr knew that what Dhariya needed now most of all was loving, tenderness, which he was more than willing to provide. And more than willing to postpone learning all that Dreshem had put her through. Thus, he kept her exhausted body held tightly against him, his heavy black velvet robe that she wore snugly enfolding her in its warmth. She nestled deeper into his protective embrace.

She was so still and she had been quiet for so long, Llyr thought she finally slept, then after a great while her voice came, in small scarce whisper, "How did you find me?"

Llyr drew a deep breath and endeavored to explain. "When I arose that eve, and stepped into my bedchamber Dacron was there as usual. Yet instead of preparing my bathwater, as was his custom, he was pacing back and forth across the carpets. At my appearance, he came rushing over and relayed the news of your disappearance in a frenzy of words."

"Dacron?" She questioned incredulously.

"Yes, seems he does indeed have a voice after all. But only uses it when absolutely necessary. Although he seems quite aloof, he too cares very much for you in his own way." He went on to say, that the young valet had even taken part in searches carried out by staff members—throughout the day they had formed into groups and, in turn—scoured the grounds and surrounding forest.

Dacron had also proved invaluable in helping with information. With his usual attention to detail, he had been able to confirm what Annie had seen—after the maid said she had seen Dhariya ride out alone early that morning and that Iain and ridden out shortly thereafter—the valet had then given an accurate time frame, as well as describe the exact direction they had both ridden off in. "Seems Dacron had been visiting one of his paramours in the sleeping quarters above the stables," Llyr told her, "and from an upper window, had seen her ride out followed moments later by Iain."

Dhariya had already been aware of the young valet's preference, having heard some of the castle's maids discussing their disappointment at discovering that the handsome angelic-looking Dacron would not be led into temptation by any of the female gender. Nor was Dhariya likely to be shocked by the idea of the two male lovers seeking their pleasure after Dreshem's graphic depictions.

Llyr explained another area where Dacron had provided invaluable details

It seems that shortly after Dhariya and her servants arrived at the castle Iain came knocking at the valet's door. Dacron was surprised by the visitor, but more surprised when the burly Scotsman pushed his way inside, held him up against the wall and began kissing his mouth wildly.

Then Iain proceeded to have his way with the younger man's body in a rough manner. All the while praising the blonde beauty, saying he was soft and sweet. Unlike that sweating pig Dreshem who had forced him into the ways of men, Iain had said. Making him succumb to pleasure despite himself, then yearn for it ever after.

From that point on Iain continued these unannounced visits with increasing regularity. Dacron did not like being used so harshly, yet he dare not refuse for fear of severe violence. Afterwards as they lay in bed together, Iain would talk as lovers often do. This was how Dacron learned that the other man was involved in some unscrupulous activities. The young valet was determined to find out all he could, so he began to encourage Iain's visits, using all of his skills to keep the burly Scotsman's interest.

Dacron's plan seemed to be working well and Iain was falling hard for the younger man. Iain spoke to him of coming into a great deal of money. Saying that when he did, he and Dacron would flee to France where they would live openly together like kings.

What Llyr kept to himself for the present however, was that when Josey had gone missing, Dacron had told him that Iain acted distraught and come to the valet for comfort. Therefore Dacron never suspected, despite the man's plans to leave her.

Dhariya was told of how Dacron had shown Llyr his written accounting of all Iain's disclosures including dates and times.

He had been trying to uncover exactly what the older man was up to so he could warn Llyr. Unfortunately however, everything had happened before he was able to do so.

"The other important detail that Dacron observed," Llyr was saying, "was the fact that Iain had left on horseback and not by the horse drawn supply wagon he always used. Obviously then supplies were not Iain's intended purpose."

Llyr then proceeded to tell her of his own horror when he had read the note Annie found. "When I saw Elysian I knew it had to be Iain. I also knew he was setting it all up to look like I was the one." He explained then that he had sent Iain to the silversmith in Edinburgh, with the diagram and written instructions, Llyr had specified for Dhariya's locket and inscription inside. "In fact you nearly spoiled my surprise when you arrived at drawing room early one evening,"

"Yes, I remember." She said softly.

"Fool that I was I thought Iain could use some extra coin for running the errand. The fact that he could read and write was helpful and highly unusual for a servant at his level and he always seemed to be hanging about making himself available. He seemed the logical choice having lived in Edinburgh and with his frequent trips into the city for supplies; he knew the city well and would easily find the address I gave him. I also had him pick the roses for your pillow and leave then outside your chamber door each eve, only when he was away did I do it myself."

Dhariya listened intently absorbing it all in silence.

"As soon as I saw those dead roses in your chamber it merely confirmed that it was indeed Iain," he was saying, "this along with Annie and Dacron having seen him following you. Jeremy Saunders arrived in the midst of it all, and when he realized what was happening, he hastened to tell me the full magnitude of his investigation and the very real suspicion of a killer stalking your family…I nearly went mad with fear."

Dhariya sensed changes in Llyr's body as he spoke, a subtle ripple of tension—a slight tightening muscles; nuances that only one as intimately acquainted with him as she, would be able to detect. The room's warmth from the hearth fire and light peat scent wafting in the air were a welcome comfort amid the icy coldness of stirring memories. Dhariya shivered in Llyr's arms as continued his recounting of all that transpired in the desperate hours following the discovery of her disappearance. He moved his hands briskly over her back, in effort to chase away the chill.

"And well, knowing you were with Iain," Llyr went on saying, "The castle staff had provided a list of six different Inns that Iain had mentioned and was known to stay in. He was speaking in harsh tones now of his own inability to find her for so long. She halted his self-rebuke by turning and pressing her fingers to his lips, telling him how grateful she was that he had found her at all.

"You did not kill Iain, did you Llyr?"

He felt a pain in his heart at the question, though he understood her need to ask it. "No, I didn't." He replied evenly, "as I approached the stable yard of the Inn, the scent of blood was overwhelming, I knew it meant someone lay dead nearby and my heart froze Dhariya, I quickly dismounted and followed the trail. When I saw Iain lying there I thanked God that it was not you, then seeing his throat so savagely slashed, I knew that although you might have been forced to stab him in self-defense, you could never have done such a vicious thing to him. I also sensed you were in even far greater danger than I had suspected. And I was right…" Feeling her shudder in his arms, Llyr held her tighter.

He went on quickly, telling all that had happened here at the townhouse after they arrived and she had lost consciousness. Llyr described the fever. About Ffyonna coming at his behest and bringing along her niece, about the fears they had all had—both spoken and unspoken. His voice shook with emotion as he recalled all the hours of waiting, not knowing if she would live or die. "You were never left alone. We all sat with you by turns." Llyr said.

"I vaguely recall hearing Ffyonna sing…yet I well remember the sound of your voice Llyr. It was so very soothing and comforting to me in that strange place where I dwelt all during that time."

She was still curled into him, with her head resting against his chest once again. He continued to stroke her back as he spoke. "It's been such a nightmare Dhariya, every moment since you bared your door to me and then left without a word." She said nothing to this. She realized she was not yet ready to talk about the rest of it. It was still far too raw to be digging around in and she was already exhausted from everything they had just spoken of. Dhariya truly appreciated everything he had done, his gentle tender care of her. The way he had made love to her the other night. She felt her own eyes burn at the magnitude of emotion that existed between them. It had only intensified even as it had altered and become something quite different. She was too afraid to examine what exactly it had now become. The time would come for that soon enough as well.

Nor did she want to drive a wedge into this closeness of the moment. There was too much to say and not enough words to adequately express her gratitude, yet she needed him to know as much as he needed to hear it. She could hear the tears in his voice and she wanted to comfort him. She turned and her arms came around him, then in the same small voice she said, "Thank you Llyr… Not only for saving my life, but also for telling me the truth if it."

Llyr seemed to divine all she was feeling and all she did not say; he hugged her tighter to him, mindful of her injured shoulder. It was going to take a long time for her inner scars to heal but she was doing remarkably well, he would not rush her, even he himself was totally overwhelmed, making words difficult. "Oh Dhariya," was all he was able to say, as he placed another kiss to the silky crown of her head.

"You don't look anything like the myths describe." Dhariya's voice cut into the room's stillness, drawing Llyr's attention from the book he was reading by the fire.

How long had she been awake? He wondered. He had been so immersed in the pages he had not felt her eyes upon him. She had slept a great deal again, in the days following their last intense discussion of her rescue. Yet he now sensed she had been watching him for quite a while.

Putting the book aside, he turned to face her and to face all that still stood between them. "Through the fallacy of myth any number of misconceptions came to be." He said as he arose and came toward her." Though most are based on some form of truth, they tend to evolve into something quite different over time."

Then, there was only silence as he crossed the room and sat in the chair next to her—facing her. His hair was loose, he was wearing riding boots, fitted black breeches, and {a rarity} a white shirt open at the neck. Yet even though he was so casually attired it made her all too aware that she was quite naked beneath the bed covers, which made her feel all the more vulnerable in their present circumstances, so she drew them closer around her in a defensive gesture.

She could not help but notice that, dressed as he was, he looked just like the night she had come to speak with him and found him in the Skara Brae Castle's drawing room, the night they had first dined together, now almost a year ago—yet it seemed more like a million with all that had happened since. Her heart clenched at the memory.

Could one's soul tear apart and bleed, until it spilled what was left of itself away entirely? Leaving only the painful torn edges of what it once had been? It seemed that's what was happening to both of them now, as they tried to fight their way through this huge obstacle between them.

Had Llyr been right when he said he was still the same person he had been before? She asked herself again for at least the thousandth time. *Was it indeed just her knowledge of him that was different?*

Why should knowing something about a person change everything? Yet the truth was it did not alter the other person at all. It was the one who had found out their secret that was altered, with the shattering of all their previous perceptions, the crumbling of all their own false beliefs. Could the pieces ever possibly be put back together in a manner that resembled what had once been? Could gaining understanding justify all that was now damaged? Of course it all depended upon what that truth was and how it impacted.

Similar questions plagued both of their minds. While only the fullness of time would bring the telling of the tale to its ultimate closure, one way or the other. In the interim all they had was the moment, which lay before them and the slim hope of bridging the distance by talking their way across the chasm.

"Tell me it's not real." Dhariya finally said the words she longed to have confirmed and in a voice trembling with emotion. "Please tell me that what I saw was merely an illusion, a deception of shadows, amid a single flame of light."

Llyr could but stare back at her. How could he possibly respond to that? What she had just said was so close to the truth, so completely accurate. Yet not in any way close to what she so dearly wished to hear—to believe.

With his elbows resting on his knees, his fingers locked together and twisting tightly against each other in his torment—he looked away from her and down to the dark wooden floor between his booted feet. Strangely aware of the grain-pattern and gleaming polished oak surface in the firelight—his answer when it finally came was brief and softly spoken. "Would that I could." was all he could manage, still unable to meet her gaze.

"Though I've seen the evidence with my own eyes," she said, a little more composed now, "it's so difficult for me to accept that…that what you are is even real. We've all grown up with the spooky tales of other-worldly creatures yet no one believes them as truth. How can this be? I try to envision…I mean…when you must feed— …"

"Don't!" He broke in more sharply than intended, then his voice gentled again. "Dhariya please do not…I myself cannot even bear the idea. Let us not bring all of that side into this. There is no place for it here. It is better left in the darkness where it belongs"

"Yes, you're right. I think it's best that I not know…certain things."

"One thing I *do* want you to know however is that even with this cursed existence, I've never before taken a life other than Dreshem, and rightly or wrongly I have no regret for sending his miserable soul to hell. But killing is completely unnecessary even for my kind to sustain ourselves or fulfill our needs, though it is not easily accomplished. Still, I have vowed never to add that sin to all my many others. As I said the only exception is Dreshem, and I killed him for totally different reasons."

"I see. I am relieved to know that Llyr."

"I thank you for allowing me say these things to you. I ask nothing more of you than the time needed to talk all of this through, let it take us where it will. I know that I'm asking a lot but"

"No Llyr, you're not asking anything more than what is fair; I know this isn't easy for you either. I ran away when I should have stayed and listened to what you wanted to tell me…the truth is that I really *do* need to know. It's important, more important I think than either of us realize."

"Yes."

"Tell me then."

He was still staring down at the floor as he spoke, "Can you imagine Dhariya, what it's like to be utterly dependent upon another for your elemental survival? To be powerless against this need while despising it and despising yourself for not being able to resist it?"

"No" came the whispered reply.

"I watched helplessly," he continued, "as my own mortality crumbled around me, leaving only the painful fragmented image of what I'd once been." He sat there, elbows still resting on his knees, head hung low and shoulders slumped. He could not look at her yet, not now as he revealed these horrid truths about himself. The thing he could not bear above all others was to look at her and see pity in her eyes as she looked back at him. Even loathing was more bearable than pity.

He just wanted her to understand, if only a little, and sought to make that so. "I have literally become a slave, bound by the limitations of being inhuman amongst humanity, faced with the despicable necessity that my survival entails, moving through the world though no longer a part of it, near enough to be teased by all that is no longer possible for one such as I—" He stopped drawing a deep ragged breath.

"Bloody hell," Llyr said a moment later in what should've been a shout, yet was all the more powerful because it was not "Do you think I wanted this-this curse? Though the whole of it is an intricately woven tangle of complications, and in all truth it is something that one, indeed draws to them."

He raked his fingers through his hair. "You see, a person's everyday choices made simple enough at the time, eventually come together like pieces of a puzzle, thus revealing the image of what they ultimately become. And so when the time came for me, the image I'd created by the decisions I'd made over the years, piece by piece, was all too clear." He drew in another harsh breath.

"I had no further choices then for the dye was cast and so too my fate. Now I am as one enslaved. It is a condition of the body. I am as powerless against it as one who must endure an illness that has no cure."

"Yet you're not the pale gaunt creature one expects. You can eat, drink, make love…How is it you seem so…so human?"

"Strangely the real answer to this question I've only just recently realized myself… and it was you Dhariya who showed it to me."

"Me?"

"Yes, for I learned that humanness is also merely a condition, having little to do with being mortal or immortal. Any being in existence can become as cold as ice if they no longer possess compassion, empathy and the ability to love. It is the caring heart that warms. I was far less human when I was a mortal man, loving you has shown me the difference."

He still could not meet her eyes, "There are also other reasons, other circumstances. You see some people wouldn't feel any coldness because we do not wish it. There are certain things that can be done to insure this, if we so choose. Mostly though, in your case, it's because of your own light Dhariya and the light that you believe is yet within me. Thus, it is your own reflection which influences your experience of what we are. This is why we can appear different to different viewers. It all depends upon each individual consciousness as does most things in life.

Dhariya remained quiet, trying to absorb the complexities of his world—his existence—of all he was trying to tell her. She had wondered so often about him, well now here it was. She was indeed learning about him, learning far more than she had ever imagined possible of anyone.

"As for the rest" He was saying, "most humans don't have any idea that there are various different species of vampyres," he explained to her "just as there are in any species of the animal kingdom. Some vampyres are barely even human and they evolve upward in various levels from there. I am of the highest order, which also explains my ability to appear among mortals as one of their own kind.

He was tending to ramble he realized, yet he could not stop himself. He wanted this all over and done with as soon as possible. Whatever the consequences, he wanted to face them now. All of the waiting had been tearing him to ribbons inside. "Not all vampyres can partake of mortal pleasures, such as eating, drinking and love making" he went on, "since I was born to darkness by the most ancient blood, I am strong enough to withstand the extreme contrasts of human pleasure and vampyre body and shall soon become a Master Vampyre once my transformation is fully complete."

He then told her that because his human bloodlines descended from one of the great Celtic warrior races, he had inherited the large proportions of a warrior's body passed down from his father. He had been able to retain this bulk because of his ability to eat regular food, thus fortifying the tissues and keeping the human elements of his body in working order. While his skin tone, which came through his mother's ancestors, had always been naturally swarthy, therefore, he would never look pale and gaunt as one might expect

Now, bent on his course he went on to more profound truths, both past and present. "During the long months of my solitude—before you came—I spent countless hours in the library. Studying all I could. Trying to understand what had befallen me. As time passed and the initial bitterness eased, I came to learn that there is indeed wisdom and truth at the basis of Holy Scripture, which is meant to guide our way—if we but listen and heed." He went on from there, explaining to Dhariya that there were good reasons for lessons such as 'do unto others as you would have done unto you' and 'as you sow so then shall you reap.' He himself was the proof of it, he told her, and again said that this existence he must endure was that of his own making.

He explained that ignorant though he was of this fact as a mortal, if he had been following the right ways of life he would not be cursed to darkness. Instead, the human person he had been was cruel and self-serving. Giving no thought anyone else that may have been hurt in pursuit of his own gain, strangely enough it was only this dark curse that initially brought about other changes in him, causing him to begin to think differently about consequences of actions.

"I cannot tell you the whole of it but I can say that through my actions and the choices I'd made in my life... I indeed drew this dark fate unto myself. 'As you sow, so shall you reap,'" he quoted again. "It seems this is a natural law which exists all around us, and there are certain rules that must be followed to maintain this ordinance." She was watching intently, taking in his every word.

Then he finally turned to her, relieved to find no evidence of pity in her expression, just a deep caring that both heartened him and cut him unto the core. "You once said you believed there was a purpose to everything in existence—tell me do you still believe that to be true Dhariya?"

Dhariya sat before Llyr now trying to find the right response.

Llyr was going through his own hell. The waiting was agony. He looked away back down at the floor. The moments crawled by in painfully slow increments, while the silence hung dark and heavy in the sandalwood scented air. If she touched him he would know all by the unspoken gesture, it had always been so between them. Though their relationship had been riddled with secrets from the beginning, strangely, there had also been absolute honesty in the emotions that bound them so tightly to one another. And the depth of their feelings was more than most would ever experience, combining all their relationships of a single lifetime, let alone with one single person.

As she had listened to his words, seeing the anguish he was so clearly going through—she was acutely aware of an unbearable pain relentlessly stabbing at her which had nothing to do with the wound in her shoulder. In spite of it all, she knew with absolute certainty that some things definitely had not changed.

Unbidden her hand reached over to him and seemed to hover in the air.

Finally her hand touched his and he knew her answer even before she spoke. He looked at her—something shifted in her eyes as she met his gaze evenly. She gave his hand a little tug and he eased himself from the chair to the bedside facing her. Then she said," "I still love you Llyr. That has never changed. I don't know where it will lead us if anywhere at all. But I can't deny my feelings any longer. Kiss me"

Llyr was taken aback; he knew when she touched him that her heart and mind were turning his way, yet he had not quite expected this. He bent his head and took her mouth tenderly and completely. It seemed forever since he had tasted her sweetness and he had thought perhaps he never would again. Now here she was, her mouth open beneath his, their tongues twirling and entwining in their own intimate dance.

Though they both hungered, the kiss was one of gentleness and savoring, of total love and joyous reunion. Those silken bonds they had forged between them, now hummed and fluttered with renewed life, as they secured their hold upon the lovers, drawing them and further uniting them as one.

When their lips finally parted moments later, they kept hold of each other's hands. It was Dhariya who spoke first. "Now as to your question—"

"Question?" It took Llyr a few seconds of mind searching to recall exactly what he had asked her.

"—the answer is yes," Dhariya was saying, "I do still believe everything happens for a reason. Though I confess, I have no ready explanation to offer, only a faith that defies understanding—an unwavering belief that all is as it should be—even after what's happened to me and my family. Even after learning your dark secret. I still believe. Perhaps because I have to believe there is a reason for it all. There has to be a greater purpose for everything than merely what we see before us. Nothing means anything or makes any sense otherwise."

"I have to agree with you on that Dhariya."

She smiled. "Oh, I just realized something."

"What's that?"

"It was two days ago that I asked you what the date was. So according to my calculations today is December 25th, Merry Christmas Llyr."

"Merry Christmas my darling"

He kissed her again.

As the days passed Dhariya continued to ask Llyr countless questions, this was understandable to him, although most of these enquiries about his dark curse were near impossible to fully express with words. Not only because of what it cost him to delve deeply into his own pain and the hating of it {he'd have paid any price, no matter how painful to ease Dhariya's fears} but also because he lacked the vocabulary. So he did his best to be as honest and forthright as he could—as she deserved. Through loving her and nearly losing her to death, Llyr had been forced to look even further within, into such previously uncharted parts of his own soul that he had still could not totally believe such depths existed within him—thus uncovering different facets to his nature long ago buried—those which made him a better person even now. Somehow she had allowed him to glimpse possibilities within him—heretofore unknown to him.

He realized what he had needed was someone who could understand the full magnitude of his pain and Dhariya did. Whether she had known it or not, from the very first she somehow understood even before he himself had. Her love had eased his way and allowed him to finally gain the courage to face all he had locked away inside of him all those years ago.

But these new facets he had discovered about himself were indeed a double edged sword, for they were also characteristics that would make the endurance of his dark existence—difficult though it was before—now nearly impossible to bear. The last thing he needed to acquire was this full clarity of conscience, which only served to intensify the loathing he had for what he was. Llyr could only hope Dhariya was right and there truly was a meaning and purpose to his existence. Then perhaps he could find some solace for his tortured soul. While he had to admit that a part of him missed the innocent adoration that had once infused the eyes she had gazed toward him with, however unmerited it was.

Yet if there was no restitution for his soul at least he had been as honest as he could, Dhariya deserved that above all others. Through her he had seen beyond *what* he now was and gained the understanding of *who* he truly was—of all that had brought him to this impasse—to this dark demise that was now his to bear. He had to find whatever peace there was to be had in that and go on from here—and perhaps, as more than just a monster—perhaps, as better person than he had been before.

Absolution

XIV

~ And still, I am drawn by faith, that which sees promise of light even within the depths of darkness ~

...I shall not live out my life in regret becoming a slave unto what might have been or if only. For each moment holds newness of life and unlimited potential ~ of which I shall find renewed courage and freely choose...

Skara Brae Castle ~ *January 1712*

~ *I* must find a way to embrace the unknown, that which lies before me now, for there is nothing else and indeed there never truly has been. Though I was once lulled by illusions of certainty and the false security of outward appearances, yet how easily that façade crumbles away, leaving only a reality that must be faced by a belief in something greater.

Who can ever truly know what the next moment may bring? All that is held dear may suddenly vanish within the blinking of an eye—and a thousand years pass unnoticed. Wise are they who treasure the precious gift of shared moments, for they come but once ...then are gone.

It seems that in spite of everything, he and I remain strangely connected in some profound, yet indefinable way—our lives intertwine like threads in a tapestry. Thus, when all is said and done, those same threads will reveal the picture of what our fate has finally become—an image to be forever etched upon our souls.

Yet where might my life be now if I had purposely plucked a different thread, followed its path down an alternate course? Where then, might it have taken me? I know not, only that there seemed an overwhelming inevitability which led toward this one particular destiny—toward him.

And, as it now appears, there could never have been any other direction.

~ D ~

~ It was late afternoon when the carriage entered the wrought iron gates of Skara Brae. The journey to the castle was far too lengthy and arduous to be undertaken at night, so it had been decided that Katie would accompany Dhariya during the daylight hours. Llyr was to ride out to join her tomorrow evening, giving Dhariya time to rest from the trip.

The weather was clear with the cold bite of frost and winter. Both women were bundle up in wools and furs with hot bricks at their feet. Dhariya's arm hung suspended in a linen cradle that tied around her neck to keep the arm bent and close to her body, ensuring as little mobility as possible while the shoulder mended. It was an added precaution that proved beneficial as the rutted roads jostled the passengers about inside the carriage.

Katie was absorbed in a book of herbals. Though Dhariya did not know how the young woman could possible read a thing with all the jarring about, she was nonetheless glad for her companion's quiet presence, which left her to her own thoughts as she gazed out the window at the passing scenery.

Dhariya was still trying to sort through all that Llyr had disclosed during these past few weeks at his Edinburgh townhome. It had proved to be the most intense interval of time the two had ever shared. From the moment he had carried her into his bedchamber and closed the door Dhariya scarcely saw another living soul—quite literally—save young Katie who checked in on her briefly each day. Otherwise, she and Llyr, for all intents and purposes, were basically locked in that one room together.

Which was perhaps for the best with neither of them being able to escape, they were forced to face the issues at hand. Llyr was with her hour upon hour, remaining by her side, answering endless questions with infinite patience, for as long as the night allowed.

When he had at length told her everything, finally revealing details of the deaths his family and the horrors of what had happened before his eyes, Dhariya had turned to him and embraced him. Then she had lifted her head, looked into his eyes and asked, "Would you, given the choice, rather have died with them?"

"Yes," had come his instant reply, "I would have gladly died with them, rather than have had to endure all the years without them—rather than have had my last memories of them be those of their blood spilling, their screams—and to bear the endless guilt of being too afraid to do anything to even try and stop it."

Shaking his head he had told her, "Sometimes the cost of survival is not worth it." He had closed his eyes then, shutting out the anguished image of himself reflected in the black depths of her pupils, his voice trailing to a breath of sound, "the lifelong pain of wounds that never heal and scars that none can see, nor could they possibly ever understand. It is too much to ask of anyone. But then after so many years of bearing the aloneness came you Dhariya, once your presence graced my life I felt there was indeed a purpose to my living on, you inspired me to dare to see a glimmer of hope on my horizon and to find the dream within myself that was buried in the darkness years ago."

She had lifted her palms to his cradle his anguished face, the soft flesh a warm comfort against his cheeks. She had whispered, "I understand." And she did. Oh how did, for she too had finally told him of her own childhood traumas. They both now had shared each other's pain in sharing the sorrows of their past. Yes, she above all others knew of what he spoke and it made the loneliness of these painful burdens, that each of them carried inside, a little easier to bear. And now she too had her dream restored because of him, even though the darkness remained with it.

After he had shared all of this and told her—as much as possible—the full scope of his dark destiny, he then offered her a choice. Saying that if she asked him to leave her, he would do so without delay and would vow never to return. Even promising to erase all knowledge of him from her memory, if she so wished.

But Dhariya could not do it. She would far rather live with the truth, even if it meant the heart-rending pain of his loss, than have the empty falseness of never having known him or his love at all.

Enduring the chill, Dhariya clung to the leather handhold with her free hand to maintain her balance, as she greedily drew in the sea-scented air and let it out again in white vaporous puffs. *Home at last*, she thought, *how long ago it seemed that I had ridden away in fear.*

As the carriage proceeded down the long winding path toward the castle Lyos and Ellyon came bounding out from the gatehouse, to provide their own brand of escort. Dhariya suddenly felt the old joy returning at the sight of the aging stones looming up ahead of her, the strange veiling of mist that always skirted the castle and never so much as stirred even in the fiercest of gales. She remembered as a child she had believed that Skara Brae floated on a cloud just above the ground. The comforting familiarity was warm and welcome.

Yet the pain of her living nightmare at Dreshem's hands remained with her, tucked away inside yet never out of reach. The wounds of his and Iain's betrayal were carved deep, though she could feel the frail seams of their newly mending edges, their scars would be no less entrenched once the balm of time had eased the rawness. Enough time perhaps could make them endurable.

There was some solace however, in knowing that Dreshem and his lesser pawn were both now dead—their evil buried in the ground along with them—and there it would stay. It had nothing to do with this beloved home of her heart.

Despite the fact Iain had lived and worked here for a time, he was not of this place. Thus the shadow he had cast had gone with him and could not tarnish what went before or what was to follow after.

All the sweet memories came rushing forth to greet her as she came home to them again. The images of her past were there too—Dhariya the small child peeped at her from behind a tree trunk along the drive. While the coltish young girl she had been raced with the carriage until her breath gave out.

Then as they pulled into the stable yard Dhariya the budding young woman strolled past and turned to smiled at the face of this Dhariya—the woman she had become—looking out of the carriage window, before the ghostly image disappeared into the garden. Welcome back to us that smile seemed to say.

This is where all the parts of her had truly flourished; fitting that here is where she must come to gather them together once more. Their presence feels distant yet they are all still with me thought Dhariya—each being an important and integral part of all that she was, of all that she would be. Yes she would be whole again, she told herself. Though she was unsure of who that whole person might be, something inside her believed in it. And it was like a warm melting relief flowing through her. Patience was what was needed—Patience and faith.

Yes, she said to herself again and reaffirmed, in time I shall heal from this into a new completeness of being. 'Nothing happens without a reason,' her father had always said, 'and nothing that happens leaves us as it found us' the rest of his words came unbidden to mind, 'all shall add to who we are in some way, yet the choice as to how is ours to make. Will it add to bitterness or to compassion?'

How many times she and her brother had heard him say this. Her mother and uncle had also echoed similar sentiments often, as this philosophy was one believed in by all the members of her family. Yet somehow her father's way of expression had always had the most impact.

But I am only human papa. Her thoughts said to him now, *and I feel overburdened by my human-ness at this moment and all the moments surrounding it.*

How hard it was not to feel bitterness toward those who had taken so much from her. Much was still to be faced in the days to come, of that Dhariya had little doubt. She had only just begun this journey. Although a great deal of healing had occurred there were demons within her yet to be conquered, some perhaps never would be. Ghosts of the past were not as easily exercised as were the poisons in ones blood or the mending of torn flesh.

The horrors of Dhariya's captivity reached out their tendrils to haunt her during sleep. She could not escape them there. She continued to suffer the ill effects from her tortuous hours spent at the mercy, more accurately lack of mercy, of Dexter Dreshem. The nightmares were all too common. That was when the doubts came and shook her up.

Could she ever get past the pain of it? Or the anger and the rage that often threatened to consume her? Could she ever find something else beyond it, something that would be far less damaging to herself? In truth, she did not know. She could only hope that someday she would, even though it seemed so impossible.

Ffyonna and Urien emerged from the servant's door as the footman helped Dhariya from the carriage. Arms open in welcome they came and ushered her into the warmth of the kitchen. Home, thought Dhariya, it was so good to be home.

After having hot tea by the kitchen fire with the older couple and her traveling companion, Dhariya turned to Katie and asked if she would mind bringing a large bouquet of flowers from the conservatory. To which Katie replied, "I'd be happy to milady.
Thus a short time later, with the blooms nestled between her body and immobile elbow, Dhariya walked out to the family plot.
She entered the quiet sanctuary and stopped to appreciate the solemn beauty. The sculpted angels of white marble, their lifelike figures stood pale and luminous against the dusk shadows. Light amid the darkness, the unbidden thought floated into her mind, though the night may come it changes them not. Nor can its blackness stain their purity. How lovely the thought was.
She felt as if another lifetime had passed since she had last been here and in a way perhaps it had. As her skirts whispered through the rows until she came to the one where her most recent family members rested, she noted there were already posies placed at the base of each headstone, their petals only just beginning to wilt. Someone had kept the up the ritual in her absence. She smiled at that. It was extremely comforting to know of such thoughtfulness.
She set her flowers beside the others and offered her prayers.
It was time to face all the shadows; all the dark corners within her must be swept clean.

———

Later Dhariya stood in the doorway of her mother's castle chambers. The chambers they had once all shared as a family, a lifetime long ago. It was one of the largest suites at Skara Brae. It was also one of the most lavish.

Dhariya had not come here since her mother's death, she had been purposely avoiding it. Now she felt compelled to be here. Closing the door she walked forward into the vast sitting room. How strange that the candles had all been lit against the night.

She placed the single flame she carried on the nearby tabletop and looked around her. Taking in the loveliness, the pale green damask of walls and furnishings, the matching thick Turkish carpets and tapestries, which were all obviously regularly maintained by the castle's cleaning staff.

Vases of fresh flowers adorned the mantle and numerous other tables. The smoldering pile of glowing embers in the hearth kept the extreme winter cold and musty dampness at bay. A family portrait hung above the vast hearth—painted when she was still an infant upon her mother's knee and DJ only a small boy, though thinking himself to be a man as he emulated their father's pose.

The faces looked out from the canvas so full of life, with the expectancy of so much future to share together. Her heart squeezed inside her chest. This too is love she had learned; this pain of its loss—was as much a part of it as its joy. She wiped her wet cheeks with her fingertips and turned to survey the rest of her surroundings.

Everything appeared exactly as it always had. Only the feeling of absolute emptiness told the truth of these chambers. She moved slowly through each room allowing the bittersweet memories to come as they would, as they did. There were so many.

Here was the bedchamber she had recovered in after … after the horrors of the deaths of her father and brother…and all that had happened to her… and there, the chair either Ffyonna or her mother had sat in by the hour, until their small patient was deemed safely out of physical danger. In time

Dhariya had indeed recovered here beneath their diligent loving care.

Her brother's chamber was exactly same as when he had last slept in this bed. His books still lined the shelves, all dusted and tidy. His desk and quill sat at the ready—As if awaiting his return at any moment.

Her parent's huge bed sat upon its dais, with its dark intricately carved frame and emerald cut velvet curtains and coverlet. She hugged one of the massive bedposts. How often she had heard her mother weeping at night in this chamber, after the tragedy on the docks.

When her child's body had finally gained enough strength, Dhariya the little girl would climb into this big bed and she and her mother would hold each other close, each weeping their own tears, feeling their own losses, while sharing the sorrow. They had both lost so much. Yet only now did Dhariya the woman, truly understand all that her mother was mourning during those dark lonely hours.

Then Dhariya thought of Llyr. He had lost his entire family at only nine years of age. Had in fact bore witness to the savage slayings, heard their screams and those of so many others. She could not imagine what that does to a child. He had said that was when the shadows first seized him. With no parent left to guide him, only a man he had been sent to live with afterward. A man he had never set eyes on before, distant eccentric uncle of wealth and title—who had immediately sent him off to boarding school—alone.

Did she have any right to judge him or any other for that matter? Dhariya asked herself. She had always thought herself to be an accepting and forgiving person. She had since learned different. She could not find forgiveness in her heart for the deliberate cruelty of Dreshem and Iain; she did not think she could ever rise far enough above the pain to allow for that.

Yet she loved Llyr. She could not deny that, despite what she had learned of him and all the fear and uncertainty this knowledge brought her. She now understood the full magnitude of this kind of love infused with passion.

She also knew the pain, which was an integral part of loving in such a way. But she did not want to feel that pain, that desperation at the thought of losing him, did not want to need him so that it was an endless ache inside of her. All of these were true however, and she was powerless against them. And even now she could not walk away from him.

Next eve Llyr and Dhariya lay atop the massive tester bed in his castle chambers. It had been another tiring day for Dhariya. Llyr himself had only just arrived a short while ago to find her awaiting him in his chambers. Now, comfortably garbed in their robes, they sipped wine and nibbled a light fare from a basket between them.

Enjoying this simple feast together, surrounded by lush deep burgundy tones of velvet bed hangings and the rich complimentary furnishings, enhancing the warm candlelit ambiance of the room about them, this was their own private celebration—so much having finally been resolved and the sense of relief was clearly reflected in both their expressions.

Llyr began hesitantly, not wanting to darken the mood, "Jeremy Saunders stopped by my town-home with news yester-eve. He told me that in the search of Dreshem's office and residence they had found numerous books where he had written out all of his activities, various plots and the like. You were right about his true feelings toward your father, seems Dreshem had detailed it all quite clearly."

Llyr took a moment to carefully observe Dhariya's reaction. Then, at her continued silence, he went on, anxious to get this all out of the way so they could finally put it behind them "Dreshem was quite proud of himself and his deeds, avidly admitted to all of it, also naming Iain as his accomplice. It seems that through Iain, Dreshem renewed his scheme of vengeance and carried out much of his plot. Saunders had Dreshem's final pages with him and I read them firsthand."

He then told her that Dreshem's notes also included such details as to the night Iain struck Dhariya over the head. Iain had in fact, arrived early from his errands in town and hid out somewhere in the castle so he would not be seen. "I didn't know about those first dead roses…you never told me about them Dhariya." He waited for her response to this.

"No I didn't, initially because I suspected you at that time. Then later with so much else was going on I simply forgot. It all makes sense now though." Dhariya replied, not meeting his gaze. "What else did Jeremy Saunders say?"

"His writings basically confirmed everything you said. That Dreshem's intent was to drive you out from safety and into his trap."

Dhariya shivered at the horrid thought and the unwanted images it evoked.

"Saunders has added these journals to his other stock pile in his offices," Llyr was saying "they've amassed a great deal of evidence. Boxes of files, a compiling of all the documented details gathered by investigators, which corroborated Dreshem's written notes which amount to a confession and also contained proof of Iain's actions and his involvement in the townhouse fire. Saunders is keeping everything on file, you can see this all for yourself at any time. "The investigation was extensive and thorough, according to the reports it seems Iain himself had been driving your mother's carriage the day it veered off the roadway, killing her."

Dhariya made no comment to any of this news. She had not known that Iain was driving the carriage when her mother died, but she was not really surprised by this news.

Llyr paused for sip of wine, watching her closely for any response, while she stared straight ahead. He specifically noted the way she had become unusually placid, and remained so all during his explanation. Her eyes fixed steadily, upon the flames in the hearth. So much trauma and too many shocking revelations, heaped one upon the other, had definitely taken its toll upon her spirit. Llyr hated seeing her this way, yet he knew she would rally—she was made of some strong stuff, his Dhariya—so much stronger than he himself ever would be. He then recalled Ffyonna saying Dhariya had the strongest spirit that she had ever known and he now knew just how true that was.

"I'm sorry to be bringing all of this about Dreshem up again and talk of Iain's betrayal, my darling, Lord knows you've had more than enough of each. But I won't keep it from you. You have a right to know all of it before it can be put to rest."

"It's all right Llyr. I must know all of it." She turned back to him seeming more herself now. "It's just so difficult to accept that Iain, a trusted member of our household staff was capable of such treachery and utter brutality, not to mention Dreshem, someone my father had loved like a brother."

"Iain was a weak pawn to be played by Dreshem's evil hand." Llyr said.

"Yes. Yet what Iain did to Josey was his own evil and is just as horrific if not more so than what Dresham has done."

"Yes it was." Llyr concurred. Recalling how sickened he himself had been upon learning the details of what Iain had done to his wife and the life she had carried within her. "No doubt Josey will not be grieving over her husband's loss."

Dhariya had of course been told the truth about her young maidservant and dear friend—shortly after she had regained consciousness she had suddenly turned to Llyr as if just remembering—and posed the question he had been dreading. "What of Josey? Is-is there any word? "Llyr had vowed to himself that when the time came, he would not lie to her about it, and he did not. Sitting down facing her he told her, as gently as possible, all that had happened to her dear friend. Fortunately Ffyonna had sent a message earlier that very day to say Josey was finally out of danger and would be transported to Skara Brae for the remainder of her recovery. So Llyr had been grateful to be able to reassure Dhariya by telling her this latest piece of good news and Dhariya, upon hearing of Josey's returning to Skara Brae, had insisted that her dear friend be given one of large lavish guest suites, feeling the beautiful surroundings would help in the healing process.

Dhariya's thoughts now turned to her visit with Josey earlier that afternoon. Upon entering the bedchamber she had been shocked by what she saw and realized why Ffyonna had refused all previous requests for the visit despite Dhariya's angry insistence. Llyr had backed up the older woman's stance, which had only infuriated Dhariya further. Though she had been kept apprized of her young maid's condition, she scarcely recognized the pale fragile figure dwarfed by the massive bed, as she had sat down on the edge of it facing its occupant.

Their reunion had been an overwhelming and emotional one. Josey's eyes held the painful memories that would always be there now. Dhariya's eyes too held the scars of her own suffering. They were both forever changed by it all.

"The babe was Bryden's." Josey had confessed in a weak wavering voice, unable to look Dhariya in the eye.

"I thought perhaps it could be."

"Yes. Iain and I…well we hadn't been intimate for some time. He knew it couldn't be his." Josey's eyes were huge brown orbs amid the thin whiteness of her face, as she turned and looked into Dhariya's, "Bryden told me you'd spoken to him…that you knew of us." The young maid's tears welled and spilled over. "And Ffyonna told me something of what you went through," her voice broke, "I-I'm so s-sorry for everything."

"Do not blame yourself." Dhariya wiped away the tears that fell freely down her friend's hollow cheeks, feeling her own tears prickling and blurring her vision. "You cannot possibly hold yourself accountable for Iain's actions."

"But if I hadn't married him—"

"Hush now." Dhariya cut in. "We'll have none of that. If Dreshem had not met up with Iain then, there would've been someone else willing enough. When those kinds of people are determined to a certain end, they'll always find a way. Besides

I'm all right now as you can see, so too are you and that's all that matters" She reassured her friend, feeling the wetness spilling down her own cheeks.

The two women hugged, each sharing the other's heartrending grief. How strange thought Dhariya, that these bonds forged in pain are so much more binding than those of shared joy—stroking her friend's back soothingly, noting the sharp knobby ridges of protruding bones beneath her palm, the reality of how close they had both came to death was fresh and frightening upon her.

"Ffyonna says they'll be other babes in time." Dhariya said gently, as she eased Josey's back against the mountain of pillows "And that's something wonderful to look forward to."

Josey nodded.

Dhariya managed a smile with no small effort, ignoring the stab of loss that she herself would never know the joy of creating life within her own body, or the emotions that only a mother feels watching the child of her blood develop and grow. Dhariya thought again of unhealed wounds, invisible scars and the high price of survival.

Josey closed her eyes looking utterly exhausted. "Take your rest now." Dhariya whispered, "I'll come again tomorrow. Leaning over she kissed Josey's forehead, then tucked the quilts around the waif-like form that was barely discernable under the bedclothes, feeling a sudden wave of weariness flooding through her own limbs, as she left the darkened chamber.

"No," said Dhariya, bringing her thoughts back to the present, "Josey isn't grieving in that way. But she's bereaved to the depths of her soul over the babe and her heart bears the heavy burden of guilt."

Dhariya sipped her wined then continued, "I feel so terrible for her Llyr, she keeps bursting into tears, saying if only she hadn't married Iain and brought him into our home, none of this would have happened. Nothing I say seems to help. I tried telling her she's not to blame, that even without Iain, a man like Dreshem would've found someone else to aid him."

"That's all too true, " Llyr replied, "unfortunately men of Iain's ilk are far too common ...Well, at least from what you've told me your pretty young maid won't be lacking for company once she's fully recovered. Bryden will no doubt offer her a comforting shoulder and Josey will be able to move forward with her life. At least Bryden does seem to be a decent and caring man."

"Yes he is and he scarcely leaves her side." she said with a smile as she thought of the all hours Llyr had stayed with her during her own recovery. Their eyes met and she knew instinctively that he thinking of the same thing.

He reached over and cradled her cheek with his palm. "Then he must truly love her greatly to show such devotion," he said with the utmost meaning.

She cupped his hand with her own and drew it to her lips. Closing her eyes, she placed a kiss to the center of his palm, just as he had once done to hers. After a moment she opened her eyes and dropped their linked fingers into her lap.

"Llyr," she said softly, "I know now how very wrong I was about everything. I should've told you right away about the threatening letters to my mother and all the rest of Jeremy Saunders' disclosures, as well as the things that were happening to me here at the castle. I too am guilty of not being honest in that regard."

Meeting his gaze evenly she tried to explain further. "But you see, I thought so much about it all when I wasn't with you, that my only escape came from you and our shared passion, nor did I wish anything to tarnish our time together. You understand that don't you?"

"How could I not understand? However, the harsh error of keeping secrets has proved itself with vengeance to us both. All we have now is hindsight, a valuable asset when one is willing to view it honestly. We've both learned a great deal through all of this. There will always be things we cannot change. Yet how we face these dragons remains the ultimate challenge. Such are life's lessons; those that are hard learned are well learned and not easily forgotten."

They lifted their goblets in a salute to these words.

"Speaking of honesty Llyr," Dhariya continued somewhat uneasily. "You know that I love and accept you in spite of everything. Yet I still have so many questions."

"Of course you do."

"Something that's been puzzling me for a long time is, how was it you were near enough to rescue me that night of the fire?"

"Well now Dhariya that involves a confession of sorts, on my part." His reply held a teasing note.

"It does?"

"Yes. You see from the moment I first saw you, I could not stop thinking about you." Reaching over, he traced the satin slope of her cheek with the backs of his fingers, while his gaze captured hers, "and in the dark hours before dawn, I'd find myself outside your town home staring longingly up at your window."

His expression now turning serious, "That particular night I was just about to turn Taranis toward your town-home when I sensed you were in danger, thus, I hastened there at once to secure your safety. Thankfully I was in time."

"But how did you manage to get to me on the second floor, from what I've heard, the entire main level was engulfed before anyone arrived?"

"Well... my ...otherworldly abilities, few though they be, amount to little more than trickery plied upon the weak minded. There is one particular technique, however, which is quite real and enables me to take to the air.

"To fly?" she asked with undisguised awe.

He nodded. "This is how I gained access to the second story window off the back alley." He replied truthfully.

"That is really quite amazing."

"I suppose it seems that way. However, if human beings developed their own consciousness and the full use of their own minds, what I do would seem as child's play, for the latent potential you and your mortal brethren carry within you is truly unlimited and without bounds.

"How can you possibly know this Llyr?"

"It's another of these oddities of a vampyre, or at least one who is of the higher order like I myself am. You see we've been given knowledge of things not yet discovered, of things yet to come. I believe it's also part our curse because we are left without the ability to use this knowledge and fore-vision to better or benefit ourselves. Like silent observers of the truth."

"How long have you been…a vampyre?"

"Not long. It happened the night before I met you in fact." He gave a brittle laugh, "the irony is if this hadn't happened to me, I never would have been at Skara Brae and never would have met you."

He paused for a moment unsure of how to proceed. "Dhariya, my fate is much more involved than what you now know… it's difficult to explain …but what I must do bears great responsibility and it is, in actuality an important component in the natural balance of these very laws of nature that I've spoken to you of."

"And it's dangerous." It was not a question.

"Yes. You see I'm to fulfill an extremely important role in the whole scheme of things, which will ultimately have great bearing on this delicate balance, for I've been chosen to succeed the one who went before me—"

"My God—" Dhariya broke into his words with a shocked gasp of understanding, and raising a trembling hand to cover her heart. She looked into his eyes and whispered "Uncle Tamas, he is the one… the one that you succeed, isn't he?"

Llyr could but stare at her dumbfounded. She turned away, looking off in the distance. "Of course, it all begins to make sense now," she was saying, her voice sounding dazed even to her own ears, "I-I'd forgotten the whispers and rumors I'd heard as a child. No, in truth I-I'd pushed them away, thinking they were only the cruel taunts of other children…and not wanting to believe them…"

Dhariya turned back to him then. Meeting his gaze, "Llyr you must tell me everything now, after all this darkness surrounds me, it's only fair that I should know. How did you and my uncle ever come to this?"

He paused again in thought, this was completely unexpected—her deciphering Tamas' true role, and although he had already told her much, there were still limits to what he could reveal, for her own safety if nothing else—it was so difficult yet of the utmost importance that he find the right words.

"First you must know that he, your uncle, bade me to never tell you and I vowed it would be so." Llyr told her, "But since you've discovered for yourself I cannot lie to you…as you said you do have a right to know…" Sighing deeply, unable to meet her eyes, he stared unseeing at the hearth fire, looking beyond the flames, into the past where the nightmare became reality.

"As I said it happened the night before I first saw you," he began, "in the forest surrounding this castle, though some distance from here." His voice had taken on a sort of trance like cadence now, as if he had returned to the forest, to that night and was no longer in the in the room with her. He told her the beginnings, how Tamas had chosen him so that, he the oldest Master Vampre, could finally take his eternal rest.

"Wait a moment." She said. "Do you mean that Uncle Tamas has gone and I'm never to see him again?" Dhariya's voice wavered, tears gathered in her eyes, glistening like jewels in the candle flame and firelight. "He never told me it was truly goodbye."

Llyr was torn, he was angry with Tamas for putting him in this position. Then again Tamas had not expected Dhariya to find out about all of it, which was one of the main reasons he had forbid the intimacy between his niece and his successor, knowing how easily the truth could come to light if they were lovers.

Llyr wouldn't lie to her now, yet how could he tell her that Tamas indeed meant to disappear forever? "Dhariya, listen to me. I know he has gone, perhaps for quite a long duration, to rest you see. He told me he was weary and needed time away—"

"Why did he not tell me he must go off to rest himself? I would've understood—"

"Come now Dhariya, think of it, how could he tell you? He would never have been able to confess the truth of it to you. And you would not have truly understood his need to leave, to be somewhere far away from you."

"Yes." She whispered. "I suppose you're right about that. Yet I feel so betrayed, so utterly betrayed by everyone. To have so much kept from me especially by those who mean the most, that they could not trust me…I feel like so much of my life was not even real and all the memories of uncle were only a lie." She bowed her head, unable to hold back the tears.

Llyr rose and went right around the bed to her to where she had turned away from him, then he picked her up lifted her into his lap, as he had done so often during this time of disclosure and confession. Holding her again now as she cried out this new pain. He had come to know that tear stained face very well of late. And even then she was still the most beautiful woman he had ever seen, if only he could spare her all of this sorrow.

"You feel that way because you're hurting so much right now my darling. There've been too many hurts one upon another and they're still far too fresh to allow you to clearly understand. Yet one thing I know for certain, if there is any part of Tamas' existence that was and is real, it is his love for you Dhariya. Nothing will ever change that."

Dhariya was still weeping against his chest and did not reply. Yet Llyr knew his words had helped, he only wished he could do more to ease her pain. She felt very fragile in his arms, so thin from the fever and the little amounts of food she managed to swallow at his insistence. He hoped it wasn't too early in her recovery for these new heart rending disclosures, but when she asked him straight out he knew he had to tell her. He would not add to her sense of betrayal by lying to her.

Even as he stroked her back in a soothing motion, Llyr was thinking that the ancient vampyre might be returning yet and sooner rather than later. And Llyr suspected this great love that Tamas bore his niece, would be the very thing that would draw him.

Llyr clearly recalled the night of their parting. *You can contact me at anytime through your thoughts,* the older vampyre had said, *I can advise you if necessary with any difficulties that may arise,* then the clear colorless eyes had pierced Llyr to the core, *I can also focus in on your thoughts at any time, even when I am at rest,* Tamas had continued his voiced chilled to ice, *So I now warn you again to stay away from Dhariya as you've foresworn. If you break this vow I will know.*

Llyr shivered despite the warmth of the crackling fire. He had indeed broken that vow. Thus he had not made any attempt to contact Tamas, but then neither had the old vampyre made any contact with him. And Llyr found that silence more frightening that anything Tamas might have to say to him.

Tamas had long since departed to make his last and final visitation to the major vampyre dwellings, *they're hidden of course,* he had said, *most of our kind cohabitate together in rather large groups or clans if you will. Very few have the courage to stay alone for it is far too difficult, as you well know.*

Once these rounds were completed Tamas would seek his eternal rest or so he had planned at the time. He had gone on to explain to Llyr that this rest was a special kind of trance that a vampyre can put himself under, so as not waken when twilight calls, but sleep on through. This trance-like sleep was only possible to induce on one specific night every two years. Only for that single night, could a vampyre either go into this trance or come out of it and rise again.

Tamas had gone on to tell him—as another form of warning—that even while under this trance, a vampyre of strong blood has an internal sense that would allow him to know when that two year doorway was near to opening again, thus offering a choice of whether to stay or go back into the world once again.

Llyr knew that doorway had opened and closed some months passed. Either Tamas had decided to wait another two years before his ultimate departure, and thus, would make his way here soon or he was now slumbering on—or perhaps he was lying in trance waiting to rise again in two years time, but he would definitely be back to seek his retribution of that Llyr was certain—for one did not break their word to a Master Vampyer.

"From as far back as I can recall," Dhariya, having now spent her tears, was saying, "Uncle Tamas had been going off on one venture or another." She sniffled into the handkerchief that Llyr kept ever at the ready, "he'd be away for a least a year. Once I was old enough to realize I thought it was because he was surely very lonely and needed to get away from the vastness of this empty castle."

How typical of Dhariya, thought Llyr, *that she would look beyond the surface, to astutely assess her uncle on a deeper level, that of his emotional need.*

"In the past, however," she went on, "he always spoke of his plans before hand; though it was obviously a fabrication, at least he gave an accurate indication of his return.

"When he came back he'd send word and ask us to come for an extended stay at Skara Brae. Thus my family, or if my father was not able to leave his duties my mother would stay with him, and just my brother and I along with our nanny Mary Anne Mackenzie, would bundle ourselves into the traveling carriage, packed full with all of the necessities and make our way to the castle.

"My brother DJ, that's what we called him instead of the full Darrien Jr., so DJ and I would be excited speculating on the stories he would tell of his adventures and what he might have brought for us—for he always lavished numerous exotic gifts upon us. Since he had no children of his own we were always spoiled when we were young. After my brother died Uncle became extremely protective of me. She heaved a heavy sigh, "Dear heaven I've never cried so much in my entire life as I have these past weeks."

"You needed to rid yourself of all the emotions and pain Dhariya," he said as he reached over and refilled their wine goblets, "it's extremely damaging to oneself to keep them buried within, I above all others know the consequences of not facing one's feelings and allowing them to be expressed, even if only acknowledged to oneself."

"Yes, I've always kept a journal precisely for that purpose."

"Very wise my darling."

They both sipped their wine, then Llyr turned to her saying, "Dhariya, there is a chance your uncle may return."

"Truly?" She brightened a little, her huge eyes looking at him held a glimmer of hope.

"Yes, you see…the truth is that he forbade me to…to get involved with you in any way. I gave him my word I would not. Now that I've betrayed him Dhariya, as you well know, I expect his wrath will bring him back for vengeance upon me."

"But that isn't fair, it was not your fault. I came to you because I wanted to. Protective or not he hasn't the right to interfere that way. I'm a woman grown now, I must make my own choices and face the consequences whatever they maybe."

"Indeed and so must I." Llyr cringed inwardly at the thought.

"I just thought of something else Llyr…If Lord Tamas is this ancient one you speak of, how then can he be my uncle? How then can he be my mother's brother?

"I don't know the answer to either question Dhariya. I only know what he told me when I went to him asked who you were. His exact words were *'she is my niece'* that's what he told me. When I pressed him further all he would say was *'the tie is a long way back, but we are indeed blood relations.'* Of course it makes no sense. Yet I thought nothing of it at the time so I questioned him no more. I'm sorry I can't answer this for you my darling."

They both knew then that they would have to accept this for with Tamas gone, there was no way to find out the truth of it all.

At last the strain of the past months had started to ease. Despite all the strangeness the discovery of both Llyr and Tamas' dark secrets, had brought with it, there was now also a new closeness between Dhariya and Llyr—that of honesty and shared truths.

As Dhariya began to understand the jeopardy she placed herself in with their every intimate encounter and the enormous demands it put upon Llyr to fight the primal impulses of his dark passion—this level of trust only deepened that which lay between them. It was an odd reversal of all that went before, yet how could they pretend, that their relationship was as any others. Only by facing their strengths and weakness could they hope to survive the dark depths of such desire.

Llyr gazed at her for long moments, eyes darkening with intensity of emotion, "You know Dhariya, it's still difficult for me to believe you love me, especially now that you know the truth … it's so much more than one such as I deserves."

"Do not say such things Llyr. Yes I love you and I love all of you…for I see the aspects of you that you deny or hide from your own self. From the very beginning I've always known you were haunted by something in the depths of your soul—that you carried dark secrets, though I could never have imagined them to be what they are. Still I've always sensed the goodness and light that yet remains within you…and at times, I could see it so clearly and when I'd see it I'd reach for it… it's there even now, whether you choose to acknowledge it or not."

Dhariya leaned over and took hold of his hand, "Though there are still things I'm curious about, I feel I know you now.

In some ways, better than you know yourself, because I know all the parts of you, even those that you repudiate."

He offered her a weak smile. Her faith in his potential was humbling and he did not wish to continue on this uncomfortable subject, so he sought to change it, "You've said you still have many questions. Tell me then, what else would you like to know Dhariya?"

"Well...you never finished telling me what happened with you and my uncle... I'll always think of him as Uncle Tamas and love him as such. Since I've now had some time to come to terms with it all, I know he cannot help what he is anymore than you can. It's just all so... so shocking and still so unbelievable."

"Of course it is. I still find it hard to believe myself. Even now there are times I think I'll awaken and find it was all just a strange dream—but then I hope it's not because you are such a part of it and couldn't bear the thought of you not being real Dhariya." Llyr told her from his heart. Then he turned his thoughts to what else he could possibly share with her to answer her remaining questions. He had already done his best to explain all that he could.

Yet perhaps there was another way...leaning over, he retrieved a thick, leather bound book from his bedside table, which he then handed to Dhariya, "Here, this should tell you all you wish to know and more."

Dhariya studied the intricate emblem painted in dark gold on the front of the soft, dark-claret leather cover. "It's the Celtic symbol of eternity, I see the significance now more than ever," she said as she placed her hand over her heart where the silver locket lay" and I also now understand why it's patterned within the castles wrought iron gates as well."

She then looked down at his hand and, stroking her finger over the black onyx of his ring—her uncle's ring, and said. "Perhaps it does indeed hold the secrets of eternity after all."

"Yes, perhaps it does indeed." Llyr concurred. "If only I knew how to decipher it for just maybe I could free myself from this eternal darkness that imprisons me."

She looked into his eyes and the sorrow held there pierced her to her soul. But before she could say anything he drew her attention back to the book.

"This is a personal journal I've begun to write, a chronicle of sorts, detailing how I came to this dark existence and its beginnings." He explained. "And since you've already concluded it was indeed by the hand of Tamas, I see no reason to keep the rest of it from you... I do ask one thing of you, however."

"And that is?" She looked to him then.

"That you wait until after I've left Skara Brae before you read it."

"If that's truly what you wish." Dhariya softly replied, her hand shaking a little as she gave it back to him, wondering what things he did not want revealed until he was far away. Well if there were, so be it. She loved him and respected his wishes. She watched him go through the motions of returning the tome to its place in the top drawer, then relocking it and slipping the key into the pocket of his robe.

"This is the only key," he told her. "It will be yours when I leave. But you must be sure to guard it carefully. These writings are for your eyes alone and could prove dangerous if it fell into the wrong hands."

Dhariya nodded her consent as he took his place next to her once again. Then, feeling suddenly overwhelmed with sadness at the thought of his leaving, she turned into his waiting arms.

"As a matter of fact, I think I'd prefer to wait." She said against the comforting strength of his chest. "It's not that I don't wish to know, it's only—"

"You are afraid." He gently stated.

"Yes," Dhariya replied honestly. "But, it's the depth of what I feel for you that frightens me more than anything ...I know it's foolish to wish for things that cannot be, yet I—"

Unable to bear hearing the words voiced aloud, Llyr pressed a finger to her lips, halting them. "Please love," he whispered.

"We've already overcome so much let us not torture ourselves further."

Lifting her head, her eyes huge and luminous in the candlelight, "but why have you not made me as you are? That we might be together for always—"

"Never!" He cut in harshly, "Dear-God—Dhariya—Never!" drawing her into a tighter, protective embrace. His voice softening at the feel of her against him, "You've no idea what blasphemy, what sacrilege you've just voiced. Never would I defile you in such a manner." Easing his hold slightly, he looked at her again, his voice taking on a sorrowful tenor, "for there is no greater desecration to the human spirit."

Then his voice further softened as he took her face between his palms, his eyes shimmered with moisture. He swallowed hard before continuing. "I love you too much." His dark gaze delving into her depths, "Enough to let you go when I must …yet I vow to you that I shall follow your soul for all eternity Dhariya, each time your soul is reborn here upon this earth I shall know and I shall find you—if only to be near you and watch from a far."

A single lonely tear escaped and began its solitary trail down his cheek. "Lifetime after lifetime, when your spirit returns, I shall know and I shall find you.

———

𝔉𝔦𝔫𝔞𝔩𝔢'

…Even if I say, surely the darkness shall cover me; night shall be light about me, darkness hideth not from thee; but the night shineth as the day; for darkness and light are both alike to thee… Psalms 139.11.1

Skara Brae Castle ~ Date & Year Unknown

~ How does a mortal woman love an immortal man, a dark and dangerous immortal man, he, whose very nearness is a threat in and of itself? How does one not fear the deadly reality of their lover and shine light into such overwhelming darkness? Is it even possible? Or will it prove to destroy us both in the end? These questions can only be answered with the passage of time and the unfolding of fate….

But I have learned so much and I know him now, as much as he can be known by anyone. In fact, I believe I've come to know him even better than he knows himself, for I can see all that he denies within his innermost depths—that fleeting glimmer of a hope, which can never be extinguished, by anyone or anything. In discovering his darkest secret, I have unveiled a greater truth, one that he—try as he may—will never be able to fully conceal again—not to the world—nor, most importantly, to himself.

Perhaps this shall be my gift to him, though he may never see it as such. For his awareness of its existence within him, shall indeed render more torment than peace to his struggling soul. And, as I gain ever-deepening understanding, I realize my own role in all of this. Not only how vastly important it is to his future, but also its impact upon what is yet to come when we are finally parted.

Yes, he will leave me one day, he has told me of commitments that will eventually see him away for an undeterminable length of time, perhaps forever. I have accepted this—or at least, I endeavor to—even as I try not to think of it. Thus I shall not mourn his loss until after he has gone and I am alone. But for now…

…My Elysian." Llyr's voice came on a soft breath of sound, lowering his lips to mine. Our robes easily slipped away. He kissed me with such excruciating slowness—such aching tenderness, weaving his gossamer web of heightening desire. Stroking my flesh with a reverent hand, my body sighed beneath his touch as pleasure whispered along each nerve ending.

Tears lodged in my throat at the utter veneration in his every gesture, stealing both breath and words away. Yet further words were no longer needed between us, for all was conveyed within the sensual promise of a lover's touch, in a tune sweetly played, unto the depths of a yearning body and longing soul.

Then, his presence fierce though it was surrounded me gently, in a caressing of one being unto another. Filling me with the full magnitude of his need and all else fell away—as desire melted into a-oneness, a rhythmic spiraling dance of unfolding ecstasy—this dance of darkness and light becoming one—merging together into a vastness, a timeless perfection of fulfillment. Behind closed eyes, I clung to it, to its each and every quaver—enveloping myself in the potent power of passion's embrace and the absolute magnificence of such a thing.

And my only wish, that it would be thus, forever more…

The End

Glossary

Absolution:	[English] formal forgiveness of sins
Chondra:	[Hindu] the moon
Elegy:	[English] dirge, lament, mournful song, funeral song, melancholy poem
Elysian:	[Greek mythology] Eden, blessed abode after death, place of ideal happiness, Paradise
Destrier:	Warhorse - Huge stallions bred for battle ñ capable of carrying the heavy weight of armor yet still remain agile on the field.
Dhariya:	[Llyr's words] She who eclipses all.
Llyr:	[Celtic] meaning: Lord of the underworld or Lord of the sea.
Ragas:	[Hindu] from Sanskrit Vedic scriptures: sustainer or keeper, activity
Sattva:	[Hindu] from the Sanskrit Vedic scriptures: creator or maker, lucidity
Suriya:	[Hindu] the sun
Tamas:	[Hindu] from Sanskrit Vedic scriptures; destroyer, death, darkness, inertia
Taranis:	[Celtic] meaning 'Thunderer'

Acknowledgements:

My mother and father Donna and Collin Wade ~ thank you for the endless ways you have given me your love and support throughout my life ~ for never ceasing to believe in me and encouraging me to believe in myself ~ I would never have seen this dream come true without you.

My aunt Diane Heiden ~ your courage and fortitude have been such a great inspiration to me ~ I'm so grateful that you are a part of my life.

Thank you to Gloria Paley ~ you are not only an amazing friend for many reasons but also a wonderful assistant in my efforts to get this novel published. Rebecca Rasbeary ~ your friendship is a true blessing in my life, so too is your immense contribution here and in helping create the promo-video for Dhariya ~ Prelude To A Dark Legacy. My brother Collin Wade, my sis-in-law Roxanne Beaton, my niece Catherine and nephew Alistair ~ for all the ways you have helped me and for your love that inspires me. My good friends Lorraine Pungente and Brenda Stringer, without your help and support I could never have done this.

Thank you to my mentor Don McQuinn for seeing something in me and my work that you believed in ~ you have taught me such invaluable tools to hone my craft, challenged me to reach farther and to never give up. To Jack Whyte and Jo Beverley ~ your encouragement and praise for my work helped get me through many difficult times. To my all time favorite writer Charlotte Bronte ~ thank you for your extraordinary gothic novels such as 'Jayne Eyre' and for helping to forge the way for female authors.

~ ~ Hope all the readers will check out the work of these four [above mentioned] highly acclaimed writers.

Thank you to Lukas Rossi and Kendra Jade Rossi for your love and friendship.

~ ~ Hope all the readers will also check out Lukas Rossi's awesome music and his incredible band Stars Down at the following websites:
www.lukasrossionline.com
www.starsdowninc.com

~ And check out my on-line writing page:
www.myspace.com/skarabrae_castle
e-mail me at: LadyKarellelynBrae@hotmail.com to view the 'Prelude To A Dark Legacy' promo-video go to: http://ca.youtube.com/LadyKarelle

original cover photo by Marcia Lippman ñ[used with permission]

~ Llyr ~

In the Presence of Darkness
The Legacy

A Gothic Novel
Depicting the embodiment of darkness and the
journey toward light

BASED ON THE PERSONAL JOURNALS &
WRITINGS OF Lord Llyr

…*"Listen well to these secrets I share with you now for they are a call to caution. I hereby break a code of silence that has existed since and angel first fell from grace. And the importance of such a revelation cannot be understated"* …

~ L ~

Exordium

*~ I am darkness ~ made flesh and given voice. My existence is an endless webbing of shadows and ill-fated desires, where naught but emptiness abounds.
Yes ~ I am darkness and the night calls me beloved ~*

*~ **My** given name is Llyr—an ancient Celtic word known to mean 'God of the Sea' yet it is ever whispered to have another secret meaning as 'God of the Underworld'—thus as you come to know me and life through the reading of these pages you will come to understand that the second offered meaning for my name, to be the accurate meaning.*

However, to protect the many who share it, my real sir name shall remain untold as it is of no consequence and thus the stains upon my own soul be not cast upon any other. Only now do I take the risk of revealing this truth and all that I shall henceforth disclose within this book you now hold in your hands, for the danger in keeping this hidden far outweighs the other.

Born in the Highlands of Scotland in the year of our Lord 1683, of Welsh mother and Scottish father, my Celtic roots are strong and firmly planted. My early life unfolded as any other young lad's of that time.

It was my ninth year when everything changed. When the shadows came to call and I began to follow them along a tenebrous path. A path which led only into further darkness, and ultimately, to this course which I now must tread without choice—a prisoner of the cold lightless chasm that exists between life and death.

Learn well from all I am here-to-fore about to tell you.

And beware the dangerous brood that walk this dark perilous path for they are ever among you, ever awaiting their chance, it is up to you if you allow them their way or not. Take your power back from the outer world around you and guard it well, for the veils are very thin which separate all worlds including mine my friend. You are always choosing just how close you will permit me and my kind to be.

Take heed and do not make the same mistakes that I have made.

I tell my tale for many reasons and on many levels. I am confident you are bright enough to discern my messages and meanings. But you must be attentive to my words, and in the end if you chose to disbelieve then the proving of these facts will be too late.

You see, once I was a man like any other, I lived, laughed, and dreamed just as you. Now I hunger for those things and so many others I shall never have and never know again.

...So turn the page and read on, then one way or another, we shall meet again once the tale is told...

~ L ~

Llyr's story will be coming next...

Author's Bio

Writing is my passion; it's as essential to my life as breathing. I am a woman of intense passion and I write stories that reflect this ~ the kinds of stories that I most love to read. By combining the old world gothic feel of such classic favorites as Jane Eyre, Wuthering Heights & Rebecca with the strong elements of sensuality in popular modern fiction, & by drawing from my years of philosophy study, fascination with British/European history, as well as my love of romance & poetry. Interweaving these threads together I offer a uniquely refreshing voice for today's readers—by creating a vivid sensually evocative world of the past with multifaceted characters that grow and evolve as they face the trials of their lives—characters that feel deeply and love passionately—within a world of light and shadows—of choices and consequences.

'Dhariya ~ Prelude To A Dark Legacy' has many exclusive elements that are self-defining & poignant—I am not alone in this opinion. It has been critiqued & received extremely high praise from such accomplished authors as Jo Beverly, Jack Whyte & Don McQuinn.

I believe my most important credentials as a writer are my passion & commitment to my craft, the willingness to give what the work demands to make it the best that it can be

I am currently writing my next novel & have ideas for many more waiting patiently for their turn to be told.

Made in the USA